THE
VISA

LIZZIE O'HAGAN studied Law and Australian Law before going into publishing, where she now works as a Publisher at an independent press. She writes and paints in her spare time and though she can usually be found drinking coffee near her flat in central London, Derbyshire will always be home.

Also by Lizzie O'Hagan:

What Are Friends For?

Writing as Elizabeth Neep:

The Spare Bedroom
Never Say No
The New Me
Twelve Days to Save Christmas

THE
VISA

LIZZIE O'HAGAN

H

REVIEW

First published in Great Britain in 2022 by
HEADLINE REVIEW
An imprint of HEADLINE PUBLISHING GROUP

1

Cataloguing in Publication Data is available from the British Library

ISBN 978 1 4722 8632 1

Typeset in Bembo Std by CC Book Production
Printed and bound in Great Britain by Clays Ltd, Elcograf S.p.A.

HEADLINE PUBLISHING GROUP
An Hachette UK Company
Carmelite House
50 Victoria Embankment
London EC4Y 0DZ

www.headline.co.uk
www.hachette.co.uk

To you, my readers, for letting me share my stories with you.

Part 1

The Proposal

Jack

'Give me six more months,' Toby's voice beckons my attention back from the corner of the room. There must be a hidden camera here somewhere. Surely, I'm getting Punk'd? 'Jack, does that make sense, mate?'

Our eyes lock and I'm almost surprised he's not a hot mess on the floor, that my glare hasn't lasered him to a crisp, Cyclops-style.

'*Six?*' I stutter again as I see the corners of Toby's mouth turn up. He knows better than to mock my New Zealand accent right now.

'*Sex? Jack, I'm flattered, but now's not the time.*' After eighteen months of working together on this damn app I just don't have the patience to explain that he's actually doing an *Australian* accent. A bad one at that.

'Yeah, just so we can secure a bit more funding.' Toby smiles through his furrowed brow. I'd feel sorry for his sleepless nights if he hadn't stolen so many of mine. 'Visas are like, real expensive, mate . . .'

I wish he'd stop calling me that. He doesn't feel like a mate right now. A mate wouldn't have told me to 'just stop worrying' every time I asked whether the sponsorship application for my visa to stay in the country was in hand.

'It's not like SoberApp is going anywhere,' Toby continues. 'We know alcohol-free drink is a growth market, and if you hang on for just another six months, we can get that visa application going . . .'

It was always meant to be *going*.

'I need to get sponsorship before then, *mate*,' I spit the word like a threat, my quickening pulse reminding me that I've never needed anything more. 'My visa runs out in five months and then I'm on the first plane back to Auckland and—'

'Just stop worrying.' Toby smiles, trying to make light of the situation, like he tries to with every three-in-the-morning pizza party, as if the smell of grease could mask the fact that we are all still working at that hour.

'Sure, but . . . I need a job that will sponsor me, so I . . .'

Even in my angry haze, I hesitate. Where else will I find an employer to sponsor my visa at such short notice? Especially given that my contact list began dwindling when I started overdosing on an app that promotes moderation. Still, it's not like I can stay here.

'I can't carry on working for you.' Literally. Not without the visa. 'I . . . I quit,' I say, not nearly as boldly as they do in the movies.

'Jack, wait,' Toby stands to stop me. 'Can you just finish the coding for—'

'Sorry, *mate*,' I say, shaking my head before leaving Toby, my dream job and my promise of staying in the UK behind, deleting SoberApp as I go.

I need a drink anyway.

Maya

Oh shit.

I open my fist to see the small gold key in my hand drawing blood. I didn't even realise I was holding onto it that tightly. I look at my mobile lying motionless on the papers scattered across my bed.

Tonight was going to be the night that I finally tell my mum about this bloody key, about that bloody apartment. The only surprising thing about the fact she has forgotten to call, is the fact I'm still surprised.

'Mum, I've got to go.' I hear my flatmate, Emmie, laugh from the other side of the door. '*Yes, Mum*, they'll be arriving soon. *No, Mum*, I won't drink too much . . .'

I can almost hear her rolling her eyes. Ever since I met Emmie, she has wanted to be independent. It's the reason she worked her arse off and lived on noodles for a questionably long time to be able to afford this flat in the first place. I want to be independent too. Turns out it's a lot easier to afford your own place if you're a management consultant, rather than a wannabe academic. I grip the key in my hand one last time, before stashing it in my jeans pocket.

'Help. Me,' Emmie mouths in my direction as I enter the living room. 'Look, Mum, I *really* have to go now—'

'Emmie, they're here!' I shout into the room to no one in

particular, kicking my bedroom door shut behind me. Moments later, Emmie manages to hang up the call.

'You're a *lifesaver*.' She beams at me, getting to her feet, her long tanned legs leading my eye to the shortest hemline I've ever seen. She's wearing an oversized shirt we found in a vintage shop last year, the cuffs pushed up to her elbows to display the countless bangles she has wrapped around her wrists. Somehow, with her dark dip-dyed hair piled high upon her head, forming a messy bun of blond tips, she looks effortless; Emmie usually does.

'Good catch-up?' I ask, moving over to the little kitchenette in the corner of the room.

'*Long* catch-up,' Emmie elongates the word dramatically but still she smiles. 'You?'

'Yeah,' I say, not looking up from pouring our drinks. 'All good.'

Emmie and I have planned our weekly family catch-ups at the same time for the whole three years we've been living here to maximise our own time together in between work. What she doesn't know is that *my* mum has missed the last three of mine.

'You sure?' Emmie asks, coming to join me in the kitchen, looking my ripped jeans up and down. At least I put on a nice top for tonight.

'Why wouldn't I be?' I say, handing her a larger-than-large glass of wine.

'Oh, I don't know,' Emmie says slowly, taking a tentative first sip. 'Because your dad just died of cancer?'

She tries to say it nonchalantly but there's a hint of pain in her eyes. It's entirely unnecessary. Yes, cancer sucks, but it's not like I've really 'lost' something when he was never a part of my life in the first place.

'And it's coming up to his birthday . . .' She studies my black top, all silky and oversized, as if she's wondering whether my choice of colour is a sign of my silent mourning.

'Not like I'll need to buy him a present,' I quip, and Emmie narrows her eyes.

'Maya!' She looks shocked and I'm not sure whether she's pretending; it's this kind of dark humour that saw us become friends in the first place but evidently it's not as funny mocking my absent father now that he's absent in every sense of the word.

'I hardly knew the man,' I say for what feels like the thousandth time since I told her.

'And he hasn't *just* died. It's been three months.'

And it's been a month since I found out about his apartment, but Emmie doesn't know about that either. We used to tell each other everything but our own catch-ups have been few and far between ever since she started dating Adrian about two months ago. But I do need one soon so I can tell her something, *ask* her something . . .

'Emmie, I—' I begin before we hear a knock at the door.

'Oh crap, they're actually here.' She takes another gulp of wine before making her way over to let our guests in. 'Let's hang out tomorrow, okay? We *need* a proper catch-up.'

'That sounds great.' I grin. A great opportunity to ask Emmie what I've been meaning to ask her all month.

Emmie opens the door to reveal the first of many friends clutching their bottles of booze. I've invited a few people; Emmie has invited everyone she knows. But then, it really doesn't matter what kind of party this turns into. All that

7

matters is that after weeks of waiting, tonight is the night that I finally get to meet him.

Jack

I hear a key turn in the door and look up to see Adrian's face, eyes wide and mouth hanging open in feigned surprise. We both know it's a double bluff. I'm never normally here.

'Do my eyes deceive me?' He laughs, as I take my feet off the coffee table.

'Yeah, I know . . . work's . . .' I stall on the sentence.

It's not long since Adrian told me he's moving in with this Emmie chick, the one he's only been seeing for two months, and that we need to move out of our own unprecedently cheap flat. And I told him I was okay with it. I *was* okay with it until I lost my already unprecedently small income. The thought of leaving the country makes me want to drink more, or be sick, but I can't deal with him worrying about me right now.

'I thought you had a date?'

'Oh *shit*,' I whisper, reaching past the three empty beer cans I have drained to grab my downturned phone from the table. I've got three missed calls. 'Crap, crap, *crap*.'

'Take it you'll be needing another one of these?' Adrian asks and I look up to see him walking from the fridge with a beer in each hand.

He comes to sit beside me, handing me a cold one. I'd completely forgotten about my third date with Daisy. Truth is, I was going to end things with her tonight anyway. I went on dating apps because I didn't know what I was looking for.

Now, I'm pretty sure I'm not looking for a relationship. I might not even be staying in the country. Maybe on some level I knew deep down I wouldn't be here long enough to make it work. The thought makes the walls feel like they're closing in. I can't go back home. Not after what I left behind. I shoot an apologetic 'rain-check?' message Daisy's way. She'll realise that she's dodged a bullet soon.

'Well, I guess now you have no excuse not to come to this party,' Adrian says and it's only then that I notice he's currently the epitome of smart-casual, his relaxed white shirt hanging over dark jeans, his short blond hair styled with just the right amount of product.

I groan, casting my eyes out of the only window in the room; it's just big enough to remind us that spring is in full swing, just thin enough for the sound of noisy streets and even noisier neighbours to remind us that the city's social life is warming up too. Still, Adrian and I both know I'd rather just stay in and drink today away. Living-to-work may be drifting into working-to-live with the passing of the seasons, but I need work to stand a chance in hell of continuing to live here. And I can't leave. I just can't.

'You'll finally get to meet Emmie,' Adrian coaxes, his keenness palpable.

'I've met her . . . apparently.'

Adrian insists Emmie was at the same university as us. That she was one of those friends-of-friends-of-friends that you have one actual conversation with, but somehow, manage to share countless memories with, without even trying.

'And Maya.' Adrian grins again.

Now, Maya I remember from first year. A petite brunette

scrappy woman with opinions ten times the size of her frame. I walked her home this one time, her ranting the whole way that she was able to walk herself. She couldn't even walk in a straight line. For some reason I can't help but smile at the thought.

Twenty dollars says she doesn't remember who I am.

Maya

'I *do* remember you,' I say, throwing my arms around Adrian as soon as I've opened the door. He looks startled as I pull away. Then, he smiles.

'And of course, I remember you too.' He grins wider, a charming toothy grin.

I'm not sure the 'of course' is justified seeing as Emmie and Adrian didn't twig that they were in the same student accommodation during our first year at uni until they'd been talking for a day or two on the dating app they matched on.

'And you remember Jack?' Adrian takes another step into the apartment before Emmie's arms engulf her new boyfriend completely, attaching herself to Adrian like a limpet.

I assumed given the sheer amount of time they've spent together over the past two months that there was some kind of force field drawing them together. Now I know for sure.

I peel my eyes away from the newly conjoined twins to look at Jack, who is still lingering in the doorway to our apartment, his deep brown eyes looking directly at me so intensely that it almost makes me feel nervous. Unlike Adrian, Jack hasn't changed a bit. He's still over six foot tall. Still permanently tanned. Still poster-boy good-looking. Even though, being two years older than the rest of us fellow freshers, he's always looked like a man. I never did work out why he didn't start university at eighteen like the rest of us. He must be twenty-four now, twenty-five at a push.

'Hi, I . . .' Jack begins, his accent catching me off guard, the same way it did when I first met him all those years ago. 'Hi.' He takes a decisive step forward as if he's just had to convince himself he wants to be here in my and Emmie's apartment.

'Hey.' I look up at him, reminding myself that the appropriate response to him taking a step forward would be to stand back, to actually let him in. But for some reason I just stand there, awkwardly close, my eyes oscillating from Jack's gorgeous brown eyes to his slightly open mouth. I trace his gaze, which is now looking past me and further into the apartment, to see Emmie and Adrian trying to devour each other. PDAs are awful at the best of times. Never mind when I'm inches apart from some random guy from uni that I'm seventy per cent sure I drunkenly tried to throw myself at when he walked me home that one time.

'How's it going?' Jack asks casually, so casually that I'm not entirely sure he's not just saying hello again. He casts another quick glance behind me and then reaches out an arm.

Cautiously, I open my arms too, ready to embrace him, before I realise that he's now reaching past me, that Adrian is handing him an open can of beer from behind me. I force my open arms down to my side immediately, like a solider that has just been called to attention. But it's too late, my sudden movement has knocked the beer in his hand, and he fumbles to save it; all of Jack's attention is now safely on me.

'I'm *so* sorry. I thought—'

11

'No, no, it's okay,' Jack replies quickly, reaching a hand forward, hoping a friendly handshake can cover over the awkwardness brimming between us. But the feeling of his hard stomach muscles against my fingers tells me that *this* time Jack was actually going for a hug.

'Oh crap, I . . .' Now it's his turn to look sheepish. 'Can I . . . ?'

I stand as still as a statue, not wanting to risk another wrong move. Can he what? Hug me? Shake my hand? Leave this apartment and never come back again?

My cheeks burn with embarrassment, and I hate that I look flustered, that he probably thinks I'm trying and failing to flirt with him somehow. I am *not* trying to flirt with him. Arrogant guys like him were the reason I spent more nights at the Feminist Debate Society than out on the sticky club floors of Hackney. Except that one night.

'Can I . . . erm . . . use your bathroom?' Jack looks for an escape.

'I'll show you.' Emmie surfaces, coming to our rescue, clearly not so submerged in snogging Adrian that she has forgotten her surroundings.

Jack gives me a strained smile before brushing past me and following Emmie across the room, the scent of his subtle aftershave catching on the air.

'Don't you go making any moves on my woman,' Adrian jokes behind them.

I swear I'm a little sick in my mouth. Emmie laughs though. Despite nights spent bemoaning dating in the digital age, that all the men online are misogynistic and, well, just *weird*, she's clearly changed her tune.

A tune that doesn't mind being called someone else's 'woman'.

I turn to watch Jack's broad shoulders disappear into the room, not knowing why I feel the need to. Then my phone buzzes in my pocket. I reach for it, feeling that damn key bite into my hand as I do. It's my mum. Apologising for missing our call. Another work meeting. It's all the reminder I need that this flustered feeling is the reason I don't really date. The reason she taught me to follow my dreams and never follow a man. And it's the reason Emmie should stop being so concerned about how I'm taking the news about my dad. We've done okay without him these past two decades. I slip my phone back into my pocket and the key jabs into my hand again. It's not like he even got in touch to say he was unwell.

And that's exactly why I have no idea what I'm going to do about this key.

Jack

I would love to say I walk across the living room, but I'm pretty sure I'm staggering.

Two hours have passed since we arrived at Maya and Emmie's party and today's sorrows still aren't drowned. But hey, can't blame a guy for trying. It's hardly on brand for SoberApp – not that that matters anymore. Still, one more drink and I'm definitely going to call it a night. Adrian will be stopping over here. It's soon to be his home anyway, but where the hell is my home going to be? My heart starts to hammer at the thought. Walking closer to the kitchen, I'm surprised to find Maya looking bored, staring down at her phone blankly.

'Tired of your own party?' I ask, and she looks up, surprised. I'm definitely not sober.

'Oh, I . . .' Maya fixes her searing green eyes on me in recognition.

I'm not sure just how far back she recognises me from. Not that it matters. It's not like I'm going to be in her future. The thought churns in my stomach again. I don't want to go back home. I *can't*.

'It's not really my party,' Maya says, her shoulders shrugging as she looks around the room. 'I don't know half these people.' She drains the last of her drink.

'Red or white?' I lift up two bottles of wine from the counter, displaying them by the neck. I try to focus on her eyes, but it's like my blurry vision is attempting to take in all her features at once, from her small and symmetrical nose and her sun-kissed cheeks to her slightly parted lips, which manage to look plump even though she's pursing them tight. Her wavy dark hair stretches down her back, looking even longer thanks to her petite stature.

'I can pour my drinks at my own party.' She rolls her eyes, reaching for the white.

She forces a laugh, trying to pass it off as a joke, but we both know she means it. Maya doesn't need anyone. I remember that much at least.

'I thought you said it wasn't your party?' I retort, pouring my own glass of red.

'It's not . . . it's . . .' she begins and then stalls, her eyes widening again at the speed at which I'm downing my drink. 'Bad day?'

'You have no idea.' I sigh, and she seems to soften before me. Misery loves company.

14

'Try me,' Maya says, looking at her phone one last time before stashing it in her back pocket.

She's probably waiting for some loser to message her back. Guys can be dicks. I should know. I can't help thoughts of Daisy, and all the other girls I couldn't commit to, from flooding my mind. But it's better than thinking about the one girl I *could* commit to.

'Rather hear about yours,' I say; it feels like the most honest thing I've said all night.

Maya

I take a sip of my wine, letting it soothe my confusion. Then, I notice Jack is still watching me, waiting intently for my reply. Oh, he actually *wants* to hear about my day. His handsome face is looking back at me, our silence speaking volumes in a room full of chatter.

'It's nothing,' I say, forcing a smile. Jack has come here for a party, not to be my agony aunt. Though from the look on his face, I'm not entirely sure he's in the party mood.

'Doesn't look like nothing,' he says back, my own face clearly saying it all.

'There's just been a lot going on,' I begin, reluctant at first.

Until three hours ago I hadn't seen this guy in years, and even then, we were never really friends; a subplot to a bigger romance − or a never-quite-a-romance − at best. And yet, somehow, him standing here in my kitchen, choosing to keep me company at a party that we both now know isn't mine at all, it kind of makes me feel safe.

15

'I finished my masters two months ago and started working on my PhD a week later,' I begin as I search Jack's face for surprise or insecurity. Usually, this admission would welcome one or the other, but Jack simply nods, encouraging me on.

'And money's pretty tight,' I admit, though I have no intention of asking anyone for help. Other than accepting Emmie's cheap rent; it's the only thing that makes perpetual studies possible in a city like London. My stomach somersaults at the thought of asking her for another rent reduction tomorrow, but despite how distant we've been since she started dating Adrian, I know the answer will be yes. We've always had each other's backs. 'Then there's some family stuff,' I say; now I've started, I can't seem to stop.

'I'm sorry,' Jack apologises, in the way people always do when they suspect something awful has happened. That stupid sympathetic head tilt.

'No, not like bad family stuff,' I correct, smiling. And I'm serious, I'm not upset about my so-called dad dying. More *confused*. 'It's just a bit complicated.'

'I guess that's one of the perks of being eleven thousand miles from home,' Jack says, taking another swig of his wine. 'Makes family stuff seem that little bit simpler.' His smile falters for a second.

'Adrian, *stop* it.' Emmie's delighted squeal steals us from the moment as we both look across the crowded room to see Adrian tickling his girlfriend.

'Oh, *please*,' Jack and I say at the exact same time before his laugh laces into mine.

'I try to tell myself it's cute, but it feels like they've moved really fast,' I say before I can stop myself. I sound jealous.

Maybe I am? But not of Adrian, and not of their relationship, but maybe of the fact that we always used to be 'Maya and Emmie' and now it's 'Adrian and Emmie'.

'I *know*.' Jack grins. 'When Aid first told me, I thought he was crazy, but now, seeing them together, this next step just makes so much sense.' What next step? Jack fixes his dark eyes on me as my cloudy mind scrambles to fill in the blanks. 'They're going to love living here.' Jack smiles again. 'What date are you moving out again?'

Jack

Shit. Shit. *Shit*. Maya's green eyes have never been bigger. Her mouth hangs open, trying to form a word before letting it go. Her neat features tell me everything I need to know: Emmie hasn't told her yet. Just when you think a day can't get any worse.

'I, err . . .' Maya tries that sentence again and then stalls. If she was an app, I'd just reboot her. But she's not, she's very much real, and I've just really, *really* put my foot in it.

'Sorry, I, err . . .' I can't help but mirror her confusion. 'I thought Emmie must have . . .'

I watch her look at Emmie and Adrian again, and I swear I see tears threatening to fall. Then she narrows her eyes and, with shaking hands, pours herself another drink.

'Maya, look, I'm sorry,' I try again. If she was anyone else, I'd try to put my arm around her. But I remember enough about Maya to know she doesn't want to be rescued.

'She should have told me,' she whispers under her breath. 'Like before now, before this party, before *you* knew . . .'

17

She looks at me in anger and I realise I'm holding my breath. I can't let her confront Emmie now. Not at this party, not in front of everyone, not until I've had a chance to collar Adrian and tell him what I've gone and done now. Maybe it's a good thing I'm leaving the country soon? Even now, I don't believe that.

'I'm just going to go and talk to her,' Maya says, slurring her words as she does. Man, we need to leave. Now is not the time for a best-friend showdown. Maya just needs some space, some fresh air, then she'll be fine.

'You know what?' I begin, daring to put my hand on her arm. 'Let's get out of here.'

She looks at me, a glimmer of vulnerability darting across her face.

'I can't, it's my part—' she begins, and against my better judgement I raise my eyebrows. She shakes her head, and with it any vulnerability disappears, her boundaries back up.

'You're right.' She reaches for two unopened bottles of wine. 'Let's get out of here.'

Maya

I don't look back when I leave the party. Instead, I walk into the cool night air. I have no idea where I'm going. I just know I'm going away from *their* apartment.

Jack keeps in step by my side, his strong arms just inches away from me. For a second, I am transported back to university, to me and Emmie watching him play in the rugby varsity finals. It's not like I even knew him, not really. And here he is watching me have a full-on meltdown. I glance at him, striding aimlessly beside me, and our eyes meet.

Are you okay? His empathetic expression is easy to read even if he knows better than to ask me when the answer is so damn obvious.

'I've spent the past few weeks just trying to find the right time to talk to my *best* friend,' I say, the wine loosening my lips. 'To ask her if I can pay *less* rent whilst I work on my PhD. I never imagined she'd been biding her time to tell me that she wouldn't be needing my rent at all.'

'What are you doing your PhD in?' Jack asks, perhaps longing to steer our conversation onto safer, only-just-acquaintances ground. I keep striding forward before stumbling on a broken paving stone. Jack's big arms wrap around me before I can fall.

'Feminist Studies,' I mumble back at him, his face inches from my own. The words feel somewhat ironic seeing as I just needed a man to catch me.

'Cool,' he whispers, the sweet scent of alcohol laced in his breath.

I shrug him off, brushing myself down.

I pick up pace, steering us down side streets until the buildings part and I can finally see the city lights dancing across the river. Jack doesn't say anything, he just tries to keep up.

'What the hell am I going to do now?' I breathe, not meaning to sound so dramatic.

'I don't know,' Jack says unhelpfully; he sounds a little hopeless too.

My feet quicken as my mind races. I know better than to ask my mum for help. *What good is bailing you out going to do, Maya? I started from nothing and I've never relied on anyone.* I can almost feel her disappointment now. She's never taken anything from anyone, not even my dad. That's why it's so damn hard to talk to her about the key in my back pocket, the apartment it leads to.

The apartment, I realise, I'm walking towards now.

Jack

I try to keep up with Maya, literally and metaphorically. I want to say something to make it better but I'm the kind of guy who can make things worse without even trying.

'Let me carry those . . .' I eventually mutter, my pathetic attempt to lighten the load.

'Being kicked out of your own home *sucks*,' Maya says, still not turning towards me, ignoring my feigned attempt at chivalry completely. She's fixed forward; I still have no idea where we're going. I'm not even sure that she does.

'So does being kicked out of the country,' I say, and, as if the sentence doesn't feel dramatic enough, the thunder fills the sky, and rain starts to fall. It's the last day of April so you could forgive the month one final April shower if this wasn't a full-blown *storm*.

'Oh *shit*.' Maya finally looks at me and for a moment I feel like I can breathe again.

'I know, shall we go and find a bar somewhere?' I say, holding my arms over my head.

'No, I mean you getting kicked out of the country,' she says, slowing to a standstill. 'Please tell me you're not a wanted man or anything?'

A wanted man? I've not felt *wanted* in years.

'That would be a curveball. Perfect Jack the Jock falls from grace,' she mocks, and I wince at the words. It's the nickname that followed me halfway around the planet.

'You think I'm perfect?' I turn to stand before her.

'You sure seemed like it at uni.' Maya goes to put a hand to her hip, forgetting that she's still holding a bottle of wine in each of them. She's wasted. I reach to relieve her of the bottles before they can slip to the floor. Nice to know my hand–eye coordination is still intact.

'You didn't even know me at uni,' I say, and it sounds meaner than I meant it to. I guess I was popular at university but that didn't mean I was *perfect*. 'But yeah, I lost my job,' I force through the lie. 'They were going to apply for a visa for me but anyway, it's a no-go. I just found out today.'

'How long have you got?' she says as if she's asking how many days I've left to live.

'Less than five months,' I answer, and I can't help my voice from cracking. I can't go home; nobody would want me to. 'So yeah.' I push away the thought. 'Shall we go and find a bar somewhere?' I suggest again.

'Nah.' Maya smiles for the first time in the hour we've been walking. 'I've got a better idea.'

I have no idea why I'm still following her but it's not like I can leave her by herself, not when she's this drunk and emotional. And I don't really want to, not when *I'm* this drunk and emotional.

As we follow the Thames, I marvel at the houses around us, four storeys high and kissing the river. Maya's eyes seem to search them too, from their flower-covered balconies to the

21

warm tall windows glowing behind large wrought-iron-railing fences, just out of reach. Then Maya stops to rest against one of the walls of a seemingly gated community, placing the wine bottles by her feet.

'What are you—' I begin, before she forces her hands beneath her, pulling her body up to sit on top of the wall as she does. Before I can stop her, she's swinging her legs over and jumping off onto the other side, out of view. Oh shit. 'Maya!' I can't help but cry behind her. Damn drunk girls. I thought I left this crap at uni too.

Then, I hear her giggle.

'What's taking you so long?' she shouts from the other side.

Oh man, she'll wake the neighbours. What the hell is she doing? More to the point, what the hell am *I* doing? I pick the wine bottles up from the pavement and reach to put them on top of the wall, using my arms to clamber up one side before pushing myself off the other.

'This way,' Maya orders, as she walks across the most manicured garden I've seen since arriving in London almost five years ago. This is crazy. We're going to get caught.

I look up at the four-storey townhouses, even more impressive close up. I follow her like a sheep; we're both already too slaughtered. She reaches into her back pocket and for a second I think she's going to stone the place; a huge *screw-you* to anyone who actually owns one of these when neither of us can't keep a roof over our head. Then I see a key, and she's turning it in a key safe, which falls open to reveal two more keys. I watch as she unlocks the front door to one of the buildings and it swings wide.

Oh crap, we're going inside.

Maya

I've looked at the photos a thousand times, ever since the lawyers contacted me out of the blue to say that it was mine – well, *his* – but I never planned on stepping a foot inside it until tonight. Ascending the pristine staircase to his floor, my legs shake as I make my way down an equally decadent corridor. How on earth can a *corridor* be decadent? I clock a huge piece of art hanging from the end of it, a velour chaise longue lining the space underneath.

That's how.

'Maya?' Jack whispers from hiding behind me. I'd almost forgotten he was here. 'Maya, where are you going? What are you doing?'

I only know the answer to one of those questions so decide it's best to keep walking. Besides, I'm too far in to go back now. Then I see it. Apartment 100; a number so perfect and complete that I'm almost convinced my dad would have paid more for it. He was always searching for perfection. With shaking hands, I turn the key in the door, and it opens with ease. I stare into the darkness, breathing deeply before reaching around for a switch.

One click and light floods the room, leaving me breathless. I force one heavy foot in front of the other until I'm standing in an entrance as big as my bedroom back home – well, at Emmie's. I could move my entire belongings into it and yet a simple single table stands in the middle, an expensive-looking vase standing proud on top of it. Apart from that, the room is empty with just more doors leading off it and one by one I open them.

23

In quick succession I scan a kitchen so big it belongs in the countryside, a bathroom covered in wall-to-wall marble, a bedroom hosting a king-size that a family of five could sleep in and, lastly, an open-plan living/dining room with views so vast that for a moment I feel like I'm dipping a toe in the Thames.

'Maya, what are you doing?' Jack hisses into the silence. 'Where are we?' I turn to see his face crinkled in concern; he knows it isn't *my* place.

'It's my dad's,' I sigh. I expect Jack to soften but his mouth hangs open all the more.

'Your dad *lives* here?' he asks, evidently incredulous. Well, he did but I don't need Jack's misplaced sympathy right now; I've had enough of that from Emmie. Wordlessly, I nod. 'And is he in?' Jack subconsciously hides the wine bottles behind his back.

'No,' I say slowly, knowing this is my time to tell the truth, but then, couldn't tonight just be about escaping instead? I look into Jack's tired eyes; we both need a break.

'He works in New York,' I explain.

The lie comes easily because, three months ago, it wasn't one. Ever since I can remember, I've known that my dad left us for a management role he couldn't refuse. Clearly, he didn't feel the same about his role as a father.

Walking further into the room, I let my legs crumple into a big armchair angled towards the view. I shouldn't be here; I don't even want to be. I'd made my mind up last week that I was going to sell it and give the money to charity, be rid of it all. Mum and I had never taken anything from Dad in his lifetime, I'm not planning to start now.

Jack comes to sit on the sofa not far from me, perching on

24

the edge of it tentatively. I have no idea why I even brought us here. For a moment I thought it would be fun, that maybe 'Jack the Jock' would be impressed by the luxury, when, really, we're surrounded by a dead man's things. I'm sure I'd picture him everywhere if I had more than his LinkedIn photos to go on. Did he live here with another woman? Another family? But then, why would he leave it to me? My mind scrambles for answers when Jack finally gives me an easier question.

'Wine?' He lifts up the bottles, relaxing into the cushions a little as he does.

'Sure.' I smile in return as his eyes linger on me. 'What?'

'Glasses?' He laughs. 'I assume your dad has some in a place like this?'

'Me too,' I agree before I realise that there should be no assumptions about it. As far as Jack is concerned, this must be my second home. 'I mean . . . I'll just go and get some.'

My stomach churns as I stand up and make my way into the kitchen. Even borrowing my dad's glasses feels like accepting too much. My mum would flip if she knew.

Heading back into the living room, I hand the glasses to Jack who starts to fill them with the over-attentive care of someone who's already had too much.

After a day like today, it still doesn't feel like enough.

'Maya?' Jack asks, one arm lining the back of the large grey sofa, the other reaching to top up my wine glass, draining the last of our two bottles.

'Jack?' I say, mirroring his tone. He laughs, both of us now drowsy with drink and resting our legs upon the sofa. It's still so strange that we're here, together, and in this place, *his* place, but somehow this combination of strange things makes both feel okay.

'You know, your dad . . .' Jack begins his sentence cautiously, as if he's been holding onto it for the whole two hours that we've been here. 'If he works away all the time, why don't you just live here?'

'Because of my mum.' I sigh, taking another swig of my wine, trying to swallow the truth with it: *it's because I never knew him, because he never wanted to know me.*

'She lives here too?' Jack asks quickly, sitting a little straighter in his seat.

'God no.' I can't help but laugh at the thought. 'They've been divorced ever since I was little. They were married for two years until my dad got his job in New York. My mum didn't see why she had to compromise her career, why women are always the ones to bend, so she refused to go with him, and he refused to stay and they just . . . stopped being married.'

Jack's eyes are fixed on me, wide and sad, and it's impossible not to feel sorry for him. He found out he needs to leave the country today, and here I am sharing my sob story for the first time in years. Maybe the fact he's leaving the country makes sharing it that bit easier.

'A couple of forms later and they were divorced,' I say, my mind feeling further from my mouth with each and every sip. 'They didn't ask each other for anything. My mum made enough of her own money to never need to take anything from him or anyone.'

And I'll never ask her for anything because all I've ever wanted from her is respect. I know better than to share this

26

last thought out loud. Still, I look to Jack, who's smiling, as if somehow something about me now makes sense.

'Divorce is brutal,' Jack says, and it sounds like he's speaking from experience.

'Divorce is *easy*,' I correct, and he looks at me like I'm a complete cynic. 'Sign a document to get married, sign a document to get out of it. Simple.'

'You can't really think that?' He laughs, and I try not to feel patronised. I bet he's used to being surrounded by swooning girls just desperate for their Mr Darcys.

'My parents are lawyers.' I shrug. 'You agree to be married until you don't.'

'Yeah, but then there's all the feelings involved.'

'So what?'

'Feelings make everything complicated.'

'Let me guess, you're a romantic? You're in love?' I don't mean to scoff. 'That's why you want to stay in the country?'

Jack

Am I a romantic? I guess I used to be, but that was before. Before everything back home came crashing down and I moved eleven thousand miles away to try to rebuild it again, rebuild *me*. And it worked, for the most part.

'There are so many reasons I want to stay in the country,' I say under my breath.

'Like what?' Maya says, clearly still so sure it's to do with love.

But then, isn't everything? There is so much I left behind me, so much I've spent the last years trying not to think about.

27

I've wrapped myself in uni, in studies and sports and one-night stands; I've drowned myself in work, in developing the app with Toby as if it is the only thing that matters. All to keep me from thinking about the one reason, the one person, I left behind. For a moment, I allow my mind to float out of the room, my gaze to drift out of the window.

'London,' I breathe, eyes fixed on the Thames before me. 'Rainbow bagels in Shoreditch and home-made pasta at Padella . . .' I begin. 'And Adrian and work: I have worked so hard on this app I've been building,' I go on, realising that though I have reasons to *not* want to go home, I do have so many reasons to stay. 'This is my home now,' I say, my voice cracking as I do. 'London is my home now.'

'Do you know what you need?' Maya's voice softens and she grabs my hand in hers. I look down at them together. Is it weird that this doesn't feel that weird?

'A visa?' I say, and her little grin tells me that's a given.

'Well, yes, but I was going to say—'

'Employer sponsorship?' I interrupt again.

'That as well.' Maya laughs before going on. 'But also, a—'

'Wife?' I say, and Maya let's go of my hand at speed. 'You fancy marrying me?'

'I was actually going to say *pizza*.'

Maya

I look back at Jack, studying his expression. I know he was joking before, but his question has lingered between us for the past half an hour. No, I silently reply for the thousandth time since he uttered the words. I never want to marry anyone. Then the buzzer rings from the hall. For a moment Jack and I just stare in the direction of the sound, like we don't quite know what it means. He has no idea that I've never heard the buzzer here before either.

'That must be the pizza?' he drawls. 'I'll get it,' he offers and before I can argue the door shuts behind him and I'm left in the apartment, completely alone.

The silence is deafening as I look around the room again. There are no photos of my dad anywhere, but I can feel his fingerprints all over the place. What did he do here? Did he sit here alone, looking out of this window? Did he ever think about my mum? Did he ever think about me? The thoughts come thick and fast without Jack here to distract me.

Tension slips down my spine and I walk towards the window, just trying to shrug it off. I get why Jack asked about my living here. I need an apartment and this one is here, mine for the taking. How can something seemingly simple be so damn complicated?

Every time I've tried to talk to my mum about it, even hazarded a conversation with her about my dad, she shuts it down before I've even had a chance to begin. I have no idea what she'd say if she found out I was here now. I just know it wouldn't be good. It stands against everything she's brought me up to believe in: work, strength, self-sufficiency. She'll probably even see it as his last lame attempt to get between the two of us or something. No, I'll just have to find somewhere else to live, let her think I'm at Emmie's until I do.

From the corner of the window, I can glimpse Jack on the street below handing some cash to a delivery man to secure our fast-food fix. If I wasn't so drunk, I'm sure I'd see some kind of serendipity in the fact we're together right now, the universe aligning my path with the one person in this city who is having a shitter day than me. I may have to move out of my apartment, but he has to move out of the whole bloody country. If he were staying, maybe we could find a place together until we figure it out, move into Adrian's apartment for a bit? But then Jack's just lost his job and it's not like I can afford to cover the rent for us both.

I look to him now, striding back to the building with the pizza box in his hand. I wish I could do *something* to help. If he was staying in the country, I may even be able to bring myself to crash here for a bit, just whilst I get my head around how to sell it. My skin prickles at the thought, my palms instantly sweaty, beading with panic or guilt or shame. My dad didn't want anything to do with me then. I don't want anything to do with him now. But then something about Jack being here makes me forget this was my dad's place to begin with. It makes it feel lighter, despite our situations feeling so heavy. Plus, I would be using the apartment for him, not me, so *technically* it would be Jack accepting my dad's help . . .

The buzzer fills the room again, and I move to the door in the hallway to buzz Jack up, almost sad he'll have to leave the country and face whatever romance drama he's clearly trying to avoid. But it's not like I can magic him a visa, or a new employer to sponsor him to stay here, or a wife. Unlike seemingly every other woman I know of my age, I don't want a ring on my finger. I don't want a big white wedding.

I've never wanted to be a wife.

But doesn't that make me precisely the kind of person who

could enter a marriage of convenience without being wholly, romantically inconvenienced?

'Honey, I'm home!' Jack emerges from the door, casting all thoughts of my dad away. Only one thought remains and it's a crazy, drunken, stupid one.

But it's one that's so bonkers I think it could actually work.

Jack

'One spicy veggie supreme, extra large,' I say, opening the pizza box like a waiter taking the silver dome off one of those fancy serving trays. Maya stares at me for a second, head tilted like she's trying to work me out. What? Why's she looking at me like that?

'Let's get married,' she says.

'Man, you must really like jalapeños.'

'No, for your visa,' she says again as if I'm the crazy one. 'We should get married.'

'Be serious,' I say, searching her tone for sarcasm, but there isn't any.

'I *am* being serious,' she says, turning from me to walk us back into the living room. 'Look, Jack, you need a visa to stay in the country. I need a place to stay and, well . . .' Maya's sentence trails off for a second whilst I struggle to get my head around it. 'My dad isn't keen on me staying here alone and I can just tell my mum I'm living with you now – she doesn't need to know *where*. So, we could just get married and stay here.'

'Maya, we can't *just* get married,' I stutter, still far from sober.

'I'll charge you rent, just a little at first but more once you've got a new job,' Maya continues, clearly ignoring my objections. 'Then I'll be able to save up to stay somewhere else once you've got permanent residence here and we're done with the thing . . .'

'The "thing" being us getting *married*?' I ask, sure I must have missed something.

'Yes, it's perfect.' She beams, standing against the city skyline.

'Maya, we can't get married,' I say, my shoulders sagging as I do.

'Why not?'

'Because what if you want to marry someone else?'

'But I don't,' Maya replies without pause, crinkling her nose at the suggestion. 'I have never wanted to and, besides, if thorugh some insane personality transplant I ever do want to embrace the man-made social construct that is marriage, we can just get divorced.'

Sign a document to get married, sign a document to get out of it. I remember Maya's words from before. I think she might be serious. But even though she may not want to get married now, I'm sure she will at some point. I mean, just look at her. She's pissed. I am too. And though I need this right now, maybe one day Maya will change her mind and want to get married for real. And then someone will fall head over heels for her and she's going to fall insanely in love with them and I'll be the loser that made life so very complicated for them both.

'We'll see other people, obviously,' Maya adds, like anything about this situation is obvious. 'We won't really be married, just legally, just a bit of paper, a document.'

'Just a bit of paper,' I mutter under my breath and I know that the heat of the pizza in my hands isn't the only thing causing my temperature to soar. She's actually serious?

'Maya, I can't let you do that . . .'

'You're not *letting* me do anything,' she says, as if the idea of me or anyone else making her do anything is preposterous. 'I don't want to get married. I don't believe in marriage. What better way to show that than making a *mockery* of marriage?'

I'm clearly drunker than I think – which is saying something – because the things Maya's saying now are starting to make sense. It's just a bit of paper to her. Just one document so that I can be granted another. I do really need a visa, and soon.

'Well, okay, then, only until we've both sorted our situations out,' I agree. I can't believe what I'm saying but I feel wine and relief rush through my veins as I do. I can stay here? I can really stay here. 'And only if you're sure?'

'I've never been surer of anything in my life,' Maya says, putting her hands to her heart in a dramatic and completely sarcastic display of affection.

'Well, okay, then,' I repeat.

Tomorrow we'll change our minds but tonight it all makes sense. It's just a piece of paper.

'Ask me properly, then,' Maya beams, still standing against the moonlit Thames.

'You're kidding, right?' I laugh, this is absurd.

'It'll be the only time I'll get proposed to.' She laughs too, pushing her long hair behind her ears. Her green eyes seem to be sparkling even more at the spontaneity of it all.

'It might not be.' I walk the few short steps between us.

'Well, it'll be the only time I say yes,' she says, rolling her eyes at the thought before fixing them bang on mine, a glint of gold glimmering within the green.

'*Fine*,' I concede, and it feels like the first of many concessions I'll be making to my assertive fake-wife. My hot fake-wife.

I look at Maya's beaming face again. Less than eight hours ago I hadn't seen her in years. Now she might be the very reason I get to stay in the UK. Screw it. Clearing my throat, I drop to my knee, still holding the open pizza box in my hands.

'Maya, do you want to get married to me and live in wedded, sexless bliss?'

Maya giggles, looking me dead in the eye before whispering the words. 'I do.'

Part 2

The Hangover

The Next Day

Maya

I open my eyes and then instantly screw them shut, blinded by the brightness. What *time* is it? I roll onto my side, half wondering why Emmie hasn't come to wake me up by now. With my eyes still closed my other senses come to life. The feel of my paper-dry tongue against the roof of my mouth. The faint smell of pizza making my stomach squirm. The taste of stale alcohol on my breath. If Emmie drank as much as me there's no wonder she isn't standing outside my bedroom trying to knock the door down.

I need water. And I need it fast. It takes all my strength to sit up, every inch of my body protesting as if it's just spent the night sleeping in the shape of a pretzel. Then I see it. Actual water surrounding me on all sides. My dry mouth hangs open at the view, light skimming across its undulating surface, breathtaking and stomach-churning at the same time.

Realisation hits me like the ton of bricks that is currently pressing on my temples. I'm in my dad's apartment. In my dead dad's apartment. Which for some strange reason makes this *my* apartment. Even though there is no good reason for it to be. Which must mean there is a bad one: a last *screw-you* to my mum or a failed attempt to buy our forgiveness. I shouldn't be here. Should never have come here. Remorse floods my mind, drowning out all other senses, except one. I hear someone stir behind me.

I turn around slowly, partly because it's the only speed my broken body can handle right now, mostly because I'm scared this next sight will tip me over the edge entirely. Jack is lying across the length of a sofa at the back of the room. Except, not actually on the sofa but along the wooden floor just in front of it. If he's fallen off at some point in the night, he's too out of it to notice or care. He looks comatose and contented, his dusty blond hair flopping across his forehead, his chiselled jaw closed shut, his shoulders look broad against the floor, the bottom half of his body cocooned in the blanket that was hanging on the back of the sofa.

I take a tentative step towards him until I can see the steady rise and fall of his naked chest, the half-smile resting on his sleeping face. What *happened* last night? My legs feel like jelly beneath me as I reach down to hold the blanket ever so slightly in my hands. I can tell in an instant that it's one hundred per cent cashmere. One hundred per cent for apartment number one hundred, my dad once again willing to give his all to something so long as he doesn't have to be present. For a moment, I think I'm going to be sick. Then the sight of Jack's jeans just visible above the blanket calms me somehow, like it's all the confirmation I need that the only stupid thing that happened last night was coming here in the first place.

'Jack?' I whisper hurriedly, a thousand regrets swirling around my stomach. He stirs again, straining to open his eyes before surrendering to his sleep. Damn it. Sweat prickles on my hands as I feel that same panic starting to crash over me again. I need to get out of here.

Looking around the room for my phone, I find it nestled down the side of the sofa cushions I seemingly slept on last night. I go to text Jack, to tell him I had to leave, to just let himself out, but my phone is dead. I search around the room, looking for something to scrawl my message on. I walk over to the writing desk pushed up against a window, looking right across the water, and try to ignore its perfection. It's easy for a place to seem perfect when no one's here to screw it up.

Reaching into one of the drawers of the desk, I riffle through my dad's things like they might bite or burn me, until I find a blank sheet of paper to write on. I don't flip it over to see if there's something important on the other side. Can't be that important seeing as he's not needed this stuff in years. I scribble my message to Jack and rest it on his toned torso so that he can read my demand to lock up and my simple P.S. *Well, last night got out of hand . . .*

I watch his sleeping half-smile for another breath before turning to leave him and this place and last night behind. It's all so random, so blurry, so wrong. But thank God we didn't do anything *really* stupid like sleep together.

Then I see the discarded pizza box by the door and it's like someone has twisted a camera lens into focus. The party. Adrian and Emmie. The wine, the walk, the wall. The apartment. Jack's visa. I reach for the box with shaking hands, the memory of Jack holding it open whilst down on one knee

39

enough to make me retch into it now. Things did get out of
hand last night. Because I'm seventy per cent sure Jack asked
for my hand in marriage.

I manage to make it back to Emmie's apartment without being
sick once, which is saying something given everything that
happened last night. But then I look up at the closed door
in front of me now, the one that leads to the only real home
I've ever known, and another wave of nausea crashes over me.
Turning my key in the door, I try to ignore the flashbacks
of finally unlocking that key safe last night. Jack will put the
apartment keys back in there, but I still have the one key I
need to unlock it nestled in my back pocket. But not for long.
Today, I'm going to come clean to my mum and she'll help me
sell the apartment quicker than my dad could say 'goodbye'.

But first, I need Emmie to finally come clean to *me*.

Holding my breath, I push open the door and walk into our
living room. I kind of expected to come home to find Emmie
and Adrian already living here, sitting on the sofa surrounded
by last night's bed sheets and feeding each other pancakes or
something. But no, she's here alone, standing in our kitchen,
cleaning away the mess from last night. My dry mouth and
hammering heart tell me that'll take a lot more than surface
spray. I urge my legs to move forward, rage rising within me
with every step. How dare she not tell me that she asked Adrian
to live here? That she's effectively forcing me to move out. That
I had to find out from some random guy from uni and not
her. Some random guy I asked to propose to me last night. I
shake the thought away and jolt my mind back into the room.

Emmie is wearing a thin blue jumper that I know for a fact is expensive, and spray-on black jeans, her hair now in a long ponytail so that I can see the perfect blend of her brown-to-blond hair. And I'm wearing the same clothes as last night, my black 'mourning' outfit morphing into my 'morning after' look.

'Hey,' I mutter weakly, because how else do I begin to confront Emmie?

It's not like we've had much practice. In all the years we've been friends we've never really fought. We've never really had to. We could talk about anything before it could become a blow-up. Clearly, Emmie feels differently now. Everything feels a bit different now.

'Oh!' She swings around, looking menacing in her Marigolds, like she wants to scrub me out with her surface spray. 'Where the hell have you been? I thought you'd been Liam-Neeson-Taken somehow.'

'I was with Jack . . .' I begin, lips pursed, her rage only maximising my own.

'We figured' — Emmie says, sounding a bit smug about being a 'we' now — 'when neither of you would pick up your damn phones.'

'We were busy,' I mumble.

Busy putting the world to rights. Busy getting betrothed.

'Well, I hope it was worth bailing on your friends for.' Emmie raises her groomed brows suggestively. We weren't busy like *that*. Even if we were, it's not like she has a right to judge me when she practically threw herself at Adrian on their first date.

'My friends?' I say, the volume of my voice creeping higher. 'They were *your* friends because this is *your* apartment.' Despite us spending three years together making it ours.

'Well, just be careful,' Emmie says, removing the Marigolds one by one, the gloves now off. 'Adrian says he's a bit fucked up.'

For some reason her talking about Jack like this is the final straw.

'No,' I breathe, seeing red; everything we've been holding back coming to a head. 'What's *fucked up* is that I had to find out about me being kicked out of this place from him.'

'He . . . I . . . we're not . . . I can . . .' Eloquent Emmie malfunctions before me.

'Explain?' I say, taking a step back, the distance between us palpable. 'Be my guest.' The words sting as I say them. Clearly, if there's a guest here it's me.

'I've been meaning to tell you,' Emmie's voice softens, her shoulders too. 'I was going to tell you . . . I was just trying to find the right time . . . It's just all happened so quickly.'

'Yes, it has,' I say, not meaning to sound so bitter.

How can two people fall in love so quickly? Put all their eggs into one basket just like that when there's so much evidence that baskets and eggs get broken all the time?

'And with everything that's happened with your dad lately . . .'

'Emmie, what have I told you?'

Emmie used to say I was the strongest person she knew. Now she's looking at me as if I'm so fragile that one mistimed conversation could break me apart completely.

'Maya. He's your *father*.'

'I thought you of all people would understand.'

'But you've not even stopped to process it.'

'I don't *need* to process it.'

'It's not a weakness to ask for help, Maya.'

'I never said it was!' I'm shouting now, thoughts of Jack asking me to marry him racing through my mind. 'Of course it's not weak to ask for help and I would if I thought I needed it, but I'm also not going to roll over and say I feel something I don't just because other people *expect* that of me.' I'm never going to do *anything* just because people expect it of me.

'Okay, *fine*.' How Emmie says this tells me things are far from fine between us now.

'So, what's happening with the flat? I can handle it.' I hate that she needs me to tell her that. It's as if she doesn't know me or what I stand for, what I thought *we* stood for, at all.

'Adrian is going to move in,' she says telling me what I already know. 'In six weeks. I was going to tell you today, I thought that was enough notice to . . . and you can stay in the spare room for as long as you want until you find another place . . .'

The fact she's calling my bedroom the spare room tells me how final this is.

'That's great,' I say, forcing a smile. Six weeks. I can find a place in six weeks. That I can afford. Even though I've barely been able to afford Emmie's mates-rates rent.

'And you could always stay at your mum's?' Emmie asks unsurely; she knows that staying there would be a last resort. What Emmie doesn't know is that I have another backup that would disappoint my mum even more. Which is exactly why I'm going to present her with my sell-it solution before it can even become a problem.

'Yeah, actually . . .' I begin, unable to stomach the tension between us a second longer. 'I'm heading over to my mum's now.'

'That sounds like a good idea,' Emmie says, a sad, sympathetic

43

smile pinned to her face. 'And, Maya, I promise you, even when Adrian moves in, I want you to feel at home here.'

I nod, even though I know by now that feeling at home somewhere is not something you can force. And for some reason it feels comforting to know that Jack understands this too.

Jack

'The prodigal son returns!' Adrian throws his arms wide as I walk into our living room. It reminds me of my and Maya's awkward first greeting yesterday before things became *much* more comfortable between us.

'Woah, dude. You look awful.' Adrian takes a step closer towards me. 'Had a *big one on the turps*?' He looks proud to be putting the Kiwi slang I taught him to good use. Proud and annoyingly chipper. And it's making me feel worse.

'Yeah, it was pretty heavy,' I say, the alcohol still sloshing around inside me, the memory of turning Maya's note over in my hands to find a faded photograph plonked haphazardly in the top left corner of the page, like someone has just pressed CTRL+P to print it at speed, still seared into my screaming head. It was a photo of a girl, six or seven years old. So random that Maya no doubt grabbed the nearest piece of paper she could find. I'm impressed she can do anything quickly after last night.

'And not a lot of sleep?' Adrian laughs, his insinuation clear. He knows I think Maya is hot. In a slightly scary, unattainable way. Clearly, Adrian thinks this last part has changed.

'Not like that.' Of all the things that were said and done last night, sex wasn't one of them.

'Oh good,' Adrian breathes, content to carry on with what he was doing when I first walked in. Which I can see from the cardboard-chaos around him looks a lot like packing his whole life into boxes. It feels a bit too close to home right now. Literally.

'Good?' I ask. Adrian used to love hearing about my dating-app misadventures.

'I mean . . . I wouldn't get too attached this time.'

'You're the one always telling me I should commit to someone.'

Of all the reasons to pass my third-date threshold, shutting Adrian up is the most compelling. But I can't. I meant what I said to Maya last night: feelings make everything complicated. But did she mean what she said to me? For a moment it felt like she might have just fixed everything. *P.S. Well, last night got out of hand* . . . Clearly, Maya thinks that everything that happened yesterday was a mistake.

'Emmie says she's a little damaged because of everything that's happened lately,' Adrian continues, walking over to our bookcase to begin packing everything on it away too.

A little damaged? After everything that's happened? I feel a surge of emotion race through my body. I don't know how to place it and I certainly don't want Adrian to see it. But it feels a bit like an urge to defend her. Which I know Maya would categorically hate.

I shrug Adrian's comment away. It doesn't feel like my place to ask. But then, Maya did ask me to marry her. Or maybe I asked her. I can't really remember which came first. Either way, I know that all of my eggs are in her basket. And it's something that she shouldn't have to carry.

45

I know all too well what it feels like to be responsible for someone else. And that's the very reason that not even the world's worst hangover laced with impending deportation doom can keep me from my plans this afternoon.

Maya

I don't hear the front door open or close, but when I emerge from my bedroom – the soon-to-be spare bedroom – hours later, Emmie is nowhere to be seen. She's no doubt headed off to see Adrian. Maybe even Adrian and his 'fucked-up' friend, Jack. Emmie's words still sting. All of them. And I can't hide out here forever. Just like I can't hide out at my so-called dad's place either.

Switching off my music, I reach to the top of my wardrobe and pull down my weekend bag, mindlessly packing everything I'll need to stay at my mum's for a week or so. Just to give me and Emmie a bit of space. And Lord knows, I'll have space at my mum's. She'll be out at the office and with clients so much that she might not even realise I'm there.

As I pack the letters from the lawyers telling me about the apartment and leave Emmie's flat behind, I can't help the tears from forming. I knew we couldn't live here forever, but I thought we'd have a few more years. That I'd have enough time to complete my PhD and work out what's next. Now it feels like I've got nothing stable to hold onto. My work, my purpose, my home; they're all frustratingly interdependent. When all my mum has ever wanted for me is to be able to stand on my own two feet. I bite back my tears as I arrive at her front door. Thankfully, last night's rain has subsided, the brighter weather reminding me it's the first day of May. My frosty mood, however, still feels like winter.

Reaching in my bag, I riffle past half-open packs of chewing gum and no less than four hair bobbles – even though, every time I need one, they are seemingly scarce – until I find the key to her front door. That it takes so long to find it reminds me of how little I've been here lately.

As I walk into the hall, I try not to draw parallels between this place and my dad's. Turns out that's tricky. For starters, they are both grand, luxurious, cold; the kind of places that scream *no kids allowed*. And then there's the fact that neither one has ever felt like home.

'Mum!' My voice echoes into the empty space. I don't hold my breath for her reply. But then she pops her head into the hallway, her designer metal glasses perched on the end of her nose, her long hair pulled up into a perfectly messy bun on the top of her head.

'Maya!' She smiles, still a floating head, her body planted firmly in the front room. 'Have you got the contract?' The contract? I see her eyes widen slightly at the sight of my weekend bag in hand and wonder, not for the first time, whether the woman has X-ray vision.

'I needed it yesterday,' she says, eyes still on me, smile fixed on her face. Does she mean the legal letters, the documents saying that he left it to me? And she's still smiling? Something doesn't add up. 'Derek, I've told you before and I'll tell you again . . .'

Derek?

Mum must see my face crinkle in confusion as she points

to her heavily jewelled ear and I see that she is wearing an earpiece. She's still on a work call. Go figure. She gives me the five-more-minutes signal and I gesture towards the kitchen. I know by now that five minutes means two hours so I may as well wait this out with snacks.

'Sorry about that, honey.'

Mum eventually emerges into the kitchen, her wide-leg trousers billowing beneath her, just skimming the floor. I know from the authoritative beat of her strides that she's wearing heels underneath. To Mum, feminism means having the choice to do whatever you please, even if it means strutting around your expensive kitchen in Louboutin, provided your hard work means you can single-handedly afford it all.

'Work crisis.' There's always a crisis. 'To what do I owe this pleasure?' My mum manages to make the word 'pleasure' sound like it's silently laced with 'inconvenience'. 'PhD going well? How were the interviews you conducted last week?'

'They were last month,' I say, and my mum begins nodding aggressively as if this is precisely what she said.

To me it seems ages since I talked to a handful of women, all sixty and over, about ageing, about how they feel about it and how the negative stereotypes surrounding the 'ageing woman' have impacted what *should* be their most powerful years. For my busy mother, this past month has clearly felt like minutes.

'They went well. Just need to analyse them for a paper now, but anyway . . .' I let my sentence trail off; we both have a habit of talking about the professional at the expense of the personal, but this conversation is too important to skirt over. 'But I actually wanted to talk to you about something else,' I say slowly, this morning's hangover lingering, as if I'm

48

unintentionally breathing black marks into this pristine room. It looks even more like a show home than the last time I came here. I didn't think that was possible.

'Great!' Mum claps her hands together and I note her manicure. I try not to feel offended that she has time to get her nails done and yet still misses our weekly calls. 'I have something to talk to you about too,' she says, as if adding to an agenda. 'Shoot!'

'Okay, well. It's a little awkward but—'

'I told you the client needed this yesterday . . .' I stall on my mum's words but then she motions to her earpiece again, mouthing more apologies. 'Look, I'm with my daughter . . .'

I hate that some kind of warmth is sparked within me at such simple words.

'Derek, of course I've mentioned that I have a daughter before . . .'

And snuffed out just as fast.

'Okay, well, I need your . . . advice . . .' I say, now that her attention is back on me.

Advice feels a better word than help. My mum gives advice for a living, but we've never needed help. Not when Dad left us. Not when Mum was juggling toddler tantrums both at home and at work. Not when I got a first at uni without any real support and she ordered the hugest bouquet of flowers to my graduation to congratulate me.

'About selling an apartment . . .' I go on, treading carefully, Mum's eyes still swinging from my face to her phone screen.

'Emmie's? I thought you guys loved it there,' Mum interjects, eyes flicking to her screen again. Something buzzes and we both pretend not to hear it. 'I'm so proud of her for bagging such a good place, it's no mean feat doing it on your own, especially before she graduated.'

I want to point out that Emmie's Year in Industry and the promise of a permanent job had no small part to play in this, but I hold my tongue. I'm proud of Emmie too, always have been. My heart lurches at the memory of our conversation today, pride and pain amalgamating in a way that makes what I have to say next feel almost impossible.

'No, not Emmie's.' I pause before adding the kicker. 'It's Dad's.'

'Yes, I know it's your dad's birthday,' Mum says absent-mindedly. That's not what I was saying. I wasn't even thinking that. I'm surprised that Mum is. 'But, Maya, we've not celebrated it for a long time, don't let it derail you now he's gone.'

'That's not what . . .' I begin, her stern look shutting down my sentence. 'It was actually more about his, erm . . . his will . . .'

'Maya-Anna,' she adds her pet name for me with such a snap that it ceases to sound sweet. 'Your father hasn't been family to us for a long time, you can't expect him to honour that commitment now. Do you need money? Is that what you've come here to—'

'No, Mum.' Now it's my turn to snap. 'I didn't come here to ask for *money*.'

'Okay, because I need to know you're okay before I—'

'Before what?' I ask, my pulse picking up pace. She's not sick too, is she?

'Maya Angela.' Mum adds my middle name, signalling the seriousness of what's to come, reminding me of the iconic feminist I'm named after, like being badged with Maya Angelou's

50

name should be confidence-boosting and not a constant reminder of how unremarkable my life is proving so far.

'I've been offered a new position. A senior one . . .' It's not like she needs to add this last point seeing as my mum wouldn't settle for anything less. 'In New York.'

'In New York?' I echo back to her, hating that it makes me sound so simple. It's just, that's where Dad lives. Or lived. I thought she liked that London was always hers.

'Yes.' She grins back at me. 'It all happened very quickly, really. And I've been meaning to tell you' – The theme of today – 'but you're so settled with Emmie and your studies that I knew it was a good time to get rid of this place, make the move.'

'Get rid of this place?' I parrot again, kicking my weekend bag further under the kitchen island we're both sitting at.

'Well, got rid. The sale went through a fortnight back, it's just been so busy. That's okay though, yes?' I stare back at my mum, my mind scrambling to make sense of her words.

'If it's not I can just . . .' She stalls.

Just what? Turn down a promotion? Her dream job? Her chance to make it in the city my dad managed to shotgun first? She stares back at me, and I see a flash of sympathy in her eyes – sympathy or disappointment.

'You're happy at Emmie's though?' She checks again and I can't take the intensity any longer.

'Yes,' I nod. I was until last night.

Mum holds my eye contact for a second longer. Then her phone rings. I need to talk to her about this apartment, about Dad's apartment, about what to do next, but I can tell from the anxious look in her eye that she really needs to take this.

'It's okay, Mum,' I say, for what feels like the thousandth time. 'I'm okay.'

'Of course you are, honey.' Mum smiles, reaching to hold my hand in hers. 'You're Maya Angela Morgan.' Her maiden name feels like another reminder. 'You are always going to be *better* than okay. Look, honey, I've got to take this, but we'll have dinner soon, yes?' I nod. Our dinners will be even fewer and further between with an ocean separating us. 'Feel free to hang out here though,' she says, getting to her feet.

The words jolt me back to the note I left for Jack this morning. Somehow last night with him now feels like the only steady island among hours of being battered by the waves. And right now, I could really do with an island. For someone to look at me like the woman I know I am, and not the grieving daughter, or the shunted housemate or the inconvenient child. Picking up my weekend bag, I reach for my phone and begin to type.

I don't know about you, but I could really do with another drink. Hair of the dog?

Jack

'Mr Wilson, you look *terrible*,' I hear one of the young women exclaim from the depths of her hoodie as soon as I make my way into the secondary school's dust-covered IT room.

I want to tell her that I *feel* terrible. That I've been having a mare of a day. A mare of a life. Then I remember I'm supposed to be something of a role model to these girls, that this good deed is another part of my penance for everything that happened back home.

'Nice to see you too, Zadie,' I say, throwing my satchel onto the teacher's desk but refusing to sit behind it. Instead, I pull out a chair and plonk it somewhere in the middle aisle of the two rows of monstrously big monitors that these twelve teenagers usually sit behind. Today there's only eleven.

'Where's Charlotte?' I ask them, unable to hide the panic in my voice; usually if one of them doesn't turn up here, it's rarely for a good reason.

'Mr Wilson,' Zadie says, her hand poised in the air as if it's about to accompany a Mariah Carey trill. Zadie's all sass and I love and loathe her for it in equal measure. 'She's probably giving up on coming because you refuse to call her *Charlie.*'

'Her mother called her Charlotte, so I'm calling her Charlotte,' I retort, and the fact I actually sound like a teacher right now makes me want to throw up.

That, and the truth: that I can't stomach using that name without thinking about my Charlie back home. It's the reason I started volunteering at Girls Code during uni in the first place, like joining a Big Sibling Scheme for underprivileged teenagers might somehow give me a second chance at being dependable, like each session might absolve me of my guilt just that little bit more.

'Charlie!' Rosa, another one of the girls, shouts, looking behind me and I swing around to see Charlotte walking into the room.

Her heavy make-up looks even more smudged than usual. If I *were* a teacher I could maybe tell them to take that stuff off. But given that I'm simply supposed to teach them how to code at the weekends, I just pull out a seat for her.

'Right, now we're all here. Who wants to learn a cool new function?'

'Isn't "cool function" an oxymoron?' Charlotte quips at the exact same time that Zadie questions: 'Mr W, are you even *fit* to function?'

Despite my hangover, I try my best not to smile. Joining the scheme may have been about Charlie but over the years I've been here, these girls have started to matter too.

'No.' I turn to Charlotte, all grins and folded arms, and yet, I can still see a sadness weighing heavy on her smile. I know that sadness too. 'And yes, I am fit.'

'Big head,' someone mutters. The girls laugh.

'Show off,' Sara says, nudging Rosa in the ribs.

'Who is she?' Charlotte says, arms still folded, a smug look that tells me that she's seen my hangover and seamlessly traced it back to the source: a date or one-night stand.

Well, she's wrong. Sure, I've had countless one-night stands since my break-up back home. But this time wasn't even an almost-one-night stand. No, I was with an almost-friend. My almost-fiancée. Even now, a small part of me is willing that blurry memory to still stand today, because how else will I be able to stay here?

'She's no one,' I say, and Charlotte's eyes light up all the more. Damn it. 'We're on Week Four of the new coding programme and things are about to get real interesting . . .'

'If you say so,' Zadie mumbles, and all the young women laugh, and another says 'nerd'.

I never got called 'nerd' in school, but behind closed doors, playing computer games into the early hours with Charlie was my happiest place to be. I push away the memory. I'm here now, doing something that matters now. But who knows for how long?

The two-hour session goes quickly, which is surprising given how bad I'm feeling. Thankfully, after their initial banter the girls settle down, they always do, because despite what so many of the grown-ups they know seem to think, they've got so much potential.

I watch as one by one they go back out into their lives, knowing that at least half of them are planning to drink themselves silly in the park with their friends this evening, even though they've got school tomorrow. And it's not like I can tell them not to, given how wasted I was last night. Still, it feels good to know that I've provided some kind of safe harbour in their otherwise hectic days. I watch as Charlotte shuts down her screen and gathers her things slowly, like it's just occurring to her that the outside world still exists. I am holding the door to the IT room open for her to walk through when she stalls.

'Mr W?' she says quietly, now that everyone's out of earshot. 'Can I chat to you for a sec?'

I kind of knew this was coming. I've seen her morph from feisty fifteen-year-old to an increasingly subdued seventeen-year-old and I know her home life is to blame. I've already spoken to the Big Sibling Scheme about the fact that I think Charlotte might benefit from some closer one-on-one mentoring, provided she doesn't think we're trying to pry.

'Sure.' I say, wedging the door to the IT room open with a chair as I do.

'I did something bad,' she says, and I can see she has no energy left to prop up her smile.

Me too. I push the thought back down, hating how often I think it even though I'm literally and figuratively miles away from who I used to be.

'Mum was drinking again,' Charlotte continues, and I see tears gathering in her lashes. I want to hold her close, because no one else does, but know better than to take a step forward. 'And she asked my sister to go and get her more booze and she went, and I was just so angry at her because, I mean, why would she go and get her more when we all just want her to—'

'Stop,' I say, barely above my breath.

'Yeah.' Charlotte sighs, her shoulders sagging as she does.

'No, I . . .' I begin, trying to find the right words to say. 'I was going to say, stop beating yourself up. This stuff is hard, Charlotte.'

It's at this point that a tear trickles down her face, as if my simple sentence has given her permission to let go. I wish I could let stuff go too. But I can't. Not after what I did. *You may be captain of the rugby club, Jack . . .* Even now my mum's words manage to force their way into my mind. *But being a big brother is the most important role you'll ever have . . .*

'But don't take it out on your sister,' I go on. I know it's the most important role. It's why I'm here. It's why I need to stay. 'You're all each other has.'

'That's not true,' Charlotte says slowly, her confidence re-assembling with every sentence shared. 'I have this place too, Girls Code, and we all have you.'

'Stop, you'll make me blush,' I joke, but an uninvited lump catches in my throat.

'Dude,' Charlotte says. 'Your face has been sheet-white the whole session. I'm not even sure you *can* blush today.'

'It's been a rough one.'

'Well, we appreciate you not bailing on us,' she says, walking through the door and out into the school hall. 'You're the only one who cares enough to show up.'

And yet, I'm the one who's going to have to leave them high and dry when I head back to Auckland. The big brother who bails all over again. The thought lodges itself in my mind, sears across my stomach. I lock up the school building behind me and look across the empty playing field, memories of me running around one of these like some kind of semi-pro or demi-god racing through my mind. I hate that guy. The one who thought his reputation was everything. Before it cost him everything. I reach into my pocket and pull out my phone, searching for something to save me from my memory.

I don't know about you, but I could really do with another drink. Hair of the dog?

The message is from an unknown number but there's only one person it could be.

I do. I type and send. *I mean . . . . I do too.*

'You look rough,' Maya says, sounding every inch like the teens at Girls Code as soon as I bump into her coming out of the doorway into her dad's apartment block.

'In a rugged, handsome way?' I'm surprised I have the energy to flirt, but something about Maya teases it out of me.

'In a *hungover* way.'

'Not my fault my fiancée got me pissed.' The words spill out of me, mostly because I've been holding onto them all day, willing them to be true, for them to fix everything.

But now that I've said them, neither one of us seems to know what to do. *Well, last night got out of hand . . .* I've still got Maya's note in the pocket of my jeans. She doesn't want this, any of this. In fact, is she *leaving* the apartment?

'Where are you—?'

'I, err . . .' Maya begins, deer in headlights. 'I went up for a bit and then it was like . . .' Her sentence trails off.

She looks worried, guilty almost. For a moment, Adrian's words from earlier dart through my mind: *Emmie says she's a little damaged.* Then I remember, I'm pretty bruised too.

'I didn't know whether you'd be able to get in.'

'I could have just buzzed up.' Thoughts of the pizza delivery, the pizza proposal itself, wedge their way between us. I can tell Maya feels it too. But what does she think now?

As I follow her back up to Apartment 100, I try my best to keep my eyes from tracing her behind. I know from my brief time with her that 'checking her out' will be met with disdain. But it's not just Maya's arse that's attractive, it's the way she walks; her confident stride, the slight swing of her hips, like she knows precisely where she's going in life.

'Home sweet home,' I say as soon as she's opened the front door. Maya winces, probably at the cheesiness of my words.

It was a lot easier to know what to say when I was knee-deep in booze. Following her into the living room, I don't know if I feel affirmed or intimidated that this place is as ludicrously luxurious as I remember from last night. Given how drunk I was, I was half expecting to discover that it was actually a shoebox.

'Hair of the dog?' Maya holds the wine bottle I've just handed to her by the neck.

This place makes me wish I'd splashed more than six pounds on it but it's not like I can afford anything else right now. If I wait to get kicked out of the country does that mean someone

58

will pay for my ticket? This thought is all it takes to make me want to drink again.

I sit on one side of a sofa facing the river, sipping my first glass of wine slowly. Maya sits on the other side doing the same. After all we had to say to each other last night, the silence between us is surprising. Surprising but not unpleasant. In fact, with Maya next to me, the swirling thoughts in my head seem to settle into one: will she actually marry me?

'Last night was fun,' I begin, studying Maya's profile, faced forward to the window.

'Which part? Leaving my party, or bemoaning your deportation?'

'Definitely not the latter,' I say, face falling, hopes falling too.

'Sorry.' She seems to soften and takes another sip of her wine. 'Today's just been . . .' I try to read her tired expression. 'I had this big fight with Emmie about the apartment.'

Maya turns to me with a sad smile, like she's decided I'm on her side again. I am on her side. I just don't know how long I'm going to be able to stay on this side of the equator.

'I'm sorry about putting my foot in it like that.'

'It's not your fault.' Except, it always is. 'And I'm glad you did,' Maya adds, her body softening even more as she inches a fraction closer. 'At least now I have more time to work out what to do next . . .' Her sentence trails off.

We both know time is the one thing I haven't got. That, and a visa.

'I'm sure Emmie and Adrian will let you stay with them as long as you need to,' I say, remembering Adrian's comment all over again: *Emmie says she's a little damaged because of everything that's happened lately.* But what does that mean?

59

'Yeah, in their *spare* room.' Maya spits the word 'spare' like it means 'superfluous'.

'And I bet your dad won't mind you staying—' Maya's narrowing eyes scare the rest of my sentence into silence. 'Oh crap, is he here?'

'He's not coming back,' Maya says quickly.

'Oh right, is everything . . .?' I stutter. 'Adrian said this thing, I don't know, like you'd been through something big lately. Do you want to talk about it?'

Maya

Do I want to talk about it?

I study Jack's expression, the one that shows he is trying to 'be there' for me. The one that clearly wants to cut me open and yank out topics like 'dead Dad' or 'leaving Mum' or 'abandoned by friend', as if pulling them out won't make my whole system flatline completely. I struggle to hold his eye, my gaze drifting to his strong, tanned forearms, exposed in his checked lumberjack shirt, pushed up to his elbows.

'I should be asking you the same thing,' I deflect, adding a smile for good measure. I'm not sure it has Jack convinced. 'Any progress on the visa issue?'

I ask the question tentatively. In the sober light of day there's no doubt that Jack's managed to sort this entire scenario out without us having to follow through with our plan. His eyes fix on me and I feel myself uncoil, relax. Last night was the first time I've hung out with this guy in years and yet somehow, I don't want him to leave. He's the only person who knows about my dad's apartment, the only person who makes being in it feel bearable.

'That depends,' he says, cautiously. 'Were you being serious last night?'

'Define "serious"?' I ask, if only to buy me some time. Since this morning the broken shards of last night have fixed themselves into place, my relationship with my best friend and my mum seeming to have shattered even further and I'm not sure what to make of it. Any of it.

'Do you seriously never want to get married?'

'No. Never.' Well, that part is easy to answer at least.

'Do you honestly think it's just a piece of paper?'

'I do,' I say, and I see Jack's face light up at the words. I can tell he really needs this, more than anything. That he's got no Plan B, nowhere left to turn. I know what that's like. 'Can you seriously not go home?'

'No. Never.' Clearly, this part is easy for Jack to answer too. 'This *is* my home.'

Jack's face is serious, his frame steady, against the increasingly dusk-lit water dancing in waves behind him. He looks at home here. Not just in the UK or in London but here in this apartment. I watch as he takes another sip of his wine, drinking from a dead man's glass. I need to sell this place, get rid of it. But with my mum leaving the country maybe I'll have a bit more time to sell it. To wait for the right price so I can help more people when I can give his guilt-money away. And with Jack staying in the country maybe I'll be able to stomach living here whilst I write my paper and begin making an impact worthy of my name . . .

'Do you seriously want to do this thing?' I ask.

'Do *you*?' Jack says, still evidently concerned that he's coercing me into something. But he needn't worry; unlike the countless people who trust their feelings, *this* marriage would be based on facts.

'Why not? It'll mean you can stay here. It'll mean I can stay here too . . .'

'Why wouldn't you be able to stay here?'

'It just means I can charge you rent once you've got another job,' I add quickly as a cover.

'What happened to "what's mine is yours"?' Jack laughs.

'Do *not* push your luck.' I narrow my eyes in his direction and he flings up his hands in defence. 'This is an administrative arrangement at best. So, no funny business.'

'I promise,' Jack says, beaming from ear to ear; it feels good to fix something today. 'Until permanent residency do us part.' He looks around *this* residency like the whole thing is a dream come true. And at least Jack staying here will stop it being my nightmare.

'Okay, then, deal.' I gaze into his big brown eyes, a strange calmness coming over me. I reach to hold his hand in mine and laugh. 'Until permanent residency do us part.'

Part 3

The Wedding

Two Weeks Later

Jack

I wake up and my first thought is *Maya*.

It has been for the past fortnight. Ever since we agreed for the second time to get married. Most guys say their fiancée makes them the 'happiest man on the planet' but I mostly just feel *relieved*; relieved to be staying on this side of it. Relieved to not have to go home and relive everything I left behind.

I turn over onto the cold side of the bed as my phone begins to buzz from somewhere beneath me. I reach for it with trepidation. I know part of me is still expecting to get a message from Maya telling me that she's changed her mind, come to her senses. It's the same niggle I've had since our second proposal two weeks ago, the same one that followed me throughout the entirety of the next day as we went to the local registry office to notify them of our forthcoming nuptials and Maya looked up to me, smiling mischievously and saying, 'Well, I guess there's no turning back now?'

The woman we spoke to there had looked Maya up and

down, exploring every inch of her, seeing if she could detect any silent cries for help or signs that this random Kiwi in front of her was coercing this beautiful young lady into the biggest mistake of her life. And I was right alongside her doing the same. The last thing I want is to trap Maya into something. But as I make my way into our almost empty living room to find Adrian pouring a cup of coffee, I know that's not entirely true: the last thing I want is to go back to New Zealand.

'That for me?' I say, and Adrian's head jolts up, surprised to see me.

'It would be if I didn't think you'd already be at work by now.'

It's a fair assumption. Adrian doesn't know that I stopped working for SoberApp in the first place, so it didn't make sense to tell him that the day after Maya and I gave our notice to get married, I called Toby to beg for my job back. Turns out that continuing to underpay me for my blood, sweat and tears began to look a lot more appealing as soon as a complicated and expensive visa sponsorship was off the table.

'Yeah, I'm actually not working today,' I say, moving around our small kitchen space to make my own coffee, Adrian seamlessly dancing out of my way in a manner only people who have lived together for a long time know how to do.

'Doesn't sound like something you'd do.' Adrian eyes me suspiciously, from my blue denim jeans to my fresh white T-shirt and open khaki shirt; he can tell I've styled my hair.

I would argue that it's a Saturday, but after spending countless of them working on the app, I know not to bother. As far as Adrian is concerned, I never lost my job, never lost my sponsorship, and my future here has never been in doubt.

'So, what's important enough to drag you away from work?'

66

He sounds a bit like a jealous spouse, given that I rarely take a day off for him.

'Nothing much,' I say quickly, and Adrian grins. He thinks I'm an easy read.

'It's that new girl, isn't it?'

Clearly, I'm not as easy to work out as he thinks. He's my best mate and he still thinks I burn through new girls because I'm a player, or aloof, or too obsessed with my job or something. Not that I'm fearful of becoming too attached to one person. He should have seen how I used to be with Laura Mae back home – downright besotted.

'A second date with . . .?' He searches for the latest name.

'I'm seeing Maya.' I tell him the truth, but not the whole truth because Maya has specifically asked me not to.

'I knew it!' Adrian's expression lands somewhere between smug and satisfied.

'No, you didn't.' He thought I was seeing a girl called Louise, someone I started chatting to online last week, mostly to take my mind off the fact that Maya's messages ran dry, and the silence soon filled with thoughts: the plan is off, you're out of options, you're going home. 'And not like that anyway, we're . . .'

'Going to the beach?' Adrian fills in my blanks.

Huh?

'Emmie said Maya was going to the beach today.'

I stare back at him. Yes, we're going to Brighton. But not for the beach.

'Yes, that's right,' I confirm, trying to work out how much he and Emmie already know, whether Maya has sworn me to secrecy but is secretly telling her friend everything.

Last I heard, things were still frosty between Maya and Emmie. I assumed she'd need to go back for her things but that perhaps she was spending more time at her dad's. I didn't like to ask. Maya may have agreed to marry me, but she never agreed we'd share everything with one another.

'How are things between the two of them anyway?' I ask cautiously.

'Your guess is as good as mine, dude,' Adrian says, with a telling smile, one that assumes that I'm falling for Maya. I'm pretty sure he'd implode if he really knew the truth. 'I'd not get into it though. Trust me, life is so much easier if you just keep out of the drama.'

Adrian folds his arms and leans against the kitchen worktop like a lecturer giving a masterclass. He has no idea that you can't keep out of the drama if you're the one causing it.

I recognise Maya from miles away, her long dark hair falling in waves down her back as she peers into a large glass shopfront. She's wearing a long cotton dress that clings to her legs, a casual grey hoodie slung over the top. It may be mid-May, but I know this country well enough by now to know that you can depend on its weather to be unpredictable. And I'm still waiting for Maya to be the same, to snap or break down or change her mind completely about marrying me. But so far, she's seemed as committed to this plan as I am. It was her idea to take the hour-long train to Brighton today, suggesting that it would be good for us to get out of the city. I suspect it's mostly because she doesn't want anyone to see what we're shopping for: our wedding rings.

As I walk further and further in the direction of her petite frame, I remind myself for the thousandth time that this plan is the right thing to do. For both of us. But as Maya swings around, her face breaking into a full and unreserved smile, I can't help but wonder again what's in this for her, whether she's just too good to be true.

'Hey, stranger.' She smiles back at me, her small frame now inches from my chest.

Strangers. That's precisely what we are, and not to throw my arms around her. And yet, after two weeks of not seeing each other, of concentrating on our own lives – me getting my job back, her working on the latest part of her PhD – I'd almost convinced myself that Maya was just a figment of my imagination. Now here she is, as tangible and real as the day I proposed, and then *she* proposed, and then we proposed our marriage to the registry office together.

'Found anything you like?' I ask as Maya's eyes explore my expression, following my gaze to the jewellery shop behind her, displaying row after row of engagement rings.

'Yes, actually.' Maya grins openly, surprising me for the umpteenth time. 'You see that one there?' She points through the window, and I stand by her side, the smell of her perfume picked up on the sea breeze. 'The gold one, with the yellow-gold diamond . . .'

I trace her pointed finger to a gargantuan yellow rock surrounded by lots of little silver spikey ones; it looks as if someone asked a toddler to draw a sunshine in precious stones. It's disgusting.

'You like that?' I try not to scoff seeing as Maya's eyes are sparkling at the sight of it.

'I really do,' she gushes, as my heart hammers harder. 'But I'm not sure it's big enough, you know? *Special* enough?'

Special? I thought this was just business. It's then that I notice it hasn't got a price tag against it.

'How much is it?'

'Ten grand, I think,' Maya says, turning from the ring to me. 'Average.'

'Average?' I say, my voice breaking like a pubescent teenager.

'I'm joking, mate.' Maya's laugh echoes down the backstreet we're standing on. 'Man, this is going to be *fun*.'

'I hate you,' I mutter sarcastically, the colour returning to my face.

'An excellent foundation for marriage.' Maya laughs again but given how lowly she views it I wonder whether she's being serious.

'Well, what are we *actually* looking for?'

Maya stops walking, turning her body to stand before me. 'We've already found everything we're looking for.' She grins up at me, fluttering her eyelashes.

'Is this all just a joke to you?' I ask, already scared of her response.

'It sort of is . . .' she says, but then she must see my face fall as her shoulders stiffen and she looks serious suddenly, as if she's just remembered something. Perhaps how serious this is to me. 'But that doesn't mean I'm not serious about going through with it too.'

'Okay,' I say, silently telling my heart to just slow down. 'Then what do we need?'

'Not an engagement ring,' Maya confirms, walking away from the marigold monstrosity and wandering further down the red-brick streets of the Lanes. 'We just need a wedding band each for when we exchange our vows.'

'Two weeks today,' I say, each sentence feeling like the next move in a game of chicken, like I'm waiting to see which utterance will make Maya back out for good.

'Two weeks today,' she nods, acknowledging the confirmation from the registry.

'Can't we just use Haribo rings or something?' I say, coming to stand outside another vintage jewellers as Maya nestles in close by my side to take a look.

Even standing there, not touching, I can tell that she'd fit perfectly under my arm, that her shoulder would provide the ideal perch for my tired head. I ignore the thought, pushing it aside. Another couple walks out of the shop we're gazing into, the man catching my eye and beaming back at me. He thinks Maya is actually my fiancée, that we're not too young to be doing this, maybe that we even look good together, *right* together? And for some reason I find myself feeling really proud of that, really proud of *her*.

'Do you *want* people to suspect it's a sham wedding?' Maya interrupts the thought.

'No,' I say quickly. 'Obviously not.'

'Then I suggest we find some bands that last longer than a week?'

'You can wear a Haribo without eating it for a *week*?'

'You know what I mean.' She shakes her head in feigned despair, and I laugh.

'Two simple wedding bands. Are they . . . ?' I begin. I sound like a novice, because I am.

'Expensive? They don't need to be.'

Maya moves on to the next shopfront and we stare into the black latticed window only to see an elderly man wave at us from the inside and begin to make his way to the door.

'Window shopping?' he asks us kindly, all rosy cheeks and unruly grey hair.

'No,' Maya begins. 'I'm *desperate* for an engagement ring but my boyfriend here can't seem to take a hint.'

My cheeks flush red. She's embarrassing me on purpose.

'Men,' the old man mutters, detecting her razor-sharp sarcasm, before ushering us into his shop, a treasure trove of jewels and diamonds and an oddly eclectic range of hats hanging from the ceiling. 'So, what type of rings would you like to look at?'

'Just plain wedding bands,' Maya says seriously now.

'No engagement ring at all?' He eyes her empty fourth finger suspiciously.

I once again feel horrible for taking her off the market. Then I feel even worse for thinking a phrase as patriarchal as *taking her off the market*.

'No, no,' Maya shakes her head, her long hair waving with it. 'Maybe with the next husband?'

The old man laughs, so does she, but I can't help but feel this is true; she must only be twenty-two right now, she's got her whole life ahead of her – once I get out of the way.

I follow Maya out of the shop, both of us now proud owners of two simple wedding bands and one step closer to tying the knot – tight enough to look convincing, lose enough so that we can simply decide to unravel it again.

'So, that's the job done, then?' I ask, as we make our way away from the Lanes.

'Today's job at least.' Maya nods, knowing that there's so much more to come.

'Great, well . . . I guess we should head back to the station?'

'Not before you take me to the beach,' Maya says, shaking her head at the thought.

'I didn't think you need me to *take you* anywhere?' I tease, even though I'm mostly just stalling for time.

I haven't been to the beach, any beach, in ages. After years of my family driving the forty-odd minutes from Auckland to Piha, I can't listen to the waves washing in and out to sea without my mind washing up back home.

'You know what I mean,' Maya says, walking in the direction of the pier.

I fall into step with her, watching her hair blowing in the breeze until the great expanse of sea coming into view grabs my attention and my heart lurches in my chest. Brighton is *nothing* like Piha Beach but the sound, *that sound*, is impossible to drown out.

Maya walks across the beach, plonking herself down on the pebbles. I come to sit beside her, pulling my shirt around me. Maya does the same with her hoodie but still snuggles a little closer to my side, the wind picking up her dark hair and whipping it across her blushed cheeks as she looks out across the ocean.

As thoughts of home threaten to surface, I reach into my back pocket and pull out the two rings, rubbing my fingers over them as if trying to beckon a genie out of a lamp. After all, they're currently the only thing with the power to keep me here. Well, Maya is.

'Here you are.' I pass her a ring. She studies it in her hands, and I try to read her thoughts. I don't have a chance of knowing what's going on in her wonderful mind.

'I never thought I'd wear one of these,' she muses. I look at her, not saying anything, hoping that she'll fill the silence with more snippets of herself. 'It's such a strange concept to me. Why would we need to brand ourselves as being "taken" or "available"? I mean, like you could be with someone for years and be fully committed but without a ring you're fair game? Then boom, one day you get married, and you need to tell the world?'

'I guess it's just a symbol of—'

'The symbol feels a bit *smug*. And don't get me started on *engagement* rings,' Maya scoffs, but somehow her ranting is soothing me, reminding me I need that marriage isn't a big deal to her. 'Why do just the women have to wear one? And the man can just strut around looking unattached?'

'I thought you said the symbol feels smug?'

'Yes, it does,' Maya confirms. 'But I also believe in equal rights to be smug.'

I laugh, beginning to look around me, searching left and right.

'Have you lost it already?' Maya looks down at my hand, the ring still there.

'No, just looking for your soapbox.'

'You dick,' she says, shoving me in the side but, I swear, snuggling closer still.

'Well, you don't have to wear this other than at the cere-mony,' I assure her. 'It doesn't need to mean anything. Well, it means everything to me but . . . not like that.'

'I know,' Maya says, looking at the ring in her hands. 'It

means I get to stay in that apartment too . . . I mean, my dad's . . . you know, as you pay rent. You got your job back?'

'I did.' I grin, knowing that in the depths of my pocket, Toby is probably calling non-stop. Good job he's one thing that's easy to silence. 'And you started your paper?'

'I did,' Maya echoes, though she doesn't look as happy about it.

'Did you sort things out with Emmie?' I ask, and she exhales deeply.

'Enough to carry on staying there until Adrian moves in, in a fortnight. I think she'd be a bit offended if I moved out before to be honest.'

'Offended about moving into your dad's?'

'She knows my dad isn't around . . . that much . . . I wouldn't want her to worry about me getting lonely or anything.'

'And you've not told her about us yet?' I ask, as nonchalantly as I can, remembering again that Emmie knows she's at the beach right now. And Adrian knows who with.

'No, no,' Maya says quickly. 'Not yet. I mean, I will. I just . . . don't want her to think it's a knee-jerk reaction, that I'm acting out because of, well . . . Adrian moving in or anything.'

'Are you?' I don't mean to size her up like the woman at the registry office did.

'No! Look, I'll tell her once we've done the thing and got settled in the apartment and we know the visa plan is going to work.'

Her sentence reminds me that this last part is still an 'if'. And as much as I hate that telling them could be a moot point, I suppose it doesn't make sense to rock her friendship unnecessarily, if she really thinks Emmie will be weird about it. I mean, it *is* pretty weird.

'So, we'll move into the apartment once our time in our current flats runs out?' Maya doesn't linger on the thought long. 'After the ceremony?'

I've clocked that she doesn't like to call it a wedding. A ceremony sounds more official, less romantic, somehow.

'Sure.' I smile, keeping my eyes on her and not the lapping of the waves; then I grin.

'What?' Maya demands, giving me another poke to the ribs.

'It's just . . . not living together until we're married. I never had you down as such a traditionalist, Maya.' I laugh, stashing my wedding band in my back pocket again.

I watch as Maya wrinkles her nose.

'Trust me, there's *nothing* traditional about this.'

Two Weeks Later

Maya

Today's the day and then there's no turning back. Except there is, I remind myself as I cut across the park, a carpet of spring pink blossom covering the floor as the early summer sends everything into full bloom. *A piece of paper to get married. A piece of paper to stop being.* It was simple enough for my parents at least.

As I trace the path across one of the city's increasingly bustling parks, I try to imagine what my mum would make of what I'm on my way to do now. A bold anti-establishment statement of a woman who knows her own mind saving a man who can't face going home. Or the silly mistake of a silly girl who needs to grow the hell up? But as I reach for my phone, feeling the hard metal of the wedding band I bought with Jack only two weeks ago, to find that she hasn't messaged once, I know that she's not thinking about me today at all. She left for New York two days ago and I'm the only trace of her she's left behind.

You've packed already! Maya and Emmie Time tonight?

I read the latest message from Emmie, remembering all the

Maya and Emmie Times we've shared before, ever since we were in Year Seven making up dances to S Club 7 in the fields by her house after school. I can imagine wine and a takeaway is more what she has in mind for this evening. Technically, it'll be my wedding night. But seeing as it's highly unlikely Jack will be whisking me away or wanting to rip off my clothes, I guess I can see her. Still, it feels like the scraps of her time, like she's just realised that three years of living together is coming to an end and I may want to mark it somehow. I bet she could never imagine I'd be marking it like this. And I've not told her yet because I know no matter what I tell her she'll hear: 'You're moving forward and I'm not getting left behind' or 'I'm grieving and feel like doing something reckless.' Something reckless like Jack.

Coming to the edge of the park, I look up at the stone pub, the one that Jack and I have agreed to meet at ahead of the ceremony. I inhale as much oxygen I can. I know this is the right decision, a logical decision, an unemotional decision, one we've sat with for the four weeks it has taken to register our marriage, buy the rings and still not back out, but it's nerve-wracking nonetheless. Still, not as nerve-wracking as staying in my dad's apartment alone.

The feeling of waking up there by myself, the day after Jack and I decided to do this thing for real, reels through my mind at random, catching me off guard when I least expect it. The tightening of my chest, the clamminess of my hands, the impending doom of knowing that I'm taking something from a dead man who never offered me anything during his life. It's all the reminder I need that helping Jack out like this is helping me out too. I can't stay in that apartment without him. And my mum's house isn't hers anymore.

Sure. Be nice to hang out before Adrian moves in and I head to my mum's.

Not that Emmie knows that. Pushing my hands against the heavy pub door, I try to force away the thought. Then I see Jack sitting at a table by the window, overlooking the pub garden, and I don't need to try anymore. A crisp white shirt stretches tightly across his broad shoulders and his caramel-coloured hair looks freshly cut and styled. I stand there for a moment, just gazing at him. At the way his forearm tenses as he reaches for his pint, at the way he keeps glancing out of the window and smiling, like seeing Brits in a beer garden is all the reason he needs to want to stay here. In less than an hour he's going to be my husband. It's a thought so bizarre and foreign that it makes me laugh out loud.

Jack looks up to see me standing there, laughing in his direction, and instantly stares down at his shirt, his shoes, his hands, as if my laughing can only mean there's something wrong with him rather than something right. I always thought his Jack the Jock persona was just something he was, something that oozed out of him naturally, but the more I know about him the more I realise that there's a multitude of pieces of him to discover. As I arrive by his side, he throws a hand to his crinkled brow before shielding his eyes. What the . . . ?

'Damn it. I'm not supposed to see you before the wedding,' Jack says as I look down at my black jeans and yellow top. He's joking, right? It's not like I was ever going to wear a gown. Then he cracks a smile. 'Meh, at least the wine is white.' He pushes a drink towards me as I take a seat. 'Can we say you "borrowed" it seeing as I bought the round?'

I take a sip of my wine, letting it soothe me all the way

to my stomach. Now I understand why all the bridesmaids gather round and pop the prosecco on the morning of the wedding. Even though it's not a real marriage, the fact we have to stand in front of someone else and exchange our make-believe vows feels akin to standing in the middle of this pub completely starkers.

I look to Jack and for some reason the memory of his naked, toned torso darts across my mind. He smiles, a deep dimple etched into his left cheek. He looks gorgeous. Even when he doesn't try, but especially now. I take another sip. This isn't about attraction, or lust, or looks, or love. It's about legalities, cold, hard facts. Jack needs a visa, and I need Jack to be able to justify staying in that apartment for more than one second.

'I can't believe this is actually happening,' Jack says, lifting his pint to his lips. I notice the slight quiver in his voice, the faint tremble of his hand. 'Maya, honestly. I don't know how to thank you . . .' He looks at me intently, so intently that my stomach flips.

'Just pay your rent on time,' I reply, matter-of-fact. 'And don't expect me to pick up your socks after you or iron your pants.'

Jack laughs, hard, and it's only then that I wonder whether he ever wanted to get married either. Whether his heartbreak back at home ever made it this far down the aisle.

'Are you sure *you* want to do this?' I ask, the sudden spike in my heart rate reminding me that I don't want him to pull out of this, that without him becoming my housemate, I'm not sure how I'm going to be able to complete this paper, my PhD. And in reality, becoming a notable academic before I'm thirty is all I've ever wanted.

'Of course,' Jack says quickly, taking my hand in his, seemingly involuntarily. 'But, Maya, honestly, if you want to back out . . . I'm not sure why you'd even agree to—'

'Excuse me, sir?' An unfamiliar voice breaks us from the moment.

Jack drops my hand as quick and automatically as he first picked it up. I spin around to see the leather-looking face of the man who has just interrupted us. With grey hair, tanned skin and laugher lines as squiggly as the pattern on his loud-coloured shirt, I'd place his age safely in the late-seventies bracket and his accent *definitely* in the American category.

'Spit it out, Ken,' a pretty and plump older woman appears by his side. From her tone and the glare she's giving him now, I assume this is Ken's wife.

'We wondered if you'd mind if we perched on the end of your table?' Ken says.

Jack's head swings around to look at me, eyes wide, like he knows this guy has just unintentionally interrupted the most important conversation we're likely to have, the one where Jack is going to give me an opportunity to back out, to ask what's really in this for me. But I don't want to back out. And I really don't want that conversation.

'Of course!' I say, gesturing to the empty seats on the other side of our table, which Ken and his wife pull out without pause, the chair legs screeching across the wooden floor of the pub nosily. If everyone in here wasn't looking at Ken's shirt before, they are now.

'Maya?' Jack lowers his voice, pulling his chair closer to mine until our knees are touching and I can hear his whisper loud and clear. I can see Ken's wife looking over at us dreamily, her chin cupped in her hands, elbows on the table, like she's just scored a front-row seat to a show about two young lovers. 'You know you don't need to do this.'

No, but I can tell from his face he needs me to.

'I want to,' I say, smiling back at him. 'And we're all set for a two p.m. kick-off?'

'This isn't a game of football.'

'You should know.'

'I played rugby, Maya.' Jack shakes his head. 'Two very different things.'

I glimpse Ken's wife again, grinning over at me. Stop grinning. We're not in love.

'But yes,' Jack says, looking from the American couple to me. He's seen them watching too. 'Everything's sorted.'

'Well, not everything.' I smile as Jack looks more concerned still.

'What?' he whispers, trying not to be overheard. I lean in closer to him too.

'I want us to write our own vows.'

Jack

'You want us to *what*?' I hiss back to Maya, the beady eyes of the older American couple still fixed in our direction, their smiles stretching from ear to ear.

'Write our own vows,' Maya repeats. 'In fact, I've already written mine.'

I watch as she reaches into her pocket to pull out her phone, swiping to Notes. I didn't know we needed to write vows. I didn't think Maya would want to. This marriage is about a formality, not heart-felt promises to one another.

Maya is still so close that I'm sure she can hear my heartbeat doubling in speed, the sweat starting to prickle on my brow. Man, it's hot in here. Her green eyes widen as she looks from her phone to me, her body so close to mine. A little smile, then she inhales deeply.

'I vow to . . .' she begins.

Oh crap, what am I going to vow to her? To cherish her in a platonic way? To like her as a friend? To try to not balls-up her life in the way I did everybody's back home? I breathe deeply, waiting for whatever bomb she's going to drop next.

'To not leave hair in the plughole,' Maya says, her frivolous laugh calming me in an instant, her words not a bomb but confetti. 'To never call you *baby* or *bae*.'

I pull my best disgusted face and can tell from Maya's giggle that she approves.

'Okay,' I begin, realising that these kind of vows I can spin on the spot. 'I promise to never leave the toilet seat up.'

'And never piss when it's down,' Maya chips in.

'Are these my vows or yours?' I cock an eyebrow; she grins again, using her hand to usher me on. 'And I vow to never use your toothbrush without asking.'

'To never use it full stop!'

I stare Maya's interruptions down again. Even if these were real vows, I get the impression she'd be making edits to my promises as I go.

'I vow to never use the terms *blue jobs* and *pink jobs*,' I go on.

Maya pretends to be sick. Out of the corner of my eye, I see the couple mutter and worry that them perhaps overhearing the word 'job' coupled with Maya's finger in mouth may lead to some unfortunate conclusions. I could promise them there will be none of *that* happening either. I finish my drink at speed, promptly offering to go and get us both another. We're going to need it today.

'I promise . . .' Maya continues as soon as I come back with our drinks, as if no time has passed at all and it hasn't just taken half an hour to get served at the increasingly sticky bar. I watch as she takes the large glass of wine, slurps at speed and then discards her phone on the table in a way that tells me she's getting into this too. 'I promise to not read into the early hours with my head torch on if it means you can't get to sleep at night.'

'Woah, you have a head torch?' I laugh, putting a palm up between us to stall her next sentence. There's a lot to unpack here. 'And you wear it to *bed*?'

'Sometimes,' Maya says, and I love that she shows not an inch of embarrassment.

'And you expect me to resist you?' I ask before she promptly jabs me in the side. 'Hey, wait. Are we going to share a bed?'

I know Maya is joking with these vows but there's a lot we haven't really spoken about. For a moment I wonder just how many couples find themselves rushing down the aisle without hammering out the finer details to make a marriage work. But this isn't a marriage is it, not a real one?

'Well, where else are you going to sleep?' Maya asks, serious all of a sudden.

'On the sofa?'

'For months?' Maya shakes her head, authoritatively. I gulp, we've not really talked about how long I'll need to stay with her; I don't want to remind her it could be years now.

'Also, in a bed that big it's hardly like we're at risk of touching each other,' Maya adds. 'I'd need a map to find you.'

'Or a head torch?'

'Shut up,' Maya snaps, but she's still smiling. 'Okay, then, I promise to never cross over onto your side of the bed.'

'Deal.' I nod, lowering my voice so that it's almost impossible to overhear in the busy pub. Maya brings her face so close to mine that I can feel her breath on my neck. 'I vow that the moment I am able to apply for permanent citizenship, this marriage will be over.'

'Oh, bae, you say the sweetest things.' She pulls away to throw her hands to her heart.

'Well, that's one vow broken already.'

'I'll keep the rules that matter,' she argues back quickly, never in the wrong.

'I thought these were meant to be *vows*?'

'Vows get broken all the time,' Maya says, reminding me just how much of a sceptic she is. 'Breaking rules has consequences.'

'Okay, so what are the rules that matter?' I ask, eyes darting to Ken and his missus at the other end of the table. They're still so close to us that I worry they feel a part of this too.

'We will both be able to date other people,' Maya confirms, leaning back, folding her arms, all business now. I nod, even though the dating has never been the hard part for me. It's been the *what comes next* that makes me fall at the first relationship-hurdle. Or, you know, the second date. I take a long, slow slurp of my pint, trying to wash the thought away. 'We will absolutely not be sleeping with one another.'

I snort out my latest sip of beer and, from across the table, Ken does the same.

'Even if you crack the head torch out?'

'*Especially* then.'

'Fine,' I joke, now my turn to fold my arms.

In reality, I have no intention of sleeping with Maya. As gorgeous as she is, I stand by my 'feelings make everything complicated' comment. And though I've perfected the art of no-strings-attached sex in recent years, something tells me that having sex with my wife will be a whole different ball game.

'And—'

'Man, you have a lot of rules.'

Maya stares my grumble away. She knows she's holding all the cards, has all the power to make or break my life here. Maybe that's why she's enjoying it all so much?

'And under no circumstances must we ever fall in love.'

I look from Maya's pursed lips to her hard stare, and know she's being serious. And I'm glad. Because as much as falling in love sounds ideal it has a way of messing everything up. I have a way of messing everything up. Loving something means having something to lose. And last time I lost my best friend and my girlfriend in one fell swoop.

'Got it.' I gulp. 'I vow to – under no circumstances – fall in love with you, Maya.'

I look into her big green eyes, the ones I have found myself thinking about so often over the last month or so since our paths crossed again, and watch her nod in confirmation.

'Well, on that note,' Maya grins, draining the last of her wine whilst simultaneously checking the time. 'We should probably go and get married. Oh *shit*!'

Maya

'Oh shit, indeed,' Jack says, laughing in a way that tells me he's not clocked my panic.

He thinks I'm talking about us getting married. But there's no way we can legally tie the knot without one tiny detail that has managed to slip our minds completely. Well, *two*.

'We need witnesses,' I mutter, cursing myself for the fact that this is only just occurring to me now, that Jack didn't think about it either.

Jack stares back at me blindly, like he's about to witness a breakdown or, worse, a runaway bride.

'Oh crap, Jack,' I curse again.

We've come too far to back out now and if we don't get married today, I fear either or both of us will realise that this is a stupid, reckless, ridiculous plan. It feels like now or never.

'Witnesses?' Jack croaks, looking like he's let me down but isn't precisely sure how.

'We need two witnesses at the wedding to make it legal,' I hiss back at him, painfully aware of our two-person audience, of the other people stood drinking around the room.

'Oh shit, okay . . . we've got' – Jack breaks off to look at his watch – 'five minutes.'

It's the reason we picked this bar today, so we could neck a couple of drinks and then become a couple for life. Well, as far as the registry office across the road is concerned.

'We need to call Emmie and Adrian,' Jack says quickly, like there's no other option.

I know the second we tell them we need them they'll be here

87

in a flash. But even a flash across central London takes longer than five minutes. Plus, they don't technically know we're about to get married yet. And everything in me is screaming to keep this our little secret. At least for now.

'Unless . . .' I begin, eyes darting to Ken and his wife on the other side of our table.

Jack's eyes follow mine across to their smiling faces, clearly hanging on our every word, before looking back to me, mouth hanging open slightly, expression aghast.

'No,' Jack hisses.

'Why not?' I whisper back.

'Because we don't *know* them.'

'We barely know each other,' I remind him, his face now inches from my own. 'And isn't that kind of the point?'

No strings. No feelings. No expectations. No disappointments.

'Won't it be obvious it's a sham? That shirt is hardly inconspicuous.'

'It's okay,' I assure him, treading the fine line between being too nonchalant about our nuptials and looking like I want this too much. I know I've not really answered Jack's question about what's in this for me. 'You don't actually need to know your witnesses for the marriage to be real. *We* just need to really look in love.'

'Well, that's one pro of asking Ken,' Jack mutters under his breath, eyes swinging once again to a shirt that would look a bit too much even in Hawaii. 'With that get-up in the registry office, no one's going to be looking at us.'

'Excuse me?' I adjust my volume to make it clear we now *want* the couple to hear.

Out of the corner of my eye, I can see Jack stiffen, he looks horrified. And I thought ignoring eye contact with strangers at all costs was just a British thing.

'See, Ken, I've been telling you they want some privacy,' the woman nudges her husband in the shoulder, not even pretending not to have been listening in.

'Fine, we're leaving,' Ken grumbles. 'But not because you said so. I've got boules.'

The woman looks to me and rolls her eyes as if to say, *husbands, eh?*

'No, no,' I say, reaching a hand out to stop her in her tracks. The fact that I don't need to move from my seat shows just how close they are. 'I . . . we were just going to ask . . .' I stall on the sentence, realising that this will be the first time I've mentioned the wedding to anyone other than Jack. It's suddenly making it feel real.

'. . . ask you a favour.' Jack fills in my blank and, for a second, we feel like a team.

'Damn it,' Ken says, slamming a hand on the table. Clearly, he doesn't like favours. I watch as he reaches into his pocket and pulls out a fiver and hands it to his wife.

'I knew you had some music in your voice,' Ken's wife says, pocketing the fiver. They had a bet on it? 'Where are you from, sonny?'

We don't have time for this. But given that we're about to ask them to spend half an hour of theirs walking across the road with us and watching us get married, I stay silent, willing our remaining four minutes to go well.

'Auckland . . . in New Zealand,' Jack adds, as if the city is such a little-known place. 'And we're actually hoping that you could—'

89

'Auckland! Oh, Kenny, remember when we went there in the campervan?'

'Remember? I'm old but I'm not demented. Of course I remember,' Ken grumbles again, but you can tell from his mischievous grin that this banter with his wife is the norm.

'We're from Austin, you see, in sunny Texas! I'm Kris ... and this is Ken ...' Kris's bubbly demeanor spills between us, like she's been trying to hold it back for too long. 'We travelled, like you ...' She nods to Jack as if they're kindred spirits somehow. I can tell from Jack's pursed lips that he no longer sees himself as a nomad. 'But now we've made a home here, have friends and a social life and hobbies here—'

'Hobbies like boules,' Ken says, eyes darting to his wife. 'At two p.m.'

'It only takes two minutes to get there,' Kris objects, but she's looking at us.

Oh crap. That's the exact same time as our appointment. I mean, our wedding.

'Oh wow, that's, erm ... great,' Jack says, his whole body shifting as if it's taking all his strength to generate the next words. 'What we're about to ask you is kind of mad, but we're really in a bit of a bind.' I swear he's cranked up his accent, hoping the 'music in his voice' might lull Kris and Ken into saying 'yes'. 'We're about to get married—'

'Damn it!' Ken cries again, reaching into his pocket to slide his wife another fiver.

'I knew it!' Kris beams, pocketing her second bet. 'When's the big day?'

'Today,' Jack and I say in perfect unison. Kris throws her hands to her face in glee.

'Like now, actually,' I add.

'We were hoping . . . maybe you could witness the wedding?' Jack says, his own hands coming together to create a pleading motion that I'm not even sure he's aware of. 'You see, we were just so excited about today, about spending our lives together' – I try not to flinch; I'm sure one day some woman will feel lucky to spend her life with Jack – 'that we completely dropped the ball on arranging for any guests or witnesses to be there. It's just across the road and we need to be there like . . . a minute ago . . . but please, please—'

'I'm afraid I've got boul—'

'It would be our *honour*,' Kris's voice cuts across her husband's.

'Oh, thank God,' Jack says, as Kris takes his hands in hers. It's an awkward gesture but no one seems to care. 'It really means the world to me and my wife.'

'Hey, I'm not your wife yet,' I say, something about the term making me revolt.

'Well, then.' Kris oozes enough excitement for all of us. 'Let's go and change that.' And with that, Kris stands, one witness at the ready. I can already tell from their dynamic that Ken has no choice but to follow suit, and as we exit the pub his grumble makes me sure.

'Guess I'll have to cancel boules, then.'

Jack

I follow Kris, Ken and Maya across the road and into the registry office, my heart in my mouth. I wish they would walk a bit quicker, we're already five minutes late for a fifteen-minute ceremony and every second feels like a moment that Maya could back out. But I know she's not going to. That for some reason, she seems to need this as much as me. Still, I wish she had told Emmie or her mum or someone before going through with this. Just a sounding board to check that she's doing the right thing. From what I know about Maya, the fact she's not told anyone, the fact she's making a completely independent call, might be the very reason she feels bold enough to be walking towards the room for our ceremony now.

'Jack Wilson and Maya Morgan?' An official-looking person pokes their head out of the main room and Kris, Ken and Maya begin to follow him in. I reach for Maya's hand.

'Are you *sure* you want to do this?' I whisper, hoping that this time Kris and Ken can't hear.

Maya's eyes look from my face to my hand, gripping hers so tightly in my own. In the silence, I try to imagine what might be running through her mind: *Why am I doing this? What if I want to marry someone else? What if I can't get out of this as easily as I think?* But she looks strangely calm and her shimmering eyes on mine slow my racing thoughts.

'Just a piece of paper, remember?' she says, squeezing my hand then letting it go.

I remind myself that she believes this, that her parents gave her countless reasons to believe this. That she genuinely doesn't ever want to get married to anyone else, other than me.

'Just a piece of paper.' I nod. 'Another to get divorced.'

'Save something for the ceremony, sweetie. Now let's go and do this thing.'

As soon as we walk into the room, I clock the tall windows welcoming the early-summer light to flood in from either side,

92

each one framed by long floral curtains. There are not one but two aisles between the empty chairs which are arranged in an arc, all leading to the focal point of a desk with two chairs behind it and two simple flower arrangements standing tall at either side of it. It's simple and it's quiet, apart from the low hum of traffic from outside, but if feels hopeful. And, as Maya reaches for my hand, I am filled with the feeling that everything might work out okay.

Tracing the short distance down the makeshift aisle together, it feels nothing like the wedding day I once imagined I'd have with Laura back home, back when I was a naive teenager who thought love could conquer all. We dreamed of tipsy guests spilling out of the stone church and onto the lawn outside it, overgrown with wildflowers. We dreamed of having our parents there and Charlie making a crude but charming Best Man's speech even though he would have only been fifteen when we first started dating, first started dreaming.

'I guess I don't need to ask everyone to stand for the entrance of the bride?' the registrar says with a warm smile as soon as we're standing in front of her. It's was Maya's idea to walk down the aisle together.

'I'm not very traditional,' Maya says. Of course, the registrar already knows that from her brief interactions with us over the past few weeks. And if she didn't, she could just look at Maya's jeans. She could have worn a dress. But then, maybe Maya thinks that would look like we're trying too hard. 'Plus, I can't wait a moment longer to stand by my husband's side,' she beams, evidently deciding she should try a little harder.

'Let's get started, then.' The registrar grins. She doesn't seem put off by our attire. Not even Ken's attire. She must see all sorts here. And, despite not wearing a wedding dress, Maya does look phenomenal, her oversized lemon shirt, tucked into her dark jeans and buckled at her tiny waist. She's got black eyeliner on, flicking out at the corners, and her lashes look even thicker and darker than usual, making her eyes look like they're sparkling.

'Good afternoon, ladies and . . . lady and gentleman.' The register looks to Ken and Kris, who are now seated in the front row; Kris looks like all her dreams are coming true, Ken looks like he's dreaming about boules.

'Welcome, on this lovely sunny afternoon, to the marriage of Jack and Maya . . .' The registrar goes on and Maya drops my hand. I look to her for signs that she's shuffling, limbering up, preparing to bolt, but she's perfectly serene, beaming beautifully.

'Today marks a new beginning in their lives together and it means a lot to both of them that you are here to witness their wedding vows and celebrate their marriage . . .'

Maya and I both turn to look at Kris and Ken. It doesn't mean so much that they, specifically, are there. But it means everything that their being here means our plan can go ahead. I imagine how disappointed my mum would be to find out I got married without her here, without her knowing. Then I remember that she couldn't be any more disappointed in me than on the day that I left the country. And the countless days before that. My hand starts to shake and my legs tremble beneath me. Until Maya reaches for my hand again.

The rest of the ceremony goes in a blur, everyone reading from their scripts, saying what we're meant to say, repeating the words we're meant to repeat. It takes all of five minutes for the course of our lives to change forever. Or at least for the time it will take me to finally be in the country long enough to apply for permanent residency. And all I can concentrate on is Maya's smile, my one fixed point as the room spins. Even as it grins uncontrollably at the absurdity of the moment. Even as it morphs into a smirk at the mention of the 'exclusion of others'; we both know from our vows in the pub that we're both mentally crossing our fingers at this part.

'It is an ancient tradition for a bride and groom to exchange rings,' the registrar continues, and I pray to God the rings are still in my back pocket, that Maya didn't make a mistake when she suggested it might look better for me to be holding onto both.

'A wedding ring is an unbroken circle which symbolises an unending and everlasting love . . .'

An unending and everlasting love that I know neither Maya nor I believe in. Her smiles holds steady as I reach for her hand and hover the ring around the top of her dainty fourth finger.

'Maya, I give you this ring . . .' I begin, my voice trembling as I do, as she looks back at me and I see my future in her eyes. Not the whole of it, but the bit that comes next.

As soon as Maya returns the favour and I feel the tight metal wrapping around my finger, I realise from the registrar's wide smile what's coming next. And I hadn't even thought about this part once. The registrar may be able to overlook Maya's jeans, our striding down the aisle together five minutes after our appointed time, but I'm not sure she'll be able to witness me refusing to kiss the bride for the first time as husband and wife. Little does she know she's about to witness me kissing Maya for the first time full stop.

'It therefore gives me great pleasure to pronounce you are husband and wife!'

Maya and I look at each other for the longest time, like two teenagers lingering at the end of a first date, neither one of us knowing if the other is going to make the first move. Then I hear the sound of Kris heckling from the front row: *kiss, kiss, kiss.* Maya laughs at the same time as I reach a hand to her cheek, and as soon as our skin touches the room falls quiet. Everything is silent except the deafening sound of my heartbeat leaping out of my chest. I gently pull her towards me, and she allows me to draw her in, ever so slowly, tilting her head until our lips are lingering a hair's breadth apart and I feel her breath heavy, catching. Then I place my lips on hers and she parts her own and we kiss, tentative and tender at first, but then with more urgency, an eagerness that nearly has me convinced it is real. Maya pulls away, breathless, stunned, but then kisses me again, and if the first felt deliberate, this one feels inevitable.

The sound of Ken and Kris cheering breaks me from the spell and soon we are ushered over to the desk to sign the documents, one step closer to getting my visa.

'Wow!' Maya grins at me and my first thought is of that kiss. 'We're *married*.'

'Yeah,' I say, beaming back at her, trying to keep my worries at bay. We're one step closer to me staying in the country. We've got a great place to stay. And we've got our rules, our boundaries, in place. I try to tell myself to stop worrying for once and *enjoy* this.

We leave the ceremony hall hand in hand, but as soon as we're out of the double doors and into the hallway, Maya lets go. I know we don't need to worry about keeping up appearances now. That kiss has everybody fooled.

'Oh wow, that was just amazing,' Kris says, throwing her arms around Maya like they are long-lost friends, Ken just lingering to one side. 'And that kiss, *that* kiss. It was like something from out of a film. I could literally *feel* the sparks flying.'

I glance at Maya, and she catches my eye, trying not to laugh at Kris's enthusiasm.

'Yeah, Jack can really . . .' Maya begins, and for a moment I want her to say 'kiss' . . . 'put on a show.' She grins in my direction, risking the briefest of winks.

'A display of true love,' Kris says, her hands now clutched to her heart.

'Yeah, erm . . .' I begin, stunned by her sincerity. 'Something like that.'

Maya hooks an arm through Kris's, steering the two of them further away from the building and back towards the bar, saving all of us from any more of my awkwardness.

'Congrats,' Ken hangs back, falling into step beside me as Kris and Maya chat away ahead of us, and I realise that as prickly as Maya can be she has the uncanny ability to make whoever she meets feel at ease.

'Thanks, Ken,' I say, before muttering feebly: 'I'm sorry you had to miss boules.'

'No bother.' He beams, before his mouth twists and relaxes again, like he's trying to choose his next words carefully. 'And it'll be no bother if you need to get in touch with us to write a reference for you guys or anything . . .' he says cautiously, quietly. 'For the visa.'

How did he know?

97

'You being from New Zealand and all . . .' he adds, even though I can tell from the grin circling his mouth that he overheard more than enough of our conversations at the pub. 'Don't worry, Kris and I had some issues staying here. I have dual citizenship but she, yeah, it was a bit of a ball ache.'

I know hearing a seventy-something-year-old man say ball ache would make Maya like this guy even more. I also know better than to share how hard this next step could be with her. She's just done the biggest favour for me I could ask for. I'm going to try to make her life with me as easy, as simple, as possible.

'Take my number in case you need it.' He hands me a physical card, rather than just airdropping me his details. 'It's worth it though, mate.'

'Yeah, this country is great.'

'I meant, *she's* worth it.' He looks ahead to his wife. I trace his eyes back to Kris and Maya, who turns her head to smile back at me as I realise, I'm now looking at *my wife* too.

Part 4

The Visa

One Day Married

Maya

I wake up in the shape of a starfish. I feel soft sheets under each limb as I stretch to the corners of the unfamiliar bed. It's pitch-black, dead quiet, and that's all the permission I need to roll over on my side and go back to sleep. And then I remember.

Where I am.

Who I'm with.

I move slowly, pushing myself up to sitting and looking across to the other side of the bed. I'm surprised to find it completely empty, the cover pulled up to meet two neat pillows that don't look slept on at all. Despite spending a painstaking half hour debating who would take which side of the bed when we settled into the apartment last night – *I don't mind, which side do you want to sleep on? No, it's your dad's apartment, which side do you want to sleep on?* – it appears that sleeping next to your wife is something you kind of have to warm up to.

Sliding down the sheets until I'm starfishing once again, I

face the empty side of the bed, wondering whether Jack is ever going to sleep there, whether this is ever going to feel normal. Because let's face it, there's nothing normal about this situation. At all. I close my eyes, imagining what it will be like to hear the steady beat of his breathing, watch the rhythm of his chest moving in and out like the roll of a wave. But there's nothing. Just silence. Dead silence. And it doesn't take long for my dad to fill the empty spaces.

How often did he sleep here? Which side of the bed did he sleep on when he did? Was the other side empty like now? Did he ever wake up in the night and think of me?

No, no, no. This is what he wanted. To leave me this apartment to mess with us. To make us think he cared when he probably wrote his will ages ago and forgot this place even existed. Forgot that I existed. I roll over again, dangerously close to 'Jack's' side.

You said you were only staying here for him, but where is he now? There's only one person sleeping in my bed. Only one person using my things, depending on me . . .

The thoughts come thick and fast until my breath is quickening, my heartbeat racing, the sheets starting to morph from slinky to sticky until they feel like they're suffocating me. I can't do this. Can't sleep in his bed without my mum knowing. Or, you know, *not* sleeping.

I reach for my phone, dreading seeing the time, not wanting to calculate how few hours Jack could stomach sleeping next to me or how many I have to wrestle through until it's a respectable time to walk into the living room and wake him up.

Get to your mum's okay?

Adrian's all settled in now.

Oh, and he does that toothpaste thing we hate.

I read Emmie's messages through blurry eyes, trying to make sense of how two people who have been dating for a minute could take the plunge and move in together. Especially without sharing enough nights to know which end of the toothpaste the other squeezes from. But mostly I'm trying to work out why she would be messaging me so late, or so early in the morning. Then I notice the time. It's gone 11 a.m.

'She lives!' Jack turns around the second I swing the door into the kitchen wide open.

'What the . . .?' I begin, heart hammering in my chest and showing no signs of stopping. Jack is standing by the hob, wearing an apron, and holding a wooden spoon in his hand, a brush of flour on the tanned skin of his cheek. He looks like a fifties housewife.

'You didn't wake me up!'

'I didn't know I had to,' Jack says, his eyes desperately trying to remain on mine as I realise that my hair must be all over the place, my make-up too. And I'm not wearing a bra.

'I don't usually sleep in,' I mumble back, subtly folding my arms to cover my chest.

'Ah, the blackout blinds got you too?' Jack says, trying and failing to seem sympathetic.

It hardly looks like he was lulled into a lie-in. His laptop is up and open on the island in the middle of the kitchen, two cups of half-drunk coffee discarded to its side. He looks like he's been up for hours. And now he's cooking?

'This apartment is amazing.' He beams back at me. 'And so is this kitchen . . .' His sentence drifts off as he sees my startled face. 'Oh but, obviously, you already know that . . .'

No, no I do not. I've not had a single meal in this place before. Other than our proposal pizza.

'Obviously,' I lie, taking a seat at the kitchen island.

'How did you sleep?' Jack asks, returning his gaze to whatever he's cooking.

'Not so good . . .' I say, but then I see Jack's face fall and add: 'But I never do the first night I sleep in a place.' He looks more confused still. 'The first night for a while.'

Jack's inquisitive look feels so intense it burns. I should just tell him, tell him that my dad died and left me this place, like I should have told him the first chance I had. Or the second chance, or the third. And especially before we got married. But how can I tell him now without him thinking he's just married a pathological liar, one that he's depending on to be able to stay in the country? He'll think I'm emotionally unstable; he'll look at me that way too. And I'm just not sure I can stomach that today.

I break our eye contact to look down at my phone, the message from Emmie still waiting for a reply. Out of the corner of my eye I can see Jack bending down to open the oven door and a heavenly scent fills the room. I look from Emmie's message about Adrian's bad toothpaste habits and back up to my husband's backside, and I can't help but smile, this morning's anxieties drifting away with his cooking, his company.

'*Bon appétit.*' Jack turns around to present me with a messily stacked sandwich oozing with runny yolk and tomato ketchup, served with a smile and a side of dimples.

Yeah, settled in. All going well. Didn't you know about the toothpaste thing already?

I rush a reply to Emmie and stash my phone away. I'll worry about telling her later, just as soon as we get the visa and know the inevitable fallout will be worth it.

'You shouldn't have,' I say, reaching for the plate whilst willing my nipples to not be visible beneath my thin pyjama top. I study the sandwich, not knowing how to eat it without getting it all down myself. It looks messy but it smells so good. Then I see why: bacon.

'It's the least I can do,' Jack says, sitting down next to me with his own breakfast.

'No, really, you shouldn't have.'

Jack eyes me suspiciously.

'I'm a vegetarian.'

Jack looks horrified for a second, reaching a hand to slowly slide my plate away from me and back towards him. I guess what's mine is his now.

'I'm so sorry,' he says, biting down into his sandwich, egg falling to his plate. He doesn't look that sorry. 'I had no idea.' He smiles sheepishly.

'I guess there's a lot we don't know about each other.'

'I'm going to learn,' Jack says decidedly, taking another bite. I wish he didn't look so grateful. The pending panic attack I've left in the bedroom is evidence I need this too. 'For the visa application . . .' he adds quickly.

'Yeah, for the visa application,' I echo back to him. 'What are the next steps?'

'So, we need to apply for leave to remain . . .' Jack begins, a momentary panic darting across his features until he seems to force a smile. 'Which should be easy now that we have a marriage certificate but—'

'But what?' I usher him on, Jack's panic seeming to placate my own.

'We might still need to make a case for our relationship,' he says, looking sorrier still.

'I guess we better start learning about each other, then,' I say, my eyes drifting from his dimples to his muscular forearms. The idea isn't horrible.

'Well, let's start simple. Where did we meet?' Jack asks, taking the last bite of his sandwich. And the first bite of mine. 'At uni?'

'I thought that was a given?' That's the truth, at least. But then there's a lot of other things we've not being truthful about; a lot of things I've not been honest about lately.

'Just checking we're going with that story. It's not like we really *knew* each other.' Jack's eyes explore my expression again. I know he remembers that evening he walked me home. But given how little I remember about that evening I decide to stay silent.

'I knew *of* you in first year,' I say, only then remembering how he seemed to fall off the face of the planet. 'But then, you seemed to—'

'I dropped out,' Jack says quickly. 'Well, technically, I managed second year, but I was spending less and less time going to lectures. Then, I got my job at SoberApp on a Youth Mobility Visa. I loved everything about the company, the ethos, investing in the NOLO industry, in a better way to drink . . .' He oozes with passion as he talks about his work, about trying to make a difference. 'I thought it was perfect and then they promised that they'd sponsor my application and then—'

'It's okay,' I remind him, putting a hand to the top of his

arm before thinking better of it. He doesn't have to tell me everything. Just enough to make our marriage seem plausible. 'Okay, well, let's say we had our first date in first year, that we've been dating since then . . .'

I'm not sure how much the visa people will even go into this stuff but, surely, it's better to be prepared.

'Em might actually have some photos of us.'

'Of us?' Jack chokes on his next bite of food.

Isn't he full yet? Though I imagine it must take plenty of calories to power his broad, rugby-guy body. I swallow the thought.

'From when she started dating Adrian.'

'Way back when,' Jack says sarcastically, but given that we've gone from barely knowing one another to being married it's not as if we can scoff at the speed of them moving in together now. Jack must realise this too as he promptly shuts up, beckoning me on.

'When she started dating Adrian, we looked back at old uni photos to see whether there was any of them together. There's one or two group shots that we're all in.'

'Okay, well, let's get hold of them,' Jack says, a little reluctantly. 'And I know you wanted to wait to tell them, but we could really do with some references from them too.'

'From Emmie and Adrian?' Now it's my turn to choke.

'We need to tell them sometime, Maya.' Jack looks more concerned still. 'Even if we don't . . . if the visa doesn't . . .'

The fact that Jack can't form this sentence tells me just how serious he is about not being able to go back home, and I find myself wondering for the thousandth time why that is. But then I remember what he said after the party, about Shoreditch and Padella and London being his home. He doesn't need to explain himself, certainly not to me.

'Then won't they want to know all about it anyway?' Jack goes on. 'It's not like we could keep this from them forever.'

'I know,' I say, putting my face into my hands. 'It's just . . . look, you won't get it.'

'Try me.'

'Emmie and I used to do everything together,' I start slowly, feeling emotion rise in my body before promptly forcing it back down. It's the first day of being legally married and I'm sure Jack doesn't want to be confronted with a crying wife. Still, I can't help scenes from my and Emmie's friendship/love story playing on a loop in my mind: Emmie and I sitting in the quad at school both reading the same novel just moments before we met. Emmie and I going to a sixth-form fancy-dress party as French and Saunders only to have everyone else joke that we were a better double act. Thumbing over university prospectuses together and knowing that us going to the same uni wouldn't hold us back but instead propel us forwards.

'We wanted all the same things,' I begin, struggling to find the words to sum it all up. 'Studied the same subjects, applied to the same universities, lived together since third year. Wanted to make money, make a mark in our industries. We were never bothered about the husband, the house, the kids, you know? And now she's met Adrian and seems to not care about any of that anymore. She just wants to move in and have babies and get married—'

'Beat her to that one,' Jack says, now his turn to reach a hand out to my arm in support; unlike me, he keeps it there, his skin soft and warm.

'That's my point.' I sigh. 'She'll think this is about her.'

About her, about her making me move out. Either that or she'll think this is about my dad, some kind of displaced grief.

'How so?' Jack goes on, genuinely curious.

Damn. I wasn't really expecting him to ask follow-up questions. Not about this.

'Emmie's competitive,' I say, and Jack raises his eyebrows. 'Okay, we're *both* competitive.' I confirm, knowing what he's getting at. 'But never with each other. We've always, always wanted the best for each other. But now, now that we're not doing everything together, she may think I'm . . . I don't know . . . pitting myself against her, trying to get one up on her somehow for not sticking to our in-sync plans.'

Even talking about it now, I feel emotion surging through my throat, my temperature starting to soar. And I don't want to talk about this, not with my *husband* the day after our wedding.

'Kris and Ken,' Jack says, changing the subject, supposedly on seeing me squirm. 'They said they'd help write a reference for us too.'

'Did they?'

'I'll get in touch.'

'You got their number?' I ask, the whole of yesterday now just a blur. Jack grins.

'Pulled more than just a wife yesterday.'

He holds my eye contact for a moment longer, before standing to make his way to the fridge. He opens it and I'm surprised to find it's full of groceries. Well, I guess he had to have got the bacon from somewhere.

'What can I make you? Eggs on toast? Fruit and yoghurt?'

I look from Jack to his empty plate and his open laptop.

'What time did you get up?' I ask, incredulously. 'Did you even *sleep*?'

'No rest for the wicked.' Jack's reply is so cliché but, on some level, I think he might actually mean it. 'In fact, I really need to be getting to work. We're developing this whole new GPS element to the app, so that you can always find your nearest sober bar. They're popping up all over the city,' he goes on, still speaking into the fridge as I wonder whether, had we been sober that night at the party, we ever would have landed up here. 'So . . . eggs or yoghurt?' Jack turns to look at me. 'Oh no, please don't tell me you're vegan.'

'Would it be an issue if it was?' I put a hand to my hip, preparing for our first fight.

'I wouldn't possibly try to tell you what you can and can't do.' Jack laughs.

'Good,' I say, my own laugh lacing into his. 'But I'm not . . .' I watch as Jack puts a hand to his strong chest, covering his heart as he takes a big, dramatic sigh. 'But don't worry about the eggs, I'll sort myself out.'

Jack smiles back at me, like he may not have known whether I'm a vegan, but he knows that I'll always be able to fend for myself. I like that about him, about the way he looks at me like I'm the kind of woman I want to be.

I watch as Jack closes his laptop and hooks his arm around it, heading out of the room. I hear the kitchen door shut behind him, the sound of the living-room door opening and closing again as he settles down to work. Of all the men I could have married for a visa, it looks like I've found one with a work ethic to rival my own. Which is saying something. Or at least, it *used* to say something before my dad's blackout blinds forced

110

me to have my first lie-in in years. Typical for an old, rich, dead guy to find new ways to hold a woman back.

I head towards the bathroom at a pace, knowing that after losing my morning to the blinds, and my weekend to the wedding, I have loads to catch up on today.

Pushing open the door, I'm greeted with steam. Through it, I glimpse the startled face of Jack holding a towel out wide behind his back, preparing to wrap it around himself. Thankfully, his body is turned away from me, facing the shower so that I can't see anything apart from the vast expanse of one of my dad's towels pulled taut between us.

'Oh God . . . sorry . . . I . . .' I stutter as Jack takes a step closer to me through the steam. He looks like he's in a Backstreet Boys music video. 'Was going to brush my . . .' I begin, distracted by his body. His modesty is covered, but I can still see so much: his broad shoulders, still slightly damp; his wet hair, flopping against his brow; his toned torso, as taut as the towel wrapped around him. I look down at my pyjamas, feeling even more exposed.

'Don't worry.' Jack smiles, the steam dissipating now to show the full extent of his cheeky grin. 'I'm just finishing. Any earlier and you would have got an eyeful.'

'I know. That would have been awful,' I say, and Jack's mouth hangs open in feigned offence. 'No, not awful. But you know . . . you know what I mean.'

Jack's laugh echoes around the bathroom as he reaches to pick up his toothbrush, his long, muscular arm almost brushing past me. He squeezes the toothpaste perfectly. Damn it.

'I'll give you some space,' I begin, turning to exit the room again.

'Don't be silly.' Jack shakes his head, mumbling now, thanks to a mouthful of toothpaste, and gesturing to the twin sinks in front of us. 'What are his and hers sinks for?'

I force my eyes to look back at my reflection, reaching for my own toothbrush as Jack and I brush away side by side. I thought he was safely in the living room, working away. But no, now we're standing here in silence, like the kind of married couple who have nothing to say to one another; the sort of his-and-hers twinset of a couple I've never wanted to be.

'Minty fresh.' Jack swivels round to me and breathes into the air.

He should be careful how vigorously he swivels. Neither one of us wants that towel to drop. I lean to spit my toothpaste into the sink, reaching a hand up to my mouth so that he doesn't see, and then put my toothbrush into the holder near his sink, the backs of our toothbrushes kissing now.

'Wow. Really can't put you in a box, can ya?' Jack laughs, nodding over to the 'hers' toothbrush holder next to my sink. I didn't even notice it there. I'm too busy trying not to notice everything else that Jack the Jock has on display. 'After you,' he gestures to the door.

'I, erm . . . I need a shower . . .'

Jack stalls for a second, looking from the shower to me, like somehow this is a strange concept. For the briefest moment I wonder whether he's imagining me in the shower or, worse, wanting to follow me in there. As soon as the thought fills my mind, I know it's ridiculous, but the air feels heavy between us, as he lingers back, and I try to scoot around his naked chest. Why is this so awkward? We're married. Except, only technically. Still, Jack's eyes are wide, like he's taking every inch of this moment in. Then he leaves, but as I undress and step into the shower, it feels so strange to see Jack's shampoo next to mine.

I open the door into the bedroom, my towel clutched around me, my hair wet and dripping onto the floor. Jack is sitting on his side of the bed, his jeans on, his top still off. Why didn't I get him to vow that he wouldn't be half-naked around me?

'Sorry, I' – Jack turns around to see me standing there before abruptly averting his gaze – 'I can leave you . . .'

Except, as awkward as this all is, it's better than being left here alone in this room.

'No, no,' I object. 'It's fine. Keep looking that way. I'll just do the knicker trick.'

'The knicker trick?' Jack's head swings around to stare at me.

'I said don't look!'

'What's a knicker trick?' He throws his hands up to cover his eyes.

'It's just something we used to do after swimming lessons when I was little,' I say, holding the towel around me as I pull out a pair of pants and start to step into them, wiggling them up my legs. Next, I grab my bra and put it on seamlessly, not dropping my cover once. 'Aha! Still got it!' I say, as I drop my towel and Jack drops his hands. 'I said don't look!'

'I thought you were done!' Jack screws his eyes shut again, blushing now.

'Did I say I was done?' I snap back but can't help laughing as I grab a clean T-shirt.

'You said you've still got it. I thought that was how the knicker trick ended.'

'You didn't know what a knicker trick was!' I pull on

yesterday's jeans, the ones I got married in. God, this is too weird. 'Okay, *now* I'm finished.'

Jack unscrews his eyes, a coy little smile turning up the corners of his mouth, before diving under his own T-shirt and making his way out of the room.

'You have still got it, by the way.' Jack grins again, before ducking out of the door.

It doesn't take long after Jack leaves the bedroom for him to be making his way out of the apartment completely. Turns out his boss, Toby, prefers it when he can actually *see* the sweat beading from Jack's forehead as he fixes algorithms and code that Toby has broken in the first place. In the silence of the kitchen, I hold Jack's compliment to my chest: *I've still got it.* I know he means more than the knicker trick, and I know I shouldn't care. I've never really cared about guys, never really made time for them. And I like it that way. It means I have the headspace to concentrate on what matters most.

I set up my laptop on the kitchen counter and click through the transcripts of my conversations about ageing. It was my supervisor who encouraged me to try to get a paper published this early into working on my PhD. I might have felt intimidated if I didn't know I was quite literally *made* for this. Ever since I was at primary school, teachers had been encouraging me to go to university, then encouraging me to stay on for a Masters, then encouraging me to do a PhD. And when I found women's studies and feminist research, feminist theory, I knew furthering the fight for equality is precisely what I wanted to give my time and energy to. Except, both my time and energy feel in short supply today.

I was a wife for fifty-five years before my husband passed away,

114

a mother for fifty-four years; my world revolved around them . . . I scan through the transcript of my interview with seventy-five-year-old Mariann, struggling to take in her words. I read the sentence once, and then for a second time, but the silence in the too-big kitchen feels distracting somehow, each new thought beginning with Mariann before drifting to my dad. My mind scrambles to remember anything tangible about him, about how he used to smell or feel or laugh, but it comes up short; I was so little when he decided to leave for New York.

Rupert may have been the 'bread winner' but it was my job to turn that bread into something that could sustain a family of six for decades. I read on, but the same thing happens, my mind drifting away. I decide to wander into the living room instead, setting my laptop up on top of my dad's writing desk, the floor-to-ceiling windows wrapping around it until I feel like I'm almost in the Thames. I refuse to switch on his Mac desktop to see whatever woman or family he last had as his computer background. What I *can* remember about my dad is that he didn't have time for his family, although this doesn't feel like a memory of him so much as a memory of my mum telling me this. Of the two of us sitting on the living-room floor, around the time I was ten, and trying to hurriedly pick out photos of our latest holiday abroad for a school project in between her afternoon work meetings. I had asked why my dad didn't come away with us, whether he ever did? Then she shut the photo album as quickly as she had shut down the conversation.

Since Rupert died, since the boys left home, I don't know what my role is anymore. I read Mariann's words, about how she shaped her entire adult life around a societal expectation. For some reason, I feel the need to remind myself that I actually *liked*

115

that my mum never gave up her job, that it was her way of modelling ambition and independence for me. Then I feel a twinge down my neck, a tightening in my shoulders, and I remember again how disappointed she'll be if she finds out about the apartment, finds out that I am here.

Get a husband, have children, raise them. No one talks about how redundant you feel when they're gone. Or how redundant it is to miss a dad who was never there in the first place. No, no, I don't miss my dad. We've been fine without him, thrived without him. I force my attention back to the transcript, but the niggle doesn't leave. I shouldn't be here, championing independence whilst mooching off a dad that didn't even tell me he was sick.

I try and fail to concentrate again and again as the minutes drag by, drifting into hours until I find myself clock-watching, just waiting for Jack to arrive home. He said he would be back almost an hour ago. I will my eyes to keep reading, analysing, but instead I find myself scrolling through the government's website, to the page about family visas, then to forums chatting about 'leave to remain' and 'life in the UK' – tests that seem to be so complicated I'm not even sure I would be able to pass them. For some reason, the visa, helping Jack, is the only thing that seems to drown out the noise of my dad, reminding me why I'm here.

'No dinner on the table?'

I whip round to see Jack standing there, face beaming, one hand on his hip. I was too engrossed in these visa forums to even hear him arrive home. And given his smug face and *that* sentence, I now have even less idea why I've wasted hours trying to keep him here.

116

'After I made you breakfast and everything . . .' he goes on. 'Call yourself a wife.'

'Firstly, you made me a sandwich I couldn't eat. Secondly, I *don't* call myself a wife. And thirdly, it's a good job I know you're joking and . . . stop looking for my soapbox!'

I notice he's pretending to look around him now. He laughs fully, coming closer towards me. I shut down the visa windows before he can see them. I'm meant to be losing myself in my PhD, the reason Jack thinks I need to stay here rent-free.

'You had a good day?' he asks, arriving by the side of the desk.

'It's been . . .'

Long? Unproductive? A little lonely?

'It's been okay. Yours?'

'Sped by, productive . . . bit too much Toby breathing down my neck.' Jack laughs. 'I hope you don't mind but I told Toby about us, I had to, otherwise how else do you explain why I'm still here? Obviously, I didn't tell him we're not in love.'

He beams back at me like I'm the genie that has made all of his wishes come true.

'Oh, and I've got a surprise for you,' he goes on and it's only then that I notice he's holding something behind his back.

'Your proof of employment?'

'Yes, got that. But it's not that,' he says, and I stand, straining to reach behind his back, praying it's not flowers or something romantic. He pulls away, pushes me off playfully, then reveals two disposable cameras.

'Oh wow. I was hoping for something bigger,' I joke.

'Tough. You get these. And a weekend taking photos and pretending to be my wife?' He asks this last part hopefully, like he's always asking too much. 'We need it for our—'

117

'Supporting evidence.' I nod.

'Woah, someone knows their stuff.'

'Thought I should scrub up.' I shrug. 'We're kind of in this thing together.'

'For better or for worse.' Jack pretends to swoon, the cameras still in his hands.

'Shut up,' I say, as he ditches his laptop and work bag and flops down onto the sofa behind him, hopeful, satisfied. 'And don't get too comfortable. You're making dinner.'

Six Days Marrried

Jack

I look at my laptop, trying to work out why the latest test I'm running keeps crashing. I set it to run again, and my screen flags up with angry, red errors. They say the definition of insanity is doing the same thing and expecting a different result.

I take a bite of my avocado on toast, forcing down the memory of Charlie spending a whole afternoon trying to fling a basketball over his head and into the hoop without looking. Same thing, same result. I should have known developing SoberApp wouldn't make me think about Charlie any less, not when too much alcohol had a part to play in what happened to us.

Fancy a drink tonight?

I look down at the message Louise has sent to me now. It's the second time she's asked, and I still haven't replied. The world is full of people doing the same thing and expecting a different result. But it's the same thing, the safety, that I like about my routine: head down, work hard, volunteer, date without going deep. Nobody gets hurt.

Hey, I had a great time last time we hung out, but I think we'd be better off as friends.

Okay, so maybe some people get momentarily bruised, but it's far better than giving your heart to one person and getting it ripped out of your chest completely.

'Morning.' Maya yawns her way into the kitchen as I slide a portion of avocado on toast her way, standing up to pour her a cup of coffee from the cafetière on the side. Over the last week that we've been living together I've become some kind of house-husband. But Maya is working so hard on her paper. Plus, she's the reason we're both here in the first place.

'Working already?' She takes a bite of toast. Her hair is messy, her face fresh; she's wearing the same pyjamas she's been wearing all week, the ones that are so thin that they leave little to the imagination. She spent the first few mornings with her arms permanently crossed but she seems to have relaxed now. We both have. And it would be typical Maya to retweet someone longing to #freethenipple anyway.

'Kind of,' I say.

I know I'm a workaholic, but I find it's better to channel my anxiety into something. My mind sort of goes quiet when I code. Even when I'm teaching teenagers how to code through the Sibling Scheme, the sheer volume of their banter seems to quieten my mind even more. My thoughts jolt forwards to tomorrow, anxious to find out how Charlotte is, how things with her family have been since last week.

'You've not forgotten about today, have you?' Maya asks, leaning against the kitchen island and lifting her toast to take another sizeable bite.

'No, not at all. I'm just about to get read—'

'Shotgun the bathroom!' Maya shoots up a hand, her toast still in it, spraying crumbs everywhere. We needed some sort of system after our first-day run-in, but the simple shotgun has not been firing in my favour. I contemplate arguing and then my phone rings. It's Adrian.

'Hey, mate,' I say, as Maya disappears out of the room.

'Hey, stranger. Just checking you're alive.'

'I'm alive,' I confirm, smiling at the sound of his voice.

'And not homeless?'

'Not homeless.'

'So where are you?' It's a simple question but I know Maya will kill me if I tell Adrian before she has a chance to come clean to Emmie.

'I found an apartment . . . a house share . . . in Wapping.' All facts so far.

'Cool. What's your housemate like?'

'Jack! I'm adding a new vow!' Maya's shout booms from the hallway. I reach to cover the microphone. 'No beard trimmings in the sink!'

'We have separate sinks!' I hiss back to her as she leans her head into the kitchen.

'Yeah, but I don't want to *see* them.'

It's then that she sees I'm on the phone, holding my finger over the microphone. I mouth Adrian's name to her, and she promptly shuts up.

'Yeah, they're cool.'

'They're? That sounded like a chick. Who is she?'

'It's no one,' I lie. I'll tell him soon, just as soon as Maya gives me the all-clear.

'It's always no one. Is it serious? You're not living with this girl, are you?'

'No, of course not!' I lie again, searching for the words to shut down this line of questioning. Shamefully, I know what they are.

'You know what I'm like, mate.' I risk a glance to Maya, who is now pretending to look busy making herself another coffee.

'Yeah, can't commit to a Hello Fresh subscription.'

I laugh, except it's committing to something too much that worries me most. As I make my excuses and hang up the call, I try not to think of Laura, of Charlie. Of all the reasons to not want to go back to Auckland, those two are at the top of the list. But today is about another list – the list of photos Maya and I need to take to form part of our visa application. I look to her now, coffee in KeepCup and raring to go. And I need this in order to be able to stay.

'Woah, you must mean business,' I say as Maya scoops up her hair to tie it in a bundle at the top of her head. She peels off her denim jacket too until she's in a plain white T and then reaches to pick up her golf club. I hand her a golf ball.

'I can't look the same in all of these photographs,' she says back to me. 'These photos are meant to span our whole relationship.'

'In that case, can you try and look nineteen?' I say, stepping back and pulling one of the disposable cameras I bought us to my face. I can still see her glaring through the lens.

'What is it with society's obsession with making women look younger?' She manages to put a hand on her hip, even with the golf ball clutched in it. To me, she doesn't look a day older than when I first met her back in first year when she actually *was* nineteen.

'Fine, look fifty for all I care, but just try and look different from the last one.'

I take the photo and Maya glares at me all over again in a way that tells me she's just told *me* that, and if it was left to me, we'd have a hundred photos of her wearing the same clothes and her hair the same way.

It was also Maya's idea to head to Junk Yard Golf Club. It's so dark in here that we could tell the authorities we're whatever age we want to be. But I've had my good ideas too. Taking Maya to get rainbow bagels, strolling down Brick Lane, taking snaps the whole way. Taking snaps of our 'relationship' full stop. It was a good idea to do this visa thing with Maya too. Sure, there were hardly people lining up around the block. But today's been *fun*.

'Hole in one!' Maya throws her hands up into the air, almost taking some poor guy out as she holds her club up into the air too. I manage to photograph her pride. 'Three, four . . .' Maya counts up as my ball hits the side for a fourth time. Unfortunately, Maya also manages to photograph my demise. 'Loser.' She makes an L-shape on her forehead.

'Says the grown woman doing the loser sign,' I banter back, but feel safe in the knowledge that, right now, Maya has no idea just how much of a loser I am.

She steers me to the next hole, turning around in intervals to take photos, the flash filling the dimly lit basement-style building. She ushers me to throw my arm around one of the dirty-looking mannequins in the middle of the holes.

123

'There were three of us in this relationship.' She throws her hand to her head, pretending to be dramatic, pretending to be Princess Diana. At least that's who I think she's being. I laugh as I unhook my arm from around the 'other woman' and one of the Junk Yard staff members takes a step forwards.

'You can't be standing on the structures, mate.'

'I told him that,' Maya says to the hipster-looking staff member and my cheeks flood red. At least no one can see them in this light. Then, Maya takes another photo, and the flash goes off. 'Come on, hubby, stop fooling around.'

The hipster walks off looking surprised. Perhaps surprised that we've seemingly chosen to get married in our early twenties. Perhaps surprised that I've managed to convince a woman like Maya to marry me. I'm still a little surprised by this too.

'Where next?' Maya asks, as we emerge into the warm evening to find millennials in jeans and T-shirts and tourists braving shorts and sandals scattered along the street, the promise of warmer weather in the air now that we've somehow stumbled into early June.

'Ever been to Tayyabs?' Maya shakes her head. 'In that case, you're in for a treat.'

We walk side by side all the way down Brick Lane, resisting every single curry-house rep who thinks they can beckon Maya in with a simple 'pretty lady' or 'beautiful woman' thrown her way. Know your audience, guys.

When we arrive at the restaurant there isn't a queue for a table so much as an orderless rabble, but no one seems too unhappy about it. Big groups of guys in suits look half-cut, families huddle around one another and there's no less than three birthday balloons floating up from the crowds, a group of dressed-up friends gathered around each. Man, I love London.

'Two?' A waiter motions at us, lifting two fingers. We nod. I guess that's what we are now. We're a two. The waiter walks at pace, weaving through crowds and down the stairs until we're descending into a dark room filled with noise and chatter.

I strain to see Maya over the large menu she's holding in front of her. She peers over the top too and I take another photo, this time on my phone. We were worried that if we took them all on our phones, they'd work out the date they were taken, that the iCloud would dob us in somehow. She smiles, her hair down again and falling to her shoulders, holding her pose for a second and then shuffling to get comfortable at a table only just big enough for two. Our knees knock together under the table, but she doesn't flinch.

'Our first date,' I joke, as another waiter places a stack of poppadoms on the table.

'You think this is our first date?' Maya asks, karate-chopping the poppadoms in half.

'Nice,' I say, reaching to pick up a piece. 'Fine, not a date, but you know—'

'No, I mean' – she interrupts me, reaching to dip her shard of poppadom in the mango chutney at the exact same time I do; our hands touch, and my skin feels hot as she breaks the contact to cram the food into her mouth – 'this is like our *fifth* date,' she mumbles.

'Our fifth?' I feel something tighten within me. I've not had a fifth date for years.

'Yeah,' Maya says, shaking her head in a way that tells me to keep up. 'Think about it. There was that time after the party,

125

then the next day when we met at the apartment, then we went to Brighton. Then we got married—'

'You count a wedding as a date?'

'You don't?' Maya scoffs, reaching for another poppadom. She has a point.

Seemingly out of nowhere a waitress arrives at our table, pretty and petite, no notepad in her hand; a fact that instantly makes me worry that she's going to forget our order. Not that I'll let Maya know that. I look over to her now, still scanning the menu. I knew what I was going to choose the second we stepped foot in here. The same thing I've always had since I came here during my first week at university, desperately trying to make this new city feel like home.

'I'll take a chicken korma and plain naan, please,' I say, smiling back at the waitress. I used to be more adventurous before I started needing something simple, so safe, so—

'*Boring!*' Maya looks across her menu at me, shaking her head in disdain.

'It's not *boring*,' I hiss back to her, the waitress still standing there, watching us.

'Well, it's not *interesting*.'

'I'll have you know it's the UK's second-favourite curry.'

'Well, the UK is boring, then,' Maya says, before her smile fades. She knows how much this country means to me or we wouldn't be here, eating dinner as husband and wife.

'What are you going to have then, Ms Reckless?' I tease through the tension.

'A garlic naan – no, peshwari naan – and the paneer tikka masala,' she says proudly, before a flirtatious smile lights up her whole face and she adds: 'Extra spicy.'

It doesn't take long for another waitress to arrive at our table, this time with countless plates and dishes dotted up her arms. If Tayyabs doesn't work out for her she could join the circus. As she places our curries and naan breads in front of us, I consider Maya's comment about our dates: if this *was* a date, this would be our fifth, which makes this the longest relationship I've had since Laura. Something that would feel dangerous and anxiety-inducing if I hadn't had three pints today and could still feel Maya's knee against mine under the table.

'Is that everything?' the waitress asks.

'Can you juggle?' I joke. Maya laughs but the waitress just stares back at me, confused. 'Could I have a beer, please?'

'Any kind of beer?' she asks, looking at me like I've never ordered one before.

'Any kind, whatever's your favourite.' I grin, and her face finally breaks into a smile, before she slowly walks away from our table, her hips swinging in time with her steps.

'Were you just flirting with her?' Maya leans forward to hiss across the table, but I can tell she's joking, that she doesn't care a bit.

'No,' I say, seriously. 'I was ordering a beer.'

'Hardly on brand for SoberApp.'

'What Toby doesn't know can't hurt him,' I say, before instantly checking around the room to confirm that he's not here. Working in Tech means you know how easy it is to keep tabs on someone. And having worked with Toby, I can tell you he's intense enough to try it. I turn back to Maya, who has just taken a massive spoonful of her curry, and I swear I see her eyes widen in shock, her cheeks beginning to pinken immediately. That curry must be *really* hot.

127

'So, what's your type?' Maya forces the words, before swallowing deeply. I think she's trying to pretend that what she's ordered isn't too spicy for her and, for some reason, watching her do this looks cute. She must notice that my thoughts are miles away from her question, as she adds: 'I'm just trying to make normal fifth-date conversation.'

'I don't know, I just fall for someone's personality, I guess.'

'Be serious.'

'Tall, blonde, surfers,' I admit, looking at Maya, a woman who categorically doesn't fit any of these boxes.

'Bodes well.' She laughs, taking a glug of her water. 'Any long-term relationships?'

'Does a marriage count?'

'Not this one,' she quips back.

'Fine, yes,' I breathe, not knowing how much to say. 'One. For five years. Childhood sweethearts, I suppose. Her name was Laura Mae.'

'Probably still is.' Maya laughs again until she realises that I'm not laughing too. 'Oh crap, she's not . . . she didn't . . . ?'

'Die?' I say, a lump catching in my throat. 'No, she didn't.' I force a smile. 'She's still in Auckland.'

'Is that why you don't want to—?'

'How about you? What's your type?' Thankfully it's noisy enough in here to change the subject with ease, to pretend I simply didn't hear her last question.

She takes a long sip of her newly materialised wine, and I mirror her, taking a slow draw of my beer. Her green eyes glass over slightly, chin tilted to the ceiling, like she's really having to think about this. I suddenly think that *tall, blonde, surfers* wasn't deep enough.

128

'Cats.'

'Cats?' I laugh. 'Now *you* be serious.'

'I am being,' she says, laughing back. 'I don't really *do* guys.' Is this why she found it so easy to marry me? Because she'd never fancy a guy like me, because she'd never fancy a guy full stop? 'And before you ask, no I'm not gay.'

I throw up my hands in surrender as if to say *wasn't gonna*.

'I've just . . . never really seen the point.' I don't say anything, hoping that Maya will go on. 'For a long time, it's just been me and my mum, and she's modelled this fantastic, whole life as someone who's single, and she's achieved so much, raised a daughter—'

'Her best achievement?'

'Something like that,' Maya says, taking another sip. She doesn't look convinced.

'So, no long relationships?'

'Not with men or cats,' Maya says, looking more disappointed about the latter. I watch as she moves her curry around with her fork, preparing herself for her next bite before she thinks better of it and reaches for a bite of her naan. 'I've always wanted a pet. But with parents who work so much, move around so much—'

'We could get a cat,' I splutter the words; I've clearly already had too much beer.

'And who would take care of it once we're divorced?'

She leans forwards to rest her chin on her hands, the sentence feels safe enough to say when we're surrounded by chatter.

'No, I'm fine thanks. No cats. No men. Just one sort-of-handsome husband.'

A silence lingers between us, before Maya reaches across the table to take a forkful of my korma sauce.

'Hey!' I say, watching as she savours the creamy taste of my dish slowly. 'I thought you were a vegetarian?'

'I'm not eating the chicken,' Maya objects.

'Well, in any case, I thought you said korma was *boring*?'

'I know,' she says, leaning forward on her elbows again, offering me a coquettish smile. 'But after tasting this lava, I'm in the market for something safer.'

'And you think I'm going to let you take it after you slagged off my beloved dish?'

Maya laughs, and her face is so close right now that if she had chosen the garlic naan, I would have practically tasted it. I wonder if that's why she didn't? But no, that's crazy.

'Well, for starters,' she says, reaching over for another forkful . 'You already have. And I may have slagged it off, but I'm allowed to change my mind.'

Her voice lowers, now more of a whisper, and I find myself leaning in further to hear.

'Then there's the fact that I'm your wife, and you're my husband and—'

'Your handsome husband?' I repeat her words from earlier at the exact same moment someone tries to squeeze past the back of my chair, I thrust myself forward until I'm inches away from Maya.

'I said *sort of.*' She grins, holding eye contact.

In the darkness of our surroundings and with our faces so close together the moment feels intense, so intense that I don't know what to do with it. She breathes deeply, her eyes darting to my lips before fixing themselves back on me. *I'm allowed to change my mind.* But just about the food? Or about me too? About what she wants from this union? Then I lean in closer, placing my lips on hers, kissing her gently until she pulls away. Unlike last time, she's not smiling. She's not having to pretend.

'You promised,' she says, her words disappearing into the noise, but I can still read her lips. Lips that I categorically shouldn't have just tried to kiss.

'I know, I'm sorry, I thought that maybe—'

'Maybe what?' Maya snaps.

'Like maybe you were flirting with me, giving me some signals.'

'Signals?' Maya scoffs and my stomach drops to the floor.

'I know, it's stupid, it's just today and all the beer and I thought that maybe this is what you want.'

'Is it what *you* want?'

'No,' I say, the blurriness of the beer sharpening into the sheer reality of the moment. 'Not really, I want to stay here. I don't want to go home.'

Damn it. I just wanted to get this right. To not screw this relationship up. The one that is keeping me here.

'I just misread the moment . . .' I say again. 'I blame the beer. I promise it won't happen again.'

'Good,' Maya says, her anger morphing into something like panic. She's made it very clear what the rules of this engagement, this marriage, are. 'And for future reference' – she goes on, and I sigh, realising just how fragile the future of this arrangement really is – 'if you sense any "signals" please refer to our earlier *vows*.'

'Vows trump signals,' I confirm back to her. 'Got it.'

'Because if this is going to work . . .' Maya softens slightly now; surely, she can see how mortified I am? 'If we're really going to keep this up until you can apply for your residency visa, I don't think that's a good idea,' she says again, and I know she's talking sense.

'It won't, I promise,' I confirm again. 'It was stupid, the beer.' I say, trust SoberApp to turn me into a lightweight. 'It won't happen again. The rules still stand.'

'The rules still stand,' Maya echoes, smile resumed. 'But can you?' She looks down to the empty plates between us, demolished just as quickly as they came.

'Come on, lightweight.' She laughs, getting to her feet. 'Let's get you home.'

Thirteen Days Married

Maya

'I can't find *anything* in this kitchen.'

'Except a sort-of-handsome husband,' Jack jokes from beside me.

'I'm not even entertaining that comment,' I tease back. Just like I didn't entertain last week's long-forgotten kiss. I yank a handle and the drawers that pull out are deceptively deep, yet another high-tech trick to hide the mess away. Typical Dad. I reach into them to grab some salt and pepper before moving across to my breakfast assembled on the side. Jack slides across the kitchen floor behind me as I do. He reaches into a top cupboard before beckoning me to chuck the salt and pepper his way. He catches them with ease. And I'd expect no less from a boy who seemingly used to spend more time on the rugby pitch than in lessons.

'Heads up,' Jack says, throwing me a carton of juice. I look up to grab it just in time.

'Dude,' I say, exasperated. 'The folder!' I motion down at

our painstaking work, the folder of supporting evidence, packed full with the photos we took on our day out in Shoreditch last weekend, the cards and love letters we've forged over the last week that we've been living together. 'It could have spilled everywhere.'

'Except you never let it drop.' Jack grins back at me.

I'm not sure if he means the juice or generally, like in an argument, that I never let things go? Which is categorically untrue seeing as I've not mentioned the kiss all week.

The beard trimmings in the sink is a different thing entirely.

'It's a bloody work of art, eh?' Jack says, looking down at the folder as he pulls out one of the chairs beside me, his bacon and avocado sandwich stacked high as per.

I take a bit of my pesto quinoa breakfast bowl. We tried to coordinate breakfast for about two days before we realised we have completely different tastes, and that's okay, seeing as we're not a real couple. Though you wouldn't know that from the file we've curated together.

'Do you really think they'll buy it?' Jack smiles but I can tell he's anxious about it.

I flick through the pages of the document, lingering on the photographs. The selfie of us standing on Brick Lane holding up our half-eaten bagels in the place of our smiles; me, in the dim light of Junk Yark holding my golf club above my head, victorious; the one I took of the back of Jack, as he wandered past one of Shoreditch's very many graffitid walls, his dark outfit popping against the bright pink background; one of me gazing into a vintage shop window, the way Jack has caught the sunlight making my hair look part-halo. And the photo of Jack sat in the Indian restaurant just moments before he kissed me for the first time since our wedding day. I turn over the next page to find the character references from Kris and Ken, from Toby and my professor, who was surprised and, I think, a bit appalled that I'd decided to enter the man-made covenant of marriage.

I turn to the next page, one that Jack put together, and scan a selection of cards and envelopes each stamped excessively as they made their journey from New Zealand to the UK. I read the dates, all sent during the last four years that we've claimed to be dating. I peer in closer to read what's on the cards but all I can see is that they are addressed to 'baby' or 'my baby' and all signed off by a single initial, either an M or an X. M? No wonder Jack thought to add these in, they look like they were sent from me to him during long-distance stints and holidays spent apart. Before I can ask who sent these, Jack makes a strange little coughing sound, reaching to turn the page over. Clearly, he doesn't want me to see them. My heartbeat quickens at the thought of who sent them, whether they still call him 'baby' now.

But before I can frame a question, I see what's on the next page. It's one of the documents I put together, the proof of our financial position and our one major asset that means we're a couple you can bank on. Jack is leaning into the page, looking closely at the fine print for the very first time.

'This is in your name . . .' Jack looks down at the page and then up at me, his mouth hanging open. 'I know this whole thing is a lie but . . . but isn't this *fraud*?' His brow crinkles with concern and his cheeks seem to drain of colour. I cross my arms, covering my chest, my throbbing heart underneath. I know I need to tell him the truth.

'Not if it's true,' I say slowly, as Jack's mouth hangs open an extra inch.

'What do you mean?' he says after what feels like the longest time.

'My dad wanted me to have the apartment in my name,' I say, looking from Jack to the document in front of me now.

'Woah, I married *up*.' He exhales, straining to study the document too. My heart throbs harder, my knees beginning to chatter underneath the table.

I read my dad's name over again, confusion clouding my vision and anxiety sparking through my veins until I can't look at it any longer. Jack's eyes are still glued to it. If he reads any more, he'll find out the truth about my dad before I can tell him. With shaking hands, I turn the page back to the one before.

'Well, we already knew that . . .' I say, trying to keep the tone light but knowing that what I'm about to tell him next will change our dynamic completely. 'Jack,' I begin, trying to hold his eye contact but it's so intense that I find my focus drifting down to the open page. *Baby, I wish we could be together again. M.* I manage to read the note word for word.

'Who is this . . . ?' I reach to finger the card, but Jack beats me to it, closing the folder completely. He looks at me, stunned into silence, as if to say *case closed too.*

'I think it's perfect,' he smiles down at the file weakly. I was just going to tell him about my dad, tell him my biggest secret, but evidently Jack doesn't want to tell me his. And I get it. We may be married but we're not that close. And our dynamic, our boundaries, work. Jack stands, picking up the folder and holding it to his chest as something falls from inside it.

'I've got it,' I say, bending to pick it up as Jack does the same, almost knocking me over in the process before he reaches out a strong arm to catch me for a second time.

We both look down at the photograph, face upwards on the kitchen floor, its corners browned with age. It's of a gorgeous young couple sat on the beach, their bare feet pressed into the sand. For a moment, I'm convinced this is a photo of Jack and Laura, but then I notice the faces of two little boys peeking out from behind them, not looking at the camera but sniggering at each other, caught in a secret joke or a stolen moment. It's the kind of picture-perfect family photo that I've never been a part of. That I didn't think I wanted to be in.

'Is this you?' I ask, picking up the photo and sitting cross-legged on the floor.

'No,' Jack says with a soft smile, proceeding to do the same. He looks so big with his long legs folded over each other, but I can tell from the meek expression on his face that he's showing me something he's not shown many people. It makes me feel warm and worried in equal measure. 'That's Charlie, my brother,' he says, his gaze pulled into the photograph. 'And this is me,' he points to the taller of the two boys.

'You're so cute! Look at those little swimming trunks! And those dimples!'

'Still got 'em.' Jack grins, his cheeks blushing now.

'The trunks or the dimples?' I laugh, his chiselled face already telling me the answer. 'Were you guys close? I bet you miss—'

'Hey,' Jack's word cuts my sentence in half. 'I didn't see a family shot of yours in there?' He gets to his feet, offering me a hand before yanking me to my feet.

'Yeah, that's because I don't have one here. My parents aren't very sentimental,' I say, looking around the room at all the paintings and photographs hung on the walls; they're all of places not people. My mum might have some in storage or in the cloud somewhere.

'I've got one of you,' Jack says, standing before me, reaching for his pocket.

'Yes, there's loads of us together.'

'No, I mean, as a little girl.' Jack's smile falters. 'At least I think I do.'

'Jack. Why on earth ... no ... *how* on earth would you have a photo of me as a little—?'

Before I can finish my sentence, Jack has placed a crumpled bit of paper in my hand, my handwriting scrawled upon it. This is the note I left him the day after the party.

'Turn it over,' Jack says, smiling as if he's just solved a puzzle or won a prize. I flip the paper over to find a faded photo printed directly onto the A4 sheet. I mean, it's hardly a vintage film photograph like Jack's, waiting to be framed, but the six- or seven-year-old girl looking into the camera and forcing a smile is most definitely me.

'Where did you get this?' I don't mean my words to sound accusatory, or for the intensity of my scare to make Jack take a step back, but he does.

'You gave it to me,' he points out.

This paper was in my dad's desk drawer. But why? Why would he have a photo of me? And at this age. He left when I was two, cut contact with us soon after. But the girl in the photo is wearing a summer school uniform, a yellow-and-white-checked dress, long dark hair flowing down her sides. I'm beaming back at the camera, probably because I'd been told to, but there's still joy in my eyes. I loved school. And my dad would have known that if he had chosen to stick around.

'Is it so surprising that there would be a photo of you here?' Jack must have noticed the colour drain from my face, and that my hand is starting to shake as I hold the photo.

'No,' I say slowly, using my free hand to steady me against the kitchen island. This doesn't add up. It doesn't make sense. 'Just caught me off guard, I guess.'

'Look, Maya, we don't have to do this,' Jack says quickly, flinching as if he's about to reach for my hand and then thinking better of it.

'Do what?'

'Any of this,' Jack says at speed, his anxiety spilling out between us as I tuck the other photos into the folder and turn the page to display our marriage certificate.

He says this but I can tell from the sheer time he's spent pacing around the apartment that he's becoming increasingly nervous about the prospect of being deported, kicked out of the city he chose to live in.

'I think we're way past that now.' I look up at him, suddenly just inches from me.

'I know, but I just feel bad,' Jack continues. 'I mean, yes I want to stay in London, yes I don't want to go back, but you're doing this huge thing for me and I just feel so responsible for—'

'Me?'

'Kind of,' he says, a hint of apology or sympathy or something in his voice.

'Well, you're not,' I snap and Jack jolts back, stung by the words.

139

Yes, he may technically be my husband now. But I chose to be in this situation. And since when has a label or a status guaranteed that someone will be there for you?

'Honestly,' I say, softening at the sight of Jack's expression; he looks like he's going to cry.

I don't know why he can't go home but I believe him when he says he needs to stay here. And helping him is helping me too. Or at least, I thought it was. But he's hardly a distraction from being at my dad's when he's finding photographs that make no freaking sense.

'I know it's stressful, that there's still a risk you might not get the visa,' I say, Jack's face falling further still. 'But I chose to do this. You've got nothing to feel responsible for.'

'Easier said than done.'

'What do you mean?'

'I've spent my whole life feeling responsible,' Jack says, opening up to me now as I will him to carry on. 'Well, since the age of three . . . since Charlie came along.'

'Were you guys close?' I finally get a second chance at that sentence.

'Yeah, we were.' Jack's smile is tinged with sadness. 'We were inseparable. Everywhere I went, Charlie came too – even when I didn't want him there.' Jack picks up his family photo again, and I can guess he's zoning in on Charlie's face. 'It was easy enough being responsible for him when we were younger but then we hit our teens and we started dating girls and well, yeah, everything got pretty messy . . .'

'Feelings make everything complicated,' I echo his favourite words back to him.

140

'Right!' He looks back at me intently, like we're on the same page.

But instead, my mind is on that printout of my dad's, a thousand questions swirling around at speed. But listening to Jack is calming me somehow. It's as though pretending to be the steady one for him reboots my whole system, reminding me of the kind of woman I want to be.

'Coming to London was a fresh start, a chance to exert my independence, to not just be "Charlie's big brother" anymore,' Jack goes on, and the more he talks the steadier I feel. 'I didn't want to feel responsible for anyone anymore, and now, I'm getting you into all this.'

'You're not getting me into anything.' I reach a hand to the top of his arm. 'And you're *not* responsible for me. I promise.' Yet another thing we're promising to each other. 'Now let's get this folder off to Croydon.'

'I don't know why their offices need to be so far away.' Jack groans.

'Closer than New Zealand.'

'True, but I have *so* much work to do.'

'Me too.' I nod, even though making ground on my paper feels like embarking on a hike up Everest. Wearing flip-flops. And now, with that photo distracting me . . .

Hey, babe, want to hang out after work?

A phone vibrates on the island, and I read the message that has just shot onto the screen. Then, Jack picks it up and I realise that the words are meant for him. I watch him read the message, beginning to type back, then he stalls.

'We don't need to do anything for the visa tonight, do we?'

'No, just need to drop this off and then the wait begins.'

141

'Okay, great. Someone wants to meet after work,' he says, typing his reply.

'You sound pretty happy about it for a commitment-phobe?'

'It's a first date.' Jack grins back at me confidently. 'First dates are always fun.'

For a moment, I feel disappointed. Then I remember that has nothing to do with Jack and everything to do with being alone here. I look down at our folder, the proof of our faux relationship, the proof of me owning this apartment, of my dad still wanting to own something of me.

'If I ever get my work done . . .'

'You should go on your date,' I say, and Jack looks a little caught in the act, but there's nothing to feel guilty for. 'Go have fun, I'll drop off the application.'

'No, you're too busy with your research.'

'Seriously,' I argue back. 'I kind of fancy the trip.'

'Maya.' Jack looks back at me with so much gratitude that I feel like I've saved everything all over again. 'What did I do to deserve a wife like you?'

'It's nothing.' I shrug, feeling the weight of the term 'wife' on my shoulders. But then Jack wraps his arms around me, my heart hammering somewhere within our hug.

'It's everything,' he whispers, and I can feel his breath on my hair. '*Bae.*'

Eighteen Days Married

Jack

I follow the Thames Path from the office back to the apartment, past rows and rows of people eating and drinking along the waterfront. London is the kind of city that has something for everyone all year round – fairy-lit markets at Christmas time, and the pink blossom trees of Greenwich Park to welcome in the spring – but summer in this city trumps them all.

My mind drifts back to work today. Toby seems to think the rising heat is nothing to me, imagining anyone from Oceania sat sunning themselves on a busy Sydney beach. But the heat in this city can feel even hotter without the cooling sea breeze. It's only mid-June and if the last few years are anything to go by, it's about to get a lot stickier than this. Still, Toby's nonchalant nagging and prying about my 'hot new wife' in the office today was a welcome relief from thinking about the visa application. Maya dropped it off over a week ago now and we've not heard anything back from them; they say it can take anywhere from two weeks to *twelve* weeks, so I guess that's normal. And this, walking back to her place, to our place, is starting to feel a bit more normal too. Now that I've stopped misreading signals and trying to screw things up. The shame of our second kiss still sears through my body from time to time. But Maya seems to have forgotten that now. And her signals are clear: we're just friends. Nothing less and certainly nothing more.

Hey. Drink tonight?

I look down at the message that has just buzzed its way into my phone, the notification pulling my attention towards the dating-app icon. It's from a new girl that I matched with soon after my date last week, the one that I wasn't sure I was going on until Maya practically forced me to, grabbing our visa application and darting out of the room.

The smell of pizza wafting up from a handful of umbrella-covered tables grabs my attention immediately and my stomach groans. It's just turned six. And though I would usually grab something and head back to the office, now I find myself wanting to head home. I walk to the menu displayed in a glass case hung up on the wall by the entrance and try to remember what toppings Maya does and doesn't like. Then, I think better of it as Maya will probably hate anything that looks even slightly like a romantic gesture – even a tasty one. I walk away, in the direction of home, wondering whether there are any other husbands out there who have to dial *down* the husbandly behaviour or whether I'm the only one.

I'm almost back at the apartment when my mobile rings. It's Adrian. I pick up the phone instantly.

'Hey, man, you good?' I swear we've been in touch more since I moved out. He's either missing me, or is convinced

144

the day has finally come and I've fallen in love with someone. Adrian doesn't know that ship sailed back in high school.

'Yeah, dude. I'm just heading back to the new digs,' I say, winding down the stone-paved streets past St Katharine's Docks and further into Wapping.

'So, let me get this straight. You're leaving the office in daylight now?'

'To be fair, the days are getting longer.'

'Either this apartment is insane, or this girl has made you crazy.'

A little bit of both. But I can't tell Adrian that, not yet, not until Maya says so. But then, as much as I owe her one – several ones, actually – it's not like I can keep this from my best mate for much longer. It's not like the stuff he doesn't know about my life before. This is happening here in the same city, it's only a matter of time until he and Emmie find out.

'Buddy, who is this girl?' Adrian goes on again. 'When can we hang out? I'm free tonight actually . . . Emmie's out with Maya.'

'Emmie's out with Maya?'

'Yes,' Adrian confirms slowly. 'Is that such a surprise?'

No, apart from the fact that I thought Maya was planning to avoid Emmie like the plague until our visa application was either approved or denied.

'Well, no . . . but hey, do you know where they're going, mate?'

'I don't know, some pub on the water by Maya's new place? They've got important things to catch up on, apparently.'

Our marriage, the visa. Is Maya really about to come clean to Emmie?

'And I've got some news too, dude.'

You and me both, mate. I can't wait to tell him everything's that happened these past few weeks. Unlike what Maya says about Emmie, Adrian will *love* what we've done. And I guess, if Maya's telling Emmie tonight it might be good to have Adrian there to soften the blow.

'Come round tonight, dude,' I say, before thinking better of it. 'I'll drop you a pin.'

Hanging up the call, I make my way to Apartment 100, excited to see Adrian, to see Maya. And yet, walking into the living room, I find her sitting at that desk, staring out of the window, and I suddenly feel like I've done something I shouldn't have. Her hair is piled up high and she's wearing a loose, pale-coloured summer dress that by now is crinkled from a day spent with her knees pulled up to her chest and resting against the computer desk.

'Emmie says you're seeing Adrian tonight?' She shoots me an accusatory glare.

'Wow, news travels fast.'

'Well, are you?' she asks again, closing a Word document; it looks blank.

'Only because he said that Emmie was heading over this way.'

'Yes, to Captain Kidd but not at the flat. Where are you seeing Adrian? And don't say *here* . . .' I don't need to. Apparently, my face says it all. 'Jack! What happened to waiting until we hear if your visa's been approved?'

'Adrian said you were talking about something important tonight?'

'Did he?' Maya's anger morphs into confusion.

'I thought you were finally going to tell Emmie everything, that it wouldn't matter.'

'We promised we'd wait until we heard back from—'

Maya's sentence is interrupted by the chime of a new email dropping into her inbox.

'Oh shit,' Maya says, barely above her breath.

'What is it?' I say, daring to move closer to her side.

'It's from the immigration office,' she says, clicking it open. I put a hand on her shoulder; she doesn't shrug me off. 'Okay . . . okay . . . our application has been received . . . I know because I bloody dropped it off . . .'

'Calm down . . .'

Maya shoots around to give me a death-glare, one that tells me these are the two worst words to say to someone who is stressed. But why is she so anxious about this? This is *my* future we're fighting for here.

'We've got to go in for an interview . . . and you have to have your *biometrics* done.' She turns back to me like the word scares her, which I'm learning is how she looks any time she doesn't understand something. Which to be fair is rare.

'That's like fingerprints and stuff.' I gulp. 'When's the interview?'

'Two weeks from now,' Maya says. 'I suppose it's time to start studying.'

'Well, you should be good at that.' I smile back at her, but her face falls.

'Not when the subject is you,' she says after a silence stretches for a second too long.

'We'll be fine,' I say, not believing it but wanting to for her. After all she's done. 'I'll cancel my plans with Adrian tonight. We can tell them when you're ready to.'

'No, it's fine.' Maya seems to surrender before me now. 'We

need to learn everything there is to know about one another. What better way to learn than from our best friends?'

'Okay, onions chopped,' I say, looking up at Maya, who is preparing the peppers.

'What's your favourite film?' she asks, the umpteenth question of the past hour.

'*Forest Gump*, it's just so beautiful.'

'Are you crying?'

'I'm chopping onions.' I signal down to the tear-inducing culprits in front of me.

'Convenient.' Maya grins, reaching to put the peppers in a bowl.

'Favourite book?' I ask her, as she dances behind me to get the seasoning.

'*Merchant of Venice*!' she shouts from the depths of a cupboard.

'That's a play,' I argue across to her.

'Yeah, that I read in a *book*.' I roll my eyes but concede. 'Memorable date?'

Twenty-first of August, almost five years ago.

'March the third,' I reply quickly.

'How come?'

'Perfect cardigan weather,' I say, and add before Maya can stare my joke away, 'Charlie's birthday.'

Maya looks back at me, her eyes imploring, clearly wanting to know more about him, more about my past. But then she looks down at her phone, sees the time.

'Crap, I need to get ready.'

Maya is going to meet Emmie at the pub, break the news

148

to her about our living together as husband and wife; Adrian is going to meet me here and I'm going to do the same. Then, the girls are going to head back here and we're all going to chow down on Mexican food like one big dysfunctional happy family. What's the worst that could happen?

'Best and worst family holiday?' Maya calls, disappearing out of the room. I don't need this latest line of enquiry to remind me that happy families don't always go to plan.

'Best, teaching Charlie to ski in Whakapapa . . .' I shout back to her.

'Whakawhatnow?' I hear her holler from the bathroom.

'And worst . . .' I try to keep my voice steady.

'Sorry. I can't really hear you!' Maya cries. That's good; I didn't really want to say.

I finish seasoning the chicken and prepping the vegetables, placing them in the fridge before turning around to see that Maya has materialised again. She's wearing a thin tight tank top, that cuts in close to her neck so that her sculpted shoulders seem even more defined. Her top is tucked into a pair of worn denim jeans that are belted around her waist. She's got a full face of make-up on for once. She's stunning without it, but whatever smoky stuff she's got on her eyelids is making the green of her eyes look like they're lit up right now.

'You look . . .' I pause, not knowing what word is appropriate for a husband looking to compliment his wife but have it not sound like a come-on.

'War paint.' Maya shrugs, adding a lick of red gloss-stuff to her lips.

'Do you really think it's going to be that bad?'

149

'Come clean to my best friend that I've married a guy we kind of used to know from university for a visa?' Maya muses. 'I think it's going to be worse.'

'Would you rather tell them together?'

'Maybe . . .' Maya says, reluctantly. She doesn't want to need anyone. 'Maybe breaking it down wouldn't be a bad thing. Tell them about living together, separately, and then tell them about our marriage and plans to separate, together?'

'A beautiful symmetry,' I laugh, nodding in agreement. 'Watch out Shakespeare.'

'And George Lucas,' Maya teases. She did not accept my claim that he's an artist.

'May the force be with you.' I press my hands together to bow. Maya laughs, turning to leave for the pub. She really does look gorgeous. And I should tell her, because something tells me that most dudes don't get a chance to.

'And before you go . . .' I begin as she shoots around, her long hair whipping around with her movement too, kissing her face. Then I think about that kiss, Maya's assurance that I'd crossed a line, and I bottle it. 'Favourite food?'

'Tacos,' Maya nods.

'In that case, make sure you hurry home, wifey.'

Maya flips me her middle finger and leaves me laughing behind her. I make my way into the living room, watching the sun begin to dip slightly, sending amber sparkles across the water. Being in this apartment is the first time I've enjoyed silence in a really long time. And then my phone buzzes. It's that girl on the dating app again. Her name's Florence. And she seems really cool. But with two weeks to learn everything there is to know about Maya, I feel like I've got my hands full.

Busy tonight but drop me some other dates that work. I hit send just as soon as I hear a hammer at the door.

'You do know there's a doorbell?' I say as I swing open the door to find Adrian standing there, wearing a blue polo shirt and chinos, an eight-pack of beer in his hands.

'But no staff?' His eyes are wide, his expression one of disbelief.

'Not that I'm aware of.' I grin. 'But I haven't checked the East Wing.'

'Well, if you find them, please tell them that I'm here for an apology.'

'An apology?'

'Yeah, here I am feeling bad for moving in with Emmie, kicking you out of our place,' Adrian says, dramatically, pushing a hand through his bright blond hair. I move to one side, so that he can step into the entrance hall and finish his tirade without upsetting the neighbours. He looks around, speech stopped in its tracks.

'Seriously, bro. When did you win the lottery?'

I grin and shrug, even though I know. It was around the time I met Maya.

Maya

'But you've only just met him!' Emmie looks back at me from across our table. The beer garden at the Captain Kidd is so busy that no one bats an eyelid at her escalating voice. Though after what I've just told her, I could do with the backup.

'And you're living together?' Emmie goes on, scooping her long

151

hair to one side of her shoulder so that it hangs like the world's silkiest scarf over her loose-fitting jumpsuit, another vintage find. The fact that Emmie is so shocked about Jack being my housemate doesn't bode well for me adding that he's my husband.

'Yes, you had moved in with Adrian and so it just kind of made sense.' I look from Emmie's incredulous expression over to the river beside us.

This place is awesome, so picturesque, especially now that the summer nights are drawing out, the sun glistening on the water. But I can't help wondering whether my dad came here, whether he sat in this place too, what he drank here, who he came with. No one seems to drown out the dad-dread like Jack and I know it's because he doesn't profess to know anything about our relationship. Unlike Emmie.

'Look, I know you've had a lot to deal with lately and that you think Adrian and I are moving too fast,' Emmie begins, softening her voice, choosing her next words carefully. Not that fast actually. Not anymore. 'But you don't need to move in with a guy too.'

'You think that's what this is about?'

'We've done everything else together,' Emmie says, not unkindly. I think both of us are nostalgic for our Maya-and-Emmie days. Up until a month or so ago they were there in full force. 'Moving in with a boyfriend is probably the first thing I've done without you.'

'Yeah, and I'm so happy for you,' I say, biting back the words: *I see your boyfriend and raise you a husband.* Thank God I get to tell her the rest of my situation when Jack is there by my side. 'And I like living with Jack.'

'That's great but . . .' Emmie begins again, reaching for my

152

hand across the table. 'Just be careful. Remember that thing Adrian said that he's a bit—'

'Fucked up,' I complete her sentence, the one I've tried and failed to forget.

'Yeah, that,' she looks apologetic. Caring but apologetic.

'It sounds like Adrian says a lot of things.' I sound mean but Emmie doesn't notice.

'Yeah, I can't wait for you to get to know him a bit more tonight!' Emmie says, throwing her hands together in glee. 'I can't believe you managed to fool us into thinking we were heading to different apartments this evening.'

Ten pounds says Emmie won't believe what else we've been keeping from them.

'And we thought we were the ones who have a secret to share!'

'What secret?' I say, and Emmie looks coy. What secret?

'Adrian's sworn me to wait until he's there,' she says, and I can almost see the cartoon love hearts floating from her eyes. Given how much she's lost her head over this guy, I can imagine the news they're excited about could be as humdrum as investing in a new clothes airer together. 'Shall we finish these and head over? Is it close to here?'

'Yeah, it's . . .' I begin, knowing it's now or never. 'It's my dad's apartment.'

'Your dad's?' Emmie looks back at me, more shocked still. I'm starting to think the husband-and-wife news might actually kill her.

'Well, it's mine, actually,' I say. 'He left it to me in his will as like a huge, expensive sorry for not being there.' I can hardly believe I'm finally telling someone out loud.

'Huge and expensive?' Emmie echoes my words back to me in disbelief.

'My dad lived there. Of course it's huge and expensive.' I roll my eyes.

'And he left it to *you*?'

'No one is more surprised than me,' I say, but Emmie's expression begs to differ.

'Why didn't you tell me?'

'I've not told anyone,' I say, honestly.

'But why? How can you keep this from me?'

'I wasn't *keeping* it from you. I guess I wanted it not to matter, to sort it out and be done with it. I tried to tell my mum before she moved to New York.'

'She moved to New York?!'

Oh crap, there's really so much I've not told her.

'Yeah, recently, *really* recently,' I add quickly. 'I was never going to stay in the apartment, never going to accept it. But then, Adrian moved in with you, and my mum moved away, and Jack needed somewhere to stay . . . and it all happened so suddenly . . .'

'It's . . .' Emmie says slowly, not usually lost for words. I hold my breath, biting my bottom lip, half expecting her to get up from the table and never return. Then I see her visibly uncoil. 'It's okay, I know I've been distracted too. That I didn't give you enough notice about moving out, and you had to find out from Jack, I still feel so awful about that.'

'I know,' I say, looking into my best friend's eyes. 'I'm sorry too.'

'I know you're going through a lot.'

'Yeah,' I say, letting her have this one. 'I've just needed a bit of time to get my head around everything,' I say. I can't believe I'm playing the sympathy card now, but it seems to be working. 'I've not actually told Jack my dad has died.'

'So, who's apartment does he think it is?' Emmie's face twists in confusion.

'Oh, he knows it's my dad's, that it's now in my name . . . he just thinks my dad is still in New York.'

'With your mum?'

'Well, not *with* my mum. He knows they're not together at least.'

'You know you have to tell him, right? He'll find out eventually.'

'I know, I just need a bit more time. To find the right way to tell him.'

'Okay, I can give you that,' Emmie says, smiling softly now. 'But you know you're not great at keeping secrets.'

'That was one time!' I say, remembering how I'd accidentally told Emmie about the eighteenth-birthday party that her parents were throwing for her. She could have won an Oscar for her reaction, not one person knew I'd let it slip. I'm a better secret-keeper now.

'I know, but still . . .' Emmie says, and I silently fill in her blanks: you *need* to tell him. 'But I guess you're not a total liar,' she goes on, and I flinch. 'If your mum and your dad were both living in New York, one of them would have killed the other by now.'

Jack

'Chicken?' Maya offers me the serving bowl, and the word feels like a threat: like who dares break the news to them first?

'Thanks,' I say, heaping more food onto my plate even though I've lost my appetite.

'I can't believe you two are actually living here,' Adrian says for the thousandth time since arriving in the apartment.

I'm not sure which bit he can't fathom, the sheer luxury of the place or the fact that I've suddenly become housemates with his girlfriend's best mate. I look at Maya and I can tell she feels uncomfortable sitting on our secret. I'm not sure sharing it is going to make her feel better. But we have to. As soon as I've plucked up the courage.

'So, that's actually not the only news we have . . .' I begin at the exact same moment that Adrian starts telling us something. I stop my sentence short. 'No, no. You first.'

Maya pokes me under the table. I know one of us needs to say the words 'we got married' and I can tell she wants it to be me. *We got married, we got married . . .*

'We're getting married!' Emmie beams.

It wasn't *Emmie's* line.

'What?' Maya and I say in unison. Below the table, I feel her reach for my hand.

'We're getting married, mate,' Adrian confirms.

'Woah, that's . . . quick,' Maya mutters beside me.

'I know how you feel about marriage, Maya,' Emmie rushes out the words. 'That has historically treated women like a commodity, that it's just a bit of paper.' Maya squeezes my

156

hand under the table. I'm not entirely sure what that means. I look at her now, her eyes wide, trying to tell me something. 'And we're not doing it on a whim, it's *means* something to us.'

'Well, you're never going to believe this—' I begin and Maya squeezes my hand so hard it hurts. Bloody hell, she's strong.

'What Jack means is *congratulations.*' Maya's words are meant for Emmie and Adrian but she's looking directly at me and now I get her message loud and clear: *abort.* I nod back at her, sharing our own silent conversation: *now's not the time to tell them.*

'Yeah, guys,' I say, turning back to them. 'That's incredible. Congratulations!'

I watch as Maya goes to get another bottle of wine. We would have bought champagne if we thought this night would be about celebrating and not explaining ourselves, defending ourselves, convincing our friends we've not gone insane.

'Thanks, guys.' Adrian beams, but Emmie is still looking for Maya's confirmation.

'I'm really happy for you both.' She smiles, puts the wine on the table and sits back, placing her hand in mine again.

'Oh, I'm so glad,' Emmie says. 'I was so scared of what you'd say. I know we used to mock marriage all the time and it looks like I've changed my mind, my morals, just like that,' she chatters on as Maya's fingers jut into my skin. 'But then I met Adrian and the idea of committing to spending my life with him didn't seem so crazy anymore.' She beams at him.

'Hey, what were you guys going to tell us?' Adrian looks between me and Maya.

'Apart from the fact we're living here in this sick apartment?' I deflect.

'Didn't you say there was something else?'

157

'Yeah, you mentioned there was something too.' Emmie looks at Maya.

'Oh yeah . . .' Maya smiles from me to them. 'We bought a clothes airer together!'

Thirty-one Days Married

Maya

I'm not having enough sex, if that's what you're asking, love.

I read the sentence again, laughing just like I did when seventy-nine-year-old Joan first said the words to me in person. When I was there in the interview room with her, just over three months ago, I felt present, passionate, my undivided attention fixed on the task in hand. But here in my dad's apartment, my mind journeys all over the place, searching for answers and stumbling on more questions. And not just about my dad, about why he'd keep a photo of me, even have it in the first place, but about Emmie. About whether, now that our decisions have diverged from one another, one of us is getting it all wrong, and whether the one who is getting it wrong is *me*.

I force my eyes away from the view, the great expanse of water in front of me, and back to the transcript on my laptop screen, set up in front of my dad's imposing desktop. With Jack out all day, I feel like I'm drowning here. *I'm not having enough*

159

sex . . . I read the sentence again, hoping I'll get further down the transcript than last time.

I don't even make it through the sentence. I know I'm not having enough sex; I'm not getting any. And my husband is having plenty. The thought sends that damn niggle down my neck again. But it's totally misplaced, it's great that Jack dates a lot. And I wouldn't even mind him being out all the time if Emmie had more time to come over. I was hoping that once I told her about this place, we'd be hanging out here all the time. Now she has a wedding to plan. And something says it's going to take a whole lot more planning than mine.

No, I've never seen my identity as dependent on servitude. I read Joan's words, letting them soothe me. The first time I heard them, they were everything I wanted to hear. Every research sample needs the exception that proves the rule. *I've lived a full life and can definitely see the benefits of being single. I've worked more and travelled more than all of my married contemporaries and I think I'm able to enjoy this time of my life more than all the empty-nesters. I never had a nest in the first place. I'm not a freaking bird, Maya.*

I smile again at the memory of her words. I'm not a freaking bird. Though that's what us women so often get called, don't we? *My bird. Duck. Chick. Mother hen.* I used to think feminism was about flying out of the cage but now I see it's learning that you weren't in a cage to begin with. Before I can stop myself, my mind scrambles to recall a memory, one that is so blurry and buried that I can't even be sure it's real. I remember creeping downstairs when I was thirteen, maybe fourteen, and overhearing my mum speaking on the phone. I'll never know who she was talking to, but I knew exactly who she was talking *about* when she said: 'I am totally capable of solving

160

this issue with the client alone, *my* client. Call *him* for legal advice? There's no way. He'd love the fact I was calling him, using him . . .'

My stomach churns, the four walls of this living room, *his* living room, closing in. But *I'm* not using him. I'm doing this for Jack. The interview for his visa is tomorrow and I feel like I now know almost everything there is to know about him. Apart from the things he's keeping behind bars. And, well, where he is now and what time he'll be coming home. As the hours tick by, I ignore the questions by revising all the answers we need to know to keep him here.

Thirty-two Days Married

Jack

The sun floods into the bedroom, which is the first sign I'm not at the apartment. I roll over on my side to see a mess of long blond hair. That would be the second.

Last night, I finally managed to meet up with Florence. And the fact we're waking up in her bed together reminds me that our date went pretty well. I reach to her bedside table, yanking my phone away from the charger I borrowed late last night when my phone battery gave up completely. Now my phone is full of energy. Which makes one of us.

I look at my screen, searching for the time, only to find a message from Maya.

Date must have gone well. Remember we've got our appointment at 10 a.m.

Oh crap. The appointment. The interview. I shoot up in bed, shocking Flo awake.

'You're not doing a runner, are you?' She smiles up at me sleepily.

'No,' I say quickly. Well, not yet.

The instinct to run usually comes in between the second date and the third, when the anxiety gets too much. But Flo doesn't need to know that yet. She said she wasn't looking for anything serious anyway.

'I do need to dash though . . .' I look down at the time again.

Oh crap. This appointment is down in Croydon. And I'm somewhere in Bethnal Green. If I play my train transport right, I could maybe get to the interview on time. And if I don't? I won't have to worry about it long because Maya will murder me within minutes of my late arrival.

'Where on earth do you need to *dash* to at eight thirty a.m. on a Saturday morning?' Flo decides that now's the time to let the duvet slip just enough so that I can see her bare chest. Well played, Florence, well played. But no. No, I really have to go. She waits for my answer.

'I've got a work thing.' I save her the drama.

'On a Saturday?' She narrows her eyes, lowering the covers. 'I don't believe you.'

'Trust me,' I say, though she's right not to. 'Start-ups don't care about Saturdays.'

Flo smiles, staring at me as I pull on last night's green jumper and black jeans. She's looking at me like I'm Jack the Jock again. But I'm never going to be; I'm never going to get distracted by trying to be The Man again. I smile back, guilty that she has no idea that I'm not technically single. I'm ninety per cent sure that's a violation of consent. But then, Maya didn't just consent to me behaving like I'm single, she insisted.

Are you even going to be at this thing?

Well apart from today. Today I'll be playing the happily married man.

163

Maya

I look down at my outfit and it's like my body belongs to someone else from the neck down. I'm wearing a blouse, tucked into a pencil skirt. I don't even own a pencil skirt. And Lord knows Emmie had questions when I asked to borrow hers. None of which I'm willing to answer until her one-woman mission to convince me that marriage matters has lost its post-engagement fervour. Or we finally get this visa and I know that the earache, the heartache, will be worth it. That all depends on today. On an appointment. That started five minutes ago. Being late to our own wedding felt a lot easier to stomach when we were in it together.

'Sorry I'm late.' Jack flurries across the car park outside the imposing building of the Visa and Immigration Service and Support Centre – or SSC for those of us who have spent a disproportionate amount of time being distracted by their spouse's upcoming deportation.

I look to him, his expression caught in a tangle between shame, relief and confusion. He's looking at my outfit, one that wouldn't look out of place on a politician giving a press conference. And now I'm looking at his. The same lightweight jumper he was wearing when he left the apartment yesterday, more crumpled now. The same denim jeans, which seem to have some kind of beer stain on them. Of course, I knew he must have stayed over at a date's last night and that's fine. Better than fine. But seeing him now, blustering in late, treating this like it's some kind of game when I'm going above and beyond for him makes my blood start to

164

boil, my palm becoming sticky against the wedding ring I'm clenching against it.

'Aren't you forgetting something?' I say, sounding more passive aggressive than I intend to. So, what if this doesn't work? It'll be his life here on the line.

'Oh, erm . . .' Jack's eyes widen, a deer in the headlights. 'You look nice.'

He sounds so much like a complacent husband right now I hate him.

'Here's your ring,' I say, holding it out for him, willing my hand not to shake.

'Oh, thanks.' His does shake as he reaches for it, clearly hungover. 'I forgot.'

I know.

'Just don't forget any of the things we've learnt about each other,' I say, forcing a smile even though I didn't sleep a wink last night. I was too busy thinking about today. Whether Jack was coming home. And whether I could stomach the night in my dad's apartment with the low hum of anxiety I feel when I'm on my own there cranked up to full force.

'I'll try not to, but that outfit is kind of throwing me off.'

'I thought you said it was *nice*?' I quip back as I turn to lead us into the building.

'It is . . . kind of . . . it's just not very you.' Jack holds the door open.

I wait for him to walk through before me, capable of holding the door open for myself, and he just rolls his eyes at my latest display of independence. I used to like how those looks made me feel. After sleeping at my dad's alone, knowing that I'm angry at Jack for not remembering his ring, I don't really feel that independent at all. And for some strange reason I feel like he's choosing his date over me. Surrendering, I walk through the door Jack is holding ajar

'Well, you look entirely *you*.' I nod to his morning-after-the-night-before attire. Jack the Jock. His face falls. 'Let's just hope the interviewers are as forgiving as our registrar or your sloppy outfit may draw attention to the fact that—'

We arrive at a waiting room to see the faces of no less than eight couples looking up at us; the most incompatibly dressed lovers to ever walk the planet. I stare back at the sea of hoodies and jeans and T-shirts and trainers as Jack arrives by my side.

'I think you'll find' – Jack leans to whisper in my ear, his smugness loud and clear – 'the only person drawing attention here is *you*.'

Jack

'Parents' names?' Maya hisses back to me, trying not to attract any more attention from the other couples sitting in the waiting room, waiting for their names to be called.

'Martin and Andrea,' I whisper back, so quietly she can barely hear me.

'Martin and . . . ?' she repeats, leaving space for me to repeat my mum's name. It's hard enough to say her name once, given that I've not uttered it in almost a year.

'Andrea,' I whisper, as another guy in the room looks over to us and nods sympathetically. 'Ruth and Dex?'

'That's right,' Maya nods back and, after this morning, the

166

death stares she gave me, I feel a strange glow of pride warming me from the inside.

'Is he obsessed with death?'

And now the pride is gone. Maya is looking back at me like I've just punched her.

'Pardon?' she croaks.

'Dexter Morgan. His name is *Dexter Morgan* . . . like from *Dexter* . . . the TV show, the forensic blood analysist-cum-serial killer?'

'Oh.' Maya doesn't get the joke. 'He doesn't have the same surname as us.'

'Okay, sorry, I . . .' I say, not knowing why I've hit a nerve.

'It's Smith.'

'Okay, that's easy, that's—'

'Forgettable,' Maya mutters under her breath.

And now I'm feeling even sicker than I was before. Clearly, she thinks I'm going to forget everything. That I should have spent last night going over all there is to know about my wife. Not getting under a woman who isn't.

'Maya Morgan?' A woman pops her head out of a door coming off the waiting room.

'You're up!' I say, as she stands to her feet and brushes down her pencil skirt.

'And Jack Wilson?' the same woman calls again.

'Together?' Maya asks her; we were expecting to be interviewed alone.

I take a seat nearest the open window; Maya takes the one beside. Our official, our interviewer, is dressed more casually than Maya and looks a little put out by it. She introduces herself – Angela – and Maya smiles back at her. *Maya Angela*. It's her middle name. *Named after Maya Angelou, Your Honour.* As she confirms our names and place of residence, I mentally prepare for the questions to come. Maya claims her favourite book is *I Know Why the Caged Bird Sings* (obviously), but I know deep down it's something by Jodi Picoult. She studied Anthropology at UCL. No siblings. Born in St Guy's Hospital on 17 March. A 'three' on the Enneagram Personality Test – whatever that means. Blood type O.

'How long have you been together?' the woman asks, her glasses perched on the end of her nose as she fills out some official-looking forms.

My phone buzzes from the depths of my pocket and I already know it'll be from Flo.

'Since our first year in university, so four and a bit years ago,' Maya beams, she's a natural. It would concern me how well she lies if I wasn't omitting so much of the truth too.

'And you got married . . . ?' She searches her paperwork.

'Three weeks ago,' I say quickly, knowing I need to say something, anything.

'*Four* weeks ago,' Maya smiles again. She reaches for my leg under the table, and it's only then that I realise my knees have been chattering. I smile at her, a secret 'thank you'.

'And how do you know your witnesses?'

'Just met them at the pub,' Maya says, and my cheeks flush red.

'She's joking,' I add quickly, forcing a laugh. 'They're old friends of ours.'

Maya squeezes my thigh even harder. My punishment for correcting her.

'Well, I can tell you love each other,' our interviewer says with a smile.

168

Can you? Maya and I look at one another, her eye contact burning through me.

'Of course,' I say, Maya's eyes still on mine. 'Of course I love her.'

Under the table, Maya's hand moves, and I know she'll be crossing her fingers.

As soon as the interview is over and we're outside, I feel like I can breathe again. I expected to be grilled for hours, an interrogation lamp held up to my eyes, someone demanding answers I'd forgotten to revise or that I've never even known. And I expected them to ask about Charlie. About why I wouldn't want to go home and be closer to him, to my family. I look at Maya and wonder whether her beauty, her feisty demeanour, her humour, might have answered the interviewer's unvoiced questions about why on earth I'd be wanting to stay.

'That seemed pretty simple?' I say to Maya, hoping she'll feel the same.

'Yeah,' she muses, turning the wedding band round and round on her fourth finger but knowing better than to take it off so close to the centre. Wearing it must be killing her. 'I made that stupid joke about Kris and Ken . . .'

'That's okay,' I say quickly. 'At least you didn't get your wedding date wrong.'

'I'm sure they didn't even notice.' Maya smiles. 'You did a good job – '

'Thanks, so did—'

' – given that you look hungover as hell.'

Forty-one Days Married

Maya

'Maybe it's because you looked hungover?' I snap back at him, looking at the almost empty document displayed on my laptop screen.

'But you were laughing about it last week.' Jack gazes across at me, his shoes up on the sofa.

There were a lot of things I was laughing about with him last week as we made our way back from the SSC in Croydon. But now that over a week has gone by without us hearing anything, things don't feel very funny; the lady at the centre promised they'd be in touch in a few days' time. I know the visa is distracting me from writing my paper, that it'll be easier to settle into it once I know whether Jack is going to be able to stay here with me.

'You got our flipping wedding date wrong,' I say, throwing a hand to my head.

The more I've thought about his mistakes over the past week or so, the more annoying they've become. That may not have

170

been the happiest day of his life, but it was meant to be the most important. When I first agreed to marry him, it felt like a matter of life or death.

'You said that didn't matter either,' Jack says, rolling his eyes at me now. 'You also said we'd picked our sole witnesses up at the pub.'

'You said that didn't matter either.'

We're bickering like husband and wife. But if we don't get this visa, we won't be for much longer. We'll be divorcees.

'But you said . . .' he begins again, more animated but still managing to keep one eye on his laptop screen open before him. The fact he enjoys work so much is a constant reminder that I used to be the same. And I will be. Once we've settled whether he's getting a visa or not and we can start to move on from all the maybes. 'Oh shit! '

I look up to see Jack staring into his computer.

'What's Toby done now?'

'It's not Toby . . .' Jack says slowly, carefully placing his laptop to one side on the sofa before getting to his feet. 'It's about the visa . . .' He arrives by my side.

'And?' I ask, a thousand more questions running through my mind: *how on earth do I sell this place? Where will I start? And at the same time as doing my PhD?*

'I'm afraid you're stuck with me for a bit longer,' Jack says, nonchalantly.

'What? As in . . . you got the visa?' I ask, taking a step closer to him.

'No,' Jack says, but he's smiling now. '*We* got the visa.' And with that he's scooping me up into a hug and spinning me around before placing me down on solid London ground.

171

Part 5

The Affair

Seventy-five Days Married

Jack

I arrive at our apartment, waiting for a moment before turning my keys in the door. Even after over two months of living here, I still feel the need to marvel at the fact it's ours – at least momentarily. But with each passing week since we heard that my visa had been granted – four weeks, six days, two hours and counting – I'm starting to get used to the fact that my being here might not be as temporary as I first feared.

I'm also getting used to being married to Maya. As I make my way into the entrance hall, I know not to expect the smell of a cooked dinner wafting out from the kitchen. I know not to expect the place to look tidy or freshly spring-cleaned. And I know that as soon as I walk into the living room, I'll find her sitting at her dad's desk, eyes fixed on her laptop screen, working away, neat features pinched as she reads her umpteenth article of the day. Kicking my shoes off in the hallway, I bend down to put them in the shoe rack before Maya can bollock me for leaving them scattered 'all over the place'.

Pushing the door into the living room open, I find Maya exactly where I anticipated, bare legs curled up on the chair, her denim hotpants and thin T-shirt top the only thing she can stand to wear in the city's rising heat. The audio recording of one of her recent focus groups blasts into the room: *I gave my all to being a wife before the fool cheated on me with another woman. I don't know why I should be surprised, there's always another woman* . . . Is it little wonder that Maya never wanted to get married when she spends her days analysing the damage done to women who have felt pressured into a societal box?

I watch her for a moment, the early-evening sunshine still shining strong, her T-shirt sleeves pushed up to her shoulders as the mid-August heat beats through the floor-to-ceiling windows, her slender tanned arms suspended over her keyboard, her long hair scrunched up messily on her head. I walk closer as she reaches for her phone, pausing the audio recording before swiping to her messages and filling the silence with an audible groan.

'Hey, what's up?'

'Shit!' She spins around, releasing the phone and holding her hand to her throbbing chest, her sudden motion making me jump too. 'What the hell are you doing here?'

'I, erm . . . I *live* here,' I say, my defiance laced with doubt; I've had nightmares about Maya waking up to realise being married to me is the last thing she wants after all.

'I know that.' She sighs, hand still to heart, breathing heavily. 'I mean, what are you doing creeping up on me?' Her eyes dart down to where I'm standing, now just inches away.

'I wasn't creeping!'

Maya rolls her eyes.

'You know, if someone hadn't made the "take the shoes off as soon as you get in" rule you might have heard me coming.'

'Don't blame me when you get the bill for a new carpet, then.' Maya closes her laptop and gets up from her chair, always one for leaning into an argument.

'Good job you know the landlord,' I say, and she is standing so close to me now that I can feel her body stiffen.

In the ten weeks we've been living together conversations about her family have been few and far between, which suits me just fine seeing as my own family are the reason I can't go back home.

'New rule,' Maya announces into the room so loudly that I take a step back. She does the same. It's too hot in here to remain that close. 'No creeping up on me.'

'Rule number one hundred and seven, is it?' I ask facetiously.

Maya grins. So far, our rules, our vows, seem to be working. Then her phone buzzes on the desk, her smile disappears and my mind springs back to her audible anguish just moments before.

'Hey, what was the matter before?'

'What do you mean?' Maya asks, moving towards the sofa; she perches on the end and I know it's because the leather is too hot to handle in this heatwave, which according to the forecast is only just getting started.

'When I walked in—'

'When you were creeping,' Maya corrects.

'I *wasn't* creeping,' I object, coming to sit beside her, and she raises her eyebrows as if to suggest that I can't seem to leave her alone. Which is categorically not true. 'You looked at your phone, like you were expecting a message . . . you've not been ghosted, have you?'

'I've never been ghosted in my life,' Maya snaps back defensively.

'Of course you have.' Now it's my turn to object. 'It's like a rite of passage in every millennial's life.'

Maya simply raises her eyebrows again. We both know she prides herself on not being like everybody else, not conforming to the so-called norms.

'Well, if I have been ghosted, I'm not aware of it,' Maya goes on.

I know her well enough by now to know that she's trying to change the subject from whatever was bothering her before, that rule one thousand and sixty-one or whatever number we're on no doubt dictates that whatever she's going through has nothing to do with me. And it's not like I can complain given everything I'm not telling her either.

'Oh, you'd *know* if you'd been ghosted.' I give in to her conversation gear-change.

'Like a *when you know you know* type thing?' Maya crinkles her nose at the naivety, and I know she's thinking about Emmie and Adrian.

It's what they've told us every time we've hung out since, every time we've tried and failed to tell them the truth about us only to be met with talk of wedmin and romance and *the best day of their lives*. Turns out it's not easy to tell a couple who are trying to convince you that they're not moving too fast that you've already pipped them to the post.

'Oh, for sure,' I continue. 'You start dating someone and, if you're honest with yourself, you know it's not going to go further than a few dates and that's fine, that's what you're in the market for,' I begin, speaking from experience as Maya listens, her eyes wide and searching, hanging on my every word. She finally surrenders into the sofa too, curling her bare legs underneath her so that her frayed denim hotpants don't damage her dignity.

'But then suddenly the time between their messages gets longer and longer, and you find yourself checking your phone more and more.' I see Maya's eyes dart to her mobile, now lying face up on the sofa beside her. 'And there's less questions from them, but your questioning goes into overdrive – why don't they want to talk to me? What don't they like about me? And as you feel them pulling away, you sense the impending rejection, the feeling like maybe you weren't too good for them after all, that maybe you are the less good-looking one, or less interesting one, or less funny one of the two of you.'

I expect Maya to scoff at this last one given how many times she tells me I'm *not* funny, but she is still listening intently, like she's really trying to work something out.

'That, actually,' I go on, as Maya rearranges her legs, moving a little closer to me in the process, 'you were pretty lucky to be on a first date with them in the first place, that perhaps you shouldn't have played it so cool. And, before you know it you've gone from not caring whether you'll see this person again to being downright obsessed with them.'

'Oh crap,' Maya whispers under her breath. 'I *have* been ghosted before.'

A flash of vulnerability darts across her face so quickly I almost miss it, and like a shooting star that shines and then fades so fast, its brevity makes it beautiful.

'You have?' I'm as shocked as she is.

Maya is ambitious, feisty and doesn't take any crap from

anyone. Plus, she doesn't even seem to date, she has better things to do with her time. Unlike me, who needs one shallow date after another to avoid falling into anything too deep. I never thought that Maya might have been *put off* dating by some loser who doesn't deserve her.

'Who in their right mind would ghost *you*?' I mean this as a compliment, but Maya's expression tells me she's heard this as: who would even *dare*?

'A couple of months ago, I tried the online dating thing, you know, just to see what all the fuss was about. It was just as my masters was coming to an end and I had some time before starting my PhD and I was bored.'

Maya continues, and although she's not saying much, I still feel like she's taking off a layer of herself. Given how little she's wearing right now the thought instantly makes my heart beat harder in my chest. Then, I register the timeline of her decision to date.

'Didn't you only have a week between finishing your masters and starting your PhD?'

Maya nods with a smile, and I know she prides herself on being the kind of person that is so busy that a week at less than a mile a minute is enough to cause said boredom. I also know this period was around the time Emmie started dating Adrian.

'I went on two dates with a guy called David and they were like, *o-kay*,' she accentuates the syllables as if to show just how mediocre her meetings with him really were. 'And he asked me on a third date and then just stopped replying somewhere in the planning of it all. I wasn't bothered, not about him, not really,' Maya stutters, and I don't know whether to believe her or not. 'But I guess for a moment, it made me feel like

180

I could have been a bit much, or not enough, or, you know, a bit *something*.'

'I do know.' I nod faintly, not wanting to make any sudden movements that would scare Maya into putting her guard back up. 'I also know it's not about you.'

Maya rolls her eyes like I've just served her the 'it's not me it's you' line.

'Some guys just aren't looking for anything serious, don't want the commitment.'

'Yeah.' Maya's smirk tells me her sharing time is over. 'Guys like you.'

Maya

As soon as I've said the words, I regret them.

And, sure enough, Jack looks back at me like he's just been slapped, and I remember that his Jack the Jock persona seems to have been something he endured rather than enjoyed.

'Guys like me?' Jack repeats, leaning away from me now. 'I'm . . .'

I feel like he was about to say 'married'. But that's only for the visa. For all the reasons he can't go back home. All the reasons he's not telling me.

'I just mean . . . you date a lot . . . different girls.'

'I'm in my twenties,' he mutters with a shrug, a defence that carries far less force now that two of our best friends are getting married to each other, for real. It's also a defence that makes me feel bad, like he's suggesting that I should be dating far more than I am.

'I choose not to date, you know?' I hate that I feel the need to explain.

'And *I'm* choosing not to get serious with anyone right now.'

'But why?'

'I could ask you the same thing.' Jack cocks his head to one side as he studies me.

It's a stalemate we've come to a thousand times over the past five weeks since he got the visa, where we see a rule, a vow, a line stretching between us and we know that if one of us crosses it, the other will have to follow.

'I don't have enough time,' I say plainly. And it's true. Ever since secondary school, my studies have had a way of spilling over into every aspect of my life; they've needed to. And yet lately, being here, being at my dad's, I feel like I'm taking my foot off the gas. My eyes drift to the beads of sweat glistening on Jack's forearm before I force them back onto his quizzical expression. Lately, I've been getting so damn distracted.

'Or you don't *make* enough time.'

'Trust me, I've seen enough people lose their heads in love to be cautious.'

Jack looks at me like I've slapped him again and I know from the brief snippets that I've managed to piece together that Jack feels this way too, and that he's thinking about Laura.

'Is that why you don't let yourself fall for anyone, because of Laura?'

His eyes widen as if I've caught him red-handed, but then he sighs.

'I've just not met anyone I can see it going the distance with,' he says, shrugging off the seriousness of the moment with a tired smile. 'In my defence, I didn't even know I *could* invest in something that would go the distance. I think I always knew that Toby's visa sponsorship was going to let me down.'

'But now you're here.'

'Now I'm here,' Jack echoes back to me, seeming to soften at the thought.

I watch as his shoulders slide an inch or two down the too-sticky sofa. I see the damp patches lightly speckled across his T-shirt, which is pulled so tightly across his chest that it leaves little to the imagination. Not that I have to imagine anything after sharing a bedroom with him for weeks. After watching him model countless different shirts for me this morning as he picked out what to wear for his twentieth second date since we've been living together.

'Hey! Aren't you meant to be on another date right now?' I ask, it only just occurring to me that despite another day of working on my paper having dragged past slowly, Jack is still back earlier than I expected him to be.

'I cancelled,' Jack says, matter-of-factly. I try my best not to roll my eyes – but of course he cancelled. It was going to be his third date with this latest girl. 'In fact, she wants to rearrange but I'm just not feeling it, so I might just—'

'Ghost them?' I snap suspiciously, having to remind myself again and again that Jack is nothing like the guys I swiped left for or the cheating men the focus group spoke of in the interview I was transcribing today. At least, I don't think he is.

'I always try to do the right thing.' Jack shakes his head. 'Be honest and whatnot.' He gulps and I wonder whether there's anything he's not being honest with me about. 'But I'm not sure why I bother, they usually write back to call me a prick or tell me where to stick it.'

'What do you say to these poor women?' I can't help but laugh.

'Just the usual. That I had a nice time, that they seem like a really good girl.'

'Good girl? They're not children!'

Jack reaches the short distance between us to give me a playful push to the side.

'Well, by all means, if you have any suggestions,' Jack begins, as I stretch out my hand, beckoning for him to place his phone in my palm.

For just a moment, I feel like the kind of jealous partner who needs to be privy to his passwords. He looks at me for the longest time, his eyes tracing the amber light of the sunset to my hair, to my lips, and I wonder whether he's thinking the same, but then he relents. It's not like he has anything to hide when I'm encouraging him to see other people, is it?

I scroll through his phone, at his latest message from a girl called Kate. Despite being far from an expert when it comes to dating, I can instantly see what he's done wrong.

'Okay, wifey, enlighten me,' Jack says.

I look up from his screen with a hard stare; calling each other hubby or wifey made its way into our rules about a fortnight ago. I continue to type at speed, clicking send before Jack can object.

'Please tell me you've not just sent her a message?' Jack says, brushing a hand through his floppy hair.

'You said I could make suggestions.' I hand the phone back to him.

'*Suggestions*, Maya.' Jack looks genuinely annoyed. 'Not direction ... wait ...' Jack looks from the phone to me again. 'This is exactly the kind of thing I usually say to the women I date. So, why does it sound so much better when you type it?' His annoyance morphs into admiration right in front of my eyes.

'I've just added the question at the end; it gives them a chance to agree, to be able to leave things with some dignity.'

I know Jack is reading it again, eight tiny words with the power to shift the tone of a text: *I'm pretty sure you felt this way too?*

'That's . . . pretty clever,' Jack says, as I grin all the more. 'Now it's my turn. I want to message this guy who ghosted you.'

Jack holds out his hand.

'No, I . . .' I begin but before I know it Jack is tickling me in the ribs, sending my body wriggling backwards to escape his touch until I'm lying horizontal on the sofa, and I can feel the weight of his torso on top of me. It's already far too hot for this.

'Maya, he needs to know that he can't waste your time,' Jack goes on, still pinning me down, and I have to stop my quickening breath from catching in my throat. 'Not when you could go on one of these dating apps and choose to spend time with any guy you want to.'

I look back at him, his eyes fixed on mine, my heart throbbing in my chest. Does he really think that? Why does it feel so nice to hear him say that? He holds the weight of his body up with one arm, his other reaching to my side, to the denim of my shorts as I catch the glimpse of his wedding ring now hanging on the gold chain against his sweat-glistening neck. Then, he pulls away to sit up on the sofa again, my phone clutched in his hands. It takes all my strength to push myself back up to sitting, to not lie there and savour his weight on

185

mine, which is weird, because this is Jack we are talking about. He hands my phone to me.

Hey. You missed out, buddy. Maya's husband x

'Tell me you didn't send that!' I already know it's too late.

'What can I say?' Jack's laugh rings through his sentence. 'He didn't deserve the dignity. And please don't let one idiot put you off dating.'

'That's not— ' I begin to object but I lose the words somewhere in Jack's jaunty smile.

'I promise there's some good guys out there.'

'And *I* promise there are women that are worth investing in.'

Jack holds my eye for the longest time, or at least what feels like it. Then, his phone buzzes and it's like I wake up. To the fact that I'm sat here in my dad's apartment. With a man who is only here to help make this bearable. So that I continue a career that I've never once doubted. Unlike the loved ones in my life that I've had cause to doubt again and again.

'You should take Florence on a third date,' I say, retreating to my side of the sofa. After all, Florence is the woman that Jack liked enough to be late to his own visa interview.

'Maybe, you're right,' Jack sighs eventually.

'I'm always right.' I try to resume our usually jovial tone, but things feel hot, sticky.

'And you,' Jack says as he stands, preparing to leave the room for his habitual post-work shower. 'You should consider taking a chance on someone too.'

Seventy-six Days Married

Jack

'Mr Wilson *definitely* has a girlfriend,' Zadie says, trademark sass-hand held high. She is so confident, so sure of herself, that it's almost admirable. Especially considering the shy and retiring fourteen-year-old who walked into Girls Code when I first started volunteering through the Big Sibling Scheme.

'Of course he does!' Charlotte chimes up now. 'Why else would he be smiling like that?' She looks towards her fellow teenagers to be greeted by seven nodding dogs.

I'm smiling because I have a visa, and a life here. I'm smiling because that means I can be here week in, week out, and that without having to jump through all the sponsorship hoops SoberApp can dream of, I have more time to spend at the scheme over the summer. Because what Maya said is true: there are women that are worth investing in.

'You can tell us who you're seeing, you're not our teacher or anything,' Sara adds. Well, no, not *technically*. I'm a volunteer, but I am hopefully teaching them something.

I know Maya wasn't talking about investing in *teenage* girls, that she was encouraging me to give dating a go, a real go. But still, if Maya knew about these students, she'd love spending time with them too. It's just that every time I try to tell her about Charlotte and co., I think about Charlie. And every time I think about Charlie, I know that I'm one breakdown from telling Maya everything, and that our inevitable break-up would follow.

'No,' I say, forcing my life outside this classroom from my mind. 'But I am here to teach you girls how to code and the only thing I'm seeing right now is a messy control structure in this script.'

The girls groan as I gesture for them to look at their monitors.

'Control freak,' one of them mutters to another.

'Control *structure*,' I repeat to let them know I heard that.

But still, their words take on more weight than they mean it to. I *am* a control freak, keeping my life here in nice, neat boxes, because that way, if anything goes wrong, I don't lose everything. All over again.

As silence descends around the IT room, or at least the fast chatter morphs into a low hum that tells me they're at least *trying* to concentrate, I reach for the chain around my neck. I haven't worn it since leaving New Zealand but knew exactly where to find it. Just because you don't wear something often doesn't mean it doesn't matter; sometimes it matters too much. And, when Maya suggested I wear my wedding ring around my neck after forgetting where I put it for the umpteenth time, I knew Charlie's old chain was the perfect solution.

As the session comes to a close, I can tell Charlotte is looking to linger behind again, that our weekly chats have come to mean a lot to her. I bet she has no idea how important they are to me too, that when I'm listening to her, the chatter in my mind falls quiet.

'Sorry about earlier,' she says, looking up at me guiltily.

'What about?' I say, standing up from the desk so that she can sit on top of it.

'About going in too hard about your personal life,' Charlotte says, fiddling with the bracelets hanging loosely around her wrist. 'I know you're a pretty private person.'

'There's not a lot to say,' I lie.

'I don't believe you,' Charlotte says.

She laughs but I can tell she's not joking, that there is something serious she wants to talk to me about. It's why I called my line manager at the Big Sibling Scheme after our session last week to ask about the best way to go about getting Charlotte some additional mentorship support. They said to keep it natural, to let our conversations develop, provided they were led by Charlotte, and that I should report back to them.

And yet, looking at her now, shifting her weight from foot to foot, I know that I'm hardly creating an environment for sharing when I'm insistent on being such a closed book.

'Well, there is this one woman,' I begin, treading the line between not-quite-her-teacher but not-actually-her-big-brother in the way I always do. Careful. Too careful. Because life is way too short to be reckless. 'She's called . . .'

I begin, not knowing who's name to say next. I messaged Flo last night, asking her out on another date. Naturally, I didn't tell her I was following orders from my wife. Or that it was Maya's insistence that I should reassess my serial-dater ways and open

189

myself up to the potential of something more. I know Maya is right, that I can't keep myself closed off from love forever, that I need to at least risk dating a girl long enough for her to see the real me. Still, that doesn't stop it feeling uncomfortable, vulnerable, really effing scary. Especially given that I messaged Flo over fifteen hours ago and she still hasn't replied. And who can blame her given that I told her I didn't want to go on a third date five weeks ago?

'She's called . . .' I begin again. Don't say Flo, not yet. 'Maya.'

'Is she your girlfriend?' Charlotte smiles, pleased to be privy to a snippet of myself.

'Not quite.' The fact that she's *not* makes this information feel stable enough to share.

'Does she have a boyfriend?'

'Not that I know of,' I say, cautious not to pique Charlotte's interest even more.

'What's that supposed to mean?' Clearly, it didn't work.

'Well, she doesn't appear to have a boyfriend, but we also agreed not to tell each other everything,' I try to keep it simple. 'She's my . . . housemate.'

'Must be nice to live with someone you actually like,' Charlotte says, crossing her arms as if to counteract the vulnerability of her sentence.

'I take it home hasn't got much better?'

'George and I had a huge fight.' Charlotte sighs, her eyes welling with tears as soon as she's uttered the words. I know by now that George is her sister. I'd think her parents were royalists if Charlotte hadn't been born way before the prince and princess. And from the sound of things, Charlotte and her sister get treated like anything but.

190

'Do you want to talk about it?' It's the kind of open question we've been trained to say, despite the fact that if Charlotte *didn't* want to talk about it, she wouldn't be here.

'It was about my mum . . .' Go figure. 'We both *know* she's a nightmare, that if she doesn't get professional help, she'll just go from bad to worse, but George just pretends the issues aren't there. She encourages my mum, aids all her bad habits, and I just look like the heartless one who is trying to change her. But she *needs* to change.'

I changed my mum too. In the very worst way a son can. I broke her heart.

'That sounds really difficult,' I say as her last sentence descends into sobs. 'I wonder whether George is struggling to know how to help too, just working it out. Like, there's no roadmap for difficult dynamics, is there?' As soon as I've said it, a lump catches in my throat.

'Yeah, maybe . . .' Charlotte softens. 'We used to be best friends.' My stomach jolts.

'You can still be best friends,' I say, knowing I'll never be able to make amends with my own brother, that one romantic relationship managed to screw it up beyond repair. 'You just need to tell her how you feel, make the most of living together, being on each other's team,' I go on, feeling emotion surge through me now. 'One day you won't live together anymore, and you'll miss it . . . you may even live in a different country.'

'Like you?' I nod. 'Do you ever think you'll go home?'

'This *is* my home.'

'I mean to New Zealand.'

Of course I know what she means.

'I don't think so,' I say, knowing I have Maya to thank for this.

'Why?' Charlotte presses on, and I'm not sure why the directness of her question catches me off guard.

'Honestly?' I say. 'I did some not great stuff at home. And I prefer my life here.'

'Good,' Charlotte says. 'Not about the bad stuff, but the staying here. Sometimes I think knowing you're here is the only thing that gets me through the week.'

'You do know you can reach out at any time.' My voice quivers but I stop it quickly.

I'm supposed to be the adult in this relationship. An adult that has just managed to convince Josie, my main contact at the scheme, that I'm stable enough to support Charlotte, to give her my number so that she can check in outside of our weekly coding sessions together if she needs to.

'Here's my number, you can message when you have no one to talk to,' I say; she looks as weighed down with worry as I used to. 'But just to be clear,' I say, feeling more like a teacher than I want to, but this part is important. 'It's part of the scheme . . . an official part . . . they'll be boundaries as to when and what I reply with and—'

'Please, Jack.' Charlotte puts her hand up to save me from having to point out the obvious: that I'm worried that in being there for her I could give her the wrong impression. 'No offence, but I see you as like my uncle or something.'

An *uncle*?!

When all this time I have been trying to be a brother? Still, as Charlotte leaves the classroom, I smile, feeling buoyed by being around enough to truly invest in Charlotte, in Girls

Code. Then, I look down at my phone to find a message from Florence, letting me know that she's willing to give me one last chance.

And thanks to Maya, it feels like I'm finally getting the life do-over that I came here searching for in the first place.

Maya

I look at the clock in the corner of my laptop and realise that I've lost at least an hour of my research time to scrolling through social media, gazing into the middle-distance and, well, checking the clock in the corner of my laptop screen. I never used to be this way. I used to hit the ground running on any academic project I set my mind to and never look back.

Sure, it sucks that he cheated on me . . . I replay the same part of my recent focus group recording, the one that Jack found me going over and over only twenty-four hours ago. *But I don't regret getting married to him, we had many happy years together, we made each other stronger, we had a family together, we were a team.* I listen to the next part, the part that makes me wonder where on earth my team went. It used to be my mum and me. Then it was Emmie and me. And for the last couple of weeks, it's started to feel like it's Jack and me. But now, Emmie isn't messaging me back and Jack is nowhere to be seen.

It's been over eight hours now since I woke up, turning over on the freshly changed sheets, my blurry morning eyes knowing to search for Jack. Our bodies may not cross the invisible line drawn between us but over the past two months or so since we've settled into post-visa life, we've taken to rolling over to

193

face each other, grunting good morning before arguing which of us should get to shower first. This morning, he was nowhere to be seen. But he did leave a note on top of his otherwise empty pillow: *Headed to gym. Sausages in the fridge. PTO.* Turning it over in my hands, I had braced myself to see another rough printout photo of me taken over twenty years ago, and about four years too late to make any sense. *PS. Don't worry, they're those Linda McCartney no-meat crap ones you like.*

I try to focus on the screen in front of me, but the memory of this morning is playing on a loop in my mind. I had made my way into the kitchen, holding Jack's note in my hands, to find the faux sausages sitting proudly in the fridge and couldn't help but smile. Then, when I took my sausage sandwich into the living room, the sight of Jack's stuff amalgamated with mine was all the evidence I needed to remind me that this, us living here, was a good idea. But then, I stumbled on something beneath me. Jack's running shoes discarded all over the place again. Even though he *said* he was spending his Sunday at the gym. Now I know for sure that he's lying to me about something, and I can't accuse him about it because when it comes to lying to your spouse, I haven't got a leg to stand on. I gaze at his running shoes again, narrowing my eyes at them accusatorily. Eight hours ago, they had felt like an annoyance. But now, after a day of trying to concentrate on my research, knowing the deadline is at the end of the month, that it will set the tone for the rest of my PhD to come, they feel like a middle finger being waved in my face. I agreed to marry Jack, to live in my dead dad's apartment for him, and now he's lying about where he is.

I click through to the next recording on my phone, this time from a woman in her eighties called Christina. *I got married at eighteen because that's what you did back then . . .* I let her voice echo into the living-room, filling the room with light. *And I was widowed at thirty-one. No, no, I never remarried. I wanted to remain faithful to him even in death.*

I listen to the words, willing my anger to rise, to feel like society had robbed her of her opportunities, just like so many of the older women I have spoken to have felt. But her contentment seems to scare my determination away.

Those were the best years of my life, and the love we shared in that relatively short time we were together, well, it's enough to sustain me for the rest of my days. Do I think marriage is a man-made construct? In some of its forms, maybe. But the choosing of someone else day-in, day-out, the lifelong commitment, that's powerful, that's brave . . .

I click pause, but my thoughts don't stop churning. Did my parents ever choose each other, or were they just convenient for each other? Was I just convenient, until I wasn't anymore? My mind scrambles for memories of my dad, the way it has ever since I walked into this room, and all I can recall is the smell of his musty-but-expensive aftershave mingled with cigar smoke. I remember asking my mum about his scent once when I was little, around ten or twelve, and I swear she smiled at the thought. Then, I asked her about it when I was older, maybe in my mid-teens, and she said she couldn't remember what he smelled like at all. But I've never been able to shake off the way she had smiled. They chose each other, once upon a time, before everything else got in the way. People choose each other every damn day. My stomach churns as it dawns on me where Jack will be right now. He'll be with Florence. Because I *told* him to be. And though he has no reason to lie about that, something tells me it's because he'll be going into it differently now, opening himself up to something serious.

I look down at my phone, no messages from him, no messages from Emmie. Everyone is busy putting themselves out there, planning for the future, taking risks on each other and whether their time together will prove productive or just a colossal waste of time. For some reason, the thoughts that once mustered so much determination now fill me with doubt. Should I be putting myself out there too?

In the silence, my fingers hover over the Hinge dating app, the one Jack claims is the best. What would he say if he saw me on there? Would he laugh and say that he's had some kind of influence on me? Or will he simply see this as me keeping my marital promises, because we *did* promise we would see other people, didn't we?

Before I can think better of it, I download the app and scroll through the profiles, the memory of minutes I've wasted dating already wrestling with Jack's words from the night before: *you should consider taking a chance on someone too.* It doesn't take any time at all to take a chance on a guy called Matt, who's profile claims he's 'just a nice guy'. And though his offer to take me out for a drink tonight feels a little *too* nice, right now and in this heat, I can't stand another minute in this room, thinking about my dad and my mum and Emmie. And now Jack. Yet another person who has pulled away. Or maybe, in reality, I've pushed.

'Mia, are you even listening?'

I look across the red-and-white-checked tablecloth to my

date. If I wasn't such a rookie on dating apps, I'd have known to have forgone dinner and suggested we just grab a drink instead. And yet, here I am with a thirty-year-old consultant who, true to profile, has referred to himself as 'just a nice guy' at least five times now. And called me *Mia* six.

'It's *Maya*,' I tell him for a seventh time.

Of all the plans I had for this year, dating wasn't one of them. But nor was marriage. Neither Emmie's nor my own. And yet, somehow, I find myself in a parallel universe where I'm the one who's falling to the back of the class.

'Do you want another one?' Nice Guy Matt asks, nodding at my empty glass.

Not really, I tell him with my eyes but still my lips say, 'Yes.'

I get that some people find love online, but I've never really understood why people would want to risk spending their precious time with a stranger and then, even worse, feel the need to stay with said stranger longer than they actually *want* to. But it turns out the desire to not be awkward is a strong one. Even for someone who has spent years trying to stand up for herself and what she believes in. Plus, I'm in no rush to head back to an empty apartment.

'What's your favourite film?' I ask, like a seven-year-old trying to make pals in the playground. Or a twenty-something trying to prep up for an interview about their husband.

'*Inception*.' Nice Guy Matt takes a swig of his pint, not taking the cue to ask me the same question back, or any question about myself really.

It's so easy with Jack. The back-and-forth, the banter. The fact he seems genuinely interested in me. Although he sort of

197

has to be, doesn't he? Or at least he has until now. I wonder if him being in a real relationship will change that?

'Shall we get the bill?' I suggest after finishing my drink, pretending to yawn.

'I'll get this,' he says, reaching into his pocket for his wallet.

'Why?'

'Because chivalry's not dead?'

'Nor is chauvinism.' This wipes the smile off Nice Guy's face. Come on, Maya. He was just trying to be *nice*. 'It's okay, I'd like to pay half,' I say, reaching into my pocket, something hard clanging to the floor as I do. Nice Guy Matt reaches to pick it up. Oh shit.

'Is this a wedding ring?' He holds the gold band between his thumb and finger. I instantly want him to give it back, to keep it safe. Which is weird. Because it's a crap symbolic gesture, a fake symbolic gesture. But it is *my* fake symbolic gesture. 'You're not married?' He looks mildly disgusted; to be fair, most people are looking to date *single* people.

'No, of course not,' I say quickly, taking the ring and stashing it in my pocket.

'Okay, cool,' Nice Guy Matt says before we're awkwardly standing outside the restaurant, him leaning in for a kiss and me swerving to give him a pat-on-the-back hug. And, as I walk the cobbled roads towards the apartment, fingering the wedding ring in my pocket, I don't look back. As weird as it sounds, the best part about this date will be laughing about it with my husband.

As I walk into the apartment, I expect to find Jack back from his day-date with Flo, sitting with his feet up, his shoes – whatever shoes he *has* been wearing today – annoyingly still

198

on as he rests them on the coffee table. I walk into the kitchen, looking left and right for sight of him. I know his date with Flo will be better than mine with Matt. It would be hard for it not to be. Still, I've refined my anecdotes about Nice Guy Matt on the walk home and they're raring to go. I know I'll have Jack in stitches in no time. Just as soon as I can *find* him.

'Jack?' I shout out loud, as I pour myself a huge glass of wine and make my way into the living room, also empty. How is it that I've spent hours looking at a screen, downloaded a dating app, been on my first Hinge date and Jack is *still* out with his date hours later?

I look to his running shoes, now tucked by the sofa thanks to my naïve hope that perhaps it was where he left them and not *why* he left them that was irritating me. My tummy flips at the sight of them; I'm not sure I can stomach another night in this apartment without him.

I take a deep glug of wine, then another, before looking at my phone screen, still blank. For a moment, I want to call my mum. It's probably just that after a dud of a date with a guy who couldn't even get my name right, I'm craving some time with my moral compass, my True Feminist North. Then, I remember that she'll still be working right now, that she's already told me she'll send me some dates for us to have a proper catch-up online once things are up and running in her new role. Part of me misses her. The other part is petrified that she'll find out where I am, what I've done, and will be more hurt than I know how to deal with. I take another gulp of wine, just topping up my tipsiness from the world's worst date.

Maybe I could try Emmie again? I know she's been busy with Adrian, with planning the wedding; that her current one-out-of-five message-back rate is leaving a lot to be desired. But she's always made space for me in the past, from the time she skived off her piano lesson to come and help me with my homework, to the evening she drunkenly raced across London to wrap her cardigan around my waist when my trousers ripped moments into a night out. Still, I'm almost surprised when Emmie answers the phone.

'Maya! It's late. Is everything okay?'

She'd know how I'm doing if she read her messages once in a while.

'I'm, well . . . I've just had a bad date . . .'

'With Jack?'

'No,' I say, taken aback by the speed at which she traced my mood back to him. 'With a guy called Matt. Why would you think it was with Jack?'

'Because you live together and seem to get on,' Emmie says nonchalantly, as a wave of guilt washes over me. Not telling Emmie felt like the right thing to do before we got the visa, then telling her felt like the *wrong* thing to do when she was so excited about her own wedding. Now I'm just so scared that this gaping distance between the offence and the confession will be far too great for our friendship to mend. 'Tell me about this date.'

'Oh, it was awful,' I begin, looking around the empty room. It's great to hear Emmie's voice but the best friend I knew still feels so far away. 'But it's not about that, not really. I've just had a bad day and I wanted to talk to you.'

'Tell me about it, we've had such a frustrating one,' Emmie goes on, ignoring my sentence completely. 'I've been trying to secure a florist all day but they're so bloody expensive, and then I found this one me and Aid both really loved, and they're fully booked!'

Emmie is now talking so quickly, her volume inching higher, until I have to hold the phone away from my ear; who is this person and what has she done with my best friend? The best friend who once insisted on wearing a suit instead of a brides-maid's dress at her cousin's wedding simply out of principle.

'Maya, are you there?'

'Yes, sorry . . . the line went a bit . . . yeah, I'm here,' I say, forcing a smile she can't see.

'Good, oh my gosh, I've needed to chat to you. Planning a wedding is stressful.'

'It doesn't need to be,' I reply, trying to muster some empathy. Emmie has been there for me countless times before, the least I can do is be there for her too. She's my best friend, my family. So what if falling in love has given her a temporary personality transplant?

'What do you know about weddings?' Emmie laughs, not unkindly, but *still*.

'I know, but like, don't some people just get married at a registry office?' I say, eyes darting around the room for Jack.

I'm dangerously close to telling Emmie everything, risking severing the ties of our friendship even further when right now, I need her the most.

'No one I know,' Emmie says, and I bite down on my lip, hard. I promised Jack that we'd tell them together. 'Oh crap, sorry, Maya. I have to go, Adrian's been on hold to another florist for hours and we've just got through.'

'But it's like . . .' I pull my phone away from my ear to look at the time. 'Gone ten.'

201

'The wedding industry never sleeps!' Emmie says, like she's just discovered the cure for cancer or the meaning of life, before saying her goodbyes and hanging up the phone.

In the silence, I down the last of my wine. The wedding industry may never sleep but after today, after that phone call, I feel too exhausted to even make it to our all too empty bed.

Jack

I stumble into the entrance hall, missing the table and the vase standing proud on top of it by millimetres.

It's not like it has any flowers in it now but I know the vase itself will cost more than my rent here to replace. One by one I kick off my shoes, suspending the boxes holding the leftover Chinese food from my date with Flo in one hand, tripping over myself as I do. Why is it that you never realise how drunk you are until you're in a place where you're meant to be sober? It's late, almost midnight, but that still doesn't mean Maya won't be up – not waiting for me to get home but working, squeezing every last drop of productivity out of the day.

Pushing open the door to the living room, I make a point of accentuating my movements. Partly because 'subtle' isn't within my repertoire right now. Mostly because I will be damned if Maya accuses me of 'creeping' up on her again, of breaking any of her iron-clad rules. It doesn't take long for me to dial down the volume though. Maya isn't at her desk but curled up in a tight ball on the sofa, long dark hair covering most of her face. I look down to see one of the huge wine glasses knocked over on the floor by her side. Is she *passed out*? And here I was thinking I'd have to dial down my drunkenness.

Moving closer to her quietly – still categorically *not* creeping – I come to kneel by her side, the sound of her slow, deep breathing filling the silence. Trying to steady my hand, I reach my fingers to her face, gently moving her hair out of it so that I can see her sun-kissed cheeks and her eyelids tightly shut, her dark thick eyelashes seeming to go on for miles. She looks fine. Better than fine, beautiful, soft, angelic – the last things Maya would want to look like. I watch her for a moment, realising that the impending guilt of returning from an amazing third date with Flo to slide into bed with Maya was completely redundant. How is it that Maya is able to take whatever it is I'm worried about next and make the problem just disappear?

Reaching behind her, I pull down the cashmere blanket from the back of the sofa, the one I slept under on my first night here, placing it on top of her gently. She stirs slightly and I stop still, willing her not to wake up, but then she curls her body tighter together, smiling in her sleep. And I smile back at her too; thanks to Maya encouraging me to break my third-date rule, I might actually have a shot at love here.

Then, she opens her eyes to see me standing there, hovering over her, smiling like I'm about to kill her or kiss her. Given her reaction last time I made the mistake of trying to kiss her, I'm not sure which of these two options Maya will think is worse.

'Jack?' She says my name in a whisper, quiet and husky, like her first words of the morning. 'What are you doing?' This second utterance comes out stronger. Why do I always feel like she's catching me out, like I'm doing something wrong? I know the answer before I've fully formed the question: because I did the worst thing you can do back home.

'Sorry, sorry,' I say in hushed tones, hands up in surrender and backing away from her. 'I've just got back, and you fell asleep here and I didn't want you to get cold.'

As soon as I've said the words, I regret them.

'That's . . .' Maya says, crinkling her nose in disdain, pushing herself to sit up. I know she's about to say 'creepy' or 'weird' or 'unnecessary'. 'That's . . . sweet,' she smiles.

Sweet?

'It has been known,' I say with a shrug. 'Coming to bed?'

I try to sound as pragmatic as possible; but my words still come out a little slurred. The expression on her face, caught between curiosity and confusion, makes me worried that she's decided to sleep out here to make a point. I'm just not sure which one. Is she angry at me? For going on a date that she told me to go on?

'Good night?' I nod to the wine glass on the floor.

'I went on a date.'

I feel a pang of jealousy dart across my chest before I can remind myself it's entirely misplaced. I've just had a great date with Flo, the best date. And I told Maya to date too. It's just, now that she has, I know a part of me is scared that she'll want to marry this guy instead.

'How was it?'

'The worst,' Maya says so forcefully that it makes me laugh. She narrows her eyes at me, trying to stare away my giggles, but it just makes me laugh even more. 'It's *not* funny.'

'I'm sorry,' I say, unable to stash my smile. 'Got to kiss a few frogs I'm afraid.'

204

'I'm not a princess.' She folds her arms in defiance, her bed-hair sprawling endlessly.

'You can say that again.'

'You wanker,' she throws a pillow at me, and though I try to duck it's the perfect shot. 'So, yeah, I came home and then rang Emmie and she was just so . . . so . . . *engaged*.'

'Well, yeah,' I say like this is obvious, still standing before her now.

Maya has said countless times that Emmie will think our getting married is about *her*, about Maya being jealous, their paths diverging in a thousand different ways. I kind of get it. Adrian has been pretty absent since he started dating Emmie too. Though, as much as Aid has been a good friend to me, I've made sure we've never gone too deep. Unlike Maya and Emmie, who seem to have entwined their lives completely. Until now.

'Want to talk about it?'

'No,' Maya says back plainly, arms still crossed angrily; she looks quite cute. 'It's just . . . Emmie is the coolest girl I know . . .'

Maya speaks tentatively, seemingly weighing up the cost of venting versus inviting me to see yet another piece of herself. I cautiously come to sit by her side, pushing any part of the blanket off myself. It may be the early hours of the morning now, but this apartment is like a greenhouse, retaining every inch of London's unrelenting sun.

'Ever since I met her at school, I wanted to be like her, *Emmie Sims*. She knew her own mind and would not stop at anything to get what she wanted. And she wanted to take me with her, into everything, but now, since Aid, it's like she doesn't *care* what I'm doing at all. I've felt so bad about not telling her about us, but really, she's not even asked.'

I look back at Maya, her eyes wide and wired all of a sudden.

'It's like she's trying to make a point or something,' Maya goes on. 'That she's a grown-up now and I need to grow up too. But since when did marriage become the gold standard? The sign that someone has chosen you to enter adulthood together?'

'You do know we're married?' I remind her.

'I know but that's not the same,' Maya shakes her head. 'If anything, what we've done will make us seem even more childish to them.'

'Not if they knew it was necessary.' I try to defend our decision, always willing Maya not to change her mind, her words rolling around my head again and again: *divorce is easy.*

'That would make sense of *your* reasons,' Maya goes on. 'But what about mine?'

A question I've tried to ask her a million times but have yet to get to the bottom of.

'And Emmie *never* wanted to get married.'

'People change,' I mutter with a shrug.

'That's what makes marriage so bonkers to me,' she continues. 'You decide to marry someone at a fixed point in time, promise to be faithful to someone for all the days of your life, and then they change. And it's not always the big changes, it's the little micro-changes they make, when they show a different version of themselves to everyone else.'

I gulp, Maya's words once again feeling too close to home. But I showed Flo enough of myself tonight, enough for her to want to go on a fourth date with me. Uncharted territory.

'Plus, falling in love sounds like you don't have a choice in the matter,' Maya rants on; it's like her nap has supercharged her for this speech. 'Like it's something inevitable. Pretty reckless if you ask me.'

'More reckless than marrying some man you'd just met?' I say and finally, *thankfully*, Maya laughs. Seeing her genuinely hurt is the last thing I want to see.

'Re-met,' Maya reminds me. 'And yeah, I don't know, I think if I were to be in love, I'd prefer to *grow* into it rather than *fall* into it.'

'A slow-burn kind of love?' Maybe if I'd had that with Laura everything would have been different. But then, we were only teenagers, our very beings supercharged with emotion. Maybe things can be different with Florence? Maybe they could be different with *Maya*? But no, she has made her thoughts about the two of us clear. And, after all this time we've spent growing our friendship, developing our boundaries, understanding one another's habits to the point that this marriage thing actually *works*, I wouldn't want to risk ruining it again.

'Yeah, and like just being with your best friend day by day,' Maya goes on, reshuffling her legs on the sofa until they are lying on top of me. I reach for her feet before her toes can tickle me in all the wrong places, allowing my hand to rest on top of them. 'And then all those days turn into a lifetime when you're not looking.'

'A best friend,' I smile back to her; I've never heard Maya talking about the future like this. That date must have really got to her. 'I like that. But with sex, right?'

'Oh yes, *lots* of sex,' Maya says, laughing fully now, all anxious tension resolved and only intimacy remaining in its place. 'But someone you don't need to keep upping the ante for with sexy lingerie and toys and gadgets and—'

'Head torches.'

'Shut up!' Maya reaches to punch me on the arm, before her tired body leans into my side. 'I'm serious. Just someone you can be yourself with, honestly, and for that to be enough.'

I look down at Maya, closer to me than ever before and more open than I've seen her yet. Someone you can be yourself with. And for that to be enough. It never was with Laura. I always had to do more and be more and prove myself more to her. I thought it was because she was in the year above me, that it was natural for her to find me running off to play computer games with my geeky little brother childish. Looking back, I can see now that I had to be Jack the Jock so much that I forgot who I really was. And now, Maya is reminding me again.

'Can you believe we're here?' She tilts her head up to me, her deep green eyes shining brightly. The heat of my body rises to the point where both our skins feel sticky against one another, her naked legs wanting to glue themselves to mine, the thin fabric of her shorts feeling like nothing between us.

'Here?' As in on the sofa, practically sitting on top of each other.

'As in . . . in this apartment . . . together . . . married.'

'Not really,' I whisper back to her. 'I have to pinch myself every day.'

'It's so random.' Maya smiles.

'And yet completely calculated.' I laugh back, but she still looks serious somehow.

'You were just some guy from uni I tried to kiss that one time and now—'

'You remember *that*?' I ask, our limbs seeming to entwine closer together.

'You *don't?*'

'Of course, I remember that,' I say, my breath catching as I do. Maya's face just inches from my own. 'I just thought you were too drunk to . . .' My sentence trails off.

Her eyes fix on mine, drifting down to my lips. I had come back here expecting to sneak into our bed, to tell her all about Flo in the morning as we faced each other, our heads resting against our pillows. To tell her that thanks to her encouragement, her assurance that some women are worth investing in, I finally broke my third-date rule for the first time since Laura. But now, Maya is looking up at me, her lips inches from my own, the lightness of her breath tickling my neck, and I remember that I've broken my third-date rule before. I broke it on the day in Shoreditch where Maya and I had four or five dates in one. When I foolishly tried to kiss her because I thought for a moment that could be what she wanted. When really it was just a reminder of all of the vows I had promised not to break. And the rules that matter most when it came to Maya: to date other people, to never sleep together and under no circumstances to ever fall in love.

Maya

I look up at Jack, my head tilted towards his. And I want to kiss him.

What the *hell?* I actually want to kiss him.

This is ridiculous.

It's just the heat, this sticky city. It's just my date, a reminder that there aren't many good men out there. It's just this apartment, a reminder that my dad is the worst of them all. It's my PhD, my paper, the woman who said that marriage was worth it. It's Emmie, it's the feeling that she's somehow leaving me behind too. It's not Jack. It's not Jack at all. I look to him now, his deep brown eyes gazing back at me, his glistening brow crinkled as he looks from my eyes to my lips, slightly parted. I look at his tanned neck, tight T-shirt, toned arms. And I want to kiss him. I want to kiss him so badly.

'Maya, I . . .' Jack croaks the word, his voice barely above a whisper, his hand on my bare shoulder, skin touching my skin. He tears his eyes away from me, and after the day I've had, I want them to be on me, to not look anywhere else, to make me know I matter.

'Jack,' I say his name, longing to repeat his words to me only moments ago: *coming to bed?* The same bed we've spent nearly three months in. Except today, in this moment, for some reason, I want things to be different. I want them to be *more*.

Then I see that Jack is looking at his running shoes placed together by the sofa we're sitting on. A timely reminder that he wasn't at the gym today like he said he was; that for some reason he's lying to me about where he is. That this, *us*, only works because we're not trying to be everything or share everything with each other. I don't know why he doesn't want to go home; he doesn't know why I have this one. I don't know why he so desperately wants to stay here. Right now, with his strong chin tilted back towards me so that his face is lingering closely to my own, part of me feels like the reason he wants to stay is *me*. But I know that's not true. That he wouldn't want to stay anywhere near me if he knew the truth. Lying about my dead dad is dark. And darkness is one thing we don't have

210

here in this room made of glass, in a situation that in this very moment feels so fragile that one missed move or broken vow might bring it tumbling down completely.

'I knew you didn't want to kiss me really,' Jack forces the words, which come out low and husky. 'That night at uni, you were drunk.'

'Yeah . . .' I mutter, looking from Jack, from his eyes to the ring around his neck, and remind myself of the vows that are keeping it there: *our promise to see other people.*

'And don't worry, I won't be trying it again.' He smiles, breathing deeply as I watch his chest rise. *To not sleep together.* My breath catches in my throat, and it takes all my strength to pull myself away. *And above all to – under no circumstances – ever fall in love.*

Part 6

The Fall

Seventy-seven Days Married

Maya

I barely sleep all night. I want to blame it on my two-hour nap, but the sinking feeling prompted by Jack's empty pillow the following morning reminds me that it's what happened *after* my nap that has been playing on my mind all night. I thought living with Jack would distract me from the memory of my dad but what on earth do I have to distract me from whatever happened – or didn't happen – between the two of us last night?

As I force myself out of our 'marital' bed, I try not to think about his eyes on mine. As I shower, I wash away the memory of his skin on mine. As I dress into the lightest long T-shirt I own; I try not to savour the feeling of his breath on mine. And, as I make my way into the living room, determined to conquer this paper on ageing that is ironically ageing me in the process, I remind myself of all of the reasons I slipped into a parallel universe in which I fancied my husband last night: the apartment, the paper, the date, the phone call . . .

'Morning,' Jack looks up from his laptop as soon as I've

215

walked into the room. His hair is floppy, his smile wide and he's completely naked apart from his boxers, which are thankfully covered by his strategically placed MacBook.

'Sorry, it's way too hot for jeans.' Jack apologises for his lack of clothes, even though I'm standing here in a top that is trying and failing to pass itself off as a dress.

'You're okay,' I say, which right now feels like a massive understatement; Jack looks like he's been cut out of one of those ludicrous hot-guy calendars; a hot, steamy August. 'I thought you'd be at work by now?'

'Toby let me work from home this morning,' Jack says, with a sheepish grin.

'He did what?' I laugh, coming to perch on the armchair across from him.

'Yeah, turns out that now that he knows I'm a married man, he trusts me.'

'Ironic,' I say, even though the interviews I've been reading lately have drifted from women who feel like their lives have been sacrificed in pursuit of being *just a wife* to women who have felt emboldened by it, supported by it, that the union has made them stronger.

'Save the niceties for Emmie and Adrian's wedding,' Jack says sarcastically, not looking up from his screen. Whatever tension was flowing between us last night seems to have gone, which is good. Really good.

'I'll try,' I tease back facetiously.

'Or you could just weave the fact we got married for a visa into your speech and that would be a real slap in the face.'

'That's actually not a bad idea.'

'Maya, I was *joking*.' Jack looks up at me, face like thunder.

216

I know we need to tell them soon, before the wedding comes around. He yawns, stretching his strong arms wide as his chest broadens before me, the sculpting of his muscles becoming even more defined.

'I need to *concentrate*,' I say out loud, berating myself for checking my husband out again. 'On my paper, I mean.' It's technically not a lie. 'My deadline is at the end of the month and then I'll be able to handle whatever fallout Emmie throws my way.'

'You can't keep putting it off, Maya,' Jack says, looking across the room to me. He doesn't know it, but he sounds every inch like Emmie telling me that I need to tell Jack about my dad. But it's not so easy for me to be vulnerable, I've never had a blueprint for that.

'I know,' I snap back. I don't like Jack feeling like he can tell me what to do. That was never what this agreement was about. It wasn't about feelings full stop.

'Okay but . . .'

'We're going to tell them, and soon. I promise.' Why does it need to be so hot in here? Why does *Jack* need to be so hot in here?

'No, I was going to say . . . but I might need to tell Florence.'

'Florence?' My heart begins to throb in my chest at the mention of her name, when just forty-eight hours ago I would have offered to ask her out for Jack myself.

'Yeah, well, like . . .' Jack begins slowly, closing his laptop as my heartbeat shoots into overdrive. 'If I'm going to try and be open to dating someone more seriously, I think we have to seriously consider telling the people we're seeing the truth about us.'

'What and risk you being deported? Or worse, *arrested*?'

217

Jack's face falls instantly, his face marred with guilt.

'*Shit*,' he mutters under his breath. 'I know but I just feel so bad about sleeping with her again and not telling her I technically have a wife if it's, you know, going to lead to something more . . .'

'Sleeping with her *again*?' I ask, before I can stop myself. Why do I need to know?

'Yeah, the day before we went to our visa interview.'

I feel my fingers clench by my sides and choose to hook my legs up onto the armchair so that Jack can't see, no doubt showing him far more of myself in the process. I knew Jack slept over at hers, and I knew Jack the Jock was the kind of man to sleep with someone on the first date. It's just, everything I've known about Jack since makes me feel like he's not really that guy. And he's not, is he? Because here he is wanting to open himself up to someone, be honest, respectful, hopeful about their future together. Because of me.

'You can't tell her,' I say, quietly now. 'Not if you don't want to risk going home . . .' The thought of Jack leaving the country now makes *me* feel sick. I feel tears starting to prickle in my eyes and he must see them because soon he's moving to put a hand to my arm.

'I know,' he says, softly. 'I wasn't thinking. I know you're right. I'll have to wait to tell her until after we're . . . yeah, when we don't need the family visa anymore . . .'

He means when *we're* not a family anymore. Which was always the plan, wasn't it?

'That's quite a long way in the future for someone who was recently scared of a third date,' I say, forcing a little laugh along with my fragile smile, as I get to my feet.

'I know,' he says, hooking an arm around me to stroke my back affectionately. 'I think you might be having a positive impact on me or something.'

Jack fixes his eyes on me, and I feel my knees growing weak. And although I know my encouragement had a massive part to play in Jack dating meaningfully again, deep down I'm fearful that Flo may throw our new life here off balance completely.

'I'm going to head into the office soon,' Jack says, breaking the relative silence that has brimmed between us as the paper I am writing finally begins to flow. 'Then I might meet Flo for another drink tonight, so that'll leave you with some peace.'

The fact Jack thinks I feel peaceful here without him shows just how little we've really told each other; working side by side in silence is the most focused I've been in weeks. And that's saying something seeing as he's still sat here in his boxers.

'Fancy a beer before you go?' I say, praying I don't come across as desperate. But I kind of am. Not to be with him, not really. But to not be left here with just my thoughts, *again*.

'It's only just gone twelve.' He must see my face fall because he adds. 'Meh, it's five o'clock somewhere, right?'

Jack returns later with two cold beers in his hands, and thankfully wearing clothes. He offers a bottle and a wide smile to me and, right now, I'm not sure which is more refreshing.

'Feeling any better about Emmie?' Jack asks, taking a deep swig of his beer.

'Yeah, a bit,' I lie, nothing has changed between now and last night, other than the confirmation that this hots-for-husband fever seems to be more than a twenty-four-hour thing. 'Sorry if it all seems a bit dramatic to you.'

'Don't apologise.' Jack smiles, walking towards the window and looking out across the Thames. Being outside is almost too hot to bear. Inside isn't much better. 'I get it. She's your family, right?' I nod, coming to stand beside him. Jack just gets it. 'And trust me, your family dramas could never be a scratch on mine.' He takes another sip from his beer, and he looks like an advert.

'Tell me about it,' I say, bizarrely longing to get under his skin. He turns to me and laughs, before he realises that I'm still waiting for his reply. For some reason it takes me back to that night at my and Emmie's party, where we both stood by the kitchen island and Jack genuinely wanted to hear all about my day even though he'd just found out he needed to leave the country. 'Do you keep in touch with them?'

'I used to, for a long time,' Jack says, brushing his spare hand through his hair. 'After things happened. Then it got really hard, you know the time difference and everything . . .'

I know by now that when he says 'things happened' he's talking about his break-up with Laura, the one that broke him so completely that it's put him off letting anyone else get close to him, until I slowly and forcefully convinced him to try. And yet, I still feel like there's so much Jack is holding back from *me*.

'Do you keep in regular touch with your parents?' He bats the question back to me and I know there's too much I've been holding back from him too.

'My mum is so busy with work, her new job in New York.'

'And your dad?' Jack asks, looking back at me, genuinely interested in me and my past, despite our future together being so temporary.

'He was really busy but . . .' Just tell him, Maya, tell him. It's the only way I can get him to trust me with any more of himself. Jack keeps looking at me, fixing his deep eyes on mine with all the intensity of the night before. I open my mouth to speak, to tell him, and then a shrill chime fills the silence and Jack is reaching into his pocket.

'Toby.' He rolls his eyes, surrendering his half-drunk beer bottle onto the writing desk. 'Sorry, Flo . . . friend,' Jack stutters. 'I'll see you later, yeah? I want to hear everything.'

And part of me wants to tell him, but from his flustered expression and the stone in my stomach, I know he was about to accidentally call me *Florence*, that she's now on his mind. Because I pressured him to put her there.

I reread the part of my paper I wrote when Jack was in the room. It's all I've been able to do since he left. Without him here, my brain has shot into overdrive, every sentence I read prompting a thousand thoughts, as I analyse how I got here, what I'm going to do next.

Women of a certain age feel the pressure to settle down. Maybe that's why Emmie threw everything into her relationship with Adrian the second a decent guy came around? But no, we're still so young, we've got years to settle down. No, no, no. This is precisely the kind of ticking-timeline thinking I'm trying to debunk.

Then there's the competition, the feeling that everyone is ahead of you. I read the next line and instantly feel hot. Though, given the heatwave everything feels hot. Maybe that's why last night felt so heated? Emmie's phone call hitting a nerve, my brain being tricked by centuries of conditioning into thinking that just because she has fallen in love that means I should start making moves on my husband. The heat prickles on my neck and the seconds seem sticky as I try to throw myself into the one thing I know I'm made for. Except, I haven't felt *made for it* in months. I feel like things are unravelling – my friendship with Emmie, my relationship with my mum, my ambition, my drive – and all that's left is the bloody thought in my head that soon Jack is going to fall for this Florence girl and I'm going to lose him too. When I never wanted a husband in the first place.

It's being here in this apartment; I know it is. I walk towards the window, where Jack and I stood hours earlier, drinking our midday beers. Everyone in this city will be gagging for water in this heat and here I am circled by the stuff. But still, I feel like I'm drowning. I thought I could do this. Thought I could live here as man and wife, without anyone knowing, without it needing to mean anything. But it's driving me insane. I think of my mum, of all the times I've asked questions about my dad just to have her tell me to concentrate on my homework, or my studies; just something that matters more than him.

I look down at my phone, blank again, and hate the fact that I feel like everyone is ghosting me. Hate that I can't concentrate, can't think straight, that I'm starting to question whether studying is my passion or just a crutch, a distraction so that I don't have to think about what might come next, because I'm just as scared of ageing as society wants me to feel. Hate the fact that Jack is out with some other girl. *Hate that I hate it.*

I slam my phone down on the desk so hard that Jack's

half-empty bottle topples, the rest of his beer spilling all over the desk, trickling down the drawers lining one side of it, the liquid dripping into the bottom drawer, pulled slightly ajar. *Oh crap.*

Without thinking, I grab the nearest blanket and begin mopping up the beer. The fact that it's cashmere should stop me but then, clearly my dad thinks it's okay to use his money to try to clear up the mess he left behind. I dab down the sides of the desk, pulling the drawer open to try to salvage the papers inside from the spillage. I have no desire to look at what's on them, no desire to riffle through my dad's things. But still, as I finish sponging them down before returning them to the drawer, I remember the first note I wrote for Jack, the paper I used from this drawer, and the random printed photograph that marred the reverse side.

In a moment of weakness, I turn the wedge of papers over and start to sift through them. It's all writing, all documents, bills and official reports, but then I see the face of an eight-year-old looking back at me – *my face*. And then a ten-year-old girl, *still me*. And a fifteen-year-old awkward teenager smiling back from the plain printer paper. How would my dad have these? Why would he print these? *Keep* these?

I put the papers back and force the sticky door shut. What on earth? My mum must have sent these to him, surely? But she said they weren't in touch, that he's not reached out to us since I was about four years old, two years after their divorce, when their contact completely dried out somewhere over the Atlantic. That's what made this apartment, the fact he left it to me, so random, such a head-fuck. What is happening? My life was so neat, so directed, so decisive – just like my mum's. I thought she'd moved on from my dad and never looked back. Without thinking, I call her number and get her voicemail. Then I call her again and get her voicemail once more. I call again and again, longing for answers, but all I get is answerphones and the onslaught of a thousand questions flooding my mind.

Jack

Six hours fly by when you're having fun. Or losing yourself in geeking out over the computer-nerd stuff you love. Or *loved*. Before the kids at school or the hot girls in the year above started telling you what you should love instead. In all the emotionless coding, I've almost forgotten that the city has morphed into the bloody Sahara until I step a jandal outside – and I'd almost forgotten slang words from back home, replacing all my 'jandals' with 'flip-flops' as this place has become more and more like home.

I refuse to take the Tube or hop on a sweatbox of a bus and so decide to walk to the bar where I'm meeting Flo for the second time in two days. As I walk through hordes of people, spilling out of bars and laughing and joking in the sun, I almost don't recognise myself. I'm the guy who buries himself in work, in volunteering; I'm the guy who says thanks but no thanks to a third date. I'm the guy who runs away when things get too serious. But thanks to Maya, I'm starting to feel excited about the future here.

Reaching for my phone to set a soundtrack to my walk, I find the screen filled with messages. One from Charlotte: *Hey,*

Mr W. Had another fight with G. Were you serious about planning a mid-week call? I smile at the sight of it; not because she's having a hard time but because thanks to the mentoring scheme, I may be able to do something to help. I have one from Adrian asking for all the details about my date with Flo tonight. And I have one from Maya wondering when I'm coming home, even though I was kind of hoping that Flo might want me to spend the night at hers

As music fills my ears, upbeat and light-hearted – the perfect soundtrack to this red-hot summer – I realise all over again that I don't want to be anywhere else but here. I like my job. I like my wife. Then my phone rings through my headphones. As I reach into my pocket, my mind tries to guess which of the people I've just messaged it could be. Florence or Charlotte or Adrian or Maya. But then I stop still, right in the middle of the busy pedestrian traffic. Because it's not any of those people calling me. It's my *mum*.

I study the letters of the name, the title, the one I've not messaged or heard from in over a year. Suddenly the temperature cranks into overdrive. There's not enough air to gulp into my lungs, not enough oxygen to steady my shaking legs.

'Yo, get out of the way, bro.' A voice somewhere in the distance calls before I feel the thump of a shoulder barging into me. He sounds angry but his barge feels soft, like only half of me is in my body. A part-time resident. The other half looking down at me screaming to get out of the way, when all my mind is thinking is: *Mum, Mum, Mum, Charlie, Mum.*

I stare down at her name, calling and calling, and my first thought is 'who's died?' Then I realise that whatever bad news she has to tell me will never be as bad as the day she yelled at me to leave. The day she screamed at me, with tears running down her face, that if it wasn't for me my brother would still be alive. That she wished it was me who'd died instead.

I hold my phone with shaking hands and watch as she stops calling. She might have clicked my name by mistake; it's been so long since we last spoke that she may even think she was calling some other guy called Jack. Then I see a notification flash up by the phone icon on my screen: she's left me a message.

Without thinking, I walk into the nearest bar and ask for a pint. What I really want is a triple whisky. On the rocks. Just something strong and stable to anchor me. But as I make my way towards a table in the corner of the dimly lit pub, I know it'll take a lot more than a drink to make this feeling, this anxiety, this adrenalin, go away. I sip then I stare at the voicemail icon, then I sip and I stare at it again. Until I can't take it anymore. I neck the last dregs of my pint, and click play, bringing the phone to my ear.

Jack. I pause the message. Just hearing her voice again, the strong accent of home, feels like my heart is being ripped in two. We were so close. The whole family was. Until that one night that changed everything; the one night where I changed everything. I press play again.

I know it's been a long time, but I've been meaning to call for a while. I've tried, so many times, I've tried, honestly. But everything got too much. Speaking to you, reminds me of how far we've both driven each other . . . It's just a lot. And I know it's selfish, but I think I'm ready to talk to you again, to face things again. Together. Jack, it's time for you to stop running, for us both to stop running. So, you know, if you're ready too, please call me back, and if you're not, then, well . . . then, well . . . know that I love you.

When I finally get back to Apartment 100 two hours later, my phone battery is almost dead from playing my mum's voicemail message over and over again, caught between wanting to torture myself for everything I've done wrong and wanting to check that it's real, that it's actually her. And my mum's message isn't the only one waiting for a reply. Florence called three times until she gave up trying. But what could I possibly say to her? A woman that I've spent one night and three evenings with, when I can't even find the words to tell the woman who I've been married to for almost three months about why I needed to leave home. And yet, she's the only one I want to be with right now. The only direction that feels right.

'Jack?' Maya says, as soon as I've walked into the living room to find her standing there, a deer caught in the headlights, a blanket held in her hands; it looks dirty, and damp. 'I thought you were out with Flo tonight?' Her voice is uncertain, her eyes a little bloodshot.

'I needed to come home,' I croak the words, they sound too much like my mum's.

'I'm glad you're here,' Maya says, and I swear she looks on the edge of tears too.

'Are you okay?' I say, bridging the gap between us unsteadily, four pints deep. Maya looks back at me, eyes wide and mouth agape before she shakes her head.

'Are *you*?' She looks me up and down, and I feel like she can see right through me.

227

She didn't want to get married to me to be my crutch or my counsellor; she's made that abundantly clear. And she wouldn't want to keep being married to me if she knew the truth about Charlie, the real reason I can't go back. Maya takes a step closer, and I have to remind myself of all of the rules, all the boundaries keeping our precarious promises to each other in place. But there is nothing stopping me from throwing my arms around her now, from holding her tiny body close to me and hoping that in some strange way our skin can communicate, saying all the things we can't say to each other out loud.

And it's a good job because right now, holding her is the only thing stopping me from breaking down completely.

Maya

I hold onto Jack tightly, not knowing why he's clinging onto me too. His head nestles into my neck, and I can smell his scent, the aftershave he no doubt put on for his date with Florence, so why is he here with me now? It feels as if the second I found those photos in my dad's draws he knew I needed him. It's like he's saving me again.

After what feels like an age, Jack releases his hold on me slightly, one arm still hooked around my body and resting on my shoulder, the other looser somehow, his hand resting on my hip as if we're in some kind of dancing hold, as if at any moment we could begin to move, circling around the already spinning room.

I should tell him, tell him all about my dad. Because I need to tell someone about those damn photos, to tell someone that my dad having them, *keeping* them, just doesn't make sense. And every piece of me wants that someone to be Jack. My *husband*.

'Jack, I . . .' I begin, struggling to find the words to say. Because how on earth do you tell someone you've been living with, married to, for almost three months that you pretended your dad was alive. How do you tell them you've been lying to them all this time and expect them to want to stay?

'There's something I need to . . .' I begin again, knowing that once I've said these words he'll be out of that front door in no time and never look back. Like my dad did. Or at least what I thought my dad did. But he's gone now. And I can't let Jack go. I don't want him to let go, to leave the country. I don't want him to leave me.

His phone buzzes between us, stashed in the depths of his jeans, and it's all the reminder I need that he is too busy dating other women, finally making a life here, a permanent one, to find himself landed with a woman who didn't want a man but now can't bring herself to let go. That he's landed himself with a dependant. A lying, abandoned dependant.

'You can get that.' I pull away from him, reaching to wipe a stray tear from my face.

'No, I don't need to,' Jack whispers.

'It's seriously okay.' I force a smile. 'It might be Florence.' The chummy tone of my voice feels strained given that we've just been embracing in the middle of the room.

'Maya, I don't want to,' Jack says. 'I want to be here, with you. You were just about to tell me something. Are you . . . ?'

He's looking at me like I'm bruised, broken. The way I never wanted him to.

'I'm okay, honestly. It's just this heat, it's driving me crazy.'

'Are you sure?' Jack reaches for my hand.

'Yes.' I shrug him off, nodding for him to answer whoever is waiting for his reply now. Because if he doesn't, if he touches me one more time, I feel like I'm going to do something reckless, something we can't reverse as easily as our marriage.

'Fine,' Jack says, reaching for his phone. We're standing so close now that as he looks at his screen, I can see that the message is from 'M' something. So not Florence at all. Just the next girl on Jack the Jock's roster. I feel another pang of jealousy surge through me, but I need him to do this, to date, to be unavailable. *Feelings make everything complicated.*

'Aren't you going to answer?' I push him further away, physically, metaphorically.

'Not right now,' Jack says, looking uncomfortable.

'Who is it?' I ask, nonchalantly, my fake smile nearly breaking my face in two.

Jack

Who is it?

Maya is looking back at me, interrupted by what she thinks is my latest date. She's stepping back, putting some distance between us, her guard back up.

It was from my mum. And I can't handle that right now. Like I can't handle her voicemail message. Not after what happened, after the things she's said to me. And yet, everything in me wants to tell Maya. All my thoughts, my raw emotion, my memories of Charlie that are floating dangerously close to the surface like the shimmering water that's wrapping around us now. In this perfect

230

apartment, in this brilliant set-up with a woman who sacrificed so much to keep me here, away from all of that.

What if I tell her and she thinks I'm going to head back to New Zealand? That after everything she's been through with getting married and getting the visa, I've changed my mind about how desperately I want to stay here anyway. *Jack, it's time for you to stop running.* Is that what my mum wants? For me to come home now. After pushing me so far away. After pushing my dad away too, breaking our whole family unit apart. Even now, I can't pretend that what happened was her fault.

'Jack, why are you being cagey about it?' Maya smiles now, but I swear it's forced. I could ask her the same thing. I watch as she walks further away from me and closer to the living-room door, planning her exit strategy at the first sign of seriousness. 'It's not like she's your mistress or anything. I want you to date other people. I *told* you to date other people,' Maya says again, willing me to confirm.

'Yeah, it's . . .' I begin, stalling slightly. It's not like I've not lied to Maya before. She still doesn't know about Girls Code. No one here knows what really went down at home. And yet, this feels different. For starters, refusing to tell her it's my mum is not just an omission but an outright lie. Then there's the fact that Maya and I keep having these moments, these brief glimpses into each other's lives that very few people get to see. And I don't want them to stop. But looking at Maya now, forced smile on her face, one hand lingering on the open door, I know that she does. 'It's Florence.' I smile, hating myself for lying to her but it's better this way.

'It's Florence?' Maya looks momentarily surprised for some reason.

231

'The girl you forced me to ask on a third date?'

'I wouldn't say *forced*?' Maya recovers her smile.

'Maya, you would have written the message for me.'

Her face falls for a moment so brief I may have missed it before she is smiling again.

'Coolest wife ever, right?' She laughs, but she still looks a little sad. *What's really going on with her?* My mum's message stops me from asking the question.

'Yeah,' I sigh, reminding myself that keeping this wall between us is the right thing, that she wouldn't still want to be married to me if she knew the truth about what I did to Charlie. Heat surges through me as I force myself to repeat the words: 'Coolest wife ever.'

Seventy-eight Days Married

Maya

'He took *photos* of you?' Emmie says, her elbows bent and leaning on the sticky picnic table in the beer garden of the Captain Kidd, her cute vintage twinset hugging tightly around her slender body, her mouth hanging open at my words. I messaged her as soon as I found them, and although she didn't reply until hours later when Jack arrived home, she'd cancelled her plans this evening to be with me now. And thank God, because it's not like I can talk to Jack about this, especially given how weird things have been between us lately. Last night, he looked like he'd seen a ghost. And I feel like I've been living with one too, the ghost of a dad I thought was dead to me long before he passed.

'Well, not him, but he had them. Photos of me printed out on scrap paper,' I explain, as Emmie's shocked face does nothing to help me make sense of this scenario.

'From when he used to keep in touch with you? When you were a toddler?' Emmie knows the timeline of my family breakdown better than anyone.

'No, after that,' I go on as her mouth hangs open all the more. 'Through the years; there's even one of me as a teenager.'

'But that's so strange, who would be sending them? Your mum?'

'Emmie, my mum wouldn't even entertain conversations about my dad when we found out he had died. I don't think she even knew he was ill. Unless she's been lying to me.'

Until recently, I didn't think my mum had *time* to lie to me. But since everything that's happened with Jack, I know sometimes it's more time-consuming to tell the truth.

'You need to talk to her,' Emmie says without pause. 'You need to tell her about your dad leaving you the apartment.'

I used to like that Emmie always knew exactly what to do, like she was standing alongside me reading my map through the mess. Since she's settled in her flat with a fiancé, I can't help but feel like she's now on a podium above looking down on me as I try to navigate my latest misstep. I readjust my strappy top, regretting wearing black in this heat.

'Emmie, believe me, I've tried a thousand times.'

'Then try a thousand and one.'

'You don't understand,' I object before watching her face fall; we used to understand one another better than anyone else.

'I'm trying,' Emmie says, reaching for my hand across the table. 'And I know your mum is hard to get through to, hard to even get hold of, but why haven't you told Jack yet?'

'I don't know,' I say with a sigh. 'I didn't think it mattered at first, and now, well, so much time has passed that the omission feels like a downright lie.'

Emmie looks at me and I know this is my time to tell her about me and Jack too.

234

'He'll understand that it's been a really hard time for you,' Emmie probes again.

'It's not been *that* hard.'

'Okay, okay.' I can tell that Emmie has to stop herself from rolling her eyes. 'But how would you feel if he finds out from someone else?'

Devastated, deceived? The same way I did when Jack was being so cagey last night.

'He's not going to, because you're the only one who knows the truth about my dad,' I say slowly, my mind pushing away the thought, scrambling to work out why she's pushing for me to come clean so fervently now. 'You've not told anyone, have you, not even Adrian?'

'No, of course not, you asked me not to and I respect that,' Emmie says quickly. 'I just think that Jack will understand. Where is he now anyway?' Emmie lightens the tone. She didn't come here to fight; maybe if she had it would finally clear the air.

'I *think* he's out on a date with this Flo girl,' I say, taking a large gulp of wine. 'Either that, or a new girl he's dating.' I remember the message he got from 'M' something last night, right around the time I thought the intensity of our embrace might kill me. 'He's not really telling me anything about her anymore.'

'And you're okay with that?' Emmie says, and I'm not sure whether the subtext of her sentence is: *it's not nice when people keep secrets from you, is it?*

'Why wouldn't I be okay with that?'

'Adrian and I just had, well, *suspicions* that there was something between you two.'

'Well, you and Adrian don't know everything,' I snap, taking another gulp of wine. 'Look, Emmie. I'm sorry,' I say, seeing her look stung. 'I've just got a lot on my mind.'

'I would too if I'd have found those photos.' Emmie offers me a soft smile and I see a glimmer of the best friend I know and love, encouraging me to go on.

'I know,' I sigh. 'And it's not just that. It's everything. The apartment, my PhD . . .'

'I thought that was going well?'

'It was,' I nod. 'At yours, and then, well, I thought moving into my dad's, not having to worry about rent, would mean I could focus on it, but it's been so hard.' I know I should have admitted this sooner, that I should have shared a lot of things with Emmie by now.

'It must be hard to hold back the memories.'

'It's not that,' I say, though the words sound pretty feeble. 'It's just . . . I keep thinking, like, how can I even call myself a feminist whilst mooching off my dad, never mind contribute some research to a canon of work that I'm basically—'

'Woah, Maya,' Emmie interrupts me. 'Why on earth would that make you not a feminist? You know that's not true.' She shakes her head, her hair shimmering in the sun.

'I know that . . . in theory . . . but since my dad left, my mum has never looked back, never taken anything from him other than the motivation to do better, be better.'

'Yes, but that doesn't make her a better feminist, it just makes her better at ignoring what's really going on.'

'But she's never needed anything from anyone and I . . . I'm here just . . .'

'Oh, babe.' Emmie smiles empathetically. 'Where is all this coming from?'

'I just feel like I'm failing lately,' I say, looking back at her, not meaning my eyes to well with tears. 'And I wanted to be like my mum, like you, just strong and ambitious and . . . I'm not sure what I even *want* anymore. Like everyone has found their thing that makes them happy, and I thought I wanted to be in academia forever, to grow a body of research, move overseas, lecture and build a life, but now, now I'm just not sure.'

'It's okay not to be sure,' Emmie says; that's easy for her to say. 'It's also okay to change your mind. Look at me, I never thought I'd want to get married and then I met Adrian and it just felt right, like what I wanted to do. I didn't overthink it.'

I didn't overthink marrying Jack either.

'Let's play a game,' Emmie says, downing the last of her wine. 'Word association. I'm going to say a word and you're going to say the first thing that pops into your mind.'

'No, Emmie. Come on, let's just get drunk and ignore everything like we used to.'

'We're not at university anymore.'

'Nor are we *children*. I don't want to play a game,' I say, draining my drink too before topping us both up from our bottle of Pinot Grigio before Emmie can object.

'Humour me! It's something my parents used to do when my brain got too tangled.' Emmie's parents are both psychiatrists and she used to mock them like crazy, saying they were too touchy-feeling, lovey-dovey; how times have changed. 'It helps unravel things.'

'Except that's the problem. I feel like I'm unravelling already.'

'Home,' Emmie says, done with my excuses. I stare back at her. 'Okay, maybe that one was too tricky to start on,' she says sadly. We know my home was with her. 'Instagram.'

'Fake.'

'Media?'

'Manipulative.'

'So, you've not lost yourself completely,' Emmie says, smirking. 'London.'

'The best.'

'Dad.'

'Absent,' I say, before adding another. 'Confusing.'

'Jack.'

'Mine,' I whisper before quickly correcting myself. 'Absent.' *With Flo. Or M. Because of me.* 'Confusing,' I add, looking back at her whilst her eyes search my expression like a shrink. This game is pointless. I'm just as confused as I was two minutes ago. Things were so blissfully simple, until . . .

'You love him, don't you?'

Tiredness hits me all at once as soon as I step foot into our apartment. My mind is circling with the conversations Emmie and I have just shared – and the many things we've left unsaid. What with my PhD paper, the photos and all the Pinot, I'm exhausted. And it's still so hot.

Heading to the bedroom, I try to hold onto her words, the ones about it being okay to change your mind, to do things differently to my mum, maybe even differently to Emmie. And yet, the only thing I can seem to capture is the question I left unanswered, shrugging it off until she let it go completely: *you love him, don't you?* As I walk into our room, I'm not surprised to find that Jack isn't home, that he's out with his mistress again even though I still feel like I'm the one who is betraying

238

him. *You love him, don't you?* The words circle around my mind once again, unwelcome, and unanswered. I pull on the biggest, coolest T-shirt I can find to sleep in, which I discover nestled in my mess of things in the back of the wardrobe. And, as I walk to the bathroom, I find myself wishing for the first time in a long time that I could sleep in the bed alone, naked and unashamed, to put some more distance between me and Jack again until Emmie's question has become moot: *you love him . . . you love him . . .*

'Just help yourself to my T-shirts, why don't you?' Jack looks up from brushing his teeth to mumble the words in my direction.

'Oh, I . . .' I say, surprised to see him standing there in his boxers.

'Don't worry,' Jack says, turning back to the mirror. 'It looks good on you.'

'Oh, erm . . . thanks,' I say, turning to look at my reflection, my legs looking longer and browner against the short hem of the plain white T. *His* plain white T, apparently. How on earth am I supposed to put some distance between us when we have to share a bathroom?

We brush our teeth in silence, as I try to hush my hectic mind. I don't want to think about my dad anymore. Or those photos, or why they are here. I don't want to think about Jack, or how good he looks in his boxers and how it now feels hotter than ever with him standing right beside me. And I don't want to think about who he has been with tonight before he arrived home to lie in bed next to me.

Pushing Jack towards a third date with Flo was meant to stop these thoughts, not escalate them. Protect our boundaries, not

239

make them even harder to keep. I catch his eye in the mirror and he grins widely, showing me his soapy, foamy teeth, and he looks so sickeningly cute that I have to leave the bathroom before I do something really stupid.

I pretend to be asleep by the time Jack is done faffing around the apartment, late-night snacking on one of his very many half-eaten cereals. How can I love a man who can't even commit to a cereal brand? I try to push away Emmie's accusation for the thousandth time. But he's changed now, hasn't he? He's allowed to change, isn't he? We all are. And yet, there's so much about Jack I don't *want* to change; the sound of his movements around the apartment now feels predictable, dependable; as comfortable as an old pair of slippers. And, against the backdrop of Emmie's question – *you love him, don't you? You love him, don't you?* – I can feel every move he makes right now. The sound of his footsteps from the doorway to the edge of the bed. The plonk of his glass of water on his bedside table, the one he can't go to sleep without and yet never once drinks. The sound of fabric being pulled off his body. Except he wasn't wearing a T-shirt, he was only wearing his boxers, which means . . . I screw my eyes shut even tighter, willing my temperature not to soar. I will not imagine Jack naked. I *will not* imagine Jack naked. I hear him get into bed, the sound of the only sheet we've been able to bear sleeping under in the heatwave pulled up around him. I feel the weight of him on the other side of the bed. Then I hear the sound of his breathing slowing, steadying, deepening, and I risk turning over to look at him.

In the darkness of the blacked-out bedroom, my eyes adjust just enough to see the steady rise and fall of his torso. And it's

240

in this moment that my thoughts fall silent, floating away like a piece of driftwood on the Thames until everything is perfectly still once again. Only one question remains and it's the question I've been trying and failing not to ask long before Emmie muttered the words: *you love him, don't you?* Then I glimpse his wedding band, resting on the chain against his chest. My heart stops and my stomach flips and I know in that moment that Emmie is right, that deep down, I know the answer to her question.

Oh *shit*, I think I'm in love with my husband.

Part 7

The Seduction

Seventy-nine Days Married

Maya

'I do,' I whisper down the line, the two little words that changed everything in the first place, except this time I'm saying them to Emmie. 'I do love him.'

Her squeal is so high-pitched that I have to pull the phone away from my ear, her voice still managing to echo around the empty kitchen. I can't help but think about all the times we have sat in the corner at parties and mocked the 'woo' girls squealing and cheering from across the room; what has become of us?

'Well,' Emmie says. 'That's what we in the psychiatrist biz call a breakthrough.'

'You're not a psychiatrist, Ems.'

'By parental-proxy I am.'

'Well, if that's a thing, I'm a wanker and a workaholic by proxy too.'

We both know I used to be the latter, now I'm not sure what I am. Apart from a lying wife who is falling uncontrollably, undeniably and entirely inconveniently in love with her own husband. A husband who I've recently forced into the arms of another woman.

'You have to tell him.'

'What is your obsession with telling everyone everything?' I laugh but then I remember the biggest thing I'm keeping from her, and my giggling stops. 'I'm scared it'll change our dynamic.'

'Oh, people are always scared about ruining the friendship, that's normal,' Emmie says, all knowing once more. It's not so much the friendship but the marriage I'm worried about, that if we end badly Jack won't just leave me but the whole bloody country.

'Yeah, but it doesn't really matter.' I sigh, looking out of the kitchen window to where Jack is sitting in the courtyard below, lounging on a picnic blanket with a beer even though it's only just gone five.

When we first moved in here, he used to work around the clock, even on the weekends. Now, he seems to have settled into summer, settled into staying here. And I know better than to think it's because of me.

'He's with Flo now and he seems to really like her. Plus, he doesn't like me like that.'

Or love me, at all. He promised not to. I keep looking at him, reclining on the blanket, and my stomach fills with butterflies, even though I thought I was incapable of feeling them.

'Only one thing for it. You have to show him what he's missing.'

'This isn't a rom-com, Ems,' I object, hot panic prickling my skin. 'And I'm not the kind of girl to chase a man.' I'm also not the kind of girl to marry one.

'I know your view of feminism might have got all mixed up in your mum's behaviour lately,' Emmie says, her empathy evident in every word. 'But need I remind you that feminism means having the freedom to fight for what you want?' Emmie says boldly, as my mind jolts back to our conversation in the Captain Kidd, the one where she encouraged me to let my mind, my *heart*, go where it truly wants to, even if that isn't quite where I expected. 'And sometimes *that* means prancing around your shared apartment in your underwear and hoping your housemate gets the hots for you.'

Well, *this* is entirely unexpected. There is no way in hell that I am doing any prancing for Jack, especially not in my underwear, no matter how nice he looks in the early-evening sunlight as I make my way to join him outside. Instead, I simply hand him another beer.

'Thanks,' he smiles softly as I sit beside him, crossing my legs beneath me.

'You've finished work early,' I say, and from Jack's crinkled brow and vacant expression I can tell that his thoughts are miles away. With Flo, or M. Whoever the hell M is? A Molly, or Matilda? Another Maya, a better one? A Milly, a May. *Laura Mae.* The thought comes from nowhere. Isn't that what Jack called his ex-girlfriend the first time he told me about her? *Her name was Laura Mae.* And my reply? *It probably still is.*

My stomach flips as it dawns on me that that's who he must be messaging so intently. And I can't believe it's taken me so long to realise. That whilst I've been joking and pushing his advances away, he's finally reconnecting with the love of his life. Maybe dating Flo has finally helped him face up to whatever happened with her? Or maybe it's being married to me.

What if they get back together? What if Jack decides to move back to Auckland?

'So have you,' Jack says back, eyes glancing to his phone again.

'Who you chatting to this time?' I try to sound nonchalant.

'It's just . . . just Adrian,' he says; I know him well enough to know he's lying again. That it's Laura Mae, the love of his life. The sun is still beating down so hard that I can see beads of sweat glistening on Jack's clavicle and my temperature soars as I try to make sense of my rising thoughts. But I can't. All I can think about is how to retain Jack's attention, to smash through the walls I erected in the first place.

Before I can think better of it, I'm taking off my top until I'm sat there in my bra, reclining on my back, propping myself up on my forearms in the least feminist move of my life to date. I'm using my body as bait. But desperate times call for, well, desperation. Jack's eyes flick from my sheepish smile to the black lace of my bra and unlike all the times that I've hidden behind outstretched towels or performed the knicker trick to perfection, this time I *want* him to watch. Jack smiles too, a soft, kind smile. He looks at his phone once more before stashing it in his pocket and I almost can't believe that he's the kind of man that simply needs to glimpse a bra before giving a woman his whole attention. Then, out of nowhere, he gets to his feet and grins down at me.

'I'll give you some space,' he mutters, before leaving me feeling entirely exposed.

Eighty Days Married

Jack

Where am I?

I look around the bomb site of a room, at the clothes scattered haphazardly across the carpet, at the fancy picture frame that is jauntily clinging with one corner to the wall. Then I turn over on my side, skin naked and sticky, to see Maya's stuff neatly stacked on her bedside table as normal. So, this is *our* room? The second question races into my blurry mind as quickly as the first. *What* happened last night?

Of course, I remember the start of it, remember yet another day of rereading my mum's text messages, of feeling the weight of the world on my shoulders even though I had naively hoped I'd be able to leave all of my baggage behind. I remember the guilt of letting Flo down, yet another broken heart left in my path. The pressure of messaging Charlotte, trying to support her when I can't even support myself. I remember needing a drink, a friend, a chance to escape my mind for just a moment, of the relief I felt when Maya came down to join me in the

249

courtyard. Then the confusion as she began acting strangely, asking too many questions, taking her top off and sitting there in her bra. On anyone else, I'd think this was an attempt to look sexy – which she did – but seeing as Maya shouts at me incessantly every time I even glance in her direction whilst she's changing, I took this as a clear sign that she wanted to be alone. So, I messaged Adrian asking for a drink. Clearly, we had a hundred.

How on earth did we get home? I try to piece my drinks with Adrian together. We talked about my mum, about her getting in touch after our blowout fight this time last year, one that I categorically couldn't hide from him as he could hear my shouting through the walls. He was there for me then and is here for me now – as much as a guy can be when someone is purposefully withholding all the details that matter most.

There's something Maya isn't telling you.

The thought comes from nowhere, along with the memory of Adrian's mouth slurring these words from behind the bar: *there's something Maya isn't telling you* . . . I feel the frustration at his half-information all over again, as a wave of sickness washes over me. *Just ask her about her dad.* I roll his cryptic words around my head again. Maybe that's why Maya wanted to be alone yesterday? Something's happened with her dad?

It takes all my effort to reach for my phone, even more to turn my screen over to look at the time. I already know from the fact that Maya is up and out of bed before me that I've overslept. It's gone eleven and I have no less than four messages waiting for me. One from Florence, no doubt telling me to stick yesterday's apology up my arse. One from Adrian, telling me he feels like the walking dead. The third is from Toby, and

250

with bile rising in my throat I click it open. Sure, I don't need a visa from him anymore, but I still need a freaking job to be able to pay my rent to Maya – if she's going to let me stay here after all the rules I've broken now: sleeping in the bed naked, not picking up my socks, trashing the place.

Hey, Jack. You didn't seem in a good place at work yesterday. If you've got personal stuff to sort out with the Mrs, feel free to take a few days off. Toby.

I read Toby's message and then read it again. Ever since he found out I got married to Maya it's like I've unintentionally entered some kind of husbands' club. I *wish* the only stuff I had to work out was with her, but I know that it's my mum's message, telling me that it's time for me to stop running away, that I'm trying to run away from. Ironically.

Hey, Mr W. Can we have a phone call later? I really need someone to talk to.

I look down at Charlotte's message, a rush of emotions coursing through me. How can I even contemplate going back to Auckland whilst she needs me so much? Whilst the others at Girls Code need me too. I promised I would be a better big brother this time. *I wish it had been you who died instead.* It's not just the words from my mum's message that have been hurtling through my mind ever since she said them, it's like they've somehow dislodged all the sentences she said before, all the ones I've been trying to forget since I left home. I can't go back there, not now. Not now that I've made a home here too. Not that Maya will let me keep living here if I don't clean up the carnage I've left in this room, and *fast*.

Forcing my broken body out of bed, I throw on some boxers – still nestled within the scrunched-up jeans I stepped

251

out of before passing out last night – and begin to pick up the clothes I scattered across the room, no doubt searching for my pyjamas in vain.

'Don't worry, I'll get those,' I hear Maya's voice from behind me as I bend down to pick up my jeans. I stop still, scared to turn around to see the anger in her eyes, her hand on her hips, a sarcastic smirk to match her sarcastic words.

Turning slowly, I'm surprised to find her standing there, a genuine smile on her face. And she looks gorgeous too, with her hair falling in effortless curls down her bronzed shoulders – even though I know by now her hair is naturally straight. She's wearing some kind of shirt dress that I've never seen her wear before, the top three or four buttons undone so that I can see a hint of the black bra that she uncovered in the courtyard yesterday.

'I'm . . .' I say, suddenly lost for words. Why does she look like that? And why is she smiling at me? The same sickness washes over me again. *There's something Maya isn't telling you.* I remember Adrian's words again from the night before and feel uneasy. There's so much I'm not telling her too. 'I'm sorry.'

I've never meant anything more.

'Don't be sorry,' Maya says, proceeding to come and pick up my socks, something she categorically promised she wouldn't do. 'You've got loads on.'

What does Maya know about what I've got on?

'With work and dating and stuff . . .'

Oh, she still thinks I'm seeing Florence, that we're going from strength to strength.

'You've got lots on too,' I force back and Maya's smile fades for a moment. *Just ask her about her dad*, Adrian's words rise up like the vomit I know is inside me. 'With your paper and everything . . . and dating,' I add. I didn't think Maya would be dating so soon after her shambles with Nice Guy Matt, but then why else would she be dressed like that?

She reaches for a discarded T-shirt at the exact same time I do and our hands touch. She looks right at me, with her kohl-rimmed smoky eyes, and for a second, I feel like she can see into my soul. That she can tell I'm hiding a thousand things, from her, from myself. And I can't tell her. Can't face it. Can't face her hating me too.

'I've . . .' I begin, her face still inches from my own as we crouch on the floor. 'I've got to go. I'm late for work . . . I'll . . .' Maya looks so disappointed in me. 'I'll tidy later.'

'No, no,' Maya says quickly, softly. 'I've got this.'

I beam back, though given how out of character she's acting, I fear what's really going on beneath her smiling surface.

Eighty-one Days Married

Maya

I can barely see Emmie's face shining out of my propped-up phone screen for all the smoke that is filling the room. I take the saucepan off the hob just before the korma sauce can catch alight.

'Emmie, what am I doing?' I pick up the phone with one hand and throw my other hand to my sweat-glistening forehead. In the corner of my screen, I can see the small picture of me, and I hardly recognise myself. I'm wearing an apron for goodness' sake.

'Well, right now, you're cooking your *love* his favourite meal in the hopes that he'll start to see you as more than just a friend.'

I cringe at the L-word. I feel like such a L-oser.

'I know, but seriously. What. Am. I. Doing?' I accentuate every word, tilting the phone downwards so that Emmie can see my pinny and just how far I've fallen from grace. There was once a time when I'd teased Jack for loving unadventurous food; now I've chained myself to the cooker in the height of summer just to cook it for him.

'You do know you could always just tell him?'

'A novel idea,' I say facetiously, seeing as this is Emmie's current party line.

'Seriously, Maya. What's the worst that could happen?'

'Well, I tell him, and he doesn't feel the same and we have to carry on living in the same house like some weird husband and wife who never talk to each other.'

'Like husband and wife?' Emmie laughs and despite the heat of the kitchen, the still-high temperature of the city outside, I shiver. Tell her, Maya. Tell her. But, after so long, I know the rift it will cause will take ages to iron out, and with Jack so MIA, I *need* her here.

'I mean, look at me. I'm already cooking his dinner!'

'Yeah, I'm not sure why you're doing that, to be honest.' Emmie crinkles up her nose, and she looks like the woman I've known and loved since we met at secondary school. The one who very publicly petitioned for unisex uniforms before anyone thought that was cool.

'I literally have no other ideas,' I say, knowing all my inspiration is coming from the damn interviews of women who were housewives in the fifties that I've been trying and failing to distract myself with for the past few months.

'I've told you, just whip your kit off and give him a kiss.'

'Emmie, that's like the most degrading thing I could do,' I argue back. 'Plus, the most embarrassing. He doesn't like me like that.'

'How do you know?' Emmie plays devil's advocate, the role she was born for.

'Well, for starters, he's been attached to his phone all week, obsessed with some girl he's messaging. And then, he's been completely checked out – even when he's here. You should have seen the way he looked at me yesterday,' I go on, recalling how I'd walked in on him hungover and tidying and had offered to help. 'It's like he didn't recognise me. Then, he said he was going to work, but left his laptop here. His whole damn life is on that laptop, Emmie.'

Apart from, I don't know his whole life, do I? Only the parts he's shown me.

'Do you think there's something going on with him?' Emmie asks, curiously.

'Yes, he's dating and regretting being marri— living with me.' I recover quickly.

'No, I mean, like something else? Something that's worrying him?'

'I don't know, I . . .' My sentence drifts off. 'Has Adrian said something?'

'No, no,' Emmie says at speed, then, I swear, looks a little shifty.

'And have you said anything to Adrian? About my dad?'

'No, of course not,' Emmie goes on. 'But you have to tell him soon.'

'I'll tell him when I'm ready.'

'Tell me what?'

If I didn't recognise Jack's voice instantly, I'd know he was here from the startled look on Emmie's face, her eyes wide and mouth pursed in the frame of my phone screen.

'I've, erm . . . got to go,' I say, and Emmie gives me a quick, unwelcome wink.

'Tell me what?' Jack says as soon as he's got my full attention. Little does he know he's had my attention for days.

'That I've made you dinner,' I say sheepishly, untying the apron as soon as I physically can. Jack looks gorgeous, all messy hair and tanned skin. But he also looks sad, really sad. Like he's got the weight of the world on his strong, muscular shoulders.

'Why?' he says, coming to stand before me, genuinely surprised.

'Can a wife not make dinner for her husband anymore?' I try to pass it off as a light-hearted joke but the heaviness clinging to Jack's features makes any flirtation flee. 'Jack, is everything okay? Is it about Florence, have things ended?' I ask, shamefully hopeful.

Jack looks at me for the longest time, that same look from yesterday – distant and detached and like he doesn't quite know who I am. Then, he shakes his head slowly.

'It's never been about Florence.'

He takes a step further forwards and my heart flutters and my breath becomes short.

'Then what is it about?' I ask, my heartbeat racing as Jack's eyes explore my face.

'I've been thinking a lot about home lately,' he says, his shoulders sagging.

'Here? The apartment?' I say, even though I'm sure he's really talking about—

'New Zealand,' Jack confirms, his lips hovering apart as if he's about to ask me a question before thinking better of it. He said his home was here, with me.

'Okay, well, let's talk about it?'

Jack is looking from me to the dinner I've just plated up and served in front of him, the dish he ate at Tayyabs just before he tried to kiss me – only this time a veggie version. He smiles kindly, genuinely, and it's like everything I love about Jack is right there in front of me. And then his smile fades.

'It's okay, I don't really feel like talking about her.' *Her.* 'Maya, is your dad okay?' Jack says before I can question him any further.

'I . . .' I begin, looking from the dinner to Jack before me. He's thinking about his ex-girlfriend, about New Zealand, maybe even about going home, and this is the one confession that will see him leave for good. 'I don't really feel like talking about him,' I say, with the shiniest smile I can muster. 'Dinner?' I say, trying to salvage something of tonight.

'I . . .' Jack begins, looking from me to his phone, which I'm only now realising has been clutched in his hand this whole time. 'Thanks, but I don't really fancy it right now.'

What he means is that he doesn't really fancy *me*.

Eighty-two Days Married

Jack

'Have you even got a social life?' Charlotte asks, hand on hip as she hangs back after our Girls Code session to chat, the other teenagers dispersing off towards whatever they've got next. You'd think after how much she's leaned on me this past week that she'd be a little nicer to me, but I know this mentoring thing isn't a two-way street.

'Yes, I have a social life,' I say, mirroring her hand-on-hip stance. Though lately, it has consisted of ignoring my mum's messages and getting pissed with Adrian.

'Then why are you here all the time?' Charlotte laughs; it's good to see her giggling. She's talking about me being here on a Saturday, but throughout the summer the scheme doubles up on classes so that the teenagers have a safe haven throughout the holidays.

'I'm only here as much as you,' I deflect, although I know Charlotte is wiser than she thinks, wiser than her years.

Sadly, family breakdown had the opposite effect on me. The

259

truth is that I want to be here for the girls as much as I can, remind myself of the reasons I can't go home, can't reply to my mum's messages, can't face her forgiveness. I don't deserve it. I deserve to pour myself into being a big sibling and make better choices this time around.

'Plus, I'm not going to be here tomorrow. I've just switched my shift,' I explain defensively.

'Hmmm,' Charlotte puts her fingers to her face, taps them on her chin. 'Seems like you're trying to avoid something . . . or *someone*.' She flings her hand into the air, index finger pointed upwards like she's just discovered gravity or solved a crime.

'I'm not avoiding you.' I laugh.

'I didn't mean me, you idiot,' Charlotte says quickly. 'I mean outside of here.'

'I thought you said I *didn't* have a life outside of here?' I laugh again.

'Is it Maya?' She narrows her eyes in my direction. 'That you're avoiding?'

'No,' I say quickly. Although aren't I? She's not seemed herself and I know that she'll be able to see the same shift in me. 'Why would you think that?'

'Because you talk about her all the time.'

'I don't talk about her all the time.' *Do* I? I didn't think I'd mentioned her much.

'Enough for all the girls to think you're in love with her.'

'I'm not in love with her.' I'm not *allowed* to be. Maya has made sure of that.

'Could have fooled me.' Charlotte looks smug, convinced that she's right.

'No, it's . . .' I say, panicked. They think I'm in love with

260

Maya? Is that what Maya thinks too? Is that why she's been acting so strange? I remember last night, when she cooked me food and was so willing to listen to me. Before I shut her out. Because that's what she wants, what she's always wanted. Boundaries, rules. 'It's complicated.'

'Too complicated for me to understand, you mean?' Charlotte's face falls.

'No, no,' I say quickly. 'In fact, you'll probably understand better than anyone.'

'Fucked-up family stuff?' She throws herself onto the desk, legs hanging off the edge.

'Charlotte! Language.'

'Oh, please.' She rolls her eyes. 'Don't they swear in your country?'

'My country is *here*, in the UK,' I correct her but the words are void of force. 'And yes, of course they do.' We swore at each other all the time after Charlie died, like now that the baby of the family was gone and all that remained was mess, it felt pointless trying to keep things clean. 'And yes, it is *screwed*-up family stuff.'

'I get it. This stuff is hard to deal with,' Charlotte says softly.

'Hey, who's the big brother here?' I say, but the words catch in my throat. Charlie taught me so much of what I know, so much of what I'm proud of now. I just didn't see his impact, his imprints all over me, until it was too late. 'Okay, fine. It's stuff with my mum. She's trying to get in touch with me,' I begin saying all the things I want to say to Maya. 'I think she's decided . . . I think she's . . . trying to get me to go back to New Zealand.'

'Will you?'

261

'I don't think I can. I didn't leave things in a good place,' I say slowly, knowing we should be wrapping up our after-hours session now. 'After my brother, Charlie, died.'

'You have a brother? Called Charlie?' Charlotte stares back at me in shock.

'I *had* a brother. And yes, I did, why do you think I call you Charlotte?'

'To annoy me?' Charlotte tries to joke, but she looks absolutely gutted for me.

'Only partly.' I force a sad smile between us. 'It's hard enough trying to forget him without having to say his name every week.'

'But why would you even want to forget him?'

Charlotte is looking at me with wide eyes and I know I've already said too much. I also know I can't run from the truth forever. That it's time to come clean, to everyone.

'I want to forget what I did to him.'

My conversation with Charlotte follows me all the way home, as guilt engulfs me again. I may not have shared any of the details, but I know I've already said too much, that I went way too far, I always do. But it's not like I have a blueprint for this mentoring thing. How the hell am I supposed to let Charlotte know she can tell me anything whilst making out like I'm the poster boy for perfection, Jack the Jock again? I instantly think of Maya.

I can't believe Charlotte and the girls think I'm in love with her. As I turn my key in the door to Apartment 100, I wonder how they got that impression, why they would even think that?

I mean, there was a moment where I fancied her, for sure. At the party, even after the wedding, photographing her all the way up Brick Lane. But that was before we got the visa, before we knew how much was on the line if we were to ever cross it ourselves. And now it feels like we've been in the friend-zone so long that I don't even see her that way.

It's then that I bump into Maya walking towards the bathroom, completely naked.

'Oh shit, I didn't think you were coming home tonight,' Maya says, flinging her arms across her body to cover herself. It's still not enough to cover her insane figure, which sends my already frantic mind into overdrive. How could anyone *not* fancy Maya?

'I'm sorry. I'm oh . . . I . . .' I stutter as if this is the first time I've seen a woman naked before. It's the first time I've seen my *wife* naked. I try to move past her, to give her some privacy, but she steps the same way as me until her body is inches away from my own. With one hand clutched to her body, she reaches with the other for the expensive vase that has sat on the hall table since the moment we first arrived here, now filled with flowers, and forces the foliage between us. I don't know if it's a good or bad thing that the vase is see-through.

'It's okay, I genuinely thought . . .' Maya looks mortified, horrified; this is precisely the type of run-in that our vows were meant to protect us from. But now that she's here, standing there, completely bare, except for the blooms, I'm not sure I want to be protected from this, from *her*. She holds my eye contact, her face covered with the vulnerability that on her looks so rare, the vulnerability that until recently she was beginning to allow me to see. Neither one of us says anything

263

and, for a moment, I feel as close to her as I did at the start of this damn heatwave. Before she pushed me towards Florence. And my mum pulled me closer to all I left behind.

Then my phone buzzes and I reach for it automatically, cursing myself for not being strong enough to ignore it, to just stay in this moment with Maya and the see-through vase.

Thanks for the chats, Mr W. It's nice to know that it's not just us teenagers who mess things up on the reg. Charlotte's message makes me smile, quelling my worries about telling her the truth about what I did to Charlie, how I was responsible for his death. But as Maya unlocks her eyes from me and scurries into the bathroom, still holding the vase, locking the door behind her, I'm not entirely sure that I told Charlotte the truth about Maya.

Because I think I might love her after all.

Eighty-three Days Married

Maya

I wake up to hear Jack stirring beside me, his body encroaching further and further into the middle of the bed. I roll over to look at him, the same way I have every morning of this past week. The rise and fall of his chest, his wedding ring moving on the chain around his neck as he repositions himself again and again. It's like he can't get settled. And I have a horrible, feeling that I'm part of the reason why. Jack married me for a visa. Because I was a safe bet. Because I wasn't like all the other silly girls that would throw themselves at Jack the Jock and try to make him fall for them, to be his teammate, his first pick. But ever since I came clean to Emmie about my feelings for him, I know I've been acting anything but myself.

As Jack breathes deeply, turning onto his side to face me, his eyes still screwed shut, I try to shake the memory of my shameful performance last night, like one naked run-in could spark some kind of realisation in him. I don't even recognise myself. I'm not the kind of girl to manipulate a man. I am a strong, independent woman who is fighting for change in all the right places, who has much better things to think about than whoever Jack is dreaming about now. His ex-girlfriend, his true love, the one with the power to woo him all the way home.

His phone vibrates on his bedside table and it's like I've willed this woman into the room. I watch as Jack's heavy eyes peel open. Oh shit, those eyes. That smile. His chest.

'Morning,' he whispers sleepily, too tired to notice how close we're lying. The covers are pulled up around him, the city's heatwave finally beginning to cool down. And this, whatever this is that I feel for Jack, can cool down now too.

'Morning,' I reply, as pragmatically as I can, rolling away from him. He lingers for a moment in the middle of the bed, before pushing himself up and over to his side. I do the same, looking down to my phone as Jack reaches for his to do the same.

Out of the corner of my eye, I see Jack smiling down at his screen. I know he's talking to her now. But why should I care? He's just doing what I told him to do. I look from my empty screen to Jack, searching for answers. Will he still like me if he knows the truth about my dad? Will he still want to be married to me if he knows I've broken my vow? This time, as I glance towards him, he catches my eye and smiles.

'You look . . .' He begins, his smile growing as my eyes grow wide. Look like what? 'No, no, nothing bad.' He laughs, those gorgeous lines drawing his grin up to his eyes. 'Maya Morgan,' he laughs again, 'I've never known someone expect the worst more than you.'

Before I can respond, Jack is discarding his phone on his bedside table and rolling himself out of bed in a comically laborious fashion. It makes me laugh but as soon as he's standing tall and I can see his strong torso and his toned body in all its glory, the scene doesn't feel that funny anymore. It feels as hot and sticky and confusing as in the heatwave and as Jack makes his way to the shower, it takes all my strength not to follow him.

As soon as I'm alone, I turn over so that my face is in my pillow. I want to scream as loud as I can or smother my feelings until they start making sense. What does Jack mean, I always expect the worst? Is that what I'm doing now? Thinking that if I come clean to Jack about my dad, or how I feel, that he'll reject me in an instant. Divorce me, even. Because going back to whatever he's left at home is better than staying here with me. A me that is so different from the woman he married. A me that is crazy, clingy, that can't seem to get him out of my mind. One that after wanting to learn everything I need to pass some kind of visa test now wants to know him to his bones. To know every inch of his history, what he left behind, his present, who he's in love with now. To know his future, and whether maybe, just maybe, he'd like to keep me a part of it. Another buzz breaks me from the thought, and I see that Jack's phone is now lit up and enticing me from his bedside table.

My eyes dart towards the bedroom door, closed shut, cocooning me inside whilst Jack is safely two doors away – three doors, if you count the shower that he'll no doubt be in for twice as long as me. I know that about him. Because I know every inch of who he is in this apartment. I just need to know who he is, who he's seeing, outside of it, for good.

Rolling over to Jack's side of the bed, I savour his crumpled sheets against my skin. I know I'm in too deep, that I should paddle to the shallows, not wade deeper into him. And yet, here I am reaching for his phone now, eyes scanning over the first glimmer of the message he's just received, displayed oh-so-clearly on his backlit screen.

Morning, Mr W. I can't wait to see you. Things are so much better since we . . .

Since they what? Starting dating. Started sleeping together? Started falling in love? It's from someone called Charlotte. But what about Mae, Laura Mae? Before I know it, my fingers are swiping to his locked screen, to the password that comes up, and I'm keying in his brother's birthday because I know this is the date that matters more than any other.

The screen opens up to me, falling open like the pages of a diary. I shouldn't be doing this, not one bit. And yet, a thrill runs through me as I feel one step closer to getting the answers that, right now, I feel like I desperately need. Because this isn't a crush that is going to blow over, dial down like the weather. It's a love I have to do something about. But what?

. . . starting really opening up to each other. I'm excited for the future again. For what happens next. I have some ideas in mind that I can't wait to tell you! Charlie x

Charlie? As in his brother Charlie? But no, the number is saved under 'Charlotte'. This is too much. And once again, I know I've come way too far to go back now. I grab my phone and take a photo of Charlotte's – or Charlie's – number, knowing that I've crossed a line. That I've become the suspicious spouse, the jealous wife, that I swore I'd never be.

I am up, dressed and heading for the door when Jack walks back into the bedroom, just a towel wrapped tightly around his middle. Like earlier, it's enough to send my heart into hysteria, my eyes searching for somewhere to land other than the small swatch of fabric. Unlike earlier, I now have another reason not to look him in the eye. The shameful truth that I have the number of the woman he's been seeing secretly stashed in my phone.

'We need to stop bumping into each other like this,' Jack says, voice low, body close.

'Yes, we do.' Another lie dangles between us. I don't want to stop.

'I've got to, erm. . .' Jack eyes dart from me to the bedroom behind us, signalling that he has places to be today, people to see. People like Charlie. 'Get ready.'

I stand still for a moment, unable to move, willing him to want to stay here with me too. I step back as Jack disappears into the bedroom, turning to me before dropping his towel, a nod to tell me to give him some privacy. All he wants is privacy. But as I walk into the living room, contemplating another Saturday sat at my dad's desk as the words stall and my raging thoughts come thick and fast, I know that I can't let this go. Can't let *him* go.

I look down at my phone, at the number now stored into mine: *Charlotte/Charlie*. Everything in me screams to stop, that this isn't me, that this is a mistake, but still I type.

Hey. I know you don't know me . . .

Then I do stop myself. Because this actually isn't me. It's so far from the woman I am it's laughable. I am not the kind of person to look through their partner's phone. I am not the kind of person to take the number of someone my partner is messaging. Except, clearly, I am that kind of person. Because I've just done both of these things. But I am *not* the kind of person to actually send a message to them. One by one, I delete the words I've just written.

I look down at my blank screen, willing me to fill the space with words, then up to the door into the living room, the one Jack will no doubt walk through soon, and suddenly another thought fills my mind: I didn't think I was the kind of person to fall for someone the way I have for Jack. And I'm certainly not the kind of person to let something go without a fight.

Hey, I know you don't know me . . . I rewrite the words I've just deleted, this time going even further. *. . . but I'm a friend of Jack's and I'm really worried about him.* I click send and continue to type. *I know this seems crazy but if you know what's going on with him, I'd really . . .*

Charlotte/Charlie: Maya?

I look down at my name on the screen. What the . . . ?

Yes, it's Maya. How did you know? I wondered if we could talk? About him.

As soon as I've sent the words, I want to delete them, reclaim them, never mention them again. This is insane. I told Jack to date, to get serious about somebody again. To keep his past in the past, to not tell me everything. And now I've crossed every line I've drawn.

Charlotte/ Charlie: King's Cross? Midday? I could meet you then?

This is too weird. Why would they even want to meet me. Does everyone know who I am but me. Because right now, I don't recognise myself.

Only if you're sure. I know this is strange. We can leave it, forget about it. I back-track immediately, knowing that if Jack knew what I was doing right now he'd kill me.

Charlotte/Charlie: It's okay. I'm glad you reached out. I'm worried about him too.

I read the words again, trying to tell myself this is crazy, trying to tell myself to stop. But I already know what my reply is going to be. If this person knows about me, I want to know what. And if they are worried about Jack too, then I need to know why.

Jack

I linger around the apartment until I can't take it anymore, storming across the pristine lawns of the gated community and out onto the cobbled streets. Once again, my thoughts of Maya follow me, spilling out of our little life in number 100. I've been just fine putting my feelings into boxes these past five years. I'm not sure whether it's Maya or my mum who has managed to mess the whole system up, ruin my neat compartmentalisation beyond repair.

As I come to stand by the waterfront, leaning against the wall, gazing up at Tower Bridge, I know what I need to do next. It's been two weeks since my mum called, and though I've tried to ignore it, tried to throw myself into my London life, I know it's not working.

Every time Maya looks at me with those big green eyes, I know I can't go back to New Zealand, but I also know I can't spend every night sleeping next to her, pretending I don't care, that I'm distant, detached, when everything in me knows I never stopped caring, about any of it. I *need* to call my mum back. And yet, even now, staring out across the Thames, with the whole day blocked out for this and the Girls Code session covered by another volunteer, I can't bring myself to dial her number. I'm just standing here, watching couples and families

271

walking across the bridge, wondering what on earth I'm going to say or do to bridge my way back to being the man I used to be. A man worthy of my wife.

Right, I'm doing this. *I'm doing this.* I look down at my phone, open on my latest message from Charlotte, telling me that there's little point in her showing up to Girls Code if I'm not going to be there, and then swipe to my mum's number.

I mentally calculate the time difference for the umpteenth time since I decided I needed to call her back, something that I used to be able to do without even trying. It's just gone 11 a.m. here, which makes it just after 10 p.m. there. But there's no way my mum will be winding down to bed. She used to be a night owl even before what happened to Charlie, now I'm not sure she lets herself sleep at all.

Hovering my finger over the call icon, I tell myself I can do this. That it's the only way I'm going to be able to make peace with my past so that I can even contemplate telling Maya that I want her to be in my future. Right, I'm counting to three and then I'm calling. One. *How can you even speak to her after what you did?* Two. *Or after what she said to you?* Three. *You said there was no going back, you moved miles away to start again and now . . .*

'Mum?' I say the name for the first time in a long time. Even in my brief conversations with Adrian about her she's been 'my mum', a descriptor, not a name.

'Jack?' she whispers back to me, and I want to hear her saying it again.

'It's me.' We both have caller ID but that doesn't stop us needing the confirmation. After a year of not speaking to one another, the connection feels fragile, make-believe. 'I've . . . I'm . . . sorry it's taken me so long to call back . . .'

272

'I'm sorry for a lot of things.' Her voice is so quiet, so distant, but I swear I hear her crying. In a moment, her face shifts into focus in my mind. I can see her howling, her face contorting in pain, the sheer brokenness of a mother who has lost a child, the kind where you know that even if, by some miracle, they manage to pull themselves together, their face will never look the same again; that it will be scarred by grief forever.

'Me too,' I say, resisting the urge to hang up, to put a lid on these feelings before they start flowing like the dirty water of the Thames before me. 'I'm so sorry.' I say the three words I've said a thousand times out loud and every moment of every day in my mind as the memory of Charlie's accident comes crashing into my mind at breakneck speed.

Maya

Emerging from King's Cross station, I stand outside the Overground platforms, gazing up at the clock in front of me, before looking to the clock tower of St Pancras, far superior to the one I've just been looking at. I wonder whether Jack feels the same way about me and this girl; that I'm the King's Cross clock – simple, serving a purpose – and she's St Pancras, the kind you capture in a photo so you can savour it for longer than a second. I look down at my ripped jeans and my light denim shirt and know that our summer is coming to an end.

'Excuse me?' I hear a voice behind me, and I spin around slowly. There I see a young girl looking back at me with wide, imploring eyes. She's dressed in Adidas tracksuit bottoms and a plain pullover, her long hair pulled into a tight ponytail on top of her head. I try to inform my throbbing heart of the false alarm, that this isn't my husband's other woman.

'Can I help you?' I say back to her politely, eyes shifting around for signs of Charlie.

'You're Maya, right?' The girl says back to me, a hand moving to her popped hip as I try to pull my jaw from the ground. What the . . .? She looks me up and down before grinning, as if something now makes sense. But nothing makes sense to me. Why has Jack been messaging a teenager? I feel a chill rush right through me as my brain becomes foggier still.

'Yes, and you're . . . *Charlotte*?'

'I prefer Charlie,' she snaps back quickly.

'Jack has a brother called Charlie . . .' I say, one of the few things I know about him. Charlotte looks back at me with all the sass of a seventeen-year-old, and then her face falls.

'He *had* a brother called Charlie.'

'What?' I say, hands shaking by my side. 'What do you mean?'

'Charlie died, like, five years ago,' she says, her mouth now twisted with concern.

'How did I not know that?' My cheeks burn hot with the sheer embarrassment of having a teenager know my husband better than me.

'He says you guys agreed not to tell each other everything,' Charlotte says, matter-of-factly, as I wonder just how much this girl really knows. How can Jack's brother have died, and I not know about it? My mind races with thoughts as Charlotte smiles back at me kindly, as if she's not witnessing a woman in her twenties having a full-scale breakdown.

'You did agree to that, right?' she goes on, trying to steer us

274

out of this silence. After all, we came here to talk. 'That you weren't going to share everything with each other?'

'Yes, but not something that . . .' I was going to say 'serious' until I remember that it doesn't get much more serious than lying about a dead relative. Though Jack didn't technically lie, did he? He just didn't *tell* me. Clearly, he's told this Charlotte everything.

'Yes,' I say, my anxiety revving into overdrive. 'But we also agreed not to share everything with other people. And now somehow you know all about our marriage and—'

'You're *married*?' Charlotte hurls the word across King's Cross Square.

'No, no, not *really*, no . . .' My face flushes bright red.

'I *knew* there was something more going on between you two!' She practically squeals. I take a step back, stunned and mute. 'He talks about you all the time.'

Even now, this sentence makes my heart flutter, bloom with hope. But why? Jack may have talked about me, but he's not talked to me about anything *real* in all these months.

'He's never . . . he's never mentioned you,' I say, as softly as I can, not wanting to upset this poor girl's feelings; clearly, she can't be the other woman, but she still seems to care about Jack or why else would she be here? 'How do you know each other?'

'Girls Code,' Charlotte says, hopping from foot to foot in a way that makes me suspect she may have ADHD. I gesture forward and she nods, beginning to walk as I fall into step beside her, physically at least. Mentally I have no freaking idea where I am.

'Girl's what?' I ask, as we wind around King's Cross station

275

towards Granary Square, everything seeming a little greyer as we slip into a darker season.

'It's a weekend club. Mr W. . . . *Jack*.' Charlotte corrects herself, 'teaches us how to code, and like, create websites and stuff; he's also been mentoring me through the scheme.'

'The scheme?'

'The Big Sibling Scheme?' Charlotte's inflected voice and even more inflected eyebrows indicate that I should have heard about this by now. I feel like I should have heard a lot of things. 'Jack started volunteering there when he was at uni.' She breaks off again to look at me, tilting her chin upward in thought. 'Hey, didn't you go to the same uni?'

'Yeah,' I say, wracking my memory for mentions of any scheme. 'But I've never heard of the Big Sibling Scheme.'

'Probs too busy studying,' Charlotte grins. 'Jack says you're a nerd.'

'Thanks.' I manage to laugh back even though my body is still shaking.

'Jack has volunteered with the scheme, with us, since then . . . every weekend, now even twice a weekend.' Charlotte shakes her pretty head. 'He needs to get a social life.'

I thought he had a social life, an active one, a romantic one. A shagging-every-girl-in-London one. I never dreamed he'd be teaching young women how to code.

'Why wouldn't he tell me about this?'

'Because you agreed not to tell each other everything,' Charlotte harps back again, rolling her eyes, as if to say: *what is wrong with you two?*

'But this is a *good* thing, a thing he should be proud of . . .'

'Except,' Charlotte says, coming to a standstill on the bridge

276

over the canal, leaning her body to look down at the murky water below. 'I think it's more complicated than that.'

'What do you mean?' I follow her gaze to the water, scared of what will surface next.

'Like it may look simple but . . .' Charlotte looks at me, a seriousness washing over her. 'I think he only joined the scheme because of what happened to Charlie, to make him feel less guilty, feel better for what he did.'

'What did he do?' I say, the look in her eyes, the tears gathering there now, making my mind go crazy, crazier than it's been all week. Crazier than finding myself contacting Charlotte in the first place. She knows something, knows more pieces of the puzzle I've been trying to put together for weeks. I hold onto the railing to stop myself from falling.

'I think . . .' Charlotte whispers, tears escaping now. 'I think he might have killed him.'

Part 8

The Fallout

Maya

My first response is to laugh.

But then, looking into Charlotte's eyes, I can tell that she is telling the truth. Why else would she be worried enough to meet me, to warn me? *I think he might have killed him.* The words bounce across my brain, until my mind is a minefield. Jack's reluctance to talk about his past. His refusal, his crippling inability, to go home. The speed at which he married a woman he'd only just met. No wonder our vows, our promises, were so convenient for him, when he's been keeping so much from me himself.

My second response is to run away. But clearly, that's what Jack has been doing all this time. Instead, I rush home, back to the apartment, as quickly as I possibly can. I know I need to find out the truth about my husband and *now*. Flinging open the front door, I shout Jack's name into the empty space. He's out. God knows where, God knows who with. For once, I'm pleased to find I'm alone. It's like the ghost of my dad has been exorcised by the only thing dreadful enough to displace it: Jack's brother is dead. And he killed him.

As I rush to the writing desk, to my research books and pointless notes stacked to the side, a small voice in my mind tells me to stop. Jack couldn't have killed someone. *He's kind, he's generous, he's intelligent* . . . But then, isn't he intelligent enough to keep me away from Girls Code because he knows I'm smart too? Smart enough to trace Girls Code back to Charlie and Charlie back to him.

Just not smart enough not to marry a man I hardly know in the first place.

Perching on the edge of the desk chair, the way I always do when I'm in the apartment alone, like I can't quite relax without Jack here, I search for my laptop. Where the hell did I put it? I storm into the bedroom, trying not to think about watching Jack sleeping this morning. I race into the bathroom, ignoring the memory of Jack brushing his teeth next to me. I fling the door open into the kitchen, refusing to remember every time he's left me treats and notes and meat-free sausages. What if nothing we shared was real? This is why I never wanted to get married. How can two people share themselves, like really share it all, their whole hearts, when hearts get broken all the time?

I look down at my phone. Of course, the battery would die now. The charger lead mocks me, useless without my laptop to plug it into. Jack could be home any second, spouting his lies about being at the gym or with a date. When all I need is the truth. I know I need to google the accident, to search Jack and Charlie's names, their town, the date, to find any reports or local news coverage about what really happened back then.

I look straight ahead, at my dad's Mac in front of me, the one I've refused to switch on all this time.

Fuck it. I reach behind the monitor and feel for the groove of the button to switch it on. The screen lights up immediately, illuminating the unlocked desktop. Clearly, my dad didn't feel the need to hide from anyone here. There, in front of me, is a photo of him. My eyes study his strong profile taking up half the picture, looking outwards over a large drop, a waterfall crashing into a view that spreads to the horizon. It looks like the Grand Canyon or one of America's national parks. Something deep inside me twists. I would love to go to the Grand Canyon. I would have loved to have gone places with a dad who wanted to see the world with me. But he didn't. I wasn't worth the sacrifice.

I'm not sure how long I'm staring at his photo before I come to. Then, I look behind me, checking Jack hasn't got back and sneaked up behind me. That's why I'm here, on my stupid dad's stupid computer, in his stupid apartment that he stupidly left to me. To find out the truth about my husband. I turn back to the screen, clicking to Safari. As soon as I do, something starts to load on the page immediately, as if the computer has just been sleeping all this time.

I look at the URL. Office 365. And then, before I can stop it, the screen is flooded with emails, my dad's emails, and I try my best not to look at them, to close the inbox quickly, but I stop on seeing a familiar name mingled within them. Ruth Morgan. *Mum?*

No, no, no. My heart hammers harder, the room spins, until it feels like the water wrapping around the apartment is crashing over me from all sides.

This doesn't make sense. At all. Mum said that she and Dad lost touch when I was four. That once he'd got wrapped up in his life in New York he didn't want anything to do with us. That we were better off alone. That's why his death felt so sudden, so final. Why leaving me the apartment felt so weird when he didn't even tell me he was sick. Everything in me wants to shut down the window, pretend I didn't see my mum's emails lined up in my dad's inbox. But I know from today that what is hidden eventually floats to the surface.

Jack

I watch the sunlight dancing along the surface of the water, listening to my mum's voice down the line, and remembering it all again, everything. Every sentence she says is like a fishing hook, cast out and reeling in each conversation, argument and decision leading up to Charlie's accident; every conversation, argument and decision that happened in its wake as we waded through our waking nightmare and lost each other somewhere in the middle of it.

'Can you remember how *obsessed* he was with that computer game?' My mum laughs down the line, stray tears falling down my face. I've not heard her laugh in years, even before we stopped trying to talk to one another.

'Of course I can remember,' I choke the words out. 'I played it with him every night for about two years after we got it.'

'Did you play it *with* him or play it *for* him?' my mum asks, pointedly, and I know what's coming next. 'Because I seem to remember you gave him the second controller without actually plugging it in and he was just content naively clicking the buttons and watching his big brother enjoying the game.'

I gulp down another wave of tears as time slows down. As I am cast back into that living room, our first living room in the big house in the countryside. I try to savour the memories, wondering for a moment why I don't let my mind drift back here more often. Then I remember the questions that have pinned themselves to every good memory of my brother until they feel as dark as the bad ones I have tried to forget. *What if my parents had never moved to the city? Would I still have distanced myself from Charlie? Would I have still met Laura Mae? Fallen in love and let it warp all my priorities? Would the accident still have happened? Can you call it an accident when it was all my fault?*

'Jack, are you okay?' My mum must be able to hear my muffled cries in the silence, as I reach my spare hand to my face to shield my tears from the tourists winding past me.

'It's just talking about him again,' I say through sobs. 'Even the good bits, the nice memories, are ruined now.' And with that my shoulders heave, I pull my phone away to hold my head in my hands. It's been years now and it still feels like yesterday.

I remember how we started at a new school in Auckland, how things began to change. Suddenly the three-year age difference between us felt like a gulf as I started playing rugby and was invited into the 'cool' crowd. I never stopped being a computer-game- and comic-loving kid like Charlie, I just started becoming really good at keeping that side of myself at home, leaning into the Jack the Jock persona I had been given like it was some sort of gift.

Charlie wasn't good at dividing himself in two, pretending to

285

be anything other than exactly who he was. I loved that about him. And other people would love this too, as soon as he got through high school. As soon as all the jocks and hot girls and nerds and drama kids graduated and realised that you didn't need to sit inside your stereotype, that you could like coding *and* rugby, that you could be a feminist *and* still love and be loved by a man. Maybe if I had learnt that sooner, I wouldn't have grown to resent being linked to my nerdy little brother, wouldn't have shrugged off my mum's warning to me that I could be the captain of the rugby team but being a big brother was still the most important role I'd ever have.

Despite all my self-doubt and objections, my wrestling with my mum that I shouldn't have to leave rugby practice early to give my brother a lift to his life-drawing class, I did an okay job at toeing the line between being Jack the Jock and my brother's keeper. Until Laura.

'The memories are all ruined now,' I whisper again, returning the phone to my ear, torturing myself once more.

'They're not ruined, Jacky.' My mum says her pet-name for me slowly, cautiously. 'They may be in *ruins* right now, but that's different; ruins you can rebuild.'

'How much therapy have you had?' I can't help but force a joke through my tears, falling freely down my face, no hope of holding them back now.

'Lots.' My mum laughs from the very depths of herself, the kind of laugh that is one moment away from a proper, visceral cry. 'I mean like, *loads*.'

'Sounds like it's working for you,' I say back, voice still hoarse.

'You should try it.'

I've not had any, not wanted to revisit it. I spent so long trying to make sense of the accident when it first happened, trying to unpick every wrong turn I made. The first one was Laura. The hot girl. The cool girl. The girl in the year above. Whatever people called her; I knew as soon as she took an interest in me that all my interests were dull in comparison to her. I fell hard and I fell fast. Laura said jump, and I'd say how high? She would want a quiet night in, and so would I. She would throw a party and she expected me to be there. I just didn't know where my desires ended and hers began.

So, when she threw a party, so that I'd already promised my mum that I'd pick her and my dad up from the airport after they'd been away for their anniversary, I knew I couldn't say no. To Laura. I tried to say no to my parents a thousand times. But I'd promised. And they wanted me to be a man of my word. But I was also a man who had gone to the party and had five beers too many by then . . .

'Do you not think it would help to talk to someone?'

'I'm talking to you,' I say, legs surrendering to the nearest bench lining the riverbank.

'I know, and I'm so glad,' she says back, no signs of tiring even though we've been talking for over an hour now. There's still so much left unsaid. 'I just mean someone *else* . . .'

'A therapist?' *My wife?* The thought of Maya floods my mind. Can I really let her into this, given how being in love with Laura Mae messed things up last time? 'What would they say though, Mum? "Yes, Mr Wilson, we have listened to all the evidence and see that you chose impressing your high-school girlfriend over picking up your parents from the airport. You manipulated your little brother to go and pick them up even though he had only just passed his driving test, even though he told you he didn't want to."'

'You were drunk.'

'So was the man who crashed into Charlie when he swerved into the wrong lane.'

'It was an accident.' Her voice is tired, raw.

'It was my fault. I should have been the one driving.'

'You were young, you were drunk, it would have been wrong for you to drive.'

'It was wrong for me to get so drunk in the first place, so obsessed with what Laura thought of me that I didn't care about my promises to you.' I sob, feeling the weight of it all again. 'I swear, if I could take it all back, if I could never have fallen in love, I would—'

'Falling in love didn't make this happen,' my mum says slowly. But she doesn't know the half of it. I was so obsessed, so insecure that I'd lose Laura to some other guy, that I needed to mould and shape into everything she wanted me to be. 'You were a *teenager.*'

'He didn't want to drive, he told me it was a bad idea, I *begged* him,' I go on, my words getting more and more hurried, like I've been holding them back, down, for so long that they're flowing out of me now, as if gushing from a freshly fixed tap. 'Charlie would have done anything for me, I was his big brother, I was meant to protect him.'

'And I was meant to protect *you*,' her words slice through my sentence.

'Pardon?'

'Do you not think I've driven myself mad going over that night, how I was trying to make you see the importance of

288

honouring your promises, keeping your word, and all just to prove a point. We could have got a taxi but, but . . . Jack, you were a child, Charlie was a child too, but I was just trying to be a good mum and teach you good—'

'I know, Mum, I know.' I say quickly, stunned by her sentences. In all my grief, in all my blaming myself, I never knew she felt this way, like she blamed herself too. I thought she blamed me. 'None of this was your fault.'

'I know,' Her voice seeming to find some strength through her sobs. 'I know that now. I've managed to forgive myself for that, but I can't forgive myself for . . .'

'What, Mum?' I say, when her silence stretches further between us. 'What is it?'

'For pushing you away. I just couldn't handle it all. Couldn't handle your grief or your father's, couldn't handle seeing Charlie in both of your faces. I'd already lost one son, but somewhere along the way I lost a husband and another son too.'

'You haven't lost me,' I say, knowing now that it's true, that after years of hiding, I can feel the first fragile flickers of wanting to be found. 'And Dad will come around.'

'He already has,' my mum says, and I can almost feel her smile.

'What do you mean?'

'We're dating again.' She's laughing now. 'Turns out divorce is a ball ache.' I hear her sarcasm loud and clear, and it reminds me of Maya; it feels like home.

'I heard it was just a piece of paper.' I laugh back.

'Well, I guess. Technically. But I promise you, Jack, once you start growing together it's surprising how entangled your roots become.'

I didn't intend to grow with Maya, but isn't she part of the reason I'm here now, building bridges back to my old self again? Getting secretly wed on a whim may have been childish but I feel like we're unintentionally growing up together too.

'That's amazing,' I say, knowing how hard it must be for them to process the loss of a child together whilst trying to make a marriage work. 'I miss him. I miss you too.'

'We miss you too, and Charlie, so much,' Mum says, and just hearing her say his name hurts like hell, but this time there's something else laced in it, the bitter-sweet weight of having loved and lost and knowing that there's a chance to love again.

Maya

Jack is still nowhere to be seen.

And even if he was here, I'm not sure his guilty face, his forthcoming confessions, could drag me away from the messages I'm looking at now. I open the most recent, the one from my mum that simply says: *I'm sorry and I miss you.* My dad never replied. And he couldn't have, because it was sent a week after the day he died.

Why on earth would my mum send that message? She hated him, despised him, loathed him, and then she moved on from it, dropped the topic of my dad completely. Because we were better without him. Supposedly.

I move down the inbox to another message brandishing my mum's name and click it open: *Please stop contacting us. I can see right through it, Maya can see right through it. She's fantastic, strong-willed, unstoppable, and you don't deserve her.* For a brief moment my mum's words make me feel warm and then the next realisation makes me prickle with heat: my dad was trying to get in touch with us?

With shaking hands, I click to my dad's outbox and flip the filter so that the list is showing his messages to her, the oldest first. It's from around a year ago and the subject bar simply reads: 'some news'. I brace myself, preparing for what could come next, but after today, I feel like nothing could surprise me, that everything I thought was true is wrong.

Ruth, I know you don't want to talk to me. For what it's worth Lisa and I called it a day about eighteen months ago. But that's not what this is about. It's about Maya.

I hold my breath, reading the words, scanning the characters for answers when all they do is raise more and more questions. Who the hell is Lisa? I want to turn away, to close this down, to launch the computer through the window, shattering the perfection of this place. But I'm powerless not to read on.

Ruth, I'm sick. Prostate cancer. They found it around two years ago and I didn't know whether to get in touch then. I know you told me not to.

I scan the words, but nothing makes sense. My mum told me he'd forgotten about us.

But it's spread and I'm not going to get better now and, I don't know, that kind of just brings everything into perspective. We've spent so long competing with each other, playing games with each other, with Maya falling somewhere in the middle of it all. And I know we tried to keep her out of that, but I feel like I've missed so much of her life and I just want her to know that I never intended for that to happen, for any of it to happen.

Tears drop from my eyes onto the desk, the desk I've been

trying and failing to work at ever since Jack and I moved in here. Cursing myself for mooching off a man who never wanted me; but what if he *did* want me?

Holding my head in my hands, I hear a deep, guttural scream, only then realising that it's my own. That I've floated out of my body, my mind so confused that it's given up its job completely. *Playing games with each other . . .* Blood rushes through my limbs, bubbling through my veins at breakneck speed. *With Maya falling somewhere in the middle of it all.* My fingers tingle, tighten, clench into fists. Was I just a pawn in everyone's plan? My dad running away to America, Jack running away from the bodies buried in his past. Well, they can't play with me anymore. I'm through with everyone who has ever pretended to care about me and then lied to my face.

I'm done with pretending full stop.

Jack

I lean against the wall outside the courtyard, the same one that a drunken Maya pushed herself onto and swung her legs off all those weeks ago. I would never have imagined that meeting her that night would have led to us tying the knot and living in this apartment together. I certainly never expected that it would become my undoing. But as I ascend the same steps to Apartment 100 and arrive at the door, I realise that's exactly what's happened. Because after years of feeling like my past was packed so deeply inside me that one serious conversation could see me unravel completely, meeting Maya has made me want to deal with that, to move past it, to move forward into my future, whether she wants to be in it or not.

As I push the door open and step into the entrance hall, I know Mum is right: love didn't make Charlie die. An accident did. An accident that robbed Charlie of the opportunity to love and be loved in this lifetime. He wouldn't want it to rob me and Mum and Dad of it too. No, I'm going to risk loving someone. Even if it's unrequited, even if it hurts. I know I need to tell Maya everything. Tell her how I feel. And I know I need to tell her now.

Walking into the living room, I see Maya sitting in her usual spot at the desk, concentrating on her research, the sun streaming in from the windows, casting shadows on her skin. This is it. My chance to tell her how I feel about her before the vulnerability hangover of my call with Mum floods out this feeling. As I step closer, I realise she's fired up her dad's desktop, the one she's not used in the whole time we've been here, choosing to stick to her laptop so that she can move rooms and dash out to coffee shops at will. No one can tie Maya Angela Morgan down. But maybe she'll let me go where she goes? I watch as she hangs her head low before releasing a frustrated groan.

'Everything okay?' I ask, a nervous energy shooting through me. Tell her. *Tell her.*

She doesn't turn around, but she must hear me as her shoulders begin to shake uncontrollably, her sobs escaping into the room, like my words have just cut her in two.

'Hey, hey.' I rush forward quickly. 'What's up?' I put a hand to her back, only to feel her body stiffen immediately. 'Maya, whatever it is, we can face it . . . together.'

'Together?' she says slowly, in little more than a whisper.

'Yes, Maya. What's wrong? Please talk to me.' I begin to panic. 'Look at me.'

'Look at you?' Maya snaps, swinging her body around to face me. But she looks nothing like she did that first time we met again, headstrong and bold and ready to take on the world. She looks bruised, marred, broken. She looks like a stranger. And she's gazing back at me like I'm one too. 'I don't even know who you are!'

'What?' I say, looking back at her, her green eyes now raw and red-rimmed. What is she talking about? She knows me better than most people this side of the equator and I was about to tell her a whole lot more. About Mum, the call, the accident, about Charlie.

'I spoke to Charlie,' she says, deadpan.

'Pardon?'

'Your *friend* Charlotte.' Maya narrows her eyes now, her arms folded across her chest, her very being closed off to me completely.

What is she on about? How could she have spoken to Charlotte? She doesn't even know Charlotte exists.

'I knew you weren't telling me something, hiding things from me.'

'Like we agreed to, like we promised,' I say, my voice inching higher now. Just moments ago, I felt like a weight had been lifted from my shoulders, my guilt drenched in grace. Now, I'm looking back at a woman who I don't recognise. 'What did you do?'

'What did *I* do?' Maya pushes against the desk, coming to stand before me now.

294

Part of me wants to grab her, to hug her, to embrace this breakdown away. The other part of me wants to push her away, to tell the stupid parts of myself that hoped for better, that I might be able to let myself love again, to close up shop, stay shut and safe.

'Yes, what did you do? How do you even know about Charlotte?'

'I know, right, because I'm just the silly wife that you think you can fool,' she snaps.

'What are you on about, Maya? You're not making any sense.' I shake my head, panic running through my veins, rage flooding into my mind too.

'I knew you were keeping something from me, and not just the normal stuff, not just the dates, but something big, something I ought to know,' Maya says, tears still streaming down her face as she takes a step towards me. I instinctively take a step back.

'So, I looked at your phone. I know I shouldn't have but I needed to find out the truth because, well—' Maya breaks off, barely able to look me in the eye. 'And Charlotte wanted to meet, knew you were keeping something from her too. And well, now I know the truth . . . about everything.'

I look at her, anger clouding over me. How dare she go through my phone? How dare she meet up with Charlotte? A young girl whose childhood is so complex that she needs good role models in her life. Not dysfunctional families and so-called friends who lie to each other. And how dare she look at me now like I'm some kind of murderer, when after years of seeing myself that way I was almost fooled that I could start to feel like me again. I can't look at her right now. Can't stomach the way she's staring at me. Can't feel the full breadth of these emotions without saying something, shouting something, I may regret. I move to turn away from her.

'Running away again?' she quips, her feigned surprise dripping with disdain.

'Maya, stop.' Her sentence halts me in my tracks, but I refuse to turn around. If I did, she'd see the tears falling from my eyes, even though, after today, I thought there were no tears left to fall. 'I need some fresh air, some space, before I say . . . this is all too much.'

'*I'm* too much?' she shouts incredulously even though that's not what I said. 'This is nothing to do with me. This is to do with you, lying, leaving.' She's sobbing now. 'Why is everybody so scared of *staying*, of saying the hard things, content to keep secrets and . . .'

Why is she saying *everybody*? I thought we were talking about me. About Charlie. Unless she's talking about her secrets too. Because I know for sure she has them too.

'What happened with your dad?' I turn to face her now.

'What do you mean?' She takes a step back, stung by the words.

'Adrian said something about your dad, to ask you what's going on with him.'

'Don't turn this around on me. I know your brother is dead. That you killed him.'

I swear my shoulders jolts forwards, winded by her words. No, I didn't. It was an accident. A terrible accident. I was drunk, I was a kid. I try to tell myself all the things my mum has just said, all the things I've longed to hear, that I knew I needed to face in order to be the kind of man deserving of Maya. Now,

296

she's looking at me like I'm capable of murder. And I can't stand it. Not from anyone. But especially, especially, not from her.

'I . . . I . . .' I stammer, not even attempting to hold back the tears now. 'I need to leave.'

'No,' Maya breathes. 'Stay . . .'

For a moment, I think she's going to soften, that she's going to say sorry – sorry she went behind my back, that she knows I'm not capable of that, that she knows what kind of man I am – but then she throws her next sentence at me.

'I'm going to be the one who gets to leave this time.'

Maya

The expression on Jack's face when I told him I was leaving follows me into the bedroom, as I grab my weekend bag and shove clothes into it at speed. I have no idea where I'm going or how long for, I just know I'm not going to be left behind this time. Not by my mum, or my dad, or Emmie, and especially, *especially,* not by Jack. A man I felt bad about lying to when he's been lying this whole time. A man I thought I was in love with even though it turns out I didn't know him at all. I didn't know a lot of things.

'Maya, wait . . .' Jack says, from behind me as soon as I open the front door.

'What?' What could he possibly say to fix this now?

'Why did you look at my phone in the first place?'

I turn around to look at him and realise, from his expression, he doesn't want to fix this. I'm not worth sticking with to work the hard stuff out. I'm the collateral damage, the one who falls through the gaps whilst people are too busy concentrating on other things.

'Why did you even care enough to go searching in the first place?' he asks, taking a step towards me, my hand trembling on the door still held ajar. I look into his dark eyes.

Because I thought I loved you. Because I think I still might. My mouth doesn't open. The words don't come. The fear of rejection. Of being seen, known. Unreservedly.

'I don't know what you want, Maya.' He throws his hands wide, exasperated.

I wanted you. I think I still might. I will myself to say something but how can I if what Charlotte said is true, if Jack is capable of killing the person he claims to love most.

'Maya, come on. Don't tell me you didn't know what you were doing, what you were looking for.' Jack is speaking quickly now. 'You always know what you want.'

'I don't . . . I . . .' The walls are caving in on our little life. The front door ajar, beckoning me away from it. From this place, from my parents, from the mess we've all made.

'Tell me what you want, Maya,' Jack says, his face heavy with emotion.

'Fine,' I say, knowing the words with the power to end this now. 'I want a divorce.'

Part 9

The Truth

Jack

I hear a knock on the front door and, for the briefest moment, part of me hopes that it's Maya. Returning for round two. Even though her words have left me wounded, I know that fighting with her feels better than this, a dead and eery silence.

'Dude,' I say, as soon as I swing open the door to see Adrian standing there. 'Thank you so much for coming.'

He's holding a four-pack of beer in his hands but right now, I don't want two beers. I want to get blind drunk or remain stone-cold sober, to feel every twist of the knife Maya has just forced into my healing heart.

'Man, you know you never need an excuse to invite me round to *this* place,' Adrian says, as I take a step back so that he can move into the hallway. He spins around, marvelling at its magnificence all over again. And my mind harps back to the first time I did the same, when an incredibly bad day turned into one of the best.

'Dude, are you *crying*?' Adrian stops his spinning to look at me now, tear marks tracking down my face before I can stop them.

I feel the sting of embarrassment, the same as I did when he first found me after fighting with my mum last year. Then I feel his arms wrapping around me, pulling me in tight, and I sob into his chest. He must think it's about her, but he doesn't know the half of it.

'This is about Maya, isn't it?'

I pull away, stunned by his words but too tired to cover over the truth. I'm done running away from the truth; it always manages to catch up with you anyway.

'Yeah, yes, it is,' I say slowly. 'It's about everything.'

'Oh, mate,' Adrian says, handing me the four-pack and turning back towards the door, opening it slightly but lingering, like Maya did. Is he leaving too?

'Where are you——?'

'Corner shop.' Adrian nods towards the four-pack. 'Sounds like we need some more.'

I pace around in silence, waiting for Adrian to return, trying to find somewhere to settle in this apartment that doesn't remind me of her. But how can I? Every inch of this place has Maya written all over it, from the faint smell of her shower gel that somehow follows her throughout the flat to the clutter of papers and books she leaves everywhere she goes.

'Talk to me,' Adrian says, as soon as he's drawn out a stool at the kitchen island.

'I don't even know where to begin.' I sigh, probably at the start. 'Maya and I . . . we . . .'

'Had sex? Had a fight?' Adrian's expression looks like he's got it all sussed, sorted.

'We got married.'

'You got *what*?' Now he looks anything but. 'Tell me you're joking!'

'I'm really not,' I say. 'We got the rings and everything.'

I reach to the neck of my T-shirt and pull out my chain, the gold wedding band hung around it.

'What the fuck? When? Why?' Adrian is on his feet now, too stunned to stay still.

'Around the time you moved in with Emmie.'

'What? Did Maya convince you to? Like getting married would be some kind of eff-you to Emmie for moving on without her?' Adrian shakes his head, throwing out his hands. I thought Maya was being paranoid when she said that Emmie would see things this way, but clearly, she had reason to, like there's been some kind of pressure to keep their lives in sync.

'No, dude,' I say, struggling to stay seated myself. 'I convinced Maya to marry me.'

'But why?'

'For a visa.'

'For a visa? I thought you *had* a visa. I thought Toby said he had it all in hand?' It only takes a raise of my eyebrow to convey that this wasn't ever the case. 'Why didn't you tell me? I could have helped out.' Another raise of the eyebrows silently asks *how*? 'Okay, okay, but couldn't you just have gone home for a bit and then—'

'That's the thing. I didn't think I *could* go home.'

'Because of your mum? Because of your fight?' Adrian asks at speed, his head oscillating from me to the door, as if he's not sure what surprises are going to barge in next.

303

'Because of what we fought about,' I say slowly. 'Charlie, and how he died.'

Adrian finally sits down, stunned, silent.

'He *died*?' He croaks, all defiance draining from his words.

'In a car accident.' I nod. 'And I thought I couldn't go home, I thought nobody would want me to go home, because, well, it should have been me who had died instead.'

'Come on, dude. That's not true.' I can tell Adrian is having to hold back tears.

'No, it is. I was meant to drive to get my parents that night, but I got drunk at a party and forced my brother to go instead. He'd literally just passed his test. He didn't want to. He wasn't ready,' I say, as Adrian's mouth hangs open. 'And some idiot who had been drinking and driving crashed into him. It was my fault he died.'

'Sounds like it was the fault of the driver who crashed into him.'

'Well, Charlie cut him up, swerved into his lane. My mum blamed me, told me she wished it had been me in that car instead.'

'Man, that's . . .'

'She also blamed herself, couldn't see clearly because everything was so screwed up, and there was nothing anyone could do to take it all back. And so I came to the UK, started uni, started volunteering, trying to earn my penance or something, have a do-over. I couldn't go back . . . I couldn't . . . and then Maya and I met at the party, and suddenly we were two people who were homeless, and she had this place but didn't want to stay here by herself.'

'Why?' Adrian asks, picking up on the most random bit of my story.

'She needed the rent and—'

'You think her dad needed rent for this place?' Adrian probes again. What is he getting at? 'Look, Jack, you can't say anything but . . . oh God, Emmie will kill me if she knows I'm telling you this . . .' Adrian winces at his own words. 'Dude, Maya's dad is dead.'

'What? No he's not. He lives in New York.'

'He *lived* in New York. He died six or seven months ago, cancer. She didn't really know him, he never tried to keep in touch after he left Maya and her mum, didn't want anything to do with them.'

I try to register what he's saying. Maya's dad is dead? And she had the gall to go on at me for not telling her about Charlie? Rage rises inside me, bubbling through my brain. But I can't help it. Despite everything Adrian is saying, a small bit of me still feels sorry for Maya. Which is the last thing she'd want. Which is why she would have chosen not to tell me in the first place.

'He left her the apartment, which was naturally a head-fuck, like she didn't want to take anything from him, her mum didn't want her to, apparently, and so—'

'She needed me to stomach staying here?' I ask, realising just how rocky my and Maya's beginnings were despite committing to the strongest union of all. How the boundaries that were meant to keep us safe have caused so much hurt to one another. Adrian nods.

'I think you guys need to talk, to just tell each other everything, have it all out.'

'I think we're a bit far past that now,' I say, mind still scrambling, sifting through everything Adrian has just said, everything I've just shared with him too. 'She went through my phone, met up with Charlotte, found out about Charlie, before I could tell her what . . .' I splutter my sentences. 'What really happened. She thinks I'm a killer.'

Adrian looks at me, placing a hand on my shoulder.

'Well, you're not.' He smiles. 'And from the things Emmie has been saying, I think Maya thinks something else, *feels* something else, about you entirely.'

Maya

It doesn't take me long to work out where I'm going. The only place in this city I've ever called home – anywhere I'm living with Emmie. Because she has always been my family, the one constant, even though her life has changed beyond recognition. So has the apartment.

'Oh, Maya,' she says, throwing her arms around me tightly. With my head resting on her shoulder, my eyes scan the room. Adrian's books have taken the space mine used to sit, he's moved in some new dark green chairs that are pulled up around the world's comfiest sofa too, the one that Emmie and I assembled together and have curled upon countless times. She will hate those green chairs with a vengeance. But they're here. A compromise. The kind you have to make if you want any relationship to work. The kind of compromise I was willing to make for Jack until I found out the truth about Charlie, the truth about my parents. The truth that lovers and liars go hand in hand, at least in my world.

'Emmie, everything's a mess . . . my mum lied to me, Jack lied to me too . . . everything's so screwed up. I just don't know what to think.'

I sob into her shoulder, and her arms tighten around me, attempting to hold me together. We both know after years of pretending I don't need anyone's help, it'll take a lot more than this.

'One thing at a time,' Emmie says, holding me closer. I don't deserve it.

'I've got so much to tell you.'

'One thing at a time,' Emmie repeats, as if talking to a child, and right now I feel like one. A shunned one, an abandoned one, one that has no bloody idea what is going on. Emmie lets go and steers us back into the apartment I slept in every night for years. I look around the place, feeling like a stranger inside it, even though I felt like a stranger at my dad's too. I only momentarily felt at home there because of Jack.

I look into Emmie's eyes, willing the words to come, but before I can tell her about Jack, our marriage, the visa, my phone begins to ring. It's my mum, calling me back, so long overdue. With so many things between us left unsaid.

'I can't . . . I . . .' I begin, looking from my phone to Emmie, my mind malfunctioning.

'What's happened?' Emmie says, her eyes fixed on my demanding phone screen. I swipe away my mum's call, sending it to voicemail and start to tell Emmie, everything. About Dad's computer desktop, about the Grand Canyon and all the gaping holes in everything I thought I knew about my parents.

'What the . . . ?' She exhales deeply.

'I know, my mum said he only tried to keep in touch for a couple of years after he moved to New York. But how do you explain the photos? The emails? The apartment?'

'I can't explain any of it,' Emmie responds slowly, her eyes drifting to my phone, the one call, the one connection that can solve this. If my mum doesn't try to explain it all away.

'I can't . . . not right now . . . things with Jack . . . I've got so much to tell you . . .'

'And we'll get to all of it,' Emmie says, reaching to put a hand to my knee, bent up on the sofa.

'Adrian's out,' she goes on. Three guesses where, or who with. The thought sends shockwaves through my body, but I will my eyes to remain on Emmie, my fixed point.

'One thing at a time,' she assures me again. 'Call her back.'

'Soon.'

'*Now.*'

I know Emmie is right, she usually is, always fighting for the best for me, even when it's not what I want for myself. Ever since I kept her out of this, shut her out of my silly decisions, my life has gone from bad to worse. As if I thought for a second that things could really work with Jack. Two broken people do not make a whole.

Reluctantly, I walk into the spare bedroom, the one that used to be mine. It's cleaner now, brighter, a fresh lick of paint covering all holes my pictures forced into the walls. Not one of them of my dad. Even though it turns out he had plenty of me. All stashed in the shadows, hidden away. And now I need my mum to finally shine a light on it all.

'Maya.' My mum picks up the phone after just one ring. It's like she knows something has happened, her 'mumtuition' kicking in when I assumed she'd worked it out of her system. 'How are you, darling? How's your research going? And findings?'

She asks the questions at speed, always somewhere better to be.

'Mum, I want to talk about Dad.'

'Maya Angela.' She says my name like a reminder again, maybe even a threat. 'I called to catch up with you, to talk about you, not your dad. Please, our time together is so rare now between my work and your studies, let's not let him waste it . . .'

I might have believed this when I was wrapped up in my research, my head stuck in a book or my laptop. But seeing as I've crashed and burned in that department lately, considering my latest *findings*, I know this excuse is all about her. I see, more clearly than ever now, that it usually is.

'Yes, but *I* want to talk about Dad.'

'Maya, *please* . . .'

'*Mum*, please,' I echo back, with all the strength she taught me to have. 'It's important.' I take her momentary silence as permission to go on. 'Dad left me an apartment, his apartment, in Wapping. He left it to me in his will.'

I let this confession dangle between us, waiting for what comes next. I listen carefully down the line, looking out of the bedroom window to the street below. Among the faint sound of traffic and people chatting just outside of the window, I hear my mum gasp, one of those double-breath inhales where there doesn't seem to be enough oxygen in the room.

'Mum? Did you hear what I said?'

'Yes, yes,' she says quickly, faintly, like she's trying to find her voice again. 'I just . . . I didn't know he kept that place.'

That's the surprising thing? Not that he left a multimillion-pound apartment to me?

'I didn't even know he *had* a place in London. Mum, why would Dad leave me an apartment when he died if he didn't even want to know me whilst he was alive?'

'I don't know, honey,' she says reluctantly now, her voice cracking. 'Maybe he was trying to make up for not being there, trying to make you miss him. But I mean, how can you miss someone who was never in your life in the first place?'

I groan, grunt in frustration.

'Mum, for a smart woman you can be pretty stupid.' It sounds harsh, it also sounds honest, more honest than I've been with her in years. 'Of course I missed him.'

'But you never really *knew* him,' she says, a last-ditch attempt to defend herself.

'No, but I missed a version of him. I missed having a dad all the time. I missed it when I won that spelling competition in Year Four. I missed him when I got into university. I missed him when I graduated. I missed him when I started my Masters . . .'

I missed him when I walked down the aisle, when I told Jack we should walk down together because I thought tradition was stupid, because even though I've never wanted to get married, I knew that my dad would never be there to walk me to the altar.

'I missed his presence all the time.'

Until I moved into his apartment, and his presence was everywhere. Taunting me, mocking me, telling me that something didn't add up, that something didn't sit right.

'You told me he didn't want me, he didn't want us.'

'He didn't.'

'Then what about the photos in his apartment, the emails you sent him?'

Everything falls quiet, deadly still apart from the sound of sobs down the line.

'Mum?'

'I was trying to protect you,' she mummers, her voice laced with fear.

'But what from?'

'From him hurting you the way he hurt me.'

'What do you mean?' Then a name darts across my mind. *Lisa.* 'Mum, who's Lisa?'

'Lisa was your dad's secretary,' she says, reluctantly, like she's having to dig deep inside herself to yank out this fact. 'The love of his life, the one he chose over us.'

As soon as this bomb drops, my stomach sinks to the floor.

'I didn't want to tell you, we *were* doing better without him,' she goes on, her sentences stumbling over one another. 'I thought it would be simpler if he left for work and not another woman. It was easier for me—'

'Mum, slow down. I need you to tell me everything.'

Mum inhales deeply, gasping for air as she promises that the story she told me was true: that my dad did get a job he couldn't refuse, that their relationship wasn't working, that they decided to go their separate ways. But then she tells me how they stayed in touch, that she sent photos of me to him all the time, that he still cared, despite his new job, his new life.

'On some strange level, it made me respect him more.' My mum sighs, and I can imagine her shaking her head, cursing herself for the thought. 'I'd never met anyone more ambitious than me before, and every time I missed him, I channelled it into my work, into climbing the ladder, into being the best lawyer I could be. Then he stopped replying, stopped taking my calls, and it drove me crazy.' She cries down the line. 'Honestly, juggling a young daughter and work alone, it was just so much. I kept sending him photos of you, kept hoping that he was just busy, that I was overthinking things, that he hadn't pulled away from us completely. Because the man I fell in love with was ambitious, but he wasn't cold. I didn't think he'd be the kind of person to turn away from his daughter just like that.'

I listen to her talking on and on, trying to take it all in. Her words are set to a backdrop of car horns and moving traffic, but somehow my mum has found enough space in the city that never sleeps to speak to her daughter. Or maybe it's that she's finally *making* space. I've never heard her talk with such emotion, never had her open up to me like this. It's only now that she is that I realise how much I've been longing for this.

'Then what happened? You threw yourself into work and forgot all about him?'

A silence stretches on for so long that I have to check the line hasn't gone dead.

'I went to New York, I went to see him, when I couldn't take the silence any longer.'

'When? Where was—?'

'You were on holiday with Emmie's family in Cornwall, and I was on gardening leave before my new job. They put me on it to rest. But I didn't want to rest, I wanted to work, keep busy, not think about your father and why he didn't want to know us anymore.'

'Did you manage to see him?'

'Yes, and, well, we kept seeing each other for a bit, going back and forth, between both cities. That's when your dad got the Wapping apartment. He said it was a good financial

312

investment, but I thought . . . I thought maybe he was investing in me.'

She sounds so broken, vulnerable, that for a moment my anger wanes.

'But something didn't feel right. He asked me to keep it a secret, even from you. I thought it was just until we were going to work out how to make the cross-Atlantic thing work this time, our second chance to start again, but he slipped up, called me Lisa by accident and then, then everything began to unravel again. Turns out he was still with Lisa at this point, that they'd been together for years. He made *me* the other woman, the mother of his child, do you know how *embarrassing* that is?'

'Is that why you stopped talking again? Because you were *embarrassed*?' I feel the rage starting to rumble inside me again, escaping into my voice.

'No, I was willing to keep in touch, figured that having a flawed father in your life may be better than not having him there at all.' Mum's voice is deep, slow, like she's having to force herself to wade through the words. 'But Lisa found out about the affair and that was that. She said that it was us or her, and . . . and he chose her. A man that didn't even choose to stay in the same country as his own flesh and blood, chose *her*.'

Tears are falling down my face now, her heartbreak hurting every part of me.

'Then your dad got sick, they broke up and he started reaching out again, but you were doing so well, had your plans and your passions and your friends, and I just . . . I don't know . . . I couldn't risk having him come back into our lives and throw everything off course again. But I'm so sorry, Maya, I'm so sorry. That wasn't my decision to make but . . .'

313

A silence simmers between us, neither one of us knowing what to fill it with.

'Love makes people do crazy things,' my mum whispers eventually. I know this now.

'You must have really loved him,' I say softly. I thought they hated each other. But I know the kind of bravery it takes to commit to spending your life with just one person now. There is so much to take in, so much information and revelation to process, but against the anger and the confusion that is swirling in my stomach, I know there is empathy there too.

'I never stopped loving him, Maya.' Mum cries. 'I was just so stubborn, refusing to surrender, and then . . . then . . . it was all too late. And I never got a chance to tell him the truth.'

Jack

'What do you mean she feels something else about me entirely?' I say, my mind literally unable to compute anything else after today. The days after Charlie's death were like a sharp decline, until I was wading through the monotony of mourning. Today has felt like a roller coaster: the refreshing wash of forgiveness before whatever shitstorm just happened with Maya. Adrian looks back at me, eyes wide, lips pursed.

'Emmie would kill me.' He shakes his head quickly.

'Then why did you *say* anything?' I throw a hand to my head in frustration.

'Because, dude, you're my best mate and I can't just have you beat yourself up like this; it sounds like you've done enough of that for a lifetime.'

The sentence lingers between us: we both know that 'life-time' is a relative term.

'Then what does Maya feel for me?' I say, thoughts of her standing there in her underwear staring back at me, rolling over on her side in the bed, the morning light hitting her as she breathed the first hello of the day, rushing through my mind. Could she like me like I like her? Even love me like I love her? But no, I saw the way she looked at me, like I was just one of many men in her life to distance myself from her and yet still be able to mess with her head completely. I can't believe her dad is dead. That she wouldn't tell me. They say marriage doesn't complete you, that two broken people don't make a whole. But all Maya and I seem to have done together is make a whole lot more mess.

'Ask her yourself,' Adrian says, in a way that tells me that even though he's my best mate, even though he doesn't want me to beat myself up, he also doesn't want to be beaten up by his fiancée. That's where his loyalties lie now; the shifting allegiance of falling in love.

Ask her yourself. For a moment it sounds so simple. But I asked her, didn't I? Just hours ago. Maya, what do you want? Tell me what you want. And she told me. A divorce. She wants a divorce. Because maybe if she wasn't grieving the loss of her dad, wasn't trying to make sense of his last-ditch attempt to provide for her, she wouldn't have agreed to marry me in the first place. I know too well what grief can do to a person.

'So, what are you going to do now?' Adrian asks, eyes darting towards the door. He thinks Maya could come home any minute, but I know she won't. Her home was with Emmie and, try as she might, she's not been able to patch up a replacement.

She helped me patch over my past too, by giving me the visa. And I know I can't deny her what she wants now. Which leaves me only one option; one that doesn't feel as impossible as it did before.

'I think it's time for me to go home.'

Maya

'How did it go?' Emmie is lingering outside the bedroom door when I emerge.

'It was . . .' I search for the words, but my head is a tangle of thoughts. 'It was *a lot*.'

'Well, I figured that much,' Emmie says. 'Given that you've been on the phone for three hours and your mum hasn't cut you short for a meeting.'

I watch as she puts her index finger and middle finger to her lips, before reaching to sort out the mascara smudges under my eyes. It's the kind of unspoken intimacy that I know takes years to curate. I laugh, a fragile laugh that could break into tears at any second. Emmie has always had my back when it comes to my parents, but I know now that I've got them all wrong. That my mum has been hiding her heartbreak in her work, that I have too. Because my studies felt safe, until my questioning felt too unruly to usher anywhere.

Emmie steers me over to the sofa, before pouring me a glass of wine.

'Now, tell me everything,' she says, as I take a tentative first sip.

And I do. I tell her about my mum, about Lisa, about

everything she's been holding back. About the photos, about the emails, about the fact that my mum's stubbornness got in the way of her saying all the things she wanted to say: *I'm sorry and I miss you*. And her secret *I love you*. I tell her how I'm angry at my mum, that she should have told me sooner. But that we've agreed to talk again, to keep talking until we've worked everything out. That when you strip away all the work and status and ambition, we're all each other really has. Even as I say this last part, I know it's not true, that my parents' instability led me straight into the arms of Emmie. That I've found my family in friendship instead.

Emmie just sits, sips, listens and nods, every now and then adding a '*no*' or a '*no way*' or simply a gasp. She doesn't interrupt or say '*me too*' or one-up my stories, she doesn't even break my eye contact until her phone starts to buzz and I nod my permission for her to read the message.

'It's Adrian, he's coming back, in about half an hour,' she says, looking up from the phone. 'You're totally welcome to stay,' she adds quickly, already looking sorry for something, 'but he's bringing Jack back here.'

'I can't see him,' I say, realising that we've not even got to this part yet, that for all of Emmie's 'one step at a time' this is the one final leap between us.

'I know,' Emmie coos, even though she doesn't know at all.

'There's something I've not told you about us,' I say slowly, as Emmie listens on. 'We got married. Jack and I got married.'

As soon as I've said the words, her supportive smile drops, her eyes widen, lips parting, hovering open in a perfect 'O' shape. It would almost be comical if the fear of losing her too wasn't too much to bear. Then she tilts her head, and she laughs.

317

'Maya, be serious,' she says, her giggles subsiding as she realises that I'm not laughing back, that I couldn't look more serious if I tried.

'When?'

'Nearly three months ago.' Emmie's jaw drops, but she says nothing so I carry on before she can stop me. 'We connected at the party, as you know, and he told me about Adrian moving in here and I was drunk and down about Mum missing another catch-up and my dad leaving me the apartment . . .'

This part makes a bit more sense now, but I wish I could tell that to Emmie's face, she looks entirely lost, like she's landed in the desert without directions.

'So, we left together, and he had just been told his visa application had fallen through, that he couldn't go home, and I couldn't stay in the apartment without him, but with my mum leaving and my PhD only just starting and . . . I just felt like I had nowhere else to go . . .'

'You could have stayed here, I told you that you could stay here.' Emmie's face is like thunder, her tone tense, as though she's about to cry or slap me or explode into some other extreme.

'And feel like a spare part, a third wheel, whilst you and Adrian set up your new lives together? It would have been unbearable, for both of us. It was time for us both to grow up.'

'So, you got married to a stranger?' Emmie is yelling now. I wince. He's not a stranger. He's her fiancé's best friend. 'Do you know how *childish* that is?'

I begin to cry, cursing the fact that I can't find a more grown-up response.

'It didn't feel it at the time,' I whisper. 'You know I've never wanted to get married, that I thought it was just a piece of

318

paper. I had no idea that my parents' break-up wasn't anything other than just business, they cut each other out so easily, so completely, that it just . . . I just thought . . . And I had no idea what Jack was running from back home.'

I think of Charlie again, of Charlotte's words: *I think he might have killed him.*

'I thought that if he could just get his visa, live in the apartment for a bit, Jack would be able to get permanent residency, and I'd be able to break the back of my studies and find some head space to sell the apartment, get rid of my dad's guilt-money.'

Emmie just looks at me, standing to her feet now, like she doesn't recognise me.

'Why didn't you tell me sooner?' she demands.

'I thought you'd tell me not to do it, that you'd think it was about my dad or . . .'

'Well, yeah,' Emmie throws her arms wide, before pinching the bridge of her nose.

'Then I thought, well, what's the point in saying anything before we know we're going to *get* the visa . . .' I go on, tears still tracking down my face. 'So, we waited . . .'

'And waited . . .' Emmie says, pacing now.

'After we got the visa, we were going to tell you, but then you told us you were engaged and you were so happy and I didn't want to steal your limelight, or make a mockery of your decision to get married because, well, I think you're actually really brave and—'

'Brave?' Emmie says, stopping her pacing to look at me now.

'I thought marriage was stupid, that people felt they needed to do it to prove something to themselves, or to other people. I thought it was to do with ownership, finances . . . but I see

319

now that it's the most vulnerable commitment you can make, that it does away with feelings and replaces it with a choice, the commitment to choose the other person, above all else, and choose them when they piss you off and choose them when they squeeze the toothpaste all wrong and choose them again and again and again.'

There was a moment where I would have chosen Jack. But he never gave me the option. Held so much of himself back.

'I am sorry I didn't tell you sooner, but I would have done, I would have told you everything. As soon as you had the perfect engagement, the perfect wedding you deserve.'

'I don't need it to be perfect,' Emmie says, softening slightly. 'I just needed you to be there. All of you. Do you not think I knew you were keeping something from me? We've been best friends for years.'

'I know, I just thought you'd be so angry and—'

'Oh, don't get me wrong,' Emmie says, looking me dead in the eye. 'I'm fucking fuming.' I flinch at the words. 'But that's the brilliant thing about family, you can be angry with each other and it doesn't do a single thing to the love.'

I didn't think I knew that love, but I know now that my mum did. That she felt so angry at my dad but never stopped loving him. She just let it be a wedge between them in all the wrong ways, thought unrequited love was worse than unspoken love before it was too late.

'So yes, I'm angry, and yes, I wish you'd told me sooner, but I love you, Maya, and love goes to all the awkward, messy, working-through-it places. So, buckle up, bestie,' she says, as she comes to sit alongside me, reaching for my hand. 'I'm in this for the long haul.'

'Me too,' I say, as she throws her arms around me.

'So, what are you going to do now?' Emmie asks, looking towards the door. 'Do you want to wait here, talk things through with Jack?'

'No, no, I'm not ready for that.'

'Okay. Then what do you want?'

I have to hold back the tears at the thought of Jack's face, screaming at me to tell him what I want, looking at me like I'm too demanding and difficult to put up with any longer.

'I think I'm going to go home . . . like, back to my dad's apartment,' I say, I can't see Jack right now, not after how we left things. I need space, I need to think. And though I never thought I'd get that at the apartment without Jack there, I think it's finally time to face the thoughts that felt so threatening when I refused to stare them right in the face.

'Do you want me to come with you?' Emmie says, squeezing my hand in hers.

'No, it's okay,' I say. 'I love you, but I think tonight, I just need to be alone.'

Somehow alone doesn't feel so lonely when someone is offering to be there with you.

Eighty-six Days Married

Jack

The low hum of traffic rouses me from my sleep, the last of the summer sun barging itself into the room through the broken blinds hanging precariously above the window. It's no ivory tower, but I can tell why Maya loved being in this place. The single-glazed windows are so thin that you can hear the chatter of locals standing just outside; it feels like you're a part of something.

Three days have passed since I spoke to Maya. If you can call what we did speaking. Shouting, crying, accusing, demanding. It's the kind of drama I thought I'd left back in Auckland, the kind of drama that back home sounds like it may be subsiding. There was once a time when I thought that our so-called friends wouldn't speak about anything else. But, after another call with my mum, after her reaction when I said I'd be flying back to see her and my dad – if they'd have me – I feel sure that people have better things to talk about now. There's always another drama, but for us – for me, my mum and my dad – we'll never,

ever forget my brother's death; we might not want to live with it, but Charlie would want us to *live*.

I pull on my jeans and a jumper before walking out into the living room. Maybe if I'd done that back at the apartment, maybe if Maya had kept her clothes on too, things wouldn't have got so heated between us. But I know any attraction I had to Maya was less to do with her body, her beauty, and more to do with her mind, her determination, her grit. It's the kind of single-mindedness that got her down the aisle, and it's the very single-mindedness that tells me that since she's decided she wants a divorce she won't settle until she's single again. As I walk into the room, I see Emmie in the kitchenette, every part of me wishing it was Maya.

'Oh, I . . .' She looks up at me like she's forgotten I'm staying here. She wraps her dressing gown further around herself and smiles. 'I'm sorry, I thought you'd be out at the office by now.'

I've been working like crazy the past two days, wrapping up my work with SoberApp, preparing handover notes for the next poor sod to come and work with Toby. Though, to his credit, when I told him things hadn't worked out between me and my wife and that I would be heading back to Auckland, he was oddly sympathetic. I guess once you're a part of the husband-crew, you stay a part of the husband-crew.

'No work today.' I'm not quite sure what Emmie knows; how much Maya has told her.

'Want one?' Emmie looks down at the orange juice she's just poured.

'Thanks.' I nod, our silent agreement that we won't go deep today, that we'll pussyfoot around the apartment together whilst Adrian is out and not talk about the elephant in the room. But like with all the vows I've made recently, this is another I can't keep. 'Is Maya . . .?'

'She's okay,' Emmie says quickly, narrowing her eyes in defence or as if to say: *I've given you an OJ so please don't ask anything more of me today.* I get it. Our lines of loyalty are clearly drawn; it's why I know Adrian will never talk to Maya about me either. Not that she wants to hear from me right now. But I wonder how much he's said to his fiancée.

'I'm assuming Adrian has told you everything?' I laugh nervously, almost hopefully. Because Lord knows Maya's version of events will not be nearly as empathetic. Emmie looks at me blankly, holding her robe even tighter around herself. 'About Charlie? And the accident?'

Her frame stiffens, like I've just applied pressure to an old bruise.

'I know . . . enough,' she says suspiciously, and I swear, looking past me, eyes searching for the nearest possible exit. Then her gaze lands on the top of my chest, just under my neck. I reach my hand to the spot she's looking at, wondering if I've just dribbled orange juice onto myself, but then I feel the cold, hard metal of my wedding band on the chain. I tuck it into my jumper.

'Good, so I hope you know that it was an accident. I didn't kill my brother or whatever crazy stuff Maya heard from my mentee at Girls Code.'

I still can't believe Maya took Charlotte's word over mine. But then, I thought I'd murdered my brother too, until I started talking about it, letting the light in, scaring the shame away. Plus, it's not like I got a chance to explain. And now I never will, but maybe, if I can convince Emmie, then somehow, some way, Maya will know the truth.

'I thought the car accident was my fault for a long time,' I go on.

'Were you the one driving?' Emmie asks.

'You genuinely don't know?'

'Look, Jack,' she says softly. 'Adrian and I have spent hours talking about you and Maya, convincing ourselves that we knew what was going on, and we *never* could have guessed you got married. So, forgive me if we've given up trying to get to the bottom of you two. Plus, I don't know if you've noticed but we've got our own wedding to plan.'

'I know, I know,' I say, putting my hands up in surrender. But she doesn't look angry, not like Maya did. She just looks tired of it all, surrendered, like: *it happened and it's over now, so deal with it*. Which is exactly what I'm going to do back in Auckland. Hug my parents, catch up on lost time, apologise to Laura Mae for cutting her out, for any of the blame I tried to apportion to her. *It's happened and it's over now, so deal with it.*

Before she can stop me, I'm telling Emmie all about the accident, how I'd blamed myself, to the point where I felt like a killer too. About losing touch with my mum, about finding her again. That she's been able to forgive herself, forgive me, and that now, I think I'm ready to forgive myself too. Since finally facing things with my mum, something has shifted inside me. My thoughts are coming thick and fast, and now that I've stopped bottling them in, started sharing them out loud, I can't seem to stop. It's like someone is bleeding a radiator inside my brain and I must drain out all the dirty liquid before the water begins to run clear.

'That's why I'm going,' I continue as Emmie simply listens

325

on. 'I am done trying to make sense of stuff, but I at least want to try and make my peace with it.'

'Going *where*?' Emmie asks, after the silence she needs to filter through my confession.

'Back to Auckland, New Zealand,' I say. Her eyes widen.

To be fair, I only told Adrian that I booked the flight last night. That I quit my job yesterday, *again*. That I couldn't keep running. And that a small part of me knows that Maya needs to be here in the spare bedroom, *her* bedroom, with Emmie, and she won't step foot in this place until she knows I've gone. We both need our families.

'When?' Emmie asks.

'Tonight.'

'But that's . . . so soon,' Emmie says, looking genuinely sorry to see me go.

'It's been five years.' I give her a sad smile. 'Trust me, it's long overdue.'

Maya

'Is the job going okay though?' I ask as Mum takes a sip of her wine, reclining into the velvet sofa she's sitting upon. I've never seen her recline in her life. The video fumbles for a second and I know that she's swinging her legs around so that they're lying along the length of the sofa, the way I often laid when I was stretching my way into Jack.

'It's great,' she says, her smile flickering slightly. And it's not the video.

'Mum?' I say sternly. This is our third call since we first

spoke about Dad and we've each had to make a constant effort not to fall back into our self-control comfort zones.

'The job is fine, good people and great work,' she goes on. 'But it's weird being here, in New York, knowing that this was your dad's place . . . you know, his city.'

We both know if either of us is in my dad's place, it's me. But then, he rarely spent any time here. Apart from the time he was making an 'other woman' out of my mum.

'He doesn't own the place,' I say softly. And he doesn't own this one anymore. I've spent the whole day with my phone off until now, not trying to work, or research or force myself to fill the silence. I've just sat in it, *with* it, until it doesn't feel so deafening anymore.

'No, I know, and I know, as I make new memories here, it'll start to feel like my own.'

'Yeah,' I smile, looking to my feet on the cushions, remembering a time when they used to hang over Jack's bare legs, back in the heatwave, when my feelings for him felt too much. But not in a bad way. I know we made some good memories here too.

'I just keep thinking about how I never got a chance to say goodbye,' Mum whispers.

'Nor did I,' I say before I can stop myself; but I wasn't thinking about Dad.

'I know, honey, and I'm so sorry, I'm so—'

'I know, Mum,' I say. I know she is. And I know she didn't mean to mess things up for me the way she did; hurt people hurt people. 'Mum, what do you think Dad would have said if you told him, you know, that you still loved him?'

'I don't know,' she says genuinely. 'I'm pretty sure he would have said he didn't feel the same way, that he only ever truly loved Lisa. I thought telling him would only make sense if he said the same things back, but . . . telling him would have still released something from me, would have still enabled me to move on . . .'

'You will move on,' I say, feeling that lump in my throat again. 'You'll keep making memories and the hard ones will come with you, but you'll have lots of good ones to carry around too.' I know as I'm saying the words, I'm trying to tell myself they're true.

'And maybe some memories with you?' My mum asks this cautiously. We've decided to take this new, honest mum-and-daughter dynamic slowly, not run before we can walk. 'It'll be nice to show you around New York a bit.'

'Yeah, I've got—'

'Yes, I know you have your PhD.' I've told her I've struggled to get into it this time, but I've not told her that I'm not sure I even *want* to do it anymore. It's a fledging thought. One that I want to give myself the time to tease out a little before letting her opinions in. Unlike all the other boundaries I've had of late, this one feels healthy.

'Maybe I can come around Christmastime? Before my bridesmaid duties really start to ramp up next year.'

'Oh, that would be amazing! You'll love Christmas in New York, ice skating by the tree at the Rockefeller Center . . .' My mum's excitement spills between us before she holds herself back, remembering again what we said about not ramping up our relationship too fast. 'Yes, yes, that sounds good,' she says, but still, her keenness makes me smile.

Then, I hear the doorbell ring. I look in the direction of

the door leading from the living room out into the hall, imagining who might be standing outside Apartment 100. Part of me hopes it's Jack.

'Look, Mum, someone's at the door, I've got to go.'

'Okay, honey, speak soon,' she says, and as we say goodbye, I know she means it.

Rushing to the door, I pause at the handle. I'm in sweatpants, a T-shirt, no make-up, no bra, but if it is Jack, I know he's seen a whole lot more of me. Physically, emotionally.

'I've been trying to call you all day!' Emmie says, slightly out of breath, her long hair messy and falling loose, her lightweight jumper slung over an old pair of jeans.

'It's only four,' I laugh, but then I see her expression. What have I done now?

'We need to talk about Jack.' What has *he* done now? Emmie barges her way into the entrance hall and through the door into the living room as if she owns the place.

'Okay, so he lied about his brother being dead but to be fair you lied about your dad. And the teenagers at Girls Code didn't have the full story. How could they? They're *teenagers*. Jack was that girl's mentor; he wasn't going to tell her—'

'He told her a whole lot more than me!' I say, remembering every bombshell of her reveal all over again, that the truth hurt almost as much as the fact he hadn't told me first.

'Yes, but he didn't tell you what really happened, that he was meant to be the one driving the night that Charlie died, that he drunkenly begged for Charlie to go to the airport to pick up his parents and his parents refused to get an Uber because they thought Jack was just trying to wiggle out of his responsibilities, they didn't know he was drunk, they didn't know he'd

329

asked Charlie to step in and then . . . then he swerved into the wrong lane and . . .'

I see it, visualise it all, the screech of the breaks, it slices through my heart.

'His mum couldn't handle the pain, said she wished it was him who died instead,' Emmie continues and I have to sit down, I feel physically sick. 'He came here for a fresh start, to not be that guy anymore and then you found out and you looked at him like—'

'Like he killed his little brother,' I say, barely audible through my bated breath.

'Like he was the kind of monster he had just convinced himself he wasn't,' Emmie continues, as the room spins.

What have I done? My mind races, adrenalin surging through me, until my limbs are shaking.

'His mum is in a better place now . . .'

Her voice softens as I think of my own mum too, about how love and losing it can make someone do and say inconceivable things. It's the reason I never wanted to fall into it in the first place. Emmie puts a hand on my leg, her chest still heaving with the urgency of travelling across town to find me and tell me. And I know that love also has the power to do inconceivably selfless things. Like be angry but still love someone.

Like finding the power to forgive.

'He's heading home,' Emmie says.

'Here? This evening?' I ask, knowing this is my chance to make things right.

'No.' Emmie shakes her head slowly. 'Home to New Zealand. His flight is tonight.'

I know in that moment I need to tell him everything.

Regardless of what he says in return. My mum didn't have the chance to come clean, to endure or enjoy the release of knowing you've given all you've got to give, said all you needed to say. I need to tell him the truth before it's too late. That I lied to him, that I've been lying to myself. That I lied when I promised that I would never, ever let myself fall in love with him.

Jack

I head to the Big Sibling Scheme Headquarters, a title far too grandiose for a modestly small room at the back of the Students' Union. Having to leave without saying goodbye to the teenagers at Girls Code sucks but I know if I don't leave now, I never will. Hopefully Charlotte will forgive me for breaking off our mentorship via text. At least as far as she's concerned, there's obviously a bit more to it behind the scenes, which is exactly why I arranged a meeting with Josie, my main contact at the scheme, before my flight tonight. But as I walk into the room, I'm surprised to find Josie and the other volunteers aren't alone. Standing there, under a banner that looks like it was made in about ten minutes, are the girls, all of them: Rosa and Zadie and Sara and Charlotte step forward as I read the banner: 'See ya' and smaller, beside it, *'wouldn't want be ya'*. I have to laugh to stop from tearing up.

'I told you he would cry,' Zadie turns to Sara. Once again, they see right through me.

'What are you all doing here?' I say, swallowing the frog in my throat.

'What do you think?' Sara pipes up now. 'That we'd let you leave the country without saying goodbye?' Well, yes. That's what happened the last time I left a country.

'But how did you know?'

'Charlie told us,' Rosa says.

'Of course she did,' I say, rolling my eyes, and the girls laugh, but Charlotte looks a little worried.

We've exchanged a few messages since her meeting with Maya, mostly on my part saying that I'm sorry Maya contacted her, that it never should have happened and was completely, one hundred per cent out of character. And that I was sorry I was so shady about my story that she got the wrong end of the stick, admitted that sometimes half-truths are just as bad as lies, given they do such a good job as masquerading as fact.

'Are you still angry at me?' she asks eventually, a good half an hour later as the girls each say goodbye and head off into the rest of their evenings.

'I was never angry at you in the first place.' I shake my head.

'But I never should have met Maya without telling you.'

'And she should have never contacted you in the first place,' I say. Charlotte is only seventeen, there's a lot of growing up that happens between her age and ours. Well, *should* happen. Maya and I have done a good job of acting like children lately.

'But are you and Maya okay?' Charlotte asks, on the verge of tears.

'Maya will be fine,' I say, and I know that she will be, that she's got through much worse before. 'And it's better this way,' I say, only then realising I mean this too. 'We were pretending to be something we weren't. I was pretending to be something I wasn't too.'

'I can't believe you are married,' Charlotte shakes her head.

'Not for long,' I smile back to her kindly. 'Not now that I can go home.'

Charlotte looks gutted for a moment, before she forces a wide smile.

'You'll be fine without me,' I say quickly, hating that I'm bailing on her, letting her down when I know just how much she's come to depend on me. 'Better than fine, you're going to thrive, Charlotte. At whatever you put your mind to. I know it.'

'I . . .' Charlotte begins, and I inhale, preparing myself for her tears. 'I know.'

'And I'll miss you,' I say, that damn lump catching in my throat again.

'I know that too,' she says softly.

'So, you don't hate me for leaving?'

'Why on earth would I hate you for leaving?' Charlotte laughs before me.

'Because you, erm . . .' I stutter, stunned by how confident she looks now. 'You said you depended on this place, on me being there, week in week out.'

'Sure,' Charlotte shrugs, smiling broadly. 'But we all know you need this place more than we do.' She laughs again. 'We thought our graduation would break your heart.'

And here I was, assuming that me not being there for them would break *them* completely. I laugh, shaking my head at my own self-importance. Charlotte's right, I did need this place as much as they needed me. I needed them to remind me of the kind of guy I wanted to be, the sort of guy that Charlie would be proud of.

'Plus, now I have a "Big Brother" in Auckland. That's pretty cool, I guess,' Charlotte says, her smile faltering once more. 'It's just, you and Maya . . .'

'Maya will be *fine*,' I repeat.

'Yeah,' Charlotte says, smiling slightly. 'It's not her I'm worried about.'

'Hey, you leave the worrying to me, I'm the big sibling, remember?' I laugh, opening my arms to give her a hug goodbye. If I don't leave here soon and head back to Adrian's to bundle my baggage into his car and head to the airport, we'll never make it on time.

'You should know by now this sibling thing works both ways,' she says.

'Thanks . . .' I whisper, memories of my brother held somewhere in our hug '. . . Charlie.'

Maya

Emmie flings open the door into her apartment. I wait at the threshold, hesitating in the exact same spot that Jack dithered when he first arrived at our house party all those months ago. I wonder if he knew I was going to be there that night, whether he and Adrian searched through our uni photos to find out just how many memories we unintentionally accrued together before they came crashing into our lives again. Crashing like Charlie; a moment so uncontrollable and irrevocable that it leaves you forever changed.

What do I say to him now? Where on earth do I find the words big enough to encompass everything that needs to be said, the mess we've just made? No wonder he didn't want to tell me about what happened to Charlie when I just cut him out at the first utterance of it. Emmie turns back to me, and I know I need to start small. One step at a time. She walks into the room and I follow, ready to say I'm sorry. For everything. I love you. I miss you . . .

'We've missed them,' Emmie says, looking up from the kitchen counter at the far side of the room, the room that I've only just about registered is empty.

'What do you mean we've missed them?' I ask, panic rising in my veins, escaping in my voice. Emmie holds up a hand-written note, scribbled at speed. 'What does it say?'

'It just says that Jack was on standby for an earlier flight, and they think they can make it. They're on their way to the airport now.'

'Crap, why didn't he tell you, tell us?' I say, my legs feeling like jelly beneath me.

'I don't know, it's not like you and Jack ended on a good note though, is it?'

As soon as she says this, I start to cry. Jack is leaving the country. Because of me. Because I said I wanted a divorce. When, in reality, I want anything but.

'That's it, then . . .' I say through sobs, a pain searing through my heart like it might break in two, Jack about to take a piece of it halfway around the world.

'No, no, it's not over,' Emmie says, quickly reaching for her phone.

What is she doing? She swipes the screen and puts the

phone to her ear. Then, another phone begins to ring, from somewhere across the room. It sounds muffled, far away, and Emmie follows the noise like a sniffer dog on the prowl. She starts flinging off the sofa cushions at speed, reclaiming the ringing phone from down the side of the cushions.

'*Crap*,' she says. 'It's Adrian's phone, he must have not had time to find it in the rush. I guess that explains the note. Call Jack.'

'And say what?' I cry back.

'All the things you want to say to his face.'

'I haven't quite worked them out,' I say, but seeing the seriousness of her expression, the tense shape of her posture, I know I don't have any time for a messy first draft. With shaking hands, I reach into my pocket and pull out my phone, swiping to his number. I call and it goes straight to voicemail. I call again and it does the same.

'We're too late,' I say, the tears flooding down my face now.

'No, we can't be,' Emmie says, flicking through her phone. 'Jack's plane was from Heathrow at 23:55. So, he must be getting on the one before, that's 21:55. And it's just gone seven p.m. . . .' She doesn't look up from her phone, but I can tell she's swiping to her Citymapper app. 'It says it'll take around ninety minutes to get there if we leave now . . . so we'll get there around half eight. And we can keep ringing him on the way.'

'Is this crazy?' I look at my best friend. 'I never thought I'd be the kind of woman to chase a man to the airport.'

'You also didn't think you'd be the kind of woman to fall in love with her husband.'

'But this is *insane*, and it might not even work.'

'Yes,' Emmie says, making her way to the door. 'But there's also a chance it might.'

336

Jack

'Dude, can we listen to some music?' I ask as I watch London drift away outside of the car window. I can't believe in just over twenty-four hours I'll be back on the streets of Auckland, on the roads where the worst thing happened. The dread of being there is soothed every time I remember my mum's voice on the phone, how much things have changed, how much I have changed. But right now, I need something to quieten, drown out my thoughts.

'Radio's bust,' Adrian shakes his head.

'Could play some on your phone?' I ask, desperate for distraction.

'I left it at home, couldn't find it before we left.'

'I'm sorry, I just thought . . .'

'Dude, stop being sorry,' Adrian says back. 'You're right, this is a better time than driving you in the dead of night. And I've left Emmie a note. Got music on yours?'

'Sure, but shit . . . the battery's pretty low already and I need it for check-in.'

'Stick it on flight mode, it'll save the battery.'

'Sure,' I repeat, no scope for independent thinking right now. I flick my screen up until the little plane icon is showing at the top of my screen. My stomach turns at the sight. I'm going to be on one of those in a matter of hours. And then I'll be on a one-way ticket out of here. Away from Maya.

'What would I do without you, mate?' I move my phone into the holder suspended from the dashboard.

'Let's hope you never have to find out.' He grins, eyes glued on the road before him.

Adrian turns the volume up and I try to concentrate on the lyrics, not listen to the small voice in my head that tells me I should have tried harder to say goodbye. But Maya didn't want that, did she? She wants a divorce; I remind myself for the thousandth time since our fight. She thinks I killed Charlie and she wants a divorce. But then Charlotte's face comes into my mind again: *It's just, you and Maya* . . . The thought of it niggles away, reminding me how strange it was that Maya went behind my back, met up with her. It's the kind of thing I would have done when I let myself fall for Laura, when I didn't know better.

It's just you and Maya . . . the thought plays on repeat as I try to listen to the music. How is it that you don't realise that almost every song ever written is about love, falling in or out of it, until you're trying to leave somebody behind?

After minutes that seem to stretch for miles, Heathrow Airport finally comes into view, and we follow the signs for the terminal until Adrian eventually pulls up at the drop-off point. 'You sure you don't want me to park up, mate?'

'Only if you want to see me cry like a baby.' I laugh but we both know I'm not joking. 'But no, mate, seriously. You've done enough. You should get back to your wife.'

I know we're both trying not to mention mine.

'Hey, she's not my wife yet.' Adrian laughs. 'But soon.' He smiles. 'And I know you'll have loads to work out and it's a lot of money and everything, but the wedding won't be the same without you, mate. You're my best man, bro.'

'I'm not your best man,' I say, shaking my head at him as I open the car door.

'Well, I mean, *technically* my brother is but that's just a glory

338

role, my mum would have killed me otherwise,' Adrian says. Once again, we both know he's not joking. 'But if I had my choice, it would have been you.'

'Now I really am going to cry, you wanker,' I say, grabbing my bags out of the boot before I can break down completely. Adrian clambers out, leaving his car door open, a clear signal to the vehicles behind that he's not parking up. 'Man, I hate goodbyes.'

'Let's not say goodbye, then,' Adrian says. 'Let's just say, see you when I see you.'

'See you when I see you,' I say, opening my arms wide to give him a hug.

'I love you, man,' Adrian says from somewhere within the hug.

'I know,' I reply, my voice cracking as I do. 'I love you too.'

Maya

I watch the Wi-Fi signal of my phone appear and then disappear as the Tube speeds through the stations on the way to Heathrow. Emmie does the same, checking and rechecking her phone for messages from Adrian saying that Jack is safely delivered and that he's made his way back home. I don't know why people celebrate the Tube as being the best way to get across London. When it comes to racing to the airport to stop your estranged husband from leaving the country, it feels impossibly, painfully, slow.

As soon as we emerge from the Tube, walking the last leg of the journey towards the terminal, I try to call Jack again, but it just goes to voicemail again and again and again, to the point where I start to think that he's probably just ignoring me. Because why would he want to talk to me after how we left things last time?

The memory of that day, meeting Charlotte, my dad's inbox, rushes through my mind again. I know now that my frustrations were only partly at Jack, that I was directing all my anger at the man who stood in front of me and not the one I didn't have the chance to scream at anymore. And my mum, the woman I admire the most, messed-up too. Because, as much as I believe in equal rights for all people, as much as I've studied the history, the present and the future of feminism, experience teaches you that humans have an equal right to cock up monumentally, as well as to feel the urge to cover their tracks.

But I don't want to cover anything up now. All I want to do is tell Jack I love him.

As we pace faster and faster towards the terminal, holiday-makers begin trundling like tourists before they even become the real thing. Emmie elbows past them to the sound of disgruntled cries and *'calm down, love'*s and *'we all want to get on holiday'*s. By the time we get to the check-in desk, we're actually running.

'Excuse me, madam, the queue is this way.' An official-looking person stops us in our tracks as I look back to the trolly-pushing people lined up in the shape of an S.

'Oh no, we're not . . .' I begin, no idea what I'm meant to say next.

'Your holiday begins at the back of that queue.' She smiles, passive aggression clear.

'We're not going on holiday,' Emmie juts in. 'We're trying

to stop someone from going on theirs. Well, not their holiday, but—'

'Please join the back of the queue.' The woman points, her face twisting in disgust.

'My friend is trying to stop the love of her life—'

'The queue for checking in starts there, madam,' she repeats her party line.

'But we're not checking in!' I cry. If this were *Love Actually* I would be Liam Neeson's son, hopping over barriers and skipping through security folk. Sadly, I do not have the agility of a prepubescent boy, nor the guts to do so. I do, however, have Emmie Sims. Who, right now, looks more like Liam Neeson circa *Taken*.

'Look, madam, we're not trying to check in and we're not trying to skip the queue. It's just we really need a strong, *powerful* official like yourself to show us the correct queue to go in for personal plane enquiries.'

'Oh, personal plane enquiries.' The official lights up for a second. 'Back of the queue.' Her face twists into a sarcastic smile and I would hate her with every ounce of my being if I didn't hate myself for pushing Jack away too.

'Next!' The man behind the check-in counter smiles only to be greeted by Emmie, red in the face, and me, with black mascara lines tracing their way down my cheeks. It's taken over forty minutes to get to this point, each one of them feeling less hopeful than the last. The tears started when I looked at my watch, because despite trying our best, between traffic and the bitch at the check-in barrier, it's somehow turned 21:15.

341

'How can I—' he begins his spiel before Emmie leans her elbow on his counter.

'Look, sir, we don't need to check in. We need to know whether someone else has checked onto the 21:55 to Auckland—'

'I'm not at liberty to disclose this information,' he says as Emmie audibly groans.

'Well, can you tell us what the status of the flight is?' I ask, hurriedly.

'It's already boarded, the gates are closed. There's a screen around the other side.'

'There should be a screen on this side!' Emmie exhales. I love her for trying so hard, but we're clearly not cut out for this.

'It's boarded? But it's not taking off for another' − I check my watch, hot tears falling onto the face of it − 'twenty-five minutes.'

'Long-haul flights often close their gates forty-five minutes early,' he says, his voice softening somewhat upon seeing the fresh tears spilling from my eyes. 'Look, if it's an emergency then we could maybe get a message to your—?'

'Husband.' I fill in the blank, knowing it'll be the last time I say the word. He got on the plane; he didn't say goodbye. I may have said I want a divorce, but Jack clearly wants to go home now. He doesn't need a visa anymore. Which means he doesn't need me.

'Oh, I'm sorry.' The man behind the counter looks genuinely gutted for me, which only makes me feel worse. 'Do you want me to try to get a message to him?'

'No,' I whisper.

I feel like I'm finally hearing Jack's message loud and clear.

342

Jack

I look out of the window, staring at the tarmac, willing the plane to just take off now. Five years I've been in this country, setting up a life here, and yet the months of knowing Maya, of being married to Maya, have by far been the best. And now all I can think about is her. *It's just you and Maya . . . It's just you and Maya . . .* Charlotte's words are lodged on repeat in my mind. What was the end of that sentence, what was she trying to say?

But the more I say them the more they feel complete, a perfectly formed sentence all on their own. Because actually, when it's just me and Maya, laughing about our dates, or talking late into the night or whispering our first faint words of the morning, it's the best it's ever been. It doesn't feel like the teenage love of Laura, insecure and obsessive. It doesn't feel like the guarded love of my last five years of dating. No, it's something else entirely. It feels like falling in love with your best friend, so slowly that you sometimes stop and wonder how your friendship morphed into love in the first place.

It's just you and Maya. But that was the problem, wasn't it? The thoughts come thick and fast as the final passengers take their places, a family of five jostling down the aisle, kids arguing over the window seat. Love includes everyone and everything you invite into it too, your families and your past and your friends and your future, all your baggage and beauty and broken bits. Maybe in a different world, I could have given Maya everything. But I know I can't give her that now, not today, not until my family can be a part of it, not until she

343

wants to bring her past, present and future into the mix too. But I can give her something. I can give her the truth. Whether she wants to hear it or not.

I reach for my phone, turning flight mode off until I'm watching the signal bars build up to two and then fall back down to one – a tiny, faint bar that may not quite be enough. This might not be enough either, but I know I need to say something. Before it's too late.

Maya, I love you, but it's time for me to go home.

I watch the message trying to send, and then the plane begins moving and a flight attendant tells me to please turn my phone off, *now, sir.* She watches me stash it away and I still don't know whether my message has sent so I say it in my heart. *Maya, I love you, but it's time for me to go home.* I say it as the plane gets into position. I say it as the wheels leave the ground. I say it over and over and over again, just praying that the words take flight.

Part 10

Another Wedding

199 Days Separated

Maya

I don't need an alarm clock to wake me up today.

For starters, the sunshine has decided to make an appearance for the first time in months. Then there's the fact that right now I have nothing to do, no obligations. For the first time since I was three years old, waltzing my way into my first Reception Class and barging my way to the front of the carpet to sit at the teacher's feet, I have finally stepped off the academic treadmill. I have officially entered my twenty-fourth year as an unemployed person living in a house share. And as I open the curtains to look at the spring pink blossoms lining the quiet streets of Pimlico, it doesn't feel half bad.

'Coffee!' my housemate Jane calls from the landing outside.

Jane is the other reason I don't need an alarm clock. She's really bloody loud. But, after a couple of months of trying to muddle through at my dad's place, it soon transpired that I could do with a bit of noise.

I thought I needed Jack's presence to drown out the thoughts

347

of my dad, when in reality it just pushed me one step closer to discovering more about my parents' story and why my dad wasn't around. One step closer to understanding what love really is. Or perhaps, understanding that there is no under-standing it, you just need to make a decision to embrace it for all it is. I'll always thank Jack for that. And for not making our quicky divorce any more painful than it needed to be.

After he left without saying goodbye, I half expected not to hear from him at all, to unintentionally stay married to a man who I'm pretty sure wonders why he ever got married to me in the first place, especially now that he's building a life back home. But, no. His emails were polite, professional, to the point. Kind but distant. Because he is, isn't he? So bloody distant. Unlike my mum, who I finally got to talk to properly about my dad as we wandered around the Christmas-lights-scattered streets of New York three months ago.

'You're an angel,' I say, as soon as I walk into the kitchen – straight out of the seventies – and Jane hands me the cup. Her get-up looks straight out of the seventies too, all patched-up denim and floaty floral tops. And, if she *was* an angel, she'd be the most colourful angel in the world. I know living here, her small acts of kindness as I began to mend my broken heart, have been exactly what I've needed.

'Did someone say *coffee*?' Henry flounces into the room, wearing a long silver robe, his long hair falling by his sides. Henry's sass is what I've needed too. He slings an arm around Jane and together they look like two models cut out of the pages of entirely different eras. After almost two decades of trying to be intentionally independent whilst being unintentionally *co-dependent* with Emmie, forcing our lives into step with each other even when they didn't fit, it feels refreshing to know that three people who have absolutely nothing in common can be patched together to create something cool.

'Thank *God* it's almost the weekend!' Henry's entire body heaves dramatically with the words.

Everything Henry does is dramatic. He loved the fact that I married Jack for a visa and accidentally fell in love with him before getting divorced in less than a year. He loved it even more when – after *much* coercing – I relented and showed him a photo of Jack. Now I'm not sure what Henry is rooting for more, the chance that my and Jack's story isn't over or that it would somehow include a love triangle with him.

I still look at that photo sometimes, the one I snapped on our day together taking pictures around Brick Lane, pretending that this date was one of many we'd shared before. It was taken in that Indian restaurant we went to, just moments before Jack tried to kiss me. I used to look at it just to torture myself, to tell myself over and over that I never should have pushed him away, not then, not when I found out the truth about my dad and jumped to all the wrong conclusions about Charlie. But now, I only catch myself looking at it from time to time and find myself smiling, remembering how I played some small part in Jack's journey to finding his way back to himself, finding his way home.

'I know,' Jane says, draining her drink and topping it up again, the slightly broken cafetière spilling drops of coffee onto the wooden breakfast table.

'Tell me about it,' I say, as their eyes shoot to me accusatorily. They both know I'm unemployed and don't technically need to find work any time soon thanks to the sale of my dad's apartment going through.

I considered keeping the apartment for a moment but then, for Mum it was filled with memories of being my dad's mistress and, for me, of being Jack's wife. It was time for it to be revitalised with someone else's memories. And we did give more than half of it away to charity like I first planned, half to further research grants into feminist studies – no surprise there – and the other half to Prostate Cancer UK – that part was more surprising.

It was also surprising to find that my mojo for my studies never came back, that after years of thinking it was what I wanted, part of me just seemed to reshape and change until it wasn't a good fit anymore. After years of fighting for change, it turns out I wanted anything but – for me personally at least. I wanted to stay with Emmie, in uni, where everything slotted into place until we outgrew it. That's what my portion of my dad's apartment money will help me find out: what I might be growing into next.

'Maya, please enlighten us,' Henry says, hand on his hip, attitude accelerating. 'How is this weekend going to look any different from your weeks?'

He doesn't say this unkindly. I know how admirable they think it is that I'm taking time to work out my next steps. It's the kind of space I should have allowed myself a long time ago. Had I not found space so scary.

'Well, for starters, I *have* been researching jobs,' I say, but the less said the better as right now every search seems to end up with me googling hostels in Chile or treks in Chang Mai. 'And this weekend is entirely different because Emmie is getting married.'

'Jane, put that pastry *down*.' Henry flings a hand up to halt Jane, who has just plated up three oven pastries and is in the process of passing one to me.

'Hey!' I say, trying to wrestle my way towards the warm, gooey goodness.

'You're a bridesmaid, aren't you? You need to look your best to bag a best man,' Henry says as Jane rolls her eyes. I knew from the first time I met her that though we may look completely different on paper, we want many of the same things. For starters, to not be put into a twenty-something-trying-to-find-a-husband box. In my defence, I was never *trying* to find a husband. Henry inhales sharply, throwing both hands to his mouth in shock.

'Is *he* going to be there? Jack? Your husband.'

'Ex-husband,' I say, a flash of pain darting across my chest. I knew I'd have to say those words one day, that was always part of the plan. I just always thought they'd feel mutual, thought-out, unemotional, not ushered in by me screaming at him, demanding a divorce.

'Well, *is* he?' Jane asks, her hand still holding the plate, not sure whether to give me the pastry or not. 'Is Jack going to be at the wedding?'

'I don't know,' I say, honestly, the panic setting in – along with a faint flicker of something else, excitement, maybe hope?

'How do you not know? Surely he's invited. He's Adrian's best mate, right?'

'He was, I mean, yeah, he is, but it's a long way to come and . . .'

I hate that I don't know more; that I just know Jack was going to try to come back for it. That he and Adrian have struggled to keep in touch more than they thought, not just because of their lives falling out of sync, but also the time difference, their busy schedules, their narrow windows to chat.

'We don't talk about him much anymore,' I add honestly.

For a long time, it was too hard, and then there wasn't much more to say. I asked for a divorce, he gave me one. He wanted to go home, he did.

'So, I doubt it but . . . yeah . . . maybe. He might even be there with someone else.' This is the thought I hate most of all, the one that started driving me crazy in the first place. After all, he went home to make peace, make amends, with all he left behind. Does that include Laura Mae?

'Maya, your phone!' Jane says, snapping my mind back into the room. I got a new one soon after Jack left, just another feigned attempt to force my mind into a fresh start. Even now, I sometimes don't recognise the ringtone, expecting the old sounds to ring and Jack's name to dance across the screen. I walk across the kitchen to pick it up. It's Emmie.

'Hey! You okay? Thought you'd be busy with all the last-minute preparations?'

'Hey, hey, yeah,' Emmie speaks quickly now, she sounds stressed, concerned. 'That's what I was calling about. Maya, it's all going wrong, it's all—'

'Woah, slow down,' I say quickly. 'Do you want me to come over?'

'Are you sure you don't mind?' Emmie asks cautiously. We've had so many chats over the past six months about how our friendship has grown and changed, that the dynamic has had to shift to accommodate her relationship and my career change, but we'll always be a priority for the other.

'Emmie, you're getting married tomorrow,' I say, feeling my usual warmth for Emmie blossom and explode. 'If you need me, you better believe I'm going to be there.'

Jack

'Jack, can you get that, buddy?' Adrian shouts from somewhere in the depths of his bedroom. I have no idea what he and Emmie are doing in there but having spent the last twenty minutes out here in the living room folding order of services, overhearing whispers and giggles, I'm pretty sure they're finding physical ways to de-stress before the big day.

'Sure thing, dude!' I shout back at him, stifling a yawn. I guess I can cut him some slack seeing as he came to pick me up from the airport in the early hours of the morning. Still, I walk towards the front door feeling like some sort of host here.

I've been helping them welcome deliveries and see off their parents as Emmie and Adrian sent them on last-minute errands before tomorrow. This place has been a hive of activity all morning. And though I don't begrudge it, I know now that my wedding should have been all of these things – flowers and parents and friends and order of services – and I do really, really need to sleep off this jet lag.

And spend some time working out what the hell I'm going to say to Maya.

'Then we need to go to this suit-fitting!' he shouts back at me.

'I don't know why you left it so late,' I hear Emmie say to Adrian. If she thinks anything about this wedding is last minute, she should have seen my wedding to Maya.

As soon as I got off the plane in Auckland, I checked my outbox, my message to her still *sending* . . . I waited and waited for it to be sent, then I was sure it had done and that my phone had just got stuck on some sort of flight-induced feedback loop. I thought about re-sending it countless times. But then I didn't want Maya to think I was hounding her. So, I waited and waited for a reply. I even messaged Flo in a moment of weakness, when Maya's silence became too much, just searching for distraction again. The fact Flo ghosted me feels like a just ending to all the things I unintentionally put her through. Plus, it was never really going to work with her, not then, not ever. It was always Maya. And, as the weeks passed waiting for my wife to reply, I found myself getting distracted in much healthier ways. There was so much to talk through back home, so many memories to face, that I knew I had to throw myself into my life there. I had spent so many years in London with half of my heart in New Zealand, I couldn't waste this time with my family longing to be back in London. And so, I took out my UK sim and readjusted to home.

The doorbell chimes again, and I let out a huge yawn before putting my hand to the door, trying to psych myself up for whatever person I need to pretend to be awake for next. In reality my mind is buzzing with the thing Emmie has just asked me to do, a favour to a friend, her one wedding wish. Which is weird because last time I spoke to Adrian about Maya he said she was doing really well without me. Well, he didn't say this last part, but I felt it. It's why I sorted the divorce so quickly in the end.

But then, why would Emmie ask me to do what she's just asked me to? I swing open the door mid-thought. And when will I get a chance before tomorrow to speak to . . .

'Maya?'

Time slows down as I say her name, as I study the shock on her face, the features I know so well, from her big green eyes to her plump rose-coloured lips, now slightly parted in genuine surprise. Of course, I knew this run-in was coming, but not here, not *now*. Her long dark hair is piled high on top of her head and she's not wearing a scrap of make-up. And I'm glad. Glad to see her natural beauty in all its glory. Glad to see her full stop. So glad that I think my heart could burst with hope or be crushed in her hands completely. So glad to be standing just inches before her now that I don't mind risking the hurt that might come next.

Maya

'Jack?' I whisper his name, my mouth hanging open, lips parted. It's like they've forgotten they're not meant to want him anymore. It's just, I wasn't expecting him to be here. My limbs begin to shake, like they are itching to reach for him, to hold him, to wrap themselves around him. And, with his gorgeous face looking back at me like this, dimples etched into the smooth skin of his cheeks, it's taking all my strength not to let them.

'Maya?' He chokes my name again. And judging from his pained expression, I assume he wasn't expecting to see me right now either. I breathe deeply, willing my chest not to betray how hard my heart is throbbing, willing Jack to say my name over and over again.

'You're here,' I say, stating the obvious, if only to convince myself the words are true, that this is actually happening and I'm not just dreaming him into existence.

He lingers in the doorway, the same way he did before

entering my and Emmie's last house party all those months ago. Except this time, I'm the one on the outside. I knew there was a chance I'd see him at the wedding tomorrow, I was hoping to find out the latest from Emmie any second. But never for one second did I think he'd be here, standing tall, tanned, broad, and a little bit blonder, before me now. *Smiling* before me now.

'You're here too,' he says, his eyes scanning every inch of me like he's trying to work out whether I'm real or not too. Whether I'm the same woman he married or the one who looked at him as if he were a killer and told him to get the hell away from me. I'm neither. Or maybe a little bit of both. I'm still working it all out, and that's, well, I think that's okay.

'I live here,' I say, still stating the obvious, my mind becoming more and more detached from my body, a body longing to touch him, that's been longing all this time.

'But Emmie said you moved to Pimlico?' Jack looks behind him quickly, perhaps to check whether she's coming to greet me too, before fixing his eyes back on mine. After six months apart, the intensity of his stare is exciting and excruciating in equal measure.

'I meant in London,' I add quickly. 'You've been asking about me?' I grin, and Jack smiles too; I'm pretty sure he'd be blushing if he wasn't so tanned. I watch as he brushes a hand through his floppy blond hair, his T-shirt tightening across his torso as he does.

'You look good,' he says after an impossibly long silence stretches between us. There's so much I want to say to him. So much I never got a chance to. But would he even want to hear it? I look down at my ripped jeans and plain white T-shirt. 'But I promise you Emmie will *kill you* if you wear white to her

356

wedding.' He laughs. Man, I miss that laugh. It's the kind of laugh you want to bottle somehow and never be without again.

'I'm not wearing this to the wedding, you idiot,' I tease him, trying to break the tension that's brimming between us, but it only fans it into flames even more.

'Well, after how you showed up to the last one . . .' He means *our* one.

'You know, that wasn't a real wedding,' I say, but suddenly he's not laughing.

'The divorce papers felt pretty real,' he says, sadness flashing across his features.

'Yeah, thanks for sorting that all out,' I say, the knife twisting in my heart. But he looks good now too, better now, more relaxed somehow, lighter. 'How's home?'

'It's . . .' Jack begins, looking behind him to see that the living room is still empty.

We're still lingering by the front door and I don't know whether Jack is reluctant to let me in or let Emmie and Adrian into a private moment I know at least I've wanted for months. Right now, I'm not sure I trust myself being alone with Jack in an empty room.

'It's a lot,' he finally finishes his sentence. 'But it's good, it was the right thing going back and facing everything I left behind.'

I watch every inch of his expression as he searches for the words carefully and I wonder whether we'll ever get the chance to have the unguarded conversations of lovers or friends again. I wonder how many of our conversations were that unguarded at all.

'I couldn't keep running from my past forever.'

'I know, me neither,' I say, risking a tiny step towards him.

'Yeah, sounds like we had a lot in common after all,' Jack says, his eyes fixed on me, his face seeming to inch forward. 'If only we'd known . . .'

'If only we had . . .'

'Maya!' Emmie appears behind Jack, blustering through our half-formed thoughts.

Jack

'Emmie!' Maya says, and I jolt around to see that she's appeared just behind us. I turn back around to Maya just in time to see her force a smile, but I can tell from a glimpse of Emmie's silent apology, mouthed in her direction before I turned away, that Maya has just been silently cursing her best friend for this orchestrated run-in. Because, surely, that's what this is? But why would she be trying so hard to force me and Maya together unless she knows something I don't, something that makes her think Maya *wants* to run in to me again.

'What's the emergency?' Maya says, her eyes widening on her best friend's. I know that as soon as I'm out of the way, Emmie will be getting an earful for this. Adrian will be getting one too. But I must admit, I'm kind of used to Maya surprising me.

'It's, erm . . .' Emmie looks between Maya and me at speed. Are *we* the emergency?

'Maya! Fancy seeing you here!' Adrian strides through to the living room, playing the knight in shining armour to his manipulative Lady Macbeth. I really hope the question Emmie has teed me up to ask next isn't her dagger to my back, a better-late-than-never way to punish me for using her best friend for a visa. 'Dude, we gotta go, we were meant to leave fifteen minutes ago.'

I watch Maya soften slightly, figuring from Adrian's comment that this awkwardly timed run-in is a genuine mistake. I know from Emmie's little nod to me now that it isn't. My heart starts to hammer, more than it is already, my palms prickling with sweat by my side.

'Jack has something to ask you,' she blurts in between us, to no one in particular. But I know this is my cue to ask Maya the one thing Emmie begged me to. Her one wedding wish. And it's been my wish too, for months now.

'Okay, well, Emmie wanted . . .' I look to her now and she shakes her head so slightly that I think Maya missed it.

'I mean, *I* wanted to ask you, whether you . . .' Maya is looking back at me, her green eyes shining brightly, the way they did when I asked her that first time to marry me, the way they did when she said *I do*. This time I can feel the gaze of Emmie and Adrian sear into me too, which is fitting seeing as they should have been our witnesses in the first place. I just hope what they're about to witness isn't a jet-lagged Kiwi falling flat on his face.

'. . . whether you wanted to be my date to the wedding?'

Maya looks back at me, her eyes still wide, her mouth parted, ready to morph into a smile, a frown, or a simple *screw-you*. Then she grins, slightly at first but it grows and grows.

'A wedding? Sure,' she says, looking from Emmie and Adrian to me. 'Whose?'

200 Days Separated

Maya

'Do you know what you're going to say to him?' Emmie asks into the mirror. She's a vision in her wedding dress, which sweeps across her shoulders and stretches down to the floor in natural waves, a crown of wildflowers circling her long blond-dipped hair, which falls naturally down her sides. She looks flawless, special and yet still one hundred per cent herself. And we should one hundred per cent be talking about *her* right now.

'I've got some thoughts . . .' I say, the understatement of the century. Ever since our run-in yesterday, I've dissected every inch of it with Emmie. Telling her off for blindsiding me. Forgiving her quickly when she said it was better this way, that she didn't want any awkwardness on her wedding day, that she wanted to get the initial shock out of the way.

'Okay, well, you have to tell him that we tried to stop him at the airport.' She grins.

We've laughed and cried about that day a thousand times since then. Of all the things we dreamed we'd do in our adulthood, chasing a man to the airport wasn't one of them. Nor was standing here as a bride and divorcee in our twenties on Emmie's wedding day.

'And you have to tell him you cried about him for weeks, that you filled that whole bloody apartment with tears until there was more water inside than out.'

'Well, as poetic as *that* sounds,' I tease her, reaching to perfect a curl, falling loose from her flower crown, 'that wasn't *all* about him.'

'And you have to tell him about your wanderlust, that you want to travel now, that you're finally wanting to let yourself change rather than just *study* change.'

'Okay, okay,' I say, ushering her towards the door, the one that opens up to the church entrance hall where the rest of her bridesmaids are already huddled out of sight, ready to walk ever so slowly down the aisle towards Adrian. And Jack.

'And you have to tell him you still love him.'

The thought floors me, but I know she's right. This is my chance.

'One thing at a time.' I beam at her, silencing my nerves for what's to come.

'Well, what's the first thing?' Emmie says. I get the impression talking about me is calming her down enough to take the next big, monumental step she's about to take.

'The first thing is getting you married to your love.' I grin at her again, reaching to place both my hands on the tops of her arms, as her dad comes to greet us in the hall.

'Oh shit, this is *happening*,' she murmurs, as I step in front of her, taking my place.

'Yes, yes it is,' I say, smiling over my shoulder as the music begins to play and all the people in the main body of the church begin to stand. At the bottom of the aisle, I see the back of Adrian facing the front of the church, turning over his shoulder to smile in our direction. Next to him, Jack is doing the same. I turn to whisper one last thing to Emmie, the words I said on *my* wedding day.

'Now, let's go and do this thing.'

Jack

The music starts, everybody stands, and I catch Adrian's eye. This is it. And I wouldn't have missed it for the world. Because even though it took me far too long to tell Adrian the truth about what happened back home, the second I did he loved me all the same. The broken bits are as much a part of me as any other. I know that now. I know that about Maya now too. And I *think* Maya feels the same.

The first of Emmie's bridesmaids comes down the aisle, doing that silly right-foot-together, left-foot-together thing that you only see during weddings or funerals, as if the steady, sober speed is indicative of the monumental size of the moment to come.

She smiles at Adrian, then at me, a weirdly flirtatious smile. She doesn't know I'm already taken. Not technically, not anymore. But as she peels off to the left and I see Maya doing the one-two-step-thing behind her, I know it all over again. I know it in my bones.

She looks gorgeous, stunning in a sweeping sage-green dress, and I have to stop my mind from drifting to what's underneath, not just physically, but mentally, emotionally; I want to peel off her layers one by one until there's nothing left to find. But I know that day will never come, there will always be more to know about Maya.

I watch as she gives Adrian a smile, full and unreserved, and looking as if she's trying not to cry. Clearly, for all of Maya's cynicism at how quickly their relationship raced from first date to here, she's started to buy in to their love, maybe started to buy in to love full stop?

Then she looks at me, and she keeps looking at me, holding my gaze the whole time. And now I have to try not to cry. After days and weeks and months of missing her, analysing our entire relationship, how it happened, how it went so wrong, she's here. Maya, as real and raw and tangible as the first day we met, but more so, now that I know so much more about her, the things she shared with me and the things I had to find out myself.

I grin at her and she beams back at me, clutching a bundle of flowers in her hands, wild and colourful, like her. How different this feels to when we rushed down the aisle, side by side, five minutes late for our appointment, Kris and Ken trailing behind. A laugh escapes at the thought, and I can tell Maya knows exactly what I'm thinking about because now she's laughing too. We did it all the wrong way round but does it really matter if it led us to this moment, to one where *if onlys* have a chance to become *thank Gods* and not even countries and miles and oceans can keep us apart?

She arrives at the top of the aisle, hovering for a moment before she too peels off left and Emmie arrives. Every single head turns back to the entrance to the church, towards the blushing bride, radiant in white. Every single head except one. Across the aisle, I'm looking to Maya and silently making a new vow: I'm going to find a way to come back to England so that I can ask my ex-wife on a real date, whatever it takes.

Maya

'Shocker, they sat us together,' I say, picking up my place card at the top table and looking down at Jack, suited and booted and already in his seat. I place my champagne down on the table and pull out a seat beside him. I've already had three of these on an empty stomach, but there's not enough champagne in the world to drink away my nerves right now.

'Well, when we RSVP'd we were married,' Jack points out, taking a sip of his drink; he looks gorgeous in his crisp white shirt, his jacket hanging off the back of his chair.

'Yeah, but they didn't technically *know* that,' I say, glad we can laugh about this now.

'Just imagine if we had a real break-up, this seating plan would be totally awkward.'

Jack tries to pass this off as a joke but I wonder whether he felt it too, the sharp rip of two conjoined lives tearing apart. It *was* a break-up. But somehow this isn't awkward. It feels long overdue, even more so since our brief time together at Emmie and Adrian's yesterday.

'Sorry we didn't get much time to talk yesterday,' I say. Of all the things I have to say sorry for, this one seems the simplest right now.

'Oh, I'm pretty sure Emmie and Adrian orchestrated it that

way, don't you?' Jack laughs, brushing his hand through his messy mop of hair. I remember the touch of his hands again, when he held my feet on top of him on the sofa, when he kissed me at our wedding.

'Yeah,' I nod. 'I think Emmie was trying to avoid any drama.'

'Drama?' Jack puts his hands to his chin now, feigning curiosity.

'Yeah, I don't know, like me searching through your phone, screaming at you that I wanted a divorce, chasing you to the airport—'

'What's that?' Jack leans in a little closer now, my heart beating faster.

'Screaming at you that I wanted a divorce. You do know that wasn't about you, right? I had just found out something about my parents, something I should have known for a long time, and I should have just told you, everything . . . and I'm sorry. Jack looks at me, head tilted quizzically, and I exhale deeply, it's like I can breathe properly for the first time in months.

'I know, Maya. I know about your dad, and I'm sorry too.' He smiles kindly.

'And I'm sorry about Charlie,' I whisper back.

'Thanks,' he says, grinning genuinely, taking another sip of his drink. 'Now, take me back to the other bit . . . the chasing-to-the-airport bit . . .'

'Yeah, well, you left without saying goodbye, so I tried to . . . but it was too late.'

'That's not technically true,' Jack says cautiously.

'Yes, it is, ask Emmie, we raced across the city and—'

'No, I mean the *I didn't say goodbye* part,' Jack says, his brow crinkling as he does.

'What do you mean?' I ask, heart leaping up into my throat.

'I sent you a message, from the plane,' Jack says, his eyes searching mine for signs of recognition but there is none. I never got a message. 'Clearly, you didn't get it?'

I shake my head slowly. 'What did it say?'

'It said I thought it was time for me to go home,' Jack says, sadly, remembering that moment again, how bad things had to get between us before we realised that running away from the mess wasn't the answer. All a little too late.

'And was it?' I ask, forcing a grin. I'm not sure what I want his answer to be. I want him to be happy, for his family to be happy, to make his peace with all the broken pieces.

'Yeah, it was.' Jack smiles, as more and more people mingle into the room. It still feels like we're the only two people in here. 'It was hard at first, being back where the accident happened, where I had some of the worst days of my life, but it also felt good, like a sore scabbing over, starting to heal. Turned out the fear of what I left behind was way worse than the real thing. I needed to stop running from what scared me and look it in the eye.'

Jack is looking into my eyes so intently that I wonder whether he's a bit scared of me. I know I am of him. Of how I feel about him. Of what he might say when I tell him. Even more so that I'll miss the opportunity to tell him the truth all over again. Come on, Maya, tell him, tell him now, before it's too late. Even so, the thought of how pointless the confession is now that he lives on the other side of the world keeps holding me back.

'Man, this tie is so tight.' Jack breaks away for a moment, as Adrian's brother announces the arrival of the bride and groom. We all get to our feet obediently and out of the corner of my eye I see Jack loosening his tie beside me and I see the glimmer of something gold underneath, his chain and his wedding band still hanging around it, even now.

'So, how has home been for you? How's the PhD?' Jack turns to me as soon as the shuffle of seats and chatter around the room indicates it's time for our meal to begin.

'I quit,' I say, and Jack's mouth hangs open. 'Like, I didn't give up,' I cover quickly.

Not because of you, I feel that same feisty streak shooting out of me; Jack seems to draw it out in me, he draws out a thousand other things as well. 'I just realised it wasn't making me happy anymore, that maybe I was just continuing my studies because it's what I know I'm good at. It was easy to feel like I was moving forward when I was studying the feminist movement, we've come so far but have got a long way to go, but I wasn't really *living* in the freedom of it all, you know, the freedom to choose my path, journey with someone else.'

Jack nods on, truly listening, and I see the chain against his neck again, the ring catching the sunlight, and I know what I need to do next. That it's okay that I don't have the answers, that I don't have a map, that I don't have it all worked out. I just know the next step.

Jack

'Sometimes you just need some time to work out what you want,' I whisper back to her, my next words catching in my throat. This is what I needed too. Time to heal, to grow, time to work out what I want. And what I want is Maya. Every messy bit of her.

367

'Look, I need to tell you something,' I go on, and she stiffens beside me.

'About Laura?' Maya says slowly, her face falling before she forces a smile.

'About Laura?' I echo back. 'Why on earth would this be about Laura?'

'Because she is the love of your life, because you went back home—'

'Maya,' I say, shaking my head, unable to stop a smile from spreading across my face, because if this is how she feels about me getting back with Laura Mae it really bodes well for what I'm about to tell her now. 'I was a *child* when I met Laura, I didn't know what love was then, I didn't know what love was until—' The sentence breaks off, Maya always managing to send my well-formed plans somewhere else entirely. 'No, this isn't about Laura but, well, she says hello, by the way.'

'Why would she say hello? Did you tell her about me? Did you—?'

'Maya, would you be quiet for one second?' I say, and she narrows her eyes at me with the kind of love-stained disdain that it takes months together to curate. 'I want to tell you something else, about the message I sent you, about the one you didn't get. It didn't just say it was time for me to go home, it also said . . .'

Maya stares back at me, with those big green eyes, silent for once.

'It also said I love you.'

The words fall out of me like bubbles blown into the wind, and I watch them floating, not sure whether they're going to pop and fade or rise up and up, dancing into the distance.

368

Maya just stares back, her silence stretching on, like she's savouring the bubbles too.

'Maya, will you . . . I don't know . . . would you like to go on a date and then, yeah, maybe just keep dating, I don't know, long distance . . .?'

I've thought about these words a thousand times in the months we've spent apart but now they fall out in shards, and I just hope that Maya can pick them up and put the pieces together again.

'Until I can find a way to come back to the UK again, without you having to marry me for a visa or anything.'

'No,' Maya says, and my stomach would plummet if she wasn't smiling so much.

'No?' I echo the word back at her. I've given her so many but this one is so final, so short. And it doesn't make any sense when she's looking at me like that.

'Do long distance with you? When you can't even send a bloody text message?'

'I was on a plane, on the fricking tarmac. I—'

Maya reaches for my hand, holding it in hers.

'Jack, would you be quiet for *one* second,' she repeats my words back to me. Maya may have stopped her research, but I know better than to think her fight for equality is over. 'I've been thinking about travelling ever since I stopped studying, even before I started, and I think I've just worked out where I want to go first . . .' She smiles in a way that tells me she'll follow me to the edge of the earth. Or, you know, Auckland.

'Not forever, only for a year or so,' Maya goes on, as I squeeze her hand and it takes all my strength not to take her in my arms and kiss these beautiful, brilliant words away.

369

'That's all I'll be able to do on my visa, you know, unless I convince some poor fool to marry me.' Maya laughs, and I laugh too, like *who would do such a thing?*

Maya

'Are you kidding me?' Jack says, and his smile looks fit to burst.

'Yes, Jack. Of course I'm kidding,' I joke sarcastically, and his face falls so quickly that it makes me reach my hand to his cheek to hold his smile intact. I'd almost forgotten how much fun messing with my husband used to be. You'd think he would have learnt by now.

'Maya, that would be . . . you could meet my family and . . . why would you do that?'

'Why do you bloody think?' I laugh, and it's at that moment that I do what I should have done all those months ago. Except I don't just *let him* kiss me, I kiss him, I take control and then lose every inch of it within our kiss as I will my lips, my mouth, to tell his: I love you, Jack Wilson, I love you, I love you to the other side of the world and back.

Somewhere in the distance I hear Emmie and Adrian cheering from down the table and we break away to look at them, to laugh with them, fully, unreservedly, Jack still cupping my cheek in his hands. Emmie winks at me and I roll my eyes as I turn back to Jack.

'That is,' I whisper, my lips inches from his own. 'Only if you want me to?'

'I do,' Jack says, laughing then kissing me and laughing again. 'I really, really do.'

Acknowledgements

Though this book may have my name on the cover, there are so many people that go into making a rom com become a reality, too many to mention by name. To all the friends and friends-of-friends whose stories of love, loss and life have wedged themselves into my mind and spilled out onto these pages, thank you.

Huge thanks must always go to my literary agent, Sallyanne Sweeney, for believing in me from the get-go and juggling my book babies so graciously whilst raising real-life little ones of her own; what a hero. And to my editor, Jess Whitlum-Cooper, thank you for championing my books and being as passionate about my characters as I am; they are all the better for your love and attention. Thank you to the entire team at Headline Review for all that you do – as someone who works in publishing myself, I know a book doesn't 'happen' without everyone playing their part from the person making the coffee to the person polishing the final pages.

Special mention must go to Mark Scoggins for the well-timed hypothetical conversation that sparked the idea for this novel and to Hamish Robertson, Gabi Code, Sarah Millar and Kezia George for helping me make the hypothetical sound something like reality.

A big thank-you to the people who witness the highs and lows of a writer 'behind the scenes': Mum, Dad, Tom, Rachel, Nick and Mango (a ginger cat, not a celebrity-baby-name ... yet). And to the friends who pray for me and keep reminding me of the One that matters most, thank you so much for being on this wild adventure with me.

**If you enjoyed *The Visa*,
then you'll love *What Are Friends For?***

Eve doesn't have time for dating, but having watched her best friend and flatmate have her heart broken one too many times, she reluctantly volunteers to play her Cupid.

Max is too much of a hopeless romantic to find the algorithms of online dating anything other than clinical, but he lives with his romantically-challenged best friend who desperately needs his advice.

And after all, what are friends for?

As Eve and Max become more involved in their best friends' relationship, they quickly realise there is a fine line between instruction and imitation.

Especially when they find they can't stop thinking about their best friends' dates . . .

Available now from Headline Review

KEEP IN TOUCH WITH LIZZIE O'HAGAN

© Juliet Trickey

 @LizzieOHagan1

@lizzie_ohagan

Bookends

When one book ends, another begins...

Bookends is a vibrant new reading community to help you ensure you're never without a good book.

You'll find exclusive previews of the brilliant new books from your favourite authors as well as exciting debuts and past classics. Read our blog, check out our recommendations for your reading group, enter great competitions and much more!

Visit our website to see which great books we're recommending this month.

Join the Bookends community:
www.welcometobookends.co.uk

 @Team Bookends   @WelcomeToBookends